Lara Adrian lives  New England, surrounded hip urban comforts, and ody Atlantic Ocean.

'Adrenaline-fueled, sizzlingly sexy, darkly intense . . . addictively readable series.'

Chicago Tribune

'Evocative, enticing, erotic . . . Enter Lara Adrian's vampire world and be enchanted'

J.R. Ward, *New York Times* bestselling author

'A thrilling blend of dark passion and heart-pounding action. Lara Adrian always delivers a keeper!

Gena Showalter, *New York Times* bestselling author

SHADES
OF
MIDNIGHT

LARA ADRIAN

ROBINSON

Constable & Robinson Ltd
3 The Lanchesters
162 Fulham Palace Road
London W6 9ER
www.constablerobinson.com

First published in the US by Bantam Dell,
1745 Broadway, New York, NY 10019

This edition published by Robinson,
an imprint of Constable & Robinson Ltd, 2010

A copy of the British Library Cataloguing in Publication
Data is available from the British Library.

ISBN: 978-1-84901-282-9

Printed and bound in the EU.

To the charming and witty, the thoroughly unforgettable,
Miss Eithne O'Hanlon of the Emerald Isle,
for being such a wonderful advocate of the series,
and a source of many giggles and much
mayhem at the message boards.
Thank you for being you!

ACKNOWLEDGMENTS

Thank you so very much to everyone who helps produce and market my books and put them into the hands of my readers, both in the United States and abroad. I feel incredibly fortunate to be associated with all of you, and I truly appreciate everything you do in support of my work.

Continued, humble thanks to my wonderful readers, whose emails, letters, and online messages keep me smiling at my keyboard, even in the midst of the most wicked deadline crunches. I can't begin to express how much your enthusiasm and friendship means to me. (((HUGS)))

None of my books would be what they are without the input and support of my husband, whose belief and encouragement – not to mention killer plot ideas – have been invaluable to me. I couldn't have dreamed of a better partner, both in life and in fiction. Thank you for all the good parts.

⊰ PROLOGUE ⊱

Under a winter-dark Alaskan sky, a wolf song carried clear and majestic into the night. The howl stretched long, a thing of pure, wild beauty that reached through the dense spruce of the boreal forest and climbed the jagged, snow-covered walls of rock that rose up along the icy banks of the Koyukuk River. When the wolf sent up his haunting call again, it was met by a discordant hoot of laughter, then a drunken voice that answered from across the flames of a small campfire.

'Ow-ow-owwoooo! Owwoooo!' One of the three guys in the group who'd come out to party tonight on this remote stretch of land cupped his gloved hands to his mouth and yowled another ear-grating reply to the wolf, which had since gone silent in the distance. 'Hear that? We're having ourselves a little communication right there.' He grabbed for the bottle of whiskey as it came around the small gathering to him. 'I ever tell you I'm fluent in wolf, Annabeth?'

Across the campfire, a soft laugh blew out on a cloud of steam from within the deep hood of the girl's parka. 'Sounded to me more like you're fluent in stuck pig.'

'Ooh, that's harsh, sweetheart. Seriously harsh.' He took a swig from the bottle and passed the Jack Daniel's to the next person in line. 'Maybe you want I should give you a little demonstration of my oral skills sometime. I promise you, I'm extremely gifted.'

'You are *such* an asshole, Chad Bishop.'

She was right, but her tone said she didn't mean it. She laughed again, a warmly flirtatious, feminine sound that made Teddy Toms's crotch go all tight and hot. He shifted on the cold rock he'd claimed for a seat, trying not to make his interest obvious as Chad announced he had to take a piss and Annabeth and the other girl with her began to chat together.

A sharp elbow jabbed Teddy in the right side of his rib cage. 'You gonna sit there and drool all night? Get off your chickenshit ass and talk to her, for crissake.'

Teddy swung a look at the tall, skinny guy sitting next to him on the rock and shook his head.

'Come on, don't be such a pussy. You know you want to. She ain't gonna bite you. Well, not unless you want her to, that is.' Skeeter Arnold had been the one who brought Teddy to this gathering. He'd also been the one who supplied the whiskey, something Teddy, at the age of nineteen, had only sampled once in his life.

Alcohol was outlawed in his father's house – outlawed in the whole six-person settlement where he lived, in fact. Tonight Teddy'd had the bottle to his lips more than ten times already. He didn't see the harm in it. In fact, he kind of liked the way it made him feel, all warm and loose inside. Grown up, like a man.

A man who wanted more than anything to stand up and tell Annabeth Jablonsky how he felt about her.

Skeeter handed Teddy the nearly empty bottle and watched him drink the last swallow. 'I think I got something else you're gonna like, my man.' He pulled off his gloves and reached into the pocket of his parka.

Teddy wasn't sure what he had, and didn't much care at the moment. He was mesmerized by Annabeth, who had taken off her hood to show her friend some of the new piercings that tracked all the way up the delicate shell of her ear. Her hair was dyed polar white except for a streak of bright pink, even though Teddy recalled that she was naturally brunette. He knew, because he'd seen her dance last spring at a strip club in Fairbanks, where Annabeth Jablonsky had been better known as Amber Joy. Teddy's cheeks flamed at the thought, and the hard-on he'd been trying to ignore was now in full bloom.

'Here,' Skeeter said, giving him something else to think about as Annabeth and her friend got up from the campfire and walked down to the frozen edge of the river. 'Take a drag on this, my man.'

Teddy took the small metal pipe and held its smoldering bowl up near his nose. A nugget of something pale and chalky burned in the bowl, emitting a foul chemical stink that wormed its way up his nostrils. He winced, sliding a doubtful look at Skeeter. 'W-w-what is it?'

Skeeter grinned, his thin lips peeling back off his crooked teeth. 'Just a little dose of courage. Go ahead, take a hit. You'll like it.'

Teddy brought the pipe to his mouth and sucked in the bittersweet smoke. He coughed only a little, so he exhaled and took another drag on the pipe.

'It's good, right?' Skeeter watched him smoke some more, then he reached out to take the pipe away. 'Easy, dude, save some for the rest of us. You know, I can get you more of this if you want it – booze, too. For a price, I can get you whatever kind of shit you like. You need a hookup, you know where to come, right?'

Teddy nodded. Even in the most remote parts of the bush, folks tended to know the name, and the general business, of Skeeter Arnold. Teddy's father hated him. He'd forbidden Teddy to hang out with him, and if he knew Teddy had sneaked away tonight – especially when they were expecting a supply delivery at home tomorrow morning – he would kick Teddy's ass from here to Barrow.

'Take this,' Skeeter was saying now, holding the pipe out to Teddy. 'Go and offer it to the ladies with my compliments.'

Teddy gaped. 'You mean, t-take it t-t-to Annabeth?'

'No, stupid. Take it to her mother.'

Teddy laughed nervously at his own awkwardness. Skeeter's smile stretched wider, making his narrow face and long razor-hook nose look even more buglike than usual.

'Don't say I never did you no favors,' Skeeter said as Teddy palmed the warm pipe and shot a glance to where Annabeth and her friend stood talking together near the frozen river.

He'd been looking for some way to strike up a conversation with her, hadn't he? This was as good a chance as any. The best chance he might ever get.

Skeeter's low chuckle followed Teddy as he began to make his way toward the girls. The ground felt uneven beneath his feet. His legs seemed rubbery, not totally in his control. But inside he was flying, feeling his heart pounding, his blood racing through his veins.

The two girls heard him approach with the crunch of the ice and stones underfoot. They turned to face him and Teddy gaped at the object of his desire, struggling to come up with just the right thing to say to win her over. He must have stood there staring for a good long while because both of them started to giggle.

'What's up?' Annabeth said, a quizzical look on her face. 'Teddy, right? I've seen you around a few times, but we haven't really had a chance to talk before tonight. You ever go to Pete's tavern down in Harmony?'

He lamely shook his head, working hard just to process the idea that she had actually just said she'd noticed him before tonight.

'You should come in sometime, Teddy,' she added

cheerfully. 'If I'm working the bar, I won't card you.' The sound of her voice, the sound of his name on her lips, almost undid him on the spot. She smiled at him, revealing the slight overlap of her two front teeth that Teddy found utterly adorable.

'Um, here.' He thrust the pipe at her and took a step backward. He wanted to say something cool. He wanted to say something – *anything* – that might make her see him in some way other than a backwoods Native kid who didn't know squat about the real world.

He knew things. He knew plenty. He knew Annabeth was a good girl, that deep down she was decent and kind. He knew that in his heart, would be willing to stake his very life on it. She was better than her reputation, and she was better than any of the losers she was hanging out with tonight. Probably even better than Teddy himself.

She was an angel, a pure and lovely angel, and she just needed someone to remind her of that.

'Okay, well, thanks,' she said now, and took a quick hit from the pipe. She passed it to her friend, and the pair of them started to turn away from Teddy in dismissal.

'Wait,' Teddy blurted. He sucked in a breath as she paused, looked back at him. 'I, um, I want you to know that I . . . I think you're really beautiful.'

Her friend stifled a laugh behind her gloved hand as Teddy spoke. But not Annabeth. She wasn't laughing. She stared at him without speaking, without blinking. Something soft shone in her eyes – confusion, maybe. Her friend was snorting now, but Annabeth was still listening, not mocking him at all.

'I think you're the most amazing girl I've ever seen. You are . . . you're amazing. I really mean that. Amazing in every way.'

Shit, he was repeating himself, but he didn't care. The sound of his own voice, free of the stammer that made him hate to talk at all, shocked him. He swallowed and took a fortifying breath, prepared to put it all out there for her – everything he'd been thinking since he saw her dancing on the poorly lit, run-down stage in the city. 'I think you're perfect, Annabeth. You deserve to be respected and . . . and cherished, you know? You're special. You're an angel, and you deserve to be honored. By a man who will take care of you and protect you and . . . and love you—'

The air next to Teddy stirred, carrying the stink of whiskey and the spice of Chad Bishop's overpowering cologne. 'K-k-kiss me, Amber Joy. P-p-please! Let me t-t-touch your p-p-perfect t-t-tits!'

Teddy felt all the blood drain from his head as Chad strode over to Annabeth and wrapped his arm possessively around her shoulders. His humiliation compounded a hundred times to witness the sloppy, tongue-heavy kiss Chad slapped on Annabeth's mouth – a kiss she didn't reject, even if she seemed less than welcoming of it.

When Chad finally let her loose, Annabeth glanced at Teddy, then gave Chad a weak shove of her palm against his chest. 'You're retarded, you know that?'

'And you're so damn hot you m-m-make my c-c-cock—'

'Shut up.' The words were out of Teddy's mouth before he could stop them. 'Sh-shut the fuck up. Don't . . . don't speak t-t-to her like that.'

Chad's eyes narrowed. 'I know you ain't talking to me, ass-hole. T-t-t-t-tell me you're not standing there, asking me to k-k-kick your sorry ass, T-T-Teddy T-T-T-Toms.'

When he started to lunge forward, Annabeth put herself in front of him. 'Leave the poor kid alone. He can't help the way he talks.'

Teddy wished he could disappear. All the confidence he'd felt a minute ago with her vanished under Chad Bishop's taunting and Annabeth's wounding pity. Nearby, he heard Skeeter and Annabeth's friend joining ranks with Chad. They were all laughing at him now. All of them mocking his stutter, their voices smashing together, ringing in his ears.

Teddy turned around and ran. He jumped on his snowmachine and cranked the starter. The second the old engine sputtered to life, Teddy opened the throttle. He gunned it, tearing away from the gathering in a state of misery and fury.

He never should have gone with Skeeter tonight. He never should have drunk that whiskey or smoked that shit in Skeeter's pipe. He should have stayed home, should have listened to his father.

That regret intensified as the miles fell away behind him and he neared home. Some five hundred yards away from the cluster of hand-hewn cabins that most of his family had lived in for generations, Teddy's anger and humiliation gave way to a knot of cold dread.

His father was still awake.

A lamp burned in the living room, the glow from the cur-tained window reaching out to the surrounding darkness like a spotlight. If his father was up, he had to know that Teddy wasn't home. And as soon as Teddy walked in, his father was going to see that he'd been partying. Which meant Teddy was in some pretty deep shit.

'God-d-dammit,' Teddy muttered as he killed the snowma-chine's headlight then steered off the main trail and cut the engine. He climbed off and stood for a minute, staring over at his house while he let his drunken legs get used to holding him upright.

Nothing he said was going to get him out of trouble. Still, he tried to come up with a reasonable excuse for where he'd been and what he'd been doing the past several hours. He was a grown man, after all. Sure, he had a responsibility to lend his father a hand where he could, but that didn't mean he couldn't have a life of his own outside the settlement. If his father gave him any shit about that, Teddy would just have to set him straight.

But as he got closer to the house, his courage began to desert him. Each careful step he took crunched loudly in the snow, amplified by the utter stillness that hung in the air. The cold swept down the collar of his parka, adding a chill to his already trembling spine. A bracing gust rolled through the center of the group of homes, and as the icy wind hit him full in the face, Teddy felt such a deep sense of dread, it made the hairs at the back of his neck rise.

He paused, glancing around him. Seeing nothing but moonlit snow and the dark silhouettes of the forest, Teddy continued on past his father's log-cabin shop that supplied the family and the handful of other folks scattered in the sur-rounding region. He peered ahead, trying to determine if there might be a way for him to sneak into the house unnoticed. His breath sawed in and out of his lungs, the only sound he could hear.

Everything seemed so quiet. Lifelessly, unnaturally quiet.

It was then that Teddy stopped walking and glanced down at his feet. The snow beneath his boots was no longer white but dark – nearly black in the moonlight, a huge, horrific stain. It was blood. More spilled blood than Teddy had ever seen in his life.

There was more a few yards away. So much blood.

Then he saw the body.

To his right, lying just near the edge of the tree line. He knew that large shape. Knew the bulky heft of the shoulders beneath the thermal undershirt that was ripped and dark with more blood.

'Dad!' Teddy raced to his father and knelt down to help him. But there was nothing to be done. His father was dead, his throat and chest shredded. 'Oh, no! Dad! Oh, God, no!'

Horror and grief choking him, Teddy scrambled to go find

his uncle and two older cousins. How could they not know what had happened here? How was it possible that his father had been attacked like this and left to bleed in the snow?

'Help!' Teddy screamed, his throat raw. He raced next door and pounded on the jamb, calling for his uncle to wake up. Nothing but silence answered. Silence in the entire cluster of cabins and outbuildings that squatted on this tiny parcel of land. 'S-s-someone! Anyone! Help me, p-p-please!'

Blinded by tears, Teddy raised his fist to bang on the door and scream again for help, but he froze in midmotion as the door drifted open. Just inside lay his uncle, as savaged and bloody as his father. Teddy peered into the darkness and saw the broken forms of his aunt and cousins.

They weren't moving. They'd been killed, too. Everyone he knew – everyone he loved – was gone.

What the hell had happened here?

Who – *or what* – in God's name could have done this?

He drifted into the center of the settlement, numb and disbelieving. This couldn't be happening. This couldn't be real. For a split second, he wondered if the shit Skeeter had made him smoke had caused him to hallucinate. Maybe none of this was happening. Maybe he was tripping out, and seeing things that weren't true.

It was a desperate, fleeting hope. The blood was real. The stench of it coated his nostrils and the back of his tongue like thick oil, making him want to heave. The death all around him was real.

Teddy sank to his knees in the snow. He sobbed, unable to contain his shock and grief. He howled and punched the frozen earth, despair engulfing him.

He didn't hear the approaching footsteps. They'd been too light, as stealthy as a cat. But in the next instant, Teddy knew he wasn't alone.

And he knew, even before he turned his head and saw the

burning glow of a predator's wild eyes, that he was about to join his kin in death.

Teddy Toms screamed, but the sound never made it past his throat.

CHAPTER ONE

Twenty-eight-hundred feet below the red single-engine de Havilland Beaver's wings, the broad swath of the frozen Koyukuk River glistened under the morning moonlight like a ribbon of crushed diamonds. Alexandra Maguire followed the long stretch of ice-jammed, crystalline water north out of the small town of Harmony, the back of her plane loaded with supplies for the day's delivery run to a handful of settlements nestled deep in the interior.

Beside her in the passenger seat of the cockpit was Luna, the best copilot she'd ever had, aside from her dad, who had taught Alex everything she knew about flying. The gray-and-white wolf dog had been standing in for Hank Maguire for a couple of years now, when the Alzheimer's had really started taking hold of him. Hard to believe he'd been gone for six months now, although Alex often felt she had been slowly losing him for a lot longer than that. At least the disease that ate away his mind and memories had also ended his pain, a small mercy to be sure.

Now it was just Luna and her living in the old house in Harmony and making the supply runs to Hank's small roster of clients in the bush. Luna sat erect next to Alex, her pointed ears perked forward, sharp blue eyes keeping a steady watch on the mountainous terrain of the Brooks Range, its dark, crouching bulk filling the northwest horizon. As they crossed the Arctic Circle, the dog fidgeted in the seat and let out a small, eager-sounding whine.

'Don't tell me you can smell Pop Toms's moose jerky from here,' Alex said, reaching out to ruffle the big furry head as they continued north along the Koyukuk's Middle Fork, past the small villages of Bettles and Evansville. 'Breakfast is still twenty minutes away, girlfriend. Make that thirty minutes, if that black storm cloud over the Anaktuvuk Pass decides to blow our way.'

Alex eyed the dark thunderhead that loomed a few miles up from their flight path. More snow was in the forecast; certainly nothing unusual for November in Alaska, but not exactly prime conditions for her delivery route today. She exhaled a curse as the wind coming off the mountains picked up speed and scuttled across the river valley to give the already bumpy ride a bit more gusto.

The worst of it passed just as Alex's cell phone began to chirp in the pocket of her parka. She dug the phone out and answered the call without needing to know who was on the other end of the line.

'Hey, Jenna.'

In the background of her best friend's house, Alex could hear a Forest Service radio chattering about sketchy weather conditions and plummeting windchill factors. 'Storm's gonna be coming your way in a couple of hours, Alex. You on the ground yet?'

'Not quite.' She rode through another round of bumps as she neared the town of Wiseman and turned the plane onto the route that would take her to the first stop on her day's delivery schedule. 'I'm maybe ten minutes from the Toms place now. Three more stops after that, shouldn't take more than an hour apiece even with the headwind I'm fighting right now. I think the storm is going to pass right by this time.'

It was hope more than qualified estimation, sympathy for

her friend's concern more than caution for her own safety. Alex was a good flier, and too well trained by Hank Maguire to do anything completely reckless, but the simple fact was the supplies she carried in her cargo hold were already a week overdue because of bad weather. She'd be damned if she was going to let a few snowflakes or gusty breezes keep her from delivering goods to the folks in the far-flung reaches of the interior who were counting on her for food and fuel.

'Everything's fine on this end, Jenna. You know I'm careful.'

'Yeah,' she said. 'But accidents happen, don't they?'

Alex might have told Jenna not to worry, but saying it wouldn't have done any good. Her friend knew as well as anyone – perhaps better than most – that the bush pilot's unofficial creed was roughly the same as that of a police officer: *You have to go out; you don't have to come back.*

Jenna Tucker-Darrow, a former Statie from a long line of Staties – and the widow of one to boot – got quiet for a long moment. Alex knew her friend's mind was likely traveling down a dark path, so she worked to fill the silence with chitchat.

'Hey, when I spoke to Pop Toms yesterday, he told me he'd just smoked a big batch of moose meat. You want me to see if I can sweet-talk him into sending me back with some extra jerky for you?'

Jenna laughed, but she sounded as though her thoughts were a million miles away. 'Sure. If you think Luna will let you get away with it, then yeah, I'd like that.'

'You got it. The only thing better than Pop's moose jerky is his biscuits and gravy. Lucky me, I get some of both.'

Breakfast at Pop Toms's place in exchange for semi-monthly supply drops had been a tradition started by Alex's father. It was one she enjoyed maintaining, even if the price of aviation gas well outweighed the price of Pop's simple meals. But Alex liked the old guy and his family. They were good, basic folks living authentically off the same rugged land that had sustained generations of their stalwart kin.

The idea of sitting down for a hot, homemade breakfast and catching up on the week's events with Pop Toms made every bump and dip in the flight out to the remote settlement worthwhile. As she crested the final ridge and began her descent toward the makeshift landing strip behind Pop's store, Alex imagined the salty-sweet smell of smoked meat and buttermilk biscuits that would already be warming on the woodstove when she arrived.

'Listen, I'd better go,' she told Jenna. 'I'm going to need both hands to land this thing, and I—'

The words caught in her throat. On the ground below, something odd caught Alex's eye. In the dark of the winter morning, she couldn't quite make out the bulky, snow-covered form lying in the center of the settlement, but whatever it was made the hair at the back of her neck prickle to attention.

'Alex?'

She couldn't answer at first, all of her focus rooted on the strange object below. Dread crawled up her spine, as cold as the wind battering the windscreen.

'Alex, are you still there?'

'I'm, uh . . . yeah, I'm here.'

'What's going on?'

'I'm not sure. I'm looking at Pop's place just ahead, but something's not right down there.'

'What do you mean?'

'I can't say exactly.' Alex peered out the window of the cockpit as she brought the plane closer, preparing to land. 'There's something in the snow. It's not moving. Oh, my God . . . I think it's a person.'

'Are you sure?'

'I don't know,' Alex murmured into the cell phone, but the way her pulse was hammering, she had no doubt that she was looking at a human being lying underneath a fresh cover of snow.

A dead human being, if whoever it was had been lying there unnoticed for anything longer than a few hours in this punishing cold.

But how could that be? It was almost nine in the morning. Even though daybreak wouldn't come until close to noon this far north, Pop would have been awake for hours by now. The other folks in the settlement – his sister and her family – would have had to be blind to miss the fact that one of them was not only unaccounted for but sprawled in a frozen heap right outside their doors.

'Talk to me, Alex,' Jenna was saying now, using her cop voice, the one that demanded to be obeyed. 'Tell me what's going on.'

As she descended to begin her landing, Alex noticed another worrisome form on the ground below – this one lying between Pop Toms's house and the tree line of the surrounding woods. The snow around the body was blood-soaked, dark stains seeping up through the blanket of fresh white in horrific intensity.

'Oh, Jesus,' she hissed under her breath. 'This is bad, Jenna. Something awful has happened here. There's more than one person out there. They've been . . . hurt somehow.'

'Hurt as in wounded?'

'Dead,' Alex murmured, her mouth gone suddenly dry with the certainty of what she was seeing. 'Oh, God, Jenna . . . there's blood. A lot of blood.'

'Shit,' Jenna whispered. 'Okay, listen to me, Alex, I want you to stay on the phone with me now. Turn around and come back into town. I'm going to call Zach on the radio while I have you on the phone with me, all right? Whatever's happened, I think we should let Zach handle it. Don't you go near—'

'I can't leave them alone,' Alex blurted. 'People have been hurt down there. They might need help. I can't just turn away and leave them now. Oh, God. I have to go down and see if I can do something.'

'Alex, dammit, don't you—'

'I have to go,' she said. 'I'm about to land.'

Ignoring Jenna's continued orders to leave the situation to Zach Tucker, Jenna's brother and the sole police officer in a hundred-mile radius, Alex cut off the call and eased the plane down onto its skis on the short landing strip. She brought the Beaver to an abrupt stop in the fresh powder, not the most graceful landing but good enough, considering that every nerve ending in her body was screaming in rising panic. She killed the engine and no sooner had she opened the cockpit door did Luna leap over her lap to bolt from the plane and run toward the center of the cluster of homes.

'Luna!'

Alex's voice echoed in the eerie quiet of the place. The wolf dog was out of sight now. Alex climbed out of the plane and called for Luna once more, but only silence answered. No one came out of the nearby houses to greet her. No sign of Pop Toms at the log-cabin store just a hundred feet away. No sign of Teddy, who, despite his teenage front of indifference, adored Luna as much as the dog loved him. There was no sign of Pop's sister, Ruthanne, either, nor her husband and grown sons, who were usually up well before the late daybreak of November and taking care of things around the settlement. The entire place was still and soundless, utterly lifeless.

'Shit,' Alex whispered, her heart jackhammering in her breast.

What the hell had happened here? What kind of dangerous situation might she be walking into when she got out of her plane?

As she reached back into the cargo hold to grab her loaded

rifle, Alex's mind latched onto the grimmest possibility. Middle of winter in the interior, it wasn't unheard of for someone to go stir-crazy and attack his neighbor or do serious harm to himself, maybe both in short order. She didn't want to think it – couldn't picture anyone in this close-knit group of people snapping like that, not even sullen Teddy, whom Pop was worried had recently fallen in with a bad crowd.

Rifle at the ready, Alex climbed out of the plane and headed in the direction Luna had run. Last night's fresh snow cover was powdery soft under her boots, muffling the sound of her footsteps as she cautiously approached Pop's store. The back door was unlatched, wedged open half a foot by snow that had blown over the threshold and begun to accumulate. No one had been out here to check on the place for a minimum of several hours.

Alex swallowed the lump of dread that was steadily growing in her throat. She didn't dare call out to anyone now. She hardly dared to breathe as she continued past the store to the cluster of cabins beyond. Luna's bark made her jump. The wolf dog was sitting several yards out. At her feet was one of the lifeless forms Alex had spotted from the air. Luna barked once more, then nosed the body as if she were trying to make it move.

'Oh, Jesus . . . how can this be?' Alex whispered, taking another look around the silent settlement as she managed a firmer grip on her weapon. Her feet felt like lead weights as she walked toward Luna and that motionless, snow-covered bulk on the ground. 'Good girl. I'm here now. Let me have a look.'

God help her, she didn't need to get very close to see that it was Teddy lying there. The teen's favorite black-and-red flannel shirt was sticking out of the shredded, bloodied mess of his heavy down parka. His dark brown hair was iced over where it rested against his cheek and brow, his olive-colored skin frozen and waxy, tinged blue where it wasn't coated brick red with coagulated blood from the torn, gaping wound where his larynx used to be.

Alex rocked back on her heels, sucking in a great gasp of air as the reality of what she was seeing slammed into her. Teddy was dead. Just a kid, for crissake, and someone had killed him and left him there like an animal.

And he wasn't the only one to suffer that fate at this remote family settlement. Shock and fear clawing at her, Alex stepped back from Teddy's body and swung her head around to look at the surrounding area and houses. A door was smashed off its hinges across the way. Another motionless bulk lay outside one of the cabins. Still another, just below the open door of a pickup truck that was parked alongside an old wooden storage shed.

'Oh, God . . . no.'

And then there was the body she'd seen on her descent into the settlement, the one that looked so like Pop Toms, dead and bloodied at the edge of the woods behind his house.

Taking a firmer hold on her rifle even though she doubted that the killer – or killers, based on the depth of carnage here – had bothered to hang around, Alex found herself drifting toward that scarlet-drenched patch of snow near the tree line, Luna following at her heels.

Alex's heart and stomach twisted together with each dreadful step. She didn't want to see Pop like this, didn't want to see anyone she cared about brutalized and broken and bloody . . . not ever again.

Yet she could no more stop her feet from moving than she could keep from kneeling beside the grisly, facedown corpse of the man who'd always greeted her with a smile and a big, warm bear hug. Alex set her gun down in the red snow next to her. A wordless cry strangling in her throat, she reached out and carefully rolled the big man's shoulder. The ruined, sightless face that gaped up at her made Alex's blood chill in her veins. His expression was one of pure terror, frozen across his once-jovial features. Alex could not even begin to imagine the horror of what he must have seen in the instant before he died.

Then again . . .

The old memory leapt out at her from the dark, locked corner of her past. Alex felt its sharp bite, heard the screams that had shattered the night – and her life – forever.

No.

Alex didn't want to relive that pain. She didn't want to think about that night, least of all now. Not when she was surrounded by so much death. Not when she was so totally alone. She couldn't bear to dredge up the past she'd left eighteen years and thousands of miles behind her.

But it crept back into her thoughts as though it were yesterday. As though it were happening again, the unshakable sense that the same horror she and her father had survived so long ago in Florida had somehow come to visit this innocent family in the isolated wilds of Alaska. Alex choked back a sickened sob, brushing at the tears that burned her cheeks as they froze against her skin.

Luna's low grunt beside her broke into Alex's thoughts. The dog was digging at the snow near the body, her muzzle buried in the powder. She moved forward, sniffing out a scent that led toward the trees. Alex got up to see what Luna had found. She didn't see it at first, then, when she did, the sight did not compute in her mind.

It was a footprint, bloodstained and partially obscured by the new-fallen snow. A human footprint that she had to guess would have fit a size fifteen or larger boot. And the foot that left it was naked – more than improbable in this deadly cold, impossible.

'What the hell?'

Terrified, Alex grabbed Luna by the scruff of her neck and held her fast at her side before the dog could follow the tracks any farther. She looked out to where they quickly grew lighter, then simply vanished into the elements. It didn't make sense.

None of this made any sense in the reality of the world as she wanted to view it.

From the direction of her plane, she heard her cell phone ringing, accompanied by the airless crackle of the Beaver's radio as an agitated male voice squawked for her to report in.

'Alex, goddamn it! Do you copy? Alex!'

Glad for the distraction, she picked up her rifle and ran back to the plane, Luna keeping pace at her side like the canine bodyguard she truly was.

'Alex!' Zach Tucker shouted her name over the airwaves again. 'If you can hear me, Alex, pick up now!'

She bent in over the seat and grabbed the radio. 'I'm here,' she said, breathless and shaking. 'I'm here, Zach, and they're all dead. Pop Toms. Teddy. Everyone.'

Zach swore a harshly whispered oath. 'What about you? Are you okay?'

'Yeah,' she murmured. 'Oh, my God. Zach, how could this happen?'

'I'm gonna take care of it,' he told her. 'Right now, I need you to tell me what you can about what you see, okay? Did you notice any weapons, any explanation for what might have gone on out there?'

Alex shot a miserable look back over at the carnage of the settlement. The lives cut short so violently. The blood that she could taste on the icy wind.

'Alex? Do you have any idea how these folks might have been killed?'

She squeezed her eyes shut against the barrage of memories that assailed her – the screams of her mother and her little brother, the anguished cries of her father as he grabbed nine-year-old Alex up into his arms and fled with her into the night before the monsters had a chance to kill them all.

Alex shook her head, trying desperately to dislodge that awful recollection . . . and to deny to herself that the killings here last night were stamped with the same kind of unthinkable horror.

'Talk to me,' Zach coaxed her. 'Help me understand what happened if you can, Alex.'

The words would not come to her tongue. They remained trapped in her throat, swallowed up by the knot of ice-cold dread that had opened in the center of her chest.

'I don't know,' she answered, her voice sounding detached and wooden in the silence of the empty, frozen bush. 'I can't tell you what could have done this. I can't . . .'

'That's okay, Alex. I know you must be upset. Just come on back home now. I've already got a call in to Roger Bemis out at the airstrip. He's going to fly me out there within the hour and we're gonna take care of the Tomses, all right?'

'Okay,' she murmured.

'Everything's going to be okay now, I promise.'

'Okay,' she repeated, feeling another tear spill down her cold cheek.

Her father had said the same words to her all those years ago – a promise that everything would be all right. She hadn't believed him. After what she had seen here today, the sense she had that something evil was closing in on her once more, Alex wondered if anything would ever truly be all right again.

Skeeter Arnold took a long drag off a fat joint as he kicked back in a battered baby blue velvet recliner, the finest piece of furniture he had in the shithole apartment he kept in the back of his mother's house in Harmony. Holding the smoke deep in his lungs, he closed his eyes and listened to the yammering of the shortwave radio on the kitchen counter. The way Skeeter saw it, the kind of enterprise he was in, it just made good business sense to keep a handle not only on the Staties but also the local yokels too stupid to keep their asses out of trouble.

And yeah, maybe he liked to listen to the dispatches partly because he got a perverted amount of enjoyment out of other people's misery, as well. Nice to be reminded sometimes that he wasn't the biggest loser in the whole state of Alaska, no matter what his bitch of a mother told him on a regular basis. Skeeter exhaled slowly, thin smoke curling around the curse he mumbled when he heard the creak and groan of the old floorboards as the perpetual pain in his ass came stomping down the hallway to his room.

'Stanley, did you hear me calling you up there? Do you intend to sleep all damn day in there?' She ham-fisted a few hard raps on the door, then gave the locked knob a good, but ineffective, jiggle. 'Didn't I tell you to run out first thing this morning and pick up some rice and canned beans? What the hell are you waiting for, the spring thaw? Get off your lazy ass and do something useful for a change!'

Skeeter didn't trouble himself to answer. Nor did he budge from his sprawl in the chair, or even so much as flinch as his mother continued to huff and puff and bang on the door. He took another lazy hit off the joint and savored the buzz, knowing the annoyance outside his room would eventually tire of him ignoring her and slink back to her harpy's perch in front of the TV where she belonged.

To help drown her out in the meantime, Skeeter reached for the radio a few feet away and cranked the volume. Harmony's one-and-only law enforcer, Trooper Zachary Tucker, sounded like he had his panties in a wad over something pretty big today.

'Stanley Arnold, don't you think you can just tune me out, you miserable no-good excuse for a son!' His mother pounded on the door again, then stormed off, her big mouth still running all the way up the hall. 'You're just like your father. Never been worth a lick and never will be!'

Skeeter got up from the recliner and moved in closer to the radio as Tucker, reporting in with the State boys in Fairbanks, rattled off the coordinates of an apparent multiple death scene – probable homicide, he'd said – some forty miles out in the bush. Tucker was awaiting air transport from one of Harmony's two resident pilots. He advised that the other one, Alex Maguire, had been the one who discovered the bodies while on a supply run and was presently on her way back into town.

Skeeter felt a twist of excitement as he listened. He knew the area in question very well. Hell, he'd been out that way just last night with Chad Bishop and a few other people. They'd been getting high and drinking by the river . . . right before they'd started tormenting Teddy Toms. In fact, the way it was sounding to him, the settlement the cops were talking about had to be the kid's family's place.

'No friggin' way,' Skeeter whispered, wondering if he could possibly be right about that. Just to be sure, he jotted the coordinates down on his palm, then riffled through a pile of unpaid bills and other trash until he found the beer-stained area map he'd been using as a coaster for the past couple of years. He triangulated the spot on the map, disbelief and a sick sort of wonderment sliding through his senses.

'Holy shit,' he said, taking a long drag off his joint before snuffing it out on the burn-scarred Formica to save the rest of the buzz for later. He was too excited to finish it now. Too lit up with morbid curiosity to keep from running a tight pace back and forth across the cramped room.

Had Pop Toms or the old man's brother-in-law gone off the deep end? Or had it been Teddy who finally snapped his leash? Maybe the kid had gone home and lost it after Skeeter and the others had driven him off in tears last night at the river?

He'd know all that soon enough, Skeeter figured. He'd always wanted to see a dead person up close. Maybe he'd just head out for a little detour on his way to the store for those beans and rice his mother wanted.

Yeah, and maybe he'd skip the errand-boy bullshit and just go do what *he* wanted for a change.

Skeeter grabbed his cell phone – the sweet new one with video capability and the cool skull-and-crossbones skin. Then he fished the key to his Yamaha sled out of the mess on his counter. He didn't bother telling his mother where he was heading, just pulled on his winter gear and strode out into the bracing chill of the day.

≒ CHAPTER TWO ≒

BOSTON, MASSACHUSETTS

Heat blasted out of the Range Rover's dashboard vents as Brock upped the temperature another few degrees. 'Damn, it's cold tonight.' The big male from Detroit cupped his hands in front of his mouth and blew into his palms. 'I hate winter, man. Feels like goddamn Siberia out there.'

'Not even close,' Kade replied from behind the wheel of the parked SUV, his gaze fixed on the decrepit brownstone they'd been surveilling for the past couple of hours. Even in the postmidnight darkness, with a fresh blanket of snow masking everything in pristine white, the place looked like total shit from the outside. Not that it mattered. Whatever they were peddling inside – drugs, sex, or a combination of both – was bringing a fairly steady stream of human traffic to the door. Kade watched as a trio of frat boys wearing university colors and a couple of bundled-up young women climbed out of a piece-of-crap Impala and went inside.

'If this was Siberia,' Kade added once the street got quiet again, 'our balls would be jingling like sleigh bells and we'd be pissing ice cubes. Boston in November is a picnic.'

'Says the vampire born on a friggin' Alaskan glacier,' Brock drawled, shaking his head as he held his dark hands in front of the vents and tried to rub off the chill. 'How much longer you think we need to wait out here before our man decides to show his ugly face? I need to start moving before my ass freezes to this seat.'

Kade grunted more than chuckled, as impatient as his partner on tonight's patrol of the city. It wasn't the humans that brought Brock and him to this address in one of Boston's roughest areas, but the individual purported to be behind the illegal activity. And if their intel proved valid – that the vampire who ran the place was also dealing in another forbidden commodity – then the night was going to end on a very unpleasant, probably bloody, note.

Kade could hardly wait.

'Here he is now,' he said, watching as a pair of headlights swung around the corner and a pimped-out black Mercedes with gold trim and gilded hubcaps prowled to a stop at the curb.

'You have got to be kidding me,' Brock said, smirking as the spectacle continued.

Music throbbed from within the sedan, the rhythmic bass and punching lyrics vibrating impossibly louder as the driver got out and went around to open the back passenger-side door. A pair of leashed white pit bulls were the first to exit the car, followed by their master, a tall Breed male trying hard to look badass even though he was wrapped in a long fox-fur coat and had gone about ten pounds beyond the respectable limits of bling and guyliner.

'Forget about the shit Gideon turned up on this asshole,' Kade said. 'We'd be in the right to waste him just for going out in public dressed like that.'

Brock grinned, showing the very tips of his fangs. 'You ask me, I think we ought to waste him just for making us freeze our stones off waiting for him out here.'

At the curb, the vampire gave his dogs a harsh yank of their studded leather leashes when they dared to take a step ahead of him. He kicked the one nearest to him as he strode toward the door of the brownstone, chuckling at the dog's sharp yelp of pain. When he and his driver and his pair of hellhounds had all disappeared inside the building, Kade killed the Rover's auxiliary power and opened his door.

'Come on,' he said. 'Let's find a way in through the back while Homeboy's busy making an entrance.'

They moved in behind the building and located a ground-level window half obscured by snow and street rubbish. Squatting on his haunches, Kade brushed away the ice and crusted-over filth, then lifted the hinged panel of glass and peered into the darkened space on the other side. It was a brick cellar, littered with a couple of rotted mattresses, spent condoms, used syringes, and a combined stench of piss, vomit, and various other expelled bodily fluids that assaulted Kade's acute senses like a sledgehammer blow to his skull.

'Jesus Christ,' he hissed, lips curling back off his teeth and fangs. 'Homeboy's housekeeper is so fired.'

He slipped inside, landing soundlessly on the rough con-crete floor. Brock followed, 280-plus pounds of heavily armed vampire lighting as quietly as a cat beside him. Kade motioned past the revolting mess on the floor to a pitch-black corner of the room, where a short length of chain and a pair of shackles lay. A strip of silver duct tape had been cast off nearby, with several strands of long, light blond hair stuck to it.

Brock met Kade's hard stare in the dark. His deep voice was more growl than words. 'Skin trader.'

Kade nodded grimly, sickened by the evidence of all that had taken place in this dank, dark basement prison. He was about to head for the stairs and crash the party above when Brock's low curse made him pause.

'We're not alone down here, my man.' Brock indicated a barred door all but obscured by shadows and the rusted skeleton of an old box spring that leaned too neatly against it. 'Humans,' he said. 'Females, just on the other side of that door.'

Hearing the quiet, broken breathing now, and feeling the current of pain and suffering that rode on the fetid air, Kade moved with Brock toward the lightless corner of the cellar. They pushed aside the old box spring, then Kade lifted the thick metal bar that locked the door from the outside.

'Holy hell,' Brock whispered into the darkness. He stepped inside the small room where three young women sat huddled together in the corner, shivering and terrified. When one of them started to scream, Brock moved faster than any of the drugged humans could track him. Reaching down, he brushed his hand over the female's brow, trancing her into silence with his touch. 'It's all right. You're safe now. We aren't going to hurt you.'

'Have any of them been bled?' Kade asked, watching as Brock willed the other two captives into similar states of quiet.

'They've been beaten recently, so there's bruising. But I don't see any bite wounds. Don't see any Breedmate marks, either,' he added, doing a quick check of the women's exposed skin and extremities, looking for the teardrop-and-crescent-moon birthmark that differentiated mortal females from their more genetically extraordinary sisters. Brock gently released the pale arm he held, then stood up. 'At least none of these three is a Breedmate.'

A small mercy, and one that hardly exonerated the vampire scum who'd been making a business out of trafficking women to the highest bidder.

'Give me a minute to scrub their memories of what they've been through and get them safely out of here,' Brock said. 'I'll be right behind you.'

Kade gave him a tight nod and a flash of fang. 'Meanwhile, I'm going to head upstairs and have a little private chat with Homeboy.'

With aggression burning like acid in his veins, Kade crept up the steps to the noise-filled main floor of the building, bypassing the orgy taking place under a cloud of narcotic smoke, trippy industrial music, and flashing strobe lights.

In a back office down the hall, he heard the thin rasp of the scumbag he was looking for.

'Fetch me the female who just came in with those Ivy League losers – no, not the blonde, the other one. If she's a true red-head, she's worth twice as much to me.'

Kade hung back, grinning as Homeboy's beefy driver-slash-bodyguard came out of the office and saw him standing there in the hallway. The male was Breed, as well, and menace flashed as amber light in his irises when he saw the threat before him now.

'Shh,' Kade said pleasantly, a dagger already gripped in his hand and ready to let fly.

He released the blade in the instant the driver reached for his own weapon, nailing the big vampire dead center in the throat. The bulky body sagged to the floor, and as the heavy thump carried over the din of music and moaning from up the hall, Kade leapt around the corpse to fill the open doorway of Homeboy's office.

The pair of white pit bulls lunged faster than their master in the ridiculous fur coat could react. Snarling and snapping, the dogs charged Kade. He didn't flinch; there was no need. He caught their wild eyes in an unblinking look of command that brought them both to a sudden halt on the carpeted floor in front of his boots.

All of the Breed were born with their own unique talents – or curses, in some cases – in addition to the longevity, strength, and bloodthirst that were traits of their kind. In Kade, his talent was the ability to connect psychically with predator animals and direct their actions with a simple thought. It was a power he had honed to lethal precision from the time he was a boy in the frozen Alaskan wild, and with animals far more dangerous than these.

'Stay,' he said calmly to the dogs, then glanced up at the Breed male who gaped at him from across the small room. 'You stay, too.'

'What the – who the fuck are you?' Panic and outrage deepened the lines around the vampire's mouth as he took in Kade's appearance, from the black fatigues and combat boots that matched the dark color of his spiky hair, to the impressive collection of blades and semi-automatic weaponry he sported at his hips and on holsters strapped to his thighs. 'Warrior,' he breathed, evidently not so arrogant – or stupid – that he didn't know some measure of fear at this unannounced visit. 'What could the Order possibly want from me?'

'Information,' Kade replied. He took a step inside the room and closed the door behind him, pausing to scratch one of the now-docile pit bulls behind the ear. 'We've heard some disturbing things about this business you're running here. We need to know more.'

The vampire lifted his shoulders and made a half-assed attempt to look confused. 'What's to tell? I dabble in a variety of ventures.'

'Yeah, I noticed. Nice little venture you've got going down in the basement of this shithole. How long have you been trafficking women?'

'I don't know what you're talking about.'

'Now, see, making me repeat myself is not a smart thing to do.' Kade crouched low and motioned to the pair of pit bulls to come up alongside him. They sat at his feet like squat gargoyles, staring at their former master and obediently awaiting Kade's command simply because that's what he wanted them to do. 'I'll bet if I told these dogs to rip your throat out, I wouldn't have to ask them twice. What do you think? Should we find out?'

Homeboy swallowed hard. 'I-I haven't been doing it for very long. A couple months short of a year, I guess. Started out with drugs and whores, then I started getting certain . . . requests.' He fidgeted with one of the many gold rings that gleamed on his fingers. 'You know, requests for services of a more permanent nature.'

'And your clients?' Kade prompted as he rose to his full six-foot-four height. 'Who are they?'

'Humans, primarily. I really don't keep good records.'

'But you do provide these *services*' – he hissed the word through his fangs – 'to members of the Breed, as well.'

It wasn't a question, and Homeboy knew it. He gave another shrug, the collar of his fox coat brushing against his diamond-studded earlobe. 'I deal in a cash business, simple supply and demand. Breed or human, the money is all the same.'

'And business is good,' Kade guessed.

'I'm getting by. Why is the Order so interested in what I'm doing, anyway? You looking for a piece of the action?' he hedged, his smile little more than a slimy split of his lips. 'I could cut Lucan in, if that's what this is about. I *am* a businessman, after all.'

'You are scum,' Kade said, incensed but not surprised that a bottom-feeder like this would think that he or any of his brethren were for sale. 'And if I told Lucan you said that, he would shred you open from chin to balls. You know what? Fuck that. I'll save him the trouble—'

'Wait!' Homeboy held up his hands. 'Wait. Tell me what you want to know.'

'Okay. Let's start with this. How many of the women you've locked up in that basement and sold were Breedmates?'

A sickening silence lengthened while the vampire considered how best to answer. Even this worthless offal had to know that those rare females bearing the Breedmate birthmark were revered, precious to all of the Breed. To bring harm to a Breedmate was to bring harm to the entire vampire race, for there were no other females on the planet who could carry

Breed young in their womb. To knowingly collect a profit from a Breedmate's pain, or to benefit in any way from her death, was about the most heinous thing one of Kade's kind could do.

He watched the other vampire as he would an insect trapped under glass, and in fact, he valued this Breed male's life even less.

'How many, you disgusting fuck? More than one? A dozen? Twenty?' He had to work to bite back his snarl. 'Did you sell them unknowingly, or did you make an even bigger profit off their suffering? Answer the goddamn question!'

With Kade's outburst, the pair of pit bulls rose up onto their feet, their compact muscles taut and straining, both of them growling with menace. The dogs were as attuned to Kade's anger as he was to them. He held the dogs back with only the barest thread of self-control, knowing that if the vampire cowering in front of him had any information of value, he was duty-bound to wring it out of him.

Then he could kill him with a clear conscience.

'Who have you been selling Breedmates to? Answer the fucking question. I'm not going to wait all night for you to cough up the truth.'

'I-I don't know,' he stammered. 'That is the truth. I don't know.'

'But you admit that's what you've been doing.' God, he wanted to waste this piece of shit. 'Tell me who you've been trafficking to, before I rip your ugly head off.'

'I swear – I don't know who wanted them!'

Kade wasn't about to let it go at that. 'Was it more than one individual who came to you for the females? What about the name Dragos – ring any bells with you?'

Kade watched with narrowed eyes, waiting for the vampire to take the bait. But the name Kade cast out to him went unacknowledged. Anyone having dealt with the Breed elder known as Dragos – a villain whose evil had only recently been discovered through the efforts of the Order – would surely register some amount of reaction at the mention of his name.

Homeboy, however, was oblivious. He exhaled a sigh and gave a weak shake of his head. 'I only dealt with one guy. He wasn't Breed. Wasn't actually human, either. Not by the time I met him, anyway.'

'A Minion, then?'

The news didn't exactly put Kade at ease. Though the creation of Minions went against Breed law, not to mention basic morality, only the most powerful of the Breed could create the human mind slaves. Drained nearly to the point of death, Minions were loyal to their Master alone. Dragos was second-generation Breed and held himself above any law, Breed or otherwise. It wasn't a question of whether Dragos kept Minions, but rather how many, and how deeply embedded into human society did they go.

'Would you know this Minion if you saw him again?'

The animal carcass wrapped around the vampire's neck lifted once more with another shrug of his shoulders. 'I don't know. Maybe. He hasn't been around for a long time now. Stopped doing business with him about three, maybe four months ago. For a while there, he was one of my regulars, then nothing out of him again.'

'You must have been so disappointed,' Kade drawled. 'Describe him to me. What did the Minion look like?'

'Tell you the truth, I never got a good look at the guy. Never really tried, either. I could tell he was Minion, and the dude paid in large bills. Nothing more I needed to know about him.'

Kade's veins tightened with animosity and a barely restrained rage to hear the ambivalence in his words. He had killed for lesser offenses than this – far less – and the urge to tear apart this worthless excuse of a male was fierce. 'So, what you're saying is you repeatedly sold him innocent females who were too drugged up to defend themselves, with zero regard for what he was doing with them or where they might end up. No questions asked. That about it?'

'I guess you could say I run my business on the basis of "don't ask, don't tell."'

'Yeah, you could say that,' Kade agreed. 'Or I could say that you run your business like an ass-licking coward and you deserve to die a slow and painful death.'

Worry spiked in an acrid stink as the vampire held Kade's stare. 'Now, let's just wait a minute. Let me think for a second, all right? Maybe I can remember something. Maybe there is some way I can help—'

'I doubt it.' Kade scrutinized him, seeing from the look of scrambling panic on his face that he wasn't going to get anything more useful out of this conversation.

Besides that, he was tired of looking at the asshole.

He reached down to lift the dogs' chins in his palms, glancing into the intense brown eyes of one, then the other. The silent command was acknowledged with a faint twitch of sinew. The pit bulls jumped up onto the desk and sat in front of their former master, their eyes unblinking, sharp-toothed maws open and dripping saliva.

'Good boys,' Kade said. He pivoted to leave.

'Wait, so . . . that's it?' Homeboy asked hesitantly from around the pair of slavering gargoyles that were now perched before him. 'I wanna be sure we're cool for now. I mean, I told you everything I know. That's all you want from me, right?'

'Not exactly,' Kade said without looking back at the skin trader. He put his hand on the doorknob. 'There is one more thing I want.'

As he walked out of the office and closed the door, he heard the pair of pit bulls launch into their attack. Kade paused there, closing his eyes and letting himself enjoy the violence of the moment through his talent's visceral connection to the animals. He felt every breaking crunch of bone, every tear of the skin trader's flesh as the dogs ripped into him. Inside the room, the vampire screamed and wailed, his pain a pleasant punctuation to the music and moaning still carrying on in the other part of the building.

Brock came striding up the hallway as Kade was stepping around the corpse of the driver.

'You take care of the females?' he asked as he and his patrol partner met up halfway.

'I scrubbed the memories of their whole captivity and sent them home,' Brock said. The big male spared only the briefest glance at the body before arching a brow at Kade. 'How about you? Did you manage to get anything out of Homeboy?'

'Turns out he wasn't actually much of a dog person,' Kade said around the continued shrieks coming from the direction of the office.

Brock's mouth quirked at the corner. 'So I hear. Anything else?'

'Yeah, unfortunately. Asshole's been trafficking Breedmates, just as our intel suggested. His client was a Minion, but he didn't know anything more than that. Never saw the mind slave up close and couldn't describe him at all.'

'Shit,' Brock said, running a big hand over the top of his head. 'So I guess Homeboy was a dead end, huh?'

Kade cocked his head as the last of the howls cut short behind him. 'He is now.'

Brock exhaled a rueful chuckle. 'Let's get this place cleaned up and shut down. Got a text from Gideon, asking us to call in when we can. Something about a situation up north.'

'Up north, as in upstate?'

'No, man. Farther north than that.' Brock met his gaze and

held it for longer than was comfortable. 'Something's evidently gone down in Alaska. He didn't say what exactly, just said that Lucan wants you to report in to headquarters asap.'

❧ CHAPTER THREE ❧

K ade understood even before he and Brock arrived at the Order's compound that the news he was about to get couldn't be good. As the founder and leader of the warriors, not to mention a first-generation Breed somewhere in the vicinity of nine hundred years old, Lucan was hardly an alarmist by nature. So the fact that he saw fit to call Kade in specifically was a major clue that whatever the so-called situation was in Alaska, it was something seriously fucked up.

Speculation swirled in Kade's gut, one disturbing scenario after another, awful things that were far too easy for him to imagine and burned like bitter bile in the back of his throat. He kept his dread to himself as he and Brock parked the Rover in the fleet garage behind the heavily secured estate at ground level, then took the hangar's elevator down some three hundred feet to the subterranean nerve center of the Order's operations.

'You cool, my man?' Brock asked as he and Kade stepped out of the elevator and into the white marble corridor that connected the labyrinthine compound's many chambers like a central artery. 'You know if this had anything to do with your kin back home, Lucan would have said so. I'm sure that whatever went down, everything's good with your family. No worries, yeah?'

'Yeah. No worries,' Kade replied, but his mouth was on automatic pilot.

He'd left his family's settlement in Alaska roughly a year ago to join the Order in Boston. It had been an abrupt departure, one spurred by the urgent summons he'd received from Nikolai, a warrior of the Order whom Kade had met decades past when his travels had taken him from Alaska's frozen tundra to that of Niko's Siberian homeland.

There were things Kade had left unfinished in Alaska. Things that haunted him still – worse, for the time and distance that had kept him away all these long months.

If anything had happened and he hadn't been there to step in . . .

Kade pushed the thought from his head as he and Brock turned down one of the corridors that would lead them to the tech lab.

Lucan, the dark-haired Gen One, was waiting there in the compound's glass-walled war room with Gideon, the blond, deceptively disheveled-looking resident genius who ran the Order's extensive collection of technology. The pair stood together in front of a flat-screen monitor. Lucan raked his fingers over his sternly set jaw just as the lab's transparent doors whisked open to permit Kade and Brock inside.

'How did the lead work out tonight in Roxbury?' he asked when the two warriors had entered the room.

Kade gave a brief rundown of what they found out from the skin trader, which wasn't much. But as Kade spoke, he couldn't keep his attention from drifting to the monitor behind Lucan. When the big male started to pace in that way he always did when he was either pissed off or deep in thought, Kade got his first good look at the image filling the computer screen.

It wasn't pretty.

A blurry photo – or maybe it was a freeze-framed video image – splashed garish red and white across the monitor. Blood and snow. A brutal killing in the frozen wilds of Alaska. Kade knew it instinctively, and the knowledge cut through him like the edge of a blade.

'What happened?' he asked, his voice so wooden it sounded apathetic, wholly undisturbed.

'Nasty bit of video showed up on the Internet today,' Lucan said. 'From what we can tell, this was captured by a cell phone camera a couple of days ago and uploaded from a Fairbanks ISP to a website that caters to crime-scene gawkers and other sick bastards who get off on viewing the dead.'

He gave a look to Gideon and with a click of the computer mouse, the frozen image onscreen came to vivid life. Over the excitable breathing and crunching footsteps of the person holding the camera, Kade watched as the crudely shot video showed the scene of what must have been a very brutal slaying.

A bloodied body lay dead on a snow-covered, gore-stained patch of land. The lens's focus was shaky, but the operator managed to zoom in tight on the victim's wounds. Shredded clothing and skin. A number of unmistakable tears and punctures that could only have been made by some very sharp teeth.

Or fangs.

'Jesus,' Kade muttered, struck by the savagery of the killing – the totality of it – as the video played past the four-minute mark and moved on to document no less than three more dead in the snow and ice.

'This looks like the work of Rogues,' Brock said, his deep voice as grim as his expression.

It was a sorry but unavoidable fact of life that there were members of the Breed population who could not – or simply would not – control their thirst for blood. While the majority of the vampire nation abided by laws and reasonable good sense, there were others who gave in to their hungers with no thought for the consequences. Those of the Breed who fed too much, or too frequently, soon found themselves addicted, lost to Bloodlust, the disease of the Rogues. Once a vampire tipped that scale, there was little hope for him to turn himself around.

Bloodlust was almost always a one-way ticket to madness . . . and death. If not by edict of the Order, then by the disease itself, which made even the most careful Breed male reckless. All a Rogue knew was his thirst. He would kill indiscriminately, take any risk, in the attempt to quench it. He would even slaughter an entire village if the opportunity was there.

'Whoever did this needs to be put down fast,' Brock added. 'Son of a bitch needs to be put down hard.'

Lucan nodded his agreement. 'The sooner, the better. That's why I called you in, Kade. The situation up there could get out of hand pretty quick, not only if we've got a Rogue problem to contend with, but also because human law enforcement has gotten wind of the killings. Gideon tracked an Alaska State Police dispatch call out of a little interior town called Harmony. Fortunately, there's fewer than a hundred people living there, but it only takes one hysterical mouth screaming the word 'vampire' to turn this whole thing into an even bigger disaster.'

'Shit,' Kade muttered. 'Do we know who shot the video?'

'Hard to say right now,' Lucan said. 'Gideon's looking into it. We do know for sure there's a trooper posted in the town – he's the one who alerted the Fairbanks dispatch to the killings. Obviously, time is critical here. We need to know who's responsible for the slayings, and we need to make sure no one up there gets anywhere close to the truth about what exactly took place out there in the bush.'

Kade listened, his veins still jangling with the brutality of what he had just seen on the monitor. In his peripheral vision was the final frame, paused on the screen, a blurred image of a young human's blood-spattered face, his open, unseeing brown eyes clouded from the cold, ice crystals clinging to his dark eyelashes. He was just a kid, for crissake. Probably barely out of his teens, if that.

It wasn't the first time Kade had seen the aftermath of a

bloody slaughter in the Alaskan bush. When he'd left home all those months ago, he'd sure as hell hoped he'd never see that kind of carnage again.

'We're spread thin here with our current operations, but we can't afford to let the situation up north go unchecked,' Lucan said. 'I need to send someone who knows the terrain and the people, and who has connections in the Breed population up there.'

Kade held Lucan's stare, knowing he could hardly refuse the assignment, even if Alaska was the last place he wanted to be. When he'd left there last year to join the Order, he'd done so with the hope that he might never return.

He wanted to forget the place where he'd been born. The wild place that had called to him like a possessive, destructive lover every moment since he'd left.

'What do you say, my man?' Lucan asked as Kade's silence grew long.

He didn't see where he had any choice. He owed it to Lucan and the Order to take care of this unexpected, unpleasant business. No matter where it led him.

Even if the search for a vampire with an uncontrollable itch to kill ended up leading Kade home to a ten-thousand-acre stretch of land in the Alaskan interior. Home, to his family's own backyard.

Grim with the idea, he gave the Order's leader an accepting nod. 'How soon do I leave?'

Forty-five minutes later, Kade was wearing a track in the rug of his private quarters, his packed duffel sitting on the end of the bed. A satellite phone lay beside the black leather bag, and for the third time in the past ten minutes, Kade reached for the device and punched in the number he hadn't called since the night he left Alaska.

This time he let the call ring through.

It was a shock to hear his father's strong voice come on the line.

'Been a while,' Kade said by way of greeting, to which his father only grunted.

It was a lame effort at contact after a year of being out of touch by his own doing. Then again, it wasn't as if his father had ever accused him of being responsible or reliable, or anything else for that matter.

The conversation was awkward, a strained attempt at hi-how-are-you as Kade worked up the nerve to ask how everything was going back home. His father talked about the hard winter, the only benefit of the season being the fact that it kept the sun in hiding for all but three hours at midday. Kade recalled the extended darkness of the north country. His pulse kicked eagerly at the thought of so much night, so many hours of freedom in which to run.

It was obvious that his father hadn't yet heard about the recent slayings. Kade didn't mention them, nor did he speak of the mission that was sending him north. Instead, Kade cleared his throat and asked the question that had been burning in his gut since the moment he heard there had been trouble in Alaska.

'How's Seth doing? Is everything all right with him?'

Kade's blood went a bit cold in the hesitant silence that preceded his father's reply. 'He is well. Why do you ask?'

Kade heard the suspicion in his father's voice, the mild disapproval that always had a way of creeping into the elder male's voice whenever Kade dared to question matters concerning his brother. 'Just wondering if he might be around, that's all.'

'Your brother had Darkhaven business to attend to for me in the city,' came the terse reply. 'He left a few weeks ago.'

'A few weeks,' Kade echoed. 'That's a long time for him to be away. Have you heard from him at all recently?'

'Not recently, no. Why?' On the other end of the line, his father seemed to go silent with impatience. 'What exactly is this about, Kade? A year without any contact from you, and now you want to interrogate me about your brother's comings and goings. What is it you want?'

'Forget it,' Kade said, instantly regretting that he'd made the call in the first place. 'Just forget I called. I gotta go.'

He didn't wait for his father's reply. Frankly, he didn't need to hear it.

Kade ended the call without another word, his thoughts swirling with the grisly images he'd seen in the tech lab a short time ago and the knowledge that his brother had not been accounted for in potentially a number of weeks.

His brother, who shared the same dark talent as Kade.

The same dangerously seductive wildness – the violent power – that could so easily slip out of control. And had, at least once, Kade acknowledged with grim recollection.

'Goddamn it, Seth.'

He tossed the phone onto the bed. Then, with a furious growl, he whirled on his heel and slammed his fist into the nearest wall.

⪥ CHAPTER FOUR ⪤

The Arctic storm had pounded the Alaskan interior for two days straight, dumping three feet of snow on the small town of Harmony and its far-flung neighbors along the river and plunging daytime temperatures all over the region to fifteen below zero. Ordinarily, weather like that tended to do one of two things to folks: keep them knuckled down at home, or send them flocking to Pete's, the local restaurant and tavern.

Today, despite the howl of the wintry wind and the skin-biting cold as the third and final hour of sunlight faded into midday dusk, nearly all of Harmony's ninety-three residents were packed into the log-cabin Congregational church for an impromptu town hall meeting. Alex sat beside Jenna in the second row of pews, trying as hard as everyone else to make sense of the recent carnage in the bush, which had brought six dead, brutally savaged bodies into makeshift cold storage at Harmony's airstrip and put the whole town into a state of anxious unrest.

Alex knew that Zach Tucker had tried to keep the news of the attack on the Toms settlement quiet, but despite the vastness of the interior, word traveled fast – faster still, in this isolated eleven-square-mile chunk of land that hugged the shore of the Koyukuk. Bad news, particularly the kind involving multiple unexplained deaths of a violent nature, tended to reach folks' ears as if flown there on a raven's wings.

In the forty-eight hours since Alex's discovery of the killings, and Zach's decision to transport the bodies from the crime scene into Harmony to await the clearing of the weather so the Staties in Fairbanks could come in and take over the investigation, the feeling around town had gone from one of shock and dismay to one of suspicion and dangerous, mounting hysteria. Forty-eight hours had been all the townspeople could take without demanding some answers about just who – or what – had so viciously attacked Pop Toms and his family.

'I simply don't understand,' said Millie Dunbar from her seat in the pew behind Alex. The old woman's voice trembled, not so much from her eighty-seven years of age but from sorrow and concern. 'Who would want to harm Wilbur Toms and his family? They were such good, kind folks. Why, when my father first settled here, he traded with Wilbur's grandfather upriver for many years. He never had a bad word for any of the Tomses. I just can't figure who could be so evil to have done something like this.'

One of the townsmen near the back of the church piped in. 'If you ask me, makes me wonder about the boy, Teddy. Too damn quiet, that one. Seen him hanging around town a bit of late, but he wouldn't even say hello when spoken to, just acted like he was too good to answer. Made me wonder what the kid was up to, and if maybe he had something to hide.'

'Oh, please,' Alex said, feeling obligated to defend Teddy since he wasn't there to do it for himself. She pivoted on the pew and shot a disapproving glance to the area behind her, where dozens of faces had hardened with suspicion because of Big Dave Grant's baseless accusation. 'Teddy was shy around people he didn't know well, that's all. He never talked much because of the teasing he always took for his stutter. And to suggest that he could somehow have anything to do with the murder of his family when he's lying right next to them on a cold slab is disgustingly callous. If any of you had seen the condition they were left in—'

Jenna's hand came down softly on Alex's wrist, but the warning was unnecessary. Alex had no intention of taking that train of thought any further. Bad enough she'd been reliving the gruesome discovery over and over in her mind since she'd stumbled upon Pop Toms, Teddy, and the rest of their kin. She wasn't going to sit there and rehash for everyone how brutal their murders had been. How savage the wounds that had rent flesh to the bone and torn open throats as if some kind of hellish beast had come out of the cold night to feed on the living.

No, not a beast.

A being out of a nightmare.

A monster.

Alex closed her eyes against the vision of blood and death that began to rise from the darkest reaches of her memory. She didn't want to go there, never again. It had taken years and thousands of miles, but she had outrun that dark reality. She had outlived it, even though it had robbed her of so very much along the way.

'Is it true there wasn't no murder weapon found?' someone shouted from the middle of the gathering. 'If they wasn't shot or stabbed, then how exactly were they killed? I heard there was a hell of a lot of blood spilled out there in the bush.'

From his position behind the pulpit, Zach held up a hand to quell the ensuing barrage of similarly curious questions from the crowd. 'Until the AST detachment arrives from Fairbanks, all I can tell you is that we are treating this as a multiple homicide. Being that I am one of the investigating officers, I am not at liberty to discuss the details of the case with anyone at this time, nor do I think it would be wise for me to speculate.'

'But what about the wounds, Zach?' This time it was Lanny

Ham who spoke up, his reed-thin voice edged with slightly more than its normal level of nervous energy. 'I heard the bodies look like they were attacked by animals. Big animals. Is that true?'

'What does Alex think, since she was the one who found the bodies?' someone else asked. 'Do either of you believe it could have been animals that killed them?'

'Roger Bemis said he saw a pair of wolves prowling around near his property on the west side of town the other day,' interjected Fran Littlejohn, who ran the town's small health clinic. Ordinarily she was a reasonable woman, but now there was a strong note of worry in her voice. 'Been a hard winter already and it's just started. What's to say it wasn't a hungry pack that decided to attack the Toms place?'

'That's a damn good point. And if it was wolves, what's to say they won't come looking around here, now that they've gotten a taste for human prey?' came another paranoid suggestion.

'Now hold on, everyone,' Zach said, his attempt to inject calm getting lost as the voices in the building escalated along with the level of hysteria.

'You know, I saw a wolf right before nightfall just last week. Big black male, sniffing around the Dumpster out back of Pete's. Didn't think nothing of it then, but now—'

'And don't forget that it wasn't more than a few months ago that wolves killed some sled dogs down in Ruby. The papers said they didn't leave anything more than entrails and a couple of leather collars—'

'Maybe the smartest thing to do is to take some action here,' Big Dave said from his post at the back of the room. 'Seeing how we're stuck waiting on the Staties to get their shit together and come out to lend us a hand, maybe what we need to do is organize a hunting party. A wolf-hunting party.'

'It wasn't wolves,' Alex murmured, her mind flashing back

unwillingly to the sight of the bloodied track she saw in the snow. It hadn't been left by a wolf, nor any other kind of animal, of that she was certain. But a small voice whispered that it wasn't exactly human, either.

So . . . what, then?

She shook her head, refusing to let her thoughts wrap around the answer she hoped – prayed – could not be true.

'It wasn't wolves,' she said again, lifting her voice over the din of paranoia running as rampant as a disease all around her. She stood up and turned to face the vengeful crowd. 'No wolf kills like this, not by itself. Not even the boldest pack together would do this.'

'Miss Maguire is right,' said Sidney Charles, one of Harmony's Native elders and the town's long-running mayor, even if he held the office in name only in recent years. He nodded to Alex from his seat in the front row of the church, the dark hair of his leather-bound ponytail shot with gray, his tanned face lined the deepest at the corners of his mouth and eyes, creases earned from his kindhearted, jovial nature. Today he was somber, however, the heavy weight of all this talk of death showing in the slump of his otherwise proud shoulders. 'Wolves have a respect for mankind, as we should respect them. I have lived a long time, long enough that I can promise you they did not do this awful thing. If I live for a hundred more years, I will never believe they would.'

'Well, all due respect, Sid, but I, for one, would rather not take that chance,' Big Dave said, to the ready agreement of several other men standing nearby. 'Last I knew, there weren't no season on dealing with problem wolves. Ain't that right, Officer Tucker?'

'No, there's not,' Zach relented. 'But—'

Big Dave went on. 'If we've got wolves threatening human settlements, folks, then it's our right to defend ourselves. Hell, it's our goddamned duty. I sure as shit don't want to wait around until some rangy pack decides to attack again.'

'I'm with Big Dave on this,' said Lanny Ham, shooting up from his seat like a rocket. He wrung his hands in front of him, his nervous gaze darting around the room. 'I say we take action before the same kind of trouble comes to roost right here in Harmony!'

'Are any of you listening at all?' Alex challenged, her anger flaring. 'I'm telling you, wolves were not responsible for what happened to Pop Toms and his family. They were attacked by something terrible, something horrific . . . but it wasn't a wolf. What I saw out there could not have been done by any kind of animal. It was something else—'

Alex's voice snagged in her throat as her gaze strayed to the back of the church and clashed with a pair of silver eyes so piercing they stole her breath. She didn't know the black-haired man who stood there in the shadows near the door. He wasn't from Harmony, or any of its far-flung neighboring towns. Alex was sure she'd never seen those lean, razor-sharp cheeks and square-cut jaw, or the startling intensity of his gaze, anywhere before in the whole of the Alaskan interior. His face wasn't the kind a woman would ever forget.

The stranger said nothing, didn't even blink his inky lashes as she went suddenly mute and lost her train of thought. He merely stared back at her over the heads of the townsfolk as if she were the only one he saw, as if the two of them were the only people in the entire room.

'What do you think it was, dear?'

Millie Dunbar's thready voice jolted Alex out of the unnerving hold of the stranger's gaze. She swallowed on her parched throat and turned back to face the sweet old woman and the other people who were now waiting in silence to hear what she believed she saw out at the Toms settlement.

'I . . . I'm not really sure,' she hedged, wishing she'd never opened her mouth. She felt the heat of the stranger's eyes on her and was suddenly unwilling to voice what she had been thinking that day in the bush, and in all the torturous hours that had passed since.

'What did you see, Alexandra?' Millie pressed, her expression a heart-squeezing mix of hope and dread. 'How can you be so certain it wasn't animals that killed those good folks?'

Alex gave a weak shake of her head. Damn it, she'd walked right into this on her own, and now, with almost a hundred pairs of eyes locked on her, awaiting her explanation, there was little she could do to back out of it. Not without making herself look like an idiot and condemning an innocent pack of area wolves to the overzealous attention of Big Dave and the posse that seemed to be waiting for permission to roll out and blow them away with no cause.

Shit.

Was there any choice but the truth here?

'I saw . . . a track,' she admitted quietly.

'A track?' This time it was Zach who spoke, his light brown brows drawn low over his eyes as he scrutinized her from his position at the pulpit above the congregation. 'You didn't tell me anything about a track. Where did you see it, Alex? What kind of track was it?'

'It was a footprint . . . in the snow.'

Zach's frown deepened. 'You mean, a print from a boot?'

Alex stood there in silence for a long moment, unsure how to phrase what she was about to say next. No one said anything in that lengthening quiet. She felt the weight of all their focus, all the town's anticipation rooted on the tall, curveless blonde who'd spent most of her life in Harmony but was still regarded as something of an outsider because she'd come with her dad from the humid swamps of Florida.

It was the recollection of those sun-baked, heat-drenched wetlands that filled Alex's senses now. She could taste the salty brine of the water on her tongue, could smell the sweet odor of moss-covered cypress trees and fragrant lilies filling the air. She could hear the trilling song of cicadas and the low creak of bullfrogs serenading the dark as she'd watched her mother rock her little brother to sleep on the screened porch of the cabin while she read to them in that soft, gentle voice that Alex missed so much. She could see the golden hunter's moon that had slowly risen toward the glittering sea of stars high above the earth.

And she could feel, even now, the bolt of fear that arrowed through her heart as the night had been shredded by violence when the monsters came to feed.

It was all still there for her.

Still so shatteringly real.

'Alex.'

Zach's voice startled her, made her shake herself back to the here and now, back to Harmony, Alaska, and the horrific dread that gripped her when she considered that the terror she fled in Florida might somehow find her again.

'What the hell is going on, Alex?' There was impatience in the clipped tone of Zach's voice. 'I need to know what you saw out there. All of it.'

'I saw a footprint,' she stated as clearly as she could manage. 'Not from a boot. It was from a bare foot. A very large foot, and very humanlike, only . . . not quite—'

'Oh, for God's sake,' Big Dave said around a snort of laughter. 'It wasn't wolves that killed them, it was Bigfoot! Now I've heard it all.'

'What are you doing, Alex? Is this some kind of joke?'

'No,' she insisted, pivoting away from Zach's disbelieving look to the rest of the townsfolk. They were all staring at her as if waiting for her to burst into laughter.

Everyone except the black-haired stranger in the back.

His silver eyes bored into her like spears of ice, only the

feeling she got the longer she held his gaze was not one of cold but of bone-melting heat. And there was no mockery in his expression. He listened with an intensity that shook her to her core.

He believed her, when every other person in the place was dismissing her with polite – and some not so polite – looks of confusion.

'It's not a joke at all,' Alex told the residents of Harmony. 'I've never been more serious, I swear to you—'

'I've heard enough,' Big Dave announced. He started lumbering toward the door, several other men laughing among themselves as they followed him outside.

'I know it sounds crazy, but you have to listen to me,' Alex said, desperate that she be believed, now that she'd laid the truth out for them.

Part of the truth, at least. If they wouldn't take her word about the track she saw in the snow, they would never accept the even more incredible – more terrifying – truth of what she feared was to blame for the murders of Pop Toms and his family.

Even Jenna was gaping at her as if she'd just gone off her rocker. 'No one could survive in that cold without proper clothing, Alex. You couldn't have seen a bare footprint out there. You know that, right?'

'I know what I saw.'

All around them, the meeting began to disband. Alex craned her neck to try to find the stranger, but she couldn't see him anymore. He was gone. She didn't know why that thought should disappoint her. Nor did she understand why she felt so compelled to search him out. She was impatient with the need, and desperate to get out of there.

'Hey, it's okay.' Jenna stood up, giving Alex a sympathetic, if bewildered, smile as she caught her in a tight hug. 'You've been through a lot. The past couple of days have been rough for everyone, but I'm sure especially you.'

Alex pulled back and gave a vague shake of her head. 'I'm fine.'

The church door opened and closed as another group of people walked out into the brisk night. Was *he* out there, too? She had to know.

'Did you see that guy in the back of the church tonight?' she asked Jenna. 'Black hair, pale gray eyes. He was standing by himself near the door.'

Jenna shook her head. 'Who are you talking about? I didn't notice anyone—'

'Never mind. Listen, I think I'm going to skip Pete's tonight.'

'Good idea,' Jenna agreed as Zach stepped down off the raised platform of the pulpit and walked over to join them. 'Go home and get some sleep, okay? You're always worrying about me, but right now you need to give yourself a little TLC. Besides, it's been a while since I had a burger and a beer with my old fart of a brother, just the two of us. He's been avoiding me lately, making me wonder if maybe he's got a secret girlfriend or something.'

'No girlfriend,' Zach said. 'Don't have time for that when I'm married to my job. You all right, Alex? That was seriously weird and not like you at all. If you want to talk about what happened, with me or even a professional—'

'I'm fine,' she insisted, getting irritated now, and thankful for the anger that was letting her put her troubling past on the back shelf where it belonged. 'Look, forget what I said tonight. I didn't mean anything by it, I was just messing with Big Dave.'

'Well, he's an asshole and he deserved it,' Jenna said, looking more than a little relieved that she wouldn't have to call in the white coats after all.

Alex smiled with a lightness she didn't really feel. 'I'm gonna go. Have fun at Pete's, you guys.'

She hardly waited for them to tell her good-bye. Her rush to the door impeded by a trio of little old ladies talking and walking in slow motion, Alex's pulse was racing by the time she got her first lungful of the frigid night outside. She stood under the snow-laden eaves of the log-cabin church and glanced in all directions, looking for the striking face that had burned itself into her memory that first instant she saw him.

He wasn't there.

Whoever he was, whatever had brought him to Harmony when the rest of civilization was barred by bad weather, he'd simply walked out into the darkness and vanished into the thin, cold air.

⇥ CHAPTER FIVE ⇤

Kade trekked deep into the frigid wilderness of the bush, leaving the tiny town of Harmony some forty miles behind him. There were only a handful of winter travel options for humans this far incountry: plane, dogsled, or snow-machine. Kade traveled on foot, his duffel and gear slung onto his back, his snowshoes carrying him over the surface of blowing drifts that could swallow a man to his earlobes. The brittle wind sawed at him as he ran up one steep rise then down through yet another gully, his inhuman speed and endurance all thanks to the part of him that was Breed.

It was his Alaskan heart and soul that relished the cold and the punishing terrain, calling to the wildness inside him – the wildness that was quick to rise again now that he was back on the familiar tundra of his homeland.

Following the frozen Koyukuk River north toward the gen-eral location of the Toms settlement was easy enough. Once he got close to the area where the killings had occurred, his acute sense of smell led him the rest of the way. Despite the thick cover of fresh-fallen snow from the storms of the past couple days, to one of his kind, the taint of spilled blood still carried on the wind like a beacon lighting the path toward the scene of the recent carnage.

What he'd seen on the Web-posted video images Gideon had obtained in Boston had prepared him somewhat for his mission. He'd gone to Harmony's airstrip after the town hall meeting to get a private look at the dead who lay on ice in the yard's sole hangar. The wounds had been grisly on the video. Seeing them up close and personal certainly hadn't been an improvement.

But Kade had studied the lacerations – the near eviscerations – with a cool head and an objective eye. He hadn't found any surprises during his visit to the makeshift morgue. It hadn't been either animal or human that killed the Toms family.

Something else had brutalized them . . . just as the young woman, the pretty brown-eyed blonde named Alexandra Maguire, had insisted in the gathering at the town church.

Now, she, on the other hand, had been a surprise.

Tall and lean, with a simple beauty that needed no enhancements, the female had stunned Kade when she stood up and declared that she had seen something strange in the snow. For one thing, Kade had not been aware of any witnesses, except the idiot who'd recorded the video and had the bad sense to post it online. Locating and silencing that particular problem was among Kade's top mission priorities for the Order, just below the priority of identifying the Rogue vampire – or vampires – responsible for the bloody attack and seeing that justice was served with a cold, swift hand.

But now there was an added complication in the form of this female, Alex.

Just one more wrinkle in a situation already full of them. Whatever she saw, whatever she knew about the killings out here in the bush, she was a problem that Kade would have to deal with before things were complicated any further. He could sure as hell think of worse things to do in the line of duty than pump the attractive blonde for information.

One of those worse things loomed ahead of him in the darkness – the shadowy cluster of houses and outbuildings that comprised the Toms family settlement. Kade's nostrils twitched with the scent of old blood beneath the white cover of snow that blanketed the site. From this distance some hundred yards away, the scene looked picturesque, peaceful. A quiet frontier outpost nestled among the spruce and birch of the boreal woods that surrounded it.

But the stench of death clung to the place even in the cold, growing more pungent as Kade walked up to the stout log building nearest the trail. He removed his snowshoes and walked up the two steps to the porch. The rough-hewn door was closed but unlocked. Kade squeezed the latch and gave the door his shoulder, pushing it open.

A large pool of frozen blood glistened like black onyx in the scant glow of the moonlight spilling in around him as he stood on the threshold of the house. His body's reaction to the sight and scent of the crystallized red cells hit him like a hammer to the skull. Even though the blood was spilled and old, of no use to Kade, whose kind could only take nourishment from the veins of living human beings, his fangs punched out from his gums in response.

He hissed a low curse through those stretching fangs as he lifted his head and caught sight of more blood – more signs of struggle and suffering – in the smeared, dark trail that led from the main room of the cabin toward the short hallway that cut down its center. One of the victims had tried to escape the predator who'd come to kill them. Kade set down his duffel and snowshoes, then followed the corridor. The human had only sealed its fate by fleeing to the back bedroom. Cornered there, the garish splatters on the walls and unmade bed told Kade enough of the brutality of this slaying, as well.

There had been two more lives cut down in this place, and Kade took no satisfaction in piecing together the horrific scenarios of their murders as he walked the rest of the settlement and analyzed the attack. He'd seen enough here. He knew with heavy certainty that the deaths had Bloodlust written all over them. Whoever killed the humans here had done so with a fervor that exceeded anything Kade had ever seen before – even that of the most savage, addicted Rogue.

'Son of a bitch,' he muttered, his gut tight with disgust as he wheeled away from the ghostly settlement and staggered toward the surrounding forest in need of fresh air. He gulped it in, dragging the taste of brisk winter deep into his lungs.

It wasn't enough. Hunger and rage twisted around him like tightening chains, suffocating him in the heat of his parka and clothing. Kade tore it all off and stood naked in the biting November night. The chill darkness soothed him, but not by much.

He wanted to run – needed to run – and felt the cold arms of the Alaskan wilderness reach out to embrace him. In the distance, he heard the low howl of a wolf. He felt the cry resonate deep in his marrow, felt it singing through his veins.

Kade threw his head back and answered it.

Another wolf replied, this one markedly closer than the first. In minutes, the pack had moved in, inching toward him through the tight clusters of spruce. Kade glanced from one pair of keen lupine eyes to another. The alpha stepped forward from the trees, a big black male with a ragged right ear. The wolf advanced alone, moving as shadow across the pristine white of the snow.

Kade stood his ground as first the alpha, then the others, walked a slow circle around him. He met their inquisitive eyes and sent a mental promise that he meant them no harm. They understood, as he knew they would.

And when he silently commanded them to take off, the pack bolted into the thick curtain of the starlit woods.

Kade fell in alongside them and ran with the wolves as one of the pack.

Elsewhere in the cold, dark night, another predator strode the frozen, forbidding terrain.

He'd been walking for hours, alone and on foot in this empty wilderness for more nights than he could recall. He thirsted, but his need was not as urgent as it had been when he'd first set out into the cold. His body was nourished now, his muscles, bones, and cells infused with power from the blood he had taken recently. Admittedly, too much blood, but already his system was leveling out from the overfill.

And now that he was stronger, his body revived, he was finding it difficult to curb the thrill of the hunt.

That's what he was, after all: the purest form of hunter.

It was those predatory instincts that pricked to awareness as the quiet of the woods he crept through was disturbed by the rhythmic gait of a two-legged intruder. The stench of wood smoke and unclean human skin assailed his nose as the dark shape of a man wrapped in a heavy parka materialized not far from where the hunter watched and waited in the darkness. A metallic jangle sounded with each step the human took, emanating from the steel chains and sharp-toothed clamps he gripped in his gloved hand. In the other hand was a dead animal held by its hind feet, a large rodentlike creature that had been gutted along the way.

The human trapper trudged toward a small log shack up the trail.

The hunter watched him walk past, unaware of the gaze that followed him with greedy interest.

For a moment, the hunter debated the merits of cornering his prey within the confines of the tiny shelter versus indulging in a bit of sport among the trees and drifts outside.

Deciding on the latter, he stepped out from the cover of his observation spot and made a low sound in the back of his throat – part warning, part invitation for the now-startled human to run.

The trapper did not disappoint.

'Oh, Jesus. What in God's name—' Fear blanched his

bearded face and rendered his jaw slack. He dropped his paltry prize into the snow at his feet, then stumbled into a terrified dash for the woods.

The hunter's lips curled off his fangs with anticipation of the chase.

He let his prey crash away some sporting distance, then he set off after him.

≼ CHAPTER SIX ≽

Alex packed up her snowmachine and hit the trail with Luna on board in front of her about an hour before day-break. She was still rattled from the town meeting the night before, and more than a bit curious about the stranger who'd apparently vanished into the bush as oddly as he'd appeared in the back of Harmony's little log church.

Who was he? What did he want in tiny, remote Harmony? Where had he come from when the recent snowstorm had left most of the interior cut off from all of the nearest major ports?

And why had he been the only person in the entire assembly last night who'd listened to her account of the footprint left in the snow out at the Toms place and not made her feel like she had lost her mind?

Not that any of that mattered today. Mr Tall, Dark, and Mysterious was long gone from Harmony, and Alex had a sled packed with as many supplies as she could carry – bare necessities for a few of the folks she'd had to neglect when her plane run to the bush was cut short the other day.

Now she had a scant three hours of daylight and just enough gasoline stowed on board and in the Polaris's oversize fuel tank to make the hundred-mile round trip.

She had no good reason to detour toward the Toms settlement about an hour into her drive. None, except the gnawing need for answers. The hope – futile as she feared it to be – that she might find some kind of explanation for the slayings that didn't involve bloodied footprints in the snow and memories dredged up from the pit of her own private hell.

As Alex steered the snowmachine onto the drifted-over trail that led to Pop Toms's place, Luna jumped off to romp in the fresh, glittering powder.

'Stay with me,' Alex warned the eager wolf dog as she slowed her sled on the approach to the small cluster of dark wood structures.

Watching Luna's eagerness to race ahead brought on an unwelcome flashback to that awful moment three mornings ago and to the grisly discovery of young Teddy's body.

And, just like that day, Luna tore off now, ignoring Alex's calls for her to wait.

'Luna!' Alex shouted into the stillness of the early afternoon. She cut the gas on the snowmachine and leapt off, then huffed and waded as best she could through the deep drifts that had hardly slowed Luna down at all. 'Luna!'

Up ahead several yards, the wolf dog ran up the steps of Pop's porch and disappeared inside. What the hell? The door was open, even though Zach had made certain everything was closed up tight before the bodies of Pop and his family had been taken away. Had the wind blown the door open?

Or had it been something more dangerous than an Arctic gale that swept through here in the time since the killings?

'Luna,' Alex said as she drew closer to the log building, hating the small shake in her voice. Her heart rate started to jackhammer in her chest. She swallowed past her anxiety and tried again. 'Luna. Come on out of there, girl.'

She heard movement inside, then a creak and a loud *pop* as a floorboard protested the cold and the weight of whoever – or whatever – was inside with her dog.

More movement, footsteps approaching the open space of the door. Fear crawled up the back of Alex's neck. She reached around to the handgun holstered under her parka at the small of her back. She drew the weapon and held it in a two-fisted grip in front of her, just as Luna came trotting nonchalantly out to greet Alex at the bottom of the stairs.

And behind her, farther inside Pop's house, was a man – the dark-haired stranger from the back of the church last night. Despite the cold, he was dressed in nothing but a pair of loose blue jeans, which he was casually fastening as if he'd just rolled out of bed.

He held Alex's incredulous gaze with a calmness she could hardly fathom, looking for all the world like staring down the barrel of a loaded .45 was something he did every day.

'You,' Alex murmured, her breath clouding in front of her. 'Who are you? What the hell are you doing out here?'

He stood unmoving, unfazed, inside the main room of the house. Instead of answering her questions, he tipped his strong, squared chin to indicate her pistol. 'You mind pointing that somewhere else?'

'Yeah, maybe I do,' she said, her pulse still pounding and not entirely from fear now.

The guy was intimidating, nearly six-and-a-half-feet tall, with broad, muscled shoulders and powerful biceps that looked capable of dead-lifting a bull moose. Beneath an unusual pattern of hennalike tattoos that danced artfully over his chest, torso, and arms in some kind of intricate tribal design, his skin had the smooth, golden color of a Native. His hair seemed to indicate the same lineage, jet black and straight, the close-chopped spikes looking as silky as a raven's wing.

Only his eyes gave him away as something other than pure Alaskan. Pale silver, piercing against the thick, inky lashes that fringed them, they held Alex in a grip that felt almost physical.

'I need to ask you to step outside where I can see you,' she said, not comfortable with this situation – or this unnerving man – in the least. Even though she was certain she was no match for him, with or without bullets to back her up, she made her best attempt at affecting Jenna's no-bullshit police officer tone. 'Right now. Out of the house.'

He cocked his head to the side and glanced past her to the soft overcast haze of the thin afternoon daylight outside. 'I'd rather not.'

He'd rather not? Was he serious?

Alex flexed her fingers to get a better grip on the pistol, and he slowly lifted his hands in a show of nonforce.

'It's about ten below out there. A man could freeze off something vital,' he said, having the nerve to quirk his lips into an amused half smile. 'My clothes are inside. As you can see, I wasn't dressed for company. Or for a shoot-out on the tundra.'

His wry, easy humor deflated most of her trepidation. Without waiting for her to reply – without any regard at all for the loaded firearm still aimed dead-center on him – he pivoted around and walked deeper inside Pop's house.

Good lord, those fascinatingly odd tattoos wrapped all the way around to his back, too. They seemed to move with him, accentuating the lean, hard muscle that bunched and flexed with his every step.

'No need for you to stand out there in the cold, either,' he said, his deep voice doing something crazy to her pulse as he disappeared from her sight. 'Stow the gun and come inside if you want to talk.'

'Shit,' Alex breathed on a huff.

She let her arms relax, not quite sure what just happened. The guy was unbelievable. Was he that arrogant or just plain crazy?

She had half a mind to squeeze off a warning shot, just to let him know she was serious, but at that same moment, Luna gave a short whine and loped back up the steps and into the house behind him. Disloyal mutt.

With a low-muttered curse, Alex lowered the pistol and

cautiously walked up to the porch and the open door of what had been almost a second home to her for the past several years. As she entered Pop's place now, it couldn't have felt more foreign to her. Wrong in every way.

Without Pop Toms's booming voice to greet her as she walked in, the house felt colder, darker, emptier than ever. Thankfully, there was no blood spilled within, as he and Teddy had either run or been chased outside before their killer managed to catch them. Everything looked just as it would be if they'd been there, only it chilled Alex like some kind of alternate reality that had collided with the one she knew.

Out of place in the cramped living room was a black leather duffel bag that sat unzipped on the skirted orange-and-brown plaid sofa. Alex stole a quick look at the contents, noting a couple changes of clothes inside and a rather nasty hunting knife that had been removed from its sheath and set atop a pair of black military-style fatigues.

But the gleaming, serrated blade that looked as though it would make short work of a grizzly's hide was merely an appetizer for the rest of the weaponry laid out in Pop's living room.

A high-powered rifle with a blunted barrel was propped in the corner nearest the door. Beside it on the scarred lamp table that Pop Toms had made with his own hands as a wedding gift for his wife some three decades ago was a book-size case of custom rounds. The tips of the big, shiny bullets were pointed and capped, the kind of ammunition that ripped through the toughest flesh and bone in an instant, showing no mercy and taking no prisoners. Another gun, a semi-automatic 9mm that easily trumped her .45 revolver, rested in a black chest holster next to the case of hollow points.

Having lived in the bush most of her life, Alex didn't cower at the sight of weapons or hunting gear, but this personal arsenal – and the awareness that the man who owned it had suddenly, silently, returned to the room with her – took her aback.

She glanced up to find him shrugging into a thick gray chamois shirt and rolling the sleeves off his forearms. The fascinating array of tattoos disappeared as he worked a couple of the buttons closed in front. In the tight confines of the room, Alex caught the scent of Arctic air and crisp pine, as well as something wilder that seemed to cling to him and made her senses come to full attention.

God, had she been so long without male companionship that her survival instinct was broken? She didn't think so, and then again, she wasn't the only female in the room to be affected by this stranger who'd appeared out of nowhere last night. Luna had parked her traitorous butt at his feet and gazed up adoringly at him while he reached down and scratched her behind the ears. Normally the wolf dog was cautious around strangers, wary of new people, but not with him.

If she needed someone to vouch for a person's character, she could do a lot worse than listen to Luna's instincts. For that matter, Alex had her own internal gauge for judging whether she could trust someone, a sort of instinctual lie-detector that she'd been aware of since she was a child. Unfortunately, in order for it to work, she needed to be close enough to touch the person – even a simple brush of her fingers against someone was usually connection enough for her to tell if she was being lied to.

Tempting as it was to put her hands on some of this guy's bare skin, it would also mean setting down her gun. Frankly, she didn't think it would be smart to get that friendly just yet.

'Who are you?' Alex demanded, wondering if he would answer this time. 'What were you doing at the town meeting in Harmony, and what business do you have being out here? This is a crime scene you're compromising, in case you hadn't noticed.'

'I noticed. And the three feet of fresh snow burying the place had compromised it long before I got here,' he said without apologizing, still rubbing his big hand over Luna's head and under her chin while the dog practically drooled with contentment.

Alex could have sworn something unspoken passed between man and canine in the moment before Luna rose and came strolling back to Alex to lick her hand.

'Name's Kade,' he said, pinning her with that shrewd, steady, silver gaze. He reached out and offered his hand, but Alex hadn't quite decided if she could trust him that far yet. He hesitated for a moment, then let his arm fall back down to his side. 'I gather from what I heard last night that you were close to the victims. I'm sorry for your loss, Alex.'

It unnerved her, the way he said her name with such easy familiarity. She didn't like the way his voice, and his uninvited, unexpected compassion seemed to reach inside her chest and wrap itself around her senses. She didn't know him, and she definitely didn't need his sympathy.

'You're not from around here,' she said abruptly, needing to maintain some sense of distance as the walls seemed to crowd in on her the longer she was in his presence. 'But you're not from Outside, either. Are you?'

He gave a vague shake of his head. 'I was born in Alaska, grew up north of Fairbanks.'

'Oh? Who's your family?' she asked, trying to sound conversational rather than interrogatory.

He blinked, just once, a slow shuttering of his remarkable eyes. 'You wouldn't know my family.'

'You might be surprised. I know a lot of people,' she said, pressing all the harder for his evasiveness. 'Try me.'

His broad lips curved at the corners. 'Is that an invitation, Alex?'

She cleared her throat, caught off guard by the innuendo,

but even more so by the sharp kick of her pulse as he let the question hang between them. He walked toward her then, an easy, long-legged stride that brought him to within arms' reach of her.

God, he was gorgeous. All the more so up close. His lean face was sharp angles and strong bones, his black brows and lashes setting off the wintry color and keen intelligence of his eyes, which tilted ever so slightly at the corners. Wolfish eyes. A hunter's eyes.

Alex felt snared in them as he came even closer. She felt the heat of his hand on hers, then a firm but gentle pressure as he carefully extracted the pistol from her fingers.

He offered it back to her in the open palm of his hand. 'You won't need to use this, I promise.'

When she mutely accepted the gun and returned it to its holster behind her back, he strode over to the sofa and sheathed the wicked blade that had been resting at the top of his open duffel.

'You must have been shaken up pretty badly, being one of the first to see what had happened here.'

'It wasn't a good day,' she said, the understatement of the year. 'The Tomses were decent people. They didn't deserve to die like this. No one does.'

'No,' he replied soberly. 'Nobody deserves this kind of death. Except the beasts responsible for what happened to your friends.'

Alex looked at him as he closed the lid on his lethal rounds and put the case back into his bag. 'Is that what brought you here – you and all these weapons? Did someone from Harmony hire you to come in and slaughter an innocent pack of wolves? Or are you here to collect on your own instead?'

He cocked his head in her direction. 'No one hired me. I'm a problem solver. That's all you need to know.'

'Bounty hunter,' she muttered, with more venom than

probably was wise. 'What happened out here had nothing to do with wolves.'

'So you said last night in that meeting.' His voice was more level than she'd heard it thus far. And when he looked at her, it was with a probing intensity that made her take a step backward on the boot heels of her Sorels. 'Nobody believed you.'

'Do you?'

If possible, that hard silver gaze mined deeper. As though he could see right through her, all the way down to the memories she could not bear to relive. 'Tell me what you know, Alex.'

'You mean, tell you more about the footprint I found outside?'

He gave the barest shake of his head. 'I mean the rest of it. How is it that you can be so certain these killings weren't done by animals? Did you see the attack?'

'No, thank God,' she answered quickly.

Too quickly maybe, because he took a step toward her, scowling now. Sizing her up.

'What about the video? Is there more of it somewhere? Something beyond the footage shot after the killings had occurred?'

'What?' Alex had no need to feign confusion now. 'What video? I have no idea what you're talking about.'

'Three days ago, a cell phone video clip was shot out here and posted to an illegal site on the Internet.'

'Oh, my God.' Appalled, Alex brought her hand up to her mouth. 'And you saw it?'

The tendon that jerked in his cheek was confirmation enough. 'If you know something more about the slayings that took place here, I need you to tell me now, Alex. It's very important that I have all the information I can get.'

If Alex had been tempted to blurt everything out last night in the town meeting, now, as she stood alone before this man

– this stranger who rattled her inexplicably on every level of her being – the words clogged up tight in her throat. She didn't know him. She wasn't at all sure she could trust him, even if she did somehow ratchet up the nerve to drag her darkest suspicions into the light.

'Why are you really here?' she asked him softly. 'What are you looking for?'

'I'm looking for answers, Alex. I'm looking for the same thing I believe you are – the truth. Maybe there's a way for us to help each other.'

The sharp trill of Alex's cell phone broke the lengthening quiet. It rang again, giving her the excuse she needed to put a few paces between herself and the man whose presence seemed to be sucking all the air out of the room. Alex turned away from him and connected to the call.

It was Jenna, phoning to remind her that they were supposed to meet up for dinner at Pete's tonight. Alex murmured a hasty confirmation but stayed on the phone after Jenna said her good-byes and disconnected. 'Yeah, no problem,' Alex said into the dead air of the receiver. 'I'm on my way right now. I'll be there in twenty minutes, tops. All right. Yep, bye.'

She stuffed the phone into the pocket of her parka and pivoted back to face Luna's new favorite person, who was now seated on the sofa with Alex's dog lying at his feet. 'I have to get going. Deliveries to make before sundown, and then I'm meeting a friend for dinner in town.'

She was anxious to get away now, but why did she feel compelled to make excuses to this man? What should he care why she was leaving as though she couldn't run out of there fast enough?

Alex subtly snapped her fingers and called Luna's name. To the wolf dog's credit, she ambled over without looking too heartbroken to be summoned away from him.

'I'll let Officer Tucker know that you were here today,' she added, figuring it couldn't hurt to remind him that she was friendly with the police.

'You do that, Alex.' He didn't get up from his negligent slouch on Pop Toms's sofa. 'Be careful out there. I'll see you around.'

Alex caught his slow-spreading grin as she rounded up Luna and headed out the door of the cabin. Although she didn't dare look behind her, she could feel those quicksilver eyes at the back of her neck, watching her as she hopped on her snow-machine with Luna and gave the motor some juice. She'd driven out a few hundred yards before another thought hit her.

She hadn't seen another sled parked anywhere.

So just how the hell had he made the forty-plus-mile trip from Harmony all the way north through the open wilderness?

✠ CHAPTER SEVEN ✠

K ade waited out the short few hours of daylight in the cabin at the Toms settlement. As soon as it was safe for him and his solar-sensitive Breed skin to venture outside, he took off on foot once more, this time heading for the ten-thousand-acre plot of land his family owned north of Fairbanks.

He wondered how he would be greeted in his father's Darkhaven compound – he, the prodigal, the unapologetic black sheep, who'd left a year ago without excuse or explanation, and never looked back. He felt some guilt for that, but didn't figure anyone would believe him if he said it.

He wondered if Seth would be at the compound when he arrived, and, if so, what his brother would say about the killings that had brought Kade home from Boston to investigate on behalf of the Order.

But more than any of that, Kade wondered what it was that Alexandra Maguire was hiding.

Kade had enough personal experience with keeping secrets to guess that the attractive female bush pilot wasn't being entirely honest about what she knew of the recent deaths – not with the townsfolk or local law enforcement, nor with him earlier today. Possibly not even with herself.

He could have pushed her for the truth when he'd met her at the Toms settlement, but Alex didn't seem the type to be forced into doing anything she didn't want to do. Kade would need to win her trust in order to win the information he needed from her.

He might even have to seduce it out of her, an idea he considered with far too much interest. Yeah. Tough job, getting close to Alexandra Maguire. Every mission should demand that onerous a task.

Thoughts of how he would play things with her the next time he saw her made the hours and miles fall away behind him. In no time, he had reached the huge tract of forested, virgin wilderness that had been in his family's possession for centuries. The familiar smell of the woods and the earth that lay dormant beneath the snow put a tightness in his chest. For so long, this expanse of land had been his home, his kingdom and domain.

How many times had he and Seth run wild and whooping through this very forest, brothers-in-arms, young lords of the chase? Too many to recall.

But Kade remembered the night that the idyll of their shared childhood had ended. He still felt the weight of that moment in the cold hand of dread that clamped down on the back of his neck as he approached the sprawling compound of hand-hewn log buildings that comprised his father's Darkhaven.

Unlike most Breed civilian communities, this Darkhaven had no perimeter fence or closed-circuit security cameras. There were no guards posted along the way, either. Then again, this far out in the bush, there was no need. The land itself acted as sentry to the many residences and the people living within them. Harsh, remote, expansive.

If the predators on four legs didn't dissuade any unwanted human visitors from stumbling onto the property, Kade's father and the roughly twenty other Breed males living inside the Darkhaven would be happy to take care of them.

Kade trudged through the snowy path that led up to the

large main house. He knocked on the doorjamb, uncomfort-able entering the place unannounced.

His father's younger brother came to the door and opened it. 'What are you doing standing out there in the snow, Seth . . . ?'

'Uncle Maksim,' Kade said, tipping his head in greeting when recognition lit up the other male's face. 'How are you, Max?'

The Breed male was nearly three hundred years old but, like all of their kind, looked to be in the prime of life with his unlined face and thick brown hair. 'I am well,' he replied. 'This is certainly a welcome surprise, Kade. Your father will be so pleased that you are home.'

Kade resisted the urge to chuckle at that sentiment, but only because he knew his uncle meant it as kindness. 'Is he here?'

Maksim nodded. 'In his study. My God, it's a relief to see you again and to know that you are alive and well. You'd been away so long without contact, I'm afraid many of us had assumed the worst about you.'

'Yeah,' Kade said, knowingly wry. 'I get that a lot. Will you tell my father I'm here?'

His uncle clapped him lightly on the shoulder. 'I'll do better than that. Come with me. I'll take you to him myself.'

Kade followed the big male through the massive residence to the private study that overlooked the broad western range of the property. Maksim rapped his knuckles on the door, then squeezed the latch and pushed it open.

'Kir. Look who's returned home, my brother.'

Kade's father turned away from an open program on his computer, rotating in his large leather chair to face them. Kade watched the stern expression darken from one of surprise and relief, to one of confusion and not-too-mild disappointment when he realized it was the prodigal son who waited at the threshold, not the favored one. The scowl deepened. 'Kade.'

'Father,' he replied, knowing there would be no emotional embraces or warm welcomes as his father got up from his seat and strode around to the front of his long desk.

He spared only the barest glance at his brother who stood behind Kade near the door. 'Leave us, Maksim.'

Kade felt rather than saw his uncle's silent, obedient retreat from the room. He watched his father instead, seeing the harsh disapproval in the dark gaze that pinned him across the distance of the private study. Kade set down his duffel of belongings and weaponry and awaited his father's displeasure.

'You failed to mention you intended to come home when we spoke a couple days ago.' When Kade offered no excuse, his father exhaled sharply. 'Then again, that's hardly surprising. You didn't bother to say much before you left us a year ago, either. Just walked away with no thought to responsibility or to your family.'

'It was time for me to go,' Kade replied after a long moment. 'There were things I needed to do.'

His father's scoff sounded brittle with animosity. 'I hope it was worth it. You broke your mother's heart, you realize that, don't you? Until you called out of the blue the other day, she was certain you'd gone off and gotten yourself killed by joining up with those warrior vigilantes back in Boston. And although Seth would be the last person to speak poorly of you, I can tell you that your leaving broke his heart, too. Your brother has changed since you've been away.'

And of course, the blame for that and everything else sat squarely on Kade's shoulders. He shook his head, knowing that it was no use trying to defend himself or the Order. Lucan and the other warriors didn't need his father's support or approval. For that matter, neither did he.

He'd survived without that for a long damned time already, and he had since given up needing to prove himself to the man.

'So, Seth is still away on business for you?'

His father met the question with a narrow look. 'He's due back soon. I presume he will also feed while he's gone, which is likely the reason for his delay.'

'What about Patrice?'

'They are not yet mated,' came his father's clipped reply.

Kade grunted in acknowledgment, and wished he could feel more surprise to hear this news. For half a dozen years, it had been accepted that Seth and Patrice, one of the Breedmates who lived in the family Darkhaven since she was a child, would eventually become a blood-bonded pair. At that time, Patrice had chosen him above all the other males in the region, and to his parents' delight, Seth had agreed to make the female his mate. Problem was, he seemed to find one good excuse after another to put her off.

Without a Breedmate to fulfill a vampire's need for blood, he was forced to feed off the mortal population for sustenance instead. Most Breed males welcomed the unbreakable, eternal bond that would release them from the slavery of their blood-thirst and provide a steady, loving source of strength and passion for the whole of a male's life.

But there were some who preferred to remain unattached, hunting where they willed, relishing the constant chase and conquest of new human prey.

Kade himself was in no rush to lock himself down with a Breedmate of his own, another point of contention with his father and mother, who had been blood-bonded and happily mated for more than a century. Instead they'd pinned their hopes on Seth. He'd been the studious one, the cerebral one, who it was assumed would one day take the reins as the leader of the family Darkhaven or form his own.

Kade had always been the raucous opposite of his brother. It was that reckless streak that had likely condemned him in his father's eyes, while Seth's careful outward control had given him seemingly limitless freedoms.

'Well,' his father said after a prolonged silence. 'Since you've come to your senses and returned home now, I trust this means you're ready to try to be part of the family once more. As it seems you've come back with barely more than the clothes on your back, I'll make arrangements to transfer some funds into your old account.'

'I didn't come here for a handout,' Kade bit off, his anger spiking at the assumption. 'And as for staying, it's not in my plan—'

'Where is my son?' Kade's words were cut short by a petite cyclone who threw open the doors of the study and breezed inside. 'It really is you! Oh, Kade!'

She pulled Kade into a fierce embrace, her body vibrating with emotion. His mother was just as beautiful and vibrant as ever – more so, her glow enhanced by the large, expectant swell of her belly beneath the loose-fitting, winter-white sweater and pants she wore. Ebony-haired with pale silver eyes that matched both his and Seth's, Kade's mother, Victoria, was a breathtaking woman. Like her mate, she, too, appeared no more than thirty years old, her aging halted by the blood bond she shared with Kir.

'Oh, my darling boy. I've been so worried about you! Thank God you've come back – and will you look at me, just in time.' She smiled, positively beaming. 'You'll have two new brothers in less than a month. Identical twins again, just like you and Seth.'

Although she seemed delighted by the prospect, Kade felt a sick twist in his gut. The talent that he and Seth shared, the ability to communicate with and command predator animals, was a unique skill passed down to them genetically from their Breedmate mother, in the same way that Seth and he shared Victoria's smooth golden skin, dark hair, and exotic eyes. But unlike her, in Kade and Seth, with their father's Breed blood running hot through their veins, the talent had a dark side. He hated to think that the pattern might repeat itself in another set of brothers.

'You look well, Mother. I'm glad to see you so happy.'

'I'm even happier now that you're here. You'll see I've kept your quarters just as you left them. Not a day passed when I didn't hope and pray that I would have both of my beloved sons safe and sound, living under our roof again as a family.'

She threw her arms around him once more, and Kade felt all the worse for what he had to say. 'I . . . I don't know how long I'll be staying. I didn't come back to live here, Mother. I'm here on business for the Order.'

She drew back, her expression falling. 'You won't stay?'

'Only until my mission is complete. Then I have to return to Boston. I'm sorry if you thought—'

'You can't go,' she murmured, tears welling in her eyes. 'You belong here, Kade. This is your home. We are your family. You have a life here—'

He gently shook his head. 'My life is with the Order now. They need me, and I have important things to do. Mother, I am sorry to disappoint you.'

She sobbed behind her hand, and took a few steps back on her heels. She wobbled unsteadily with the sudden movement, and Kade's father was right at her side, wrapping her protectively under his arm. He spoke softly to her, tenderly, private words that seemed to soothe her somewhat. But her tears and sobs did not stop completely.

Kade's father escorted her carefully to the door, pausing only to lift his head and level a hard look on his son. Their gazes met and clashed, neither one of them willing to back down. 'You and I are not finished here, Kade. I will expect you to wait for me until I finish looking after your mother.'

He waited as ordered, but only for a minute. Time away had made him forget what it had been like to be in this place. He couldn't live under his father's roof any more than he could live under Seth's shadow. It killed him to cause his mother distress, but if he'd needed a reminder that he didn't belong here, he'd gotten it as clearly as possible in the look his father gave him as he was walking out the door.

'Shit,' Kade hissed, as he grabbed his duffel bag and exited the study.

He walked outside, thinking the frigid air would help clear his head. Instead his gaze was snagged by the sight of his brother's cabin. He knew he shouldn't go inside – he had no right, actually – but the need for answers was more powerful than any sense of guilt at invading Seth's privacy. Kade opened the door and walked inside.

He wasn't sure what he'd expected. Some sense of chaos or the scattered clutter of a troubled mind? But Seth's quarters were as neat as ever, not a single thing out of place. All of his furnishings and belongings were orderly and precisely arranged. There was a philosophy book on the reading table beside the sofa, a collection of classical music on rotation in the stereo CD player. On Seth's computer workstation, a file folder containing spreadsheet printouts he was obviously working on for their father lay neatly closed underneath a crystal paperweight.

Seth, the perfect son.

Except, the more Kade looked around, the more the cabin seemed staged rather than lived in. Things were too neat. Too carefully arranged, as though put there on the chance that someone might be poking about, searching for something amiss. Or for some overt sign of deception, just as Kade was doing now.

But Kade knew his brother better than anyone else. He was a part of Seth, unlike anyone else could be because of the inextricable bond they'd been born with as identical twins. From the time they were boys they'd been two parts of one whole, inseparable, with an unspoken mutual understanding of each other.

Kade had believed that he and Seth were alike in every way . . . until the first time he saw his brother command a wolf pack to pursue and slaughter a grizzly.

They were just boys then, fourteen years old and eager to test the boundaries of both their strength and their preternatural abilities. Seth was showing off, bragging about how he'd befriended an area wolf pack and could command the minds of more than one animal at a time. Kade had never done that – he hadn't even realized he could – which made Seth all too willing to demonstrate.

He'd summoned the pack with a howl, and before Kade realized what was happening, he and Seth were running with the wolves in search of prey. They came across a grizzly bear catching salmon in a river. Seth told the pack to take the bear down. To Kade's astonishment, they obeyed. But even more stunning – infinitely more abhorrent – was the sight of Seth participating in the slaughter.

It was a bloody, prolonged battle . . . and Seth had reveled in it. Slick with the animal's blood and gore, he'd called Kade to join in, but Kade had been appalled. He'd vomited in the weeds, never feeling so sick with misery in all his life.

Seth had teased him privately for weeks afterward. He'd goaded Kade, acting as the devil on his shoulder, challenging him to test the limits of his talent to determine which of them was the more powerful twin. Kade had stupidly given in. Pride had made him a fool, and so he'd picked up the gauntlet Seth had thrown.

He'd honed his ability until it came as naturally to him as breathing. He'd learned to love the feel of the untamed wild on his skin, drenching his senses, caught between his teeth and fangs. He'd become so adept, so addicted to the power of his talent, it was soon nearly impossible to hold it under rein.

Seth had been furious that Kade's ability had exceeded his own. He was jealous and insecure, a dangerous combination.

He'd suddenly found something more to prove to Kade, and his violent inclinations took on a more disturbing focus.

At some point, Seth had quietly advanced his dark talent toward other prey.

He and his pack had killed a human.

It happened just months before Kade was recruited by the Order. Repulsed, furious, he'd intended to drag Seth in front of their father and the rest of the Darkhaven and expose his inexcusable breach of Breed law. But Seth had pleaded with him. He'd sworn up and down that it had all been a terrible mistake – a game somehow gotten completely out of hand. He had begged Kade not to turn him in. He'd promised that the killing had been accidental, and that it would never happen again.

Kade had doubted him even then. He should have exposed Seth's secret. But Seth was his beloved brother – the other half of him. Kade knew what the news of Seth's crime would do to his parents, particularly his mother. So Kade had kept the secret, even though holding it had been eating away at him constantly every moment since.

He'd protected Seth from the truth and sheltered his parents from the pain of it, and when the call came from Nikolai in Boston that the Order needed new recruits, Kade jumped on the chance to join.

Now the slayings of the Toms family had brought it all back. He hoped like hell his brother wasn't capable of killing an entire family in cold blood, but he feared Seth's promise a year ago was proving too hard for him to keep.

With that fear heavy on his mind, Kade started to walk toward the door. He didn't realize until he was halfway there that he was walking on the thick pelt of a grizzly. The skin covered the living room floor, and although the bear Seth and his wolves had killed all those years ago was long lost to time and the elements, the frozen snarl of this dead bear's head gave Kade pause. He walked back and knelt down near the open jaw of the animal.

'Ah, Christ. Let me be wrong,' he whispered as he carefully stuck his hand into the sharp-toothed maw.

He reached back as far as he could and swore tightly as his fingers brushed the soft cloth and loose bulk of a hidden pouch at the back of the grizzly's throat.

Kade withdrew the small drawstring bag, hearing a metallic jingle as it came to rest in his palm. He loosened the strings and poured out the contents. Several gold rings slid into his hand, along with a braided leather bracelet with a bear tooth dangling from it and small locks of clipped hair collected from a variety of human heads. Dried blood caked some of the items.

There could be no mistaking them for anything but what they were . . .

Souvenirs that Seth had apparently been collecting. A killer's hidden cache of mementos, taken from his victims.

'You son of a bitch,' Kade ground out harshly. 'You sick, fucking son of a bitch.'

Anger and grief collided in the pit of his stomach. He didn't want to believe what he was seeing. He wanted to make excuses, grasp for any possible explanation except the one that was clanging around like a warning bell in his skull.

His brother was a killer.

Had he attacked the Toms family so heinously, too?

Something deep inside Kade just could not reconcile the wholesale slaughter of an entire family.

Despite the dread that was sitting like ice in his gut, he needed more answers before he was willing to convict Seth of being that kind of monster. He needed proof. Hell, he needed to look his brother in the face and demand the truth from him, once and for all.

And if it turned out that Seth was guilty, then Kade was

prepared to do what needed to be done. What by rights he should have done when he'd first seen evidence of Seth's apparent disregard for human life.

He would hunt his goddamn brother down and he would kill him.

⫸ CHAPTER EIGHT ⫷

Most of the crowd at Pete's that night was gathered in the bar area out front, the din of conversation competing with the racket of a hockey game on satellite TV and an old Eagles song wailing on the jukebox that squatted near the unisex restroom and the entryway to the game room in back. Alex and Jenna sat across from each other at one of the tables in the center of the place. They'd finished dinner some time ago and were now splitting a piece of Pete's homemade apple pie while they nursed the warming dregs of their microbrews.

Jenna had been yawning off and on for the past hour or so and checking her watch, but Alex knew her friend was too polite to bail on her. Selfishly, Alex wanted to prolong their visit. She had insisted on the pie and one last beer, had even fed a couple of quarters to the jukebox so she had the excuse to wait for her song to play before they left.

Anything to avoid going home to her empty house.

She missed her dad, now more than ever. For so long, he had been her closest friend and confidant. He'd been her strong, willing, and capable protector when the world around her had been turned upside-down by violence. He would be the only one who'd understand the unspeakable fears that were swirling in her now. He'd be the only one she could turn to, the only one who could tell her that everything would be all right and almost convince her that he believed it.

Now, except for her dog, she was alone, and she was terrified.

The urge to pull up stakes and run from what she'd seen that awful day at the Toms settlement was almost overwhelming. But where to? If running from Florida to Alaska hadn't been far enough to escape the monsters that lurked in her memories, then where could she possibly hope to escape them next?

'You gonna twirl that fork all night, or are you going to have some of this pie?' Jenna downed the last of her beer and set the bottle on the rough wood table with a soft *thump*. 'You wanted dessert, but you're making me eat most of it.'

'Sorry,' Alex murmured as she put down her fork. 'I guess I wasn't as hungry as I thought I was.'

'Everything okay, Alex? If you need to talk about what happened the other night at the meeting, or out at the Toms place—'

'No. I don't want to talk about it. What's to say anyway? Shit happens, right? Bad things happen to good people all the time.'

'Yeah, they do,' Jenna said quietly, her eyes dimming under the glare of the tin lamp overhead. 'Listen, I was over at Zach's for a little while this afternoon. Sounds like the Alaska State Troopers in Fairbanks have their hands full at the moment, but they'll be sending a unit out to us in a few days. In the meantime, they discovered video footage of the crime scene on the Internet, of all places. Some asshole apparently went out there with a cell phone camera not long after you'd been there, then uploaded the video to an illegal site that allegedly pays a hundred bucks for actual blood-and-guts material.'

Alex sat forward in her chair, her attention snapped sharply back into focus to hear a confirmation of what Kade had told her out at the Toms place. 'Do they know who?'

Jenna rolled her eyes and gestured toward the game room, where a small group of the local stoners were shooting darts.

'Skeeter Arnold,' Alex said, unsurprised that the slacker, perpetually unemployed yet never without a drink in one hand and a smoke in the other, would be the one so lacking in respect for the dead that he would sell them out for a few dollars. 'What a bastard. And to think that he and Teddy Toms had been hanging out together quite a bit before . . .'

She couldn't finish the sentence; the reality was still too raw.

Jenna nodded. 'Skeeter has a way of latching on to kids he can manipulate. He's a user and a loser. I've been telling Zach for the past year or more that I have a hunch the guy is pushing drugs and alcohol on the dry Native populations. Unfortunately, cops need to have this sticky thing called evidence before they arrest and prosecute, and Zach keeps reminding me that all I have on Skeeter Arnold is suspicion.'

Alex watched her friend, seeing the tenacity sparking in Jenna's eyes. 'Do you miss it? Being a cop, I mean.'

'Nope.' Jenna frowned as though considering, then gave a firm shake of her head. 'I couldn't do that job anymore. I don't want to be responsible for cleaning up someone else's tragedies or fuck-ups. Besides that, every time I'd walk up to a traffic accident, I'd be wondering whose heart was going to be torn apart once I called in my report. I don't have the stomach for police work now.'

Alex reached out and gave her friend's hand a gentle, understanding squeeze. 'For what it's worth, I think you're a great cop, and that's because you do care. It was never just a job to you, and it showed. We need more people like you looking out for the rest of us. I keep thinking that maybe one day you'll go back to it.'

'No,' she replied, and through the link of their hands, Alex's inner sense told her that Jenna meant it. 'I lost my edge when

I lost Mitch and Libby. Do you realize it will be four years later this week?'

'Oh, Jen.'

Alex recalled very well the November night that took the lives of Jenna's trooper husband and their little girl. The whole family had been traveling home from a special dinner in Galena when an icy snow kicked up and sent their Blazer sliding into oncoming traffic. The eighteen-wheeler that hit them was hauling a full load on its oversize trailer – five tons of timber on its way to the Lower Forty-eight.

Mitch had been driving the Blazer and was killed on impact. Libby held on for two days in the hospital, broken and bruised on life support, before her little body simply gave up. As for Jenna, she had lain in a coma for a month and a half, only to wake up to the terrible news that Mitch and Libby were gone.

'Everyone says that in time it won't hurt so bad. Give it time, and I'll be able to console myself with happy memories of what I had, not dwell on what I've lost.' Jenna blew out a hitched breath as she withdrew her hand from Alex's loose grasp and picked at the label on her empty beer bottle. 'It's been four years, Alex. Shouldn't I have some closure by now?'

'Closure,' Alex scoffed. 'I'm the wrong one to ask about that. Dad's only been gone six months, but I don't think I'll ever give up hoping to see him walk through the door again. That's part of the reason why I'm thinking I might . . .'

Jenna stared at her as the words trailed off. 'Might what?'

Alex shrugged. 'I guess it's just that I've been wondering lately if things might be better for me if I sold the house and moved on.'

'Move on, as in leave Harmony?'

'As in leave Alaska, Jen.' And hopefully leave behind all of the death that seemed to follow her wherever she ran. Before it had the chance to catch up to her again. 'I'm just thinking that maybe I need a fresh start somewhere, that's all.'

She couldn't read Jenna's expression, which seemed trapped somewhere between misery and envy. Before her highly persuasive friend could launch into a counteroffensive argument for why Alex needed to stay, a loud roar of masculine enthusiasm went up from the area of the bar.

'What's all that about?' Alex asked, unable to tell what was going on with her back to the ruckus. 'Did Big Dave's team win or something?'

'I don't know, but he and his crew just bellied up to the bar in a hurry.' Jenna glanced back at her then and exhaled a soft curse. 'You are my best friend, Alex, and you know I'm damned picky when it comes to my friends. You can't sit there over a half-eaten slice of pie in the middle of hockey night at Pete's tavern and casually drop a bomb on me about you're thinking of moving away. Since when? And why haven't you talked to me about any of this? I thought as friends we shared everything.'

Not everything, Alex admitted silently. There were some things she wasn't brave enough to share with anyone. Things about herself and things she'd seen that would label her either mentally unstable or positively deranged. Jenna didn't even know that Alex's mom and little brother were murdered, let alone how.

Slaughtered.

Attacked by creatures out of the worst nightmare.

Alex and her father had concocted a more believable lie as they'd made the trip to Alaska to begin their lives without the other, missing half of their family. To anyone who asked, Alex's mother and kid brother were killed by a drunk driver down in Florida. They had died instantly, painlessly.

Nothing could have been farther from the truth.

Alex had felt guilty for perpetuating the lie, especially to Jenna, but she'd consoled herself that she was only protecting her friend. No one would want to know the horror that Alex

awake all night once she finally did work up the nerve to go home.

God, she was being ridiculous. What she really needed was to go home, feed Luna before the dog tore up the house in retaliation for being abandoned all night, then try to get some solid sleep for a change. She could think about everything else in the morning, when her head was clearer. Things would make more sense then. At least, she hoped so, because she wasn't sure what could possibly happen to throw her off balance any more than she was now.

As soon as she stood up and shrugged into her parka, Alex felt the two beers she'd consumed make a quick rush to her bladder. Great. Using the restroom at Pete's meant walking right past the bar – and Kade. She considered ignoring the urgent press of her plumbing, but the two blocks to her house from the tavern, in the frigid cold, would be torture. Maybe even disastrous.

So what if Kade might see that she was there? She sure as hell didn't need to talk to him. She didn't even need to so much as look at him.

Yeah, brilliant plan. Too bad it fell apart the moment she took two paces away from her table.

She felt Kade's quicksilver eyes slicing through the crowd to zero in on her like twin laser beams. His gaze went through her every nerve ending in much the same way – hot, electric. Alex tried to ignore the effect he had on her, which was made a bit easier when she separated Big Dave's grating voice from the others and heard him bragging about his recent hunting exploits while Kade smiled and nodded along like he was hanging out with his best friends.

Twenty-four hours in town and he was one of the good ol' boys already. How freaking nice for him.

Disgusted, Alex continued on past the jukebox to the restroom. Breathing a small sigh of relief to find it unoccupied, she went right in and did her business, rolling her eyes as the good times and laughter continued on the other side of the locked door. It wasn't until she was at the sink washing her hands that she happened to look up into the mirror and saw a tired, haggard reflection of herself staring back at her.

'Oh, my God,' she whispered, wishing she'd at least taken the time to dab on some mascara when she left the house tonight. And maybe paused long enough to drag a brush through her windblown, wrecked mop of hair.

She made a futile attempt at smoothing some of the blonde flyaways, but there wasn't a lot she could do. No wonder Kade stared as he had. She looked like a walking Medusa who hadn't had a decent night's sleep in about a week straight – which was just about accurate, come to think of it.

Had she looked this bad when she saw him earlier today? She hoped not. She hoped he hadn't thought—

'For crying out loud. Why should you give a rat's ass what he thinks, huh?' she told the hopeless face in the mirror. 'That man out there is the last person you need to impress.'

Alex nodded at her own advice, at the same time wondering if everything that had happened lately had pushed her past some invisible line where it was suddenly acceptable to have conversations with her own reflection. Bad enough she talked to Luna as if the wolf dog could understand every word; this was taking things just a bit too far.

Taking a deep breath, Alex hooked her unruly hair behind her ears, then opened the bathroom door and stepped outside.

'Everything all right in there?'

Kade. Oh, God.

He leaned on the edge of the jukebox, which she noticed had finally coughed up the song she'd chosen nearly an hour ago. He was grinning at her, humor playing at the corners of his broad mouth and in the pale light of his eyes. Had he possibly heard her berating herself over the irony of Sheryl Crow singing about her favorite mistake?

'I see you're making friends in Harmony already.'

He grunted, shot a casual look over at the knot of men who were still pounding down beers before turning all of his attention back on her. 'Big Dave and some of the others are going to track the wolf pack that's been spotted around here lately. They asked me to join them.'

Alex scoffed. 'Congratulations. I'm sure you'll all have a great time.'

As she brushed past him, he said, 'I also heard tonight about a death in the bush late last winter that seemed suspicious. A Native man, living by himself in a cabin ten miles northwest of Harmony. Big Dave seems to think wolves were responsible for that one, too.'

Alex pivoted back, shaking her head. 'You're talking about Henry Tulak? He was a drinker and a little bit crazy. He most likely did something stupid and died of exposure.'

Kade lifted one thick shoulder. 'Big Dave and the others said nothing could be proven because Tulak's body wasn't discovered until the spring thaw. Nothing left of him by then but a few bones.'

'And if you lived in the interior for any amount of time – as you claim – you'd know that nothing lasts for long in the bush. If the elements don't absorb you, the scavengers will. It doesn't mean that wolves killed that man.'

'Maybe not,' Kade said. 'Except the rumor is that the last time anyone saw Tulak alive, he was talking about seeing a wolf pack prowling around his place. Said he felt like they were sizing him up, waiting for the chance to strike.'

Alex's frustration spiked to hear this kind of bullshit perpetuated, and especially by Kade, whom she would have guessed to be smarter than Big Dave Grant and his band of boneheads. 'Big Dave would say anything to get folks riled up. That's his nature. If I were you, I wouldn't put too much stock in what he says.'

'I'm here to gather information, Alex. Right now, Big Dave seems to be the most forthcoming. All I'm getting from everyone else in this town is evasions and half-truths, neither of which interests me.'

Okay, now she was offended. Her internal barometer blazed right through frustration and into fury. 'Why are you really here? Talk about evasions and half-truths! Look at you. You show up here, nobody knows you, nobody even knows where you came from—'

'I told you, north of Fairbanks. By way of Boston, if we're going to start being honest with each other now.'

So, he wasn't actually from Alaska, just flew in from Outside. She couldn't have been less surprised. As casually as she could, she put her hand down on top of his forearm and leaned in closer, as though she were a cop questioning an uncoopera- tive witness. 'How did you get to Harmony when everyone else has been grounded by bad weather the past several days? For that matter, how did you get out to the Toms settlement after you left Harmony last night?'

'I walked. On snowshoes, of course.'

'You walked more than forty miles in the middle of the night.' Alex laughed, but without humor. She listened for the prickling of her instincts as she kept her hand resting on his arm, waiting for her senses to tell her whether he was trust- worthy. Nothing registered. He was as clear as glass, unreadable. Still, that didn't change the crock he was trying to feed her. 'Such bullshit. You stand there and accuse me of lying to you, when you've told me nothing about yourself other than your name is Kade and you're a bounty hunter looking to cash in on an innocent pack of wolves.'

He gave only the barest shake of his head. 'I never said I came here to hunt wolves, for a bounty or otherwise. You made an assumption. And you are wrong.'

'Okay, I give up then. What are you doing here, and why

did you come loaded up with a hell of a lot of serious fire-power? What exactly do you want, Kade, the non-wolf hunter from north of Fairbanks by way of Boston?'

'I told you that when we talked earlier today. I want answers. I need to have the truth – the entire truth – about what happened to your friends. I think you can help me with that, Alex. I think you might be the only person who can.'

He glanced down to where her hand was still settled on his arm. Alex abruptly drew it away, his deep voice vibrating inside her, his words making her feel that she possibly could trust him, whether her instincts could confirm it or not.

She did not want to warm to him, dammit. She didn't want to put her trust in anything he said when her heart was racing at hyperspeed and everything in her screamed for her to run. Run, before she made the mistake of letting this man into her private hell when she didn't know anything about him.

'What are you trying to pull?' she asked softly, wishing she had the strength just to walk away and leave him standing there instead of giving in to the curiosity that made her want to know more. 'What kind of game are you playing here?'

'I don't know what you mean,' he said, despite the intense steadiness of his gaze that said there wasn't much that escaped his keen intellect. 'What game do you think I'm playing?'

Alex stared back at him, forcing herself to try to read in his eyes all the things he probably wouldn't tell her. 'You tell me you're not a wolf hunter, but you let Big Dave and the other men believe that you are. You tell me you want information from me, yet you give up nothing in return. You're either one of the good guys, or you're not. So, which one are you, Kade?'

Something flickered across his expression. 'Do you view everything in terms of right or wrong, black or white? Is everyone either good or bad in your judgment?'

'Yes, they are.' She hadn't really thought about it in those terms, but she had to admit she took a certain comfort in the clarity of that. Right was right and wrong was wrong. In her experience, there was a very distinct line between good and bad.

And Kade still hadn't answered her question.

To her astonishment, he reached out and brushed his fingers across her cheek where some of her tangled hair had fallen into her face. She knew she should balk at the uninvited touch, but the warmth of his caress – even as fleeting as it was – felt too good to deny. 'You can be honest with me, Alex. You can trust me that whatever you tell me, I mean you no harm.'

God help her, but she was tempted to blurt out everything right then and there.

She didn't know this man from Adam, really, and yet when she was looking in his eyes, still feeling the trailing heat of his touch on her skin, she wanted to believe that she truly could trust him. In some frightened, little-girl corner of her heart, she actually hoped that he might be able to help her banish some of the demons that had haunted her nearly all her life.

She felt, inexplicably, that if she told him about the beasts that killed her mom and her little brother – the same beasts she felt certain had killed the Toms family, as well – Kade would understand. That he, of all people, would be her strongest ally.

'You can tell me,' he said, his deep voice so gentle and coaxing. 'Tell me about the track in the snow. You know what made that footprint, don't you? Tell me, Alex. I want to help you, but I need you to help me first.'

'I . . .' Alex swallowed hard, finding it took more effort than she expected to work up her courage. 'What I saw . . . it's hard to say the words . . .'

'I know. But it's okay, I promise. You're safe with me.'

She drew in a nervous breath and got a sudden whiff of acrid smoke and the odor of unwashed clothing from somewhere nearby. No sooner had she registered the stale stench than she saw Skeeter Arnold and a couple of his stoner buddies shuffling from the bar back to the game room. A cell phone decorated in a skull-and-crossbones motif in one hand, a beer in the other, Skeeter tipped his bottle in Kade's direction as he passed. 'Thanks for the brewskies, dude. That was straight-up righteous of you, man.'

Kade hardly spared Skeeter a glance, but Alex couldn't hide her revulsion. And she was glad for it, because the disgust she felt for Skeeter Arnold doused some of the temporary insanity that was making her think she could trust the stranger who was playing her like an instrument of his own design.

'I take it you aren't fond of that guy,' Kade said as Alex weathered an inward shudder of repugnance.

She grunted. 'You know that video you mentioned to me, the footage of the Toms family that had been uploaded to the Internet? Well, that's the creep who did it.'

Kade's eyes narrowed as they locked on to Skeeter from across the room. His gaze was more than intense – it was lethal. And as Alex watched him, she noticed that the pattern of tattoos on his forearms, part of them just visible under the pushed-up sleeves of his shirt, were not the henna color she remembered but a dark shade of deep blue-black.

Well, that was certainly odd.

Maybe she'd had one beer too many if she was seeing his tattoos change colors. Or maybe she simply remembered wrong. She'd been so gobsmacked by the unexpected sight of him at the Toms place earlier today, not to mention the fact that his incredible body had been half naked besides, it was completely possible that she'd mistaken the color of his ink. Except she'd never seen such an amazing work of body art ever in her life, and the image of him standing there, buttoning up his jeans like she'd just roused him out of bed, was a sight burned indelibly into her memory.

After a long minute of searing Skeeter Arnold with his eyes, Kade finally looked back at Alex. 'I'll deal with him later. What you have to say is more important.'

Alex took a step back now, sensing the danger in the man even though he was speaking to her in the same gentle tones as before. But something was different. There was an air of menace about him that put her on edge.

And there remained the fact that when she'd asked him if he was good or bad, he hadn't answered her.

'I think I'd better go now,' she murmured, retreating another step before making a quick dodge past him.

'Alex,' she heard him call from behind her.

But she kept moving, cutting through the knot of people packed into the bar and desperate for some cold, sobering air – and freedom from her troubling, visceral response to Kade.

✥ CHAPTER NINE ✥

Kade exhaled a low growl as he watched Alex cut through the tavern and all but run for the exit.

He had pushed a little too hard with her, a tactic he should have known would fail just from the brief time he'd spent around her, studying the way she operated. Alexandra Maguire only dug in her heels harder if someone attempted to lean on her.

And then, on top of that, he'd made everything worse by having the bad sense to touch her.

He hadn't been able to resist, and some part of him acknowledged even as it was happening that she'd seemed to welcome the contact. Right up until the moment that greasy slacker with the burnout's gaze and thin beak of a nose came walking up and disrupted them. Kade had a serious urge to pound the guy for that alone, never mind the fact that the stoner had also been the one to broadcast visual evidence of a vampire attack all over the World Wide Web.

As for dealing with Alex, Kade had seen the fear in her eyes as he pressed her for answers. She'd been terrified to spit the words out, but he was certain he'd been very close to getting her to open up completely about what exactly she knew. And the cold-as-ice feeling in his gut was telling him that what she knew went a whole lot deeper than just the recent attack and slaying of the family in the bush.

Could she possibly be aware of the Breed's existence?

Had she seen one of his kind before?

Jesus Christ, what if she'd found more than just an unexplainable footprint out there at the Toms settlement?

If she had information that might implicate Seth in the killings – or clear him, slim as that hope seemed – Kade had to know. He had to know right now.

And if she did, in fact, have any inkling about the Breed, Kade figured it would be a hell of a lot easier to strip the memory from her outside in the shadows of the dimly lit parking lot than in the middle of a crowded restaurant and bar.

He stalked out after her to the snow-covered lot. She was already halfway across the short span of plowed tundra, walking briskly past the couple of pickup trucks and the half-dozen snowmachines parked outside Pete's. She didn't even break stride as the clank of the bell on the door sounded behind Kade as he leapt off the squat, covered porch and fell in, hot on her heels.

'Do you always run away when you get scared?'

That brought her up short. She pivoted around, an odd look on her face, as though his comment hit too close to home. But then she blinked and the look was gone, replaced with a narrowed gaze and a stubborn tilt of her hooded head. 'Do you never give up, even when you know you're not going to win?'

'Never,' he said, zero hesitation.

She muttered a particularly vivid curse and kept on walking, headed in the direction of the street. Kade caught up to her in a few long strides.

'You were going to tell me something back there in the tavern, Alex. Something important that I really need to know. What was it?'

'God!' She spun toward him, anger flashing in her brown doe eyes. 'You're impossible, you know that?'

'And you're beautiful.'

He didn't know why he said it, other than that he found it too hard to keep the thought inside his head when she was standing there looking windblown and wild, her cheeks carrying the pink kiss of the Arctic chill, her blonde hair framing her face in tousled waves beneath the fur ruff of her parka's hood.

If Brock or any of the other warriors in Boston had heard him just now, they'd guess that he was just playing this female, plying her with flattery to get what he wanted from her. Kade himself wanted to believe that was the cause of his ham-handed blurt. But as he looked at Alexandra Maguire, her simple beauty lit up by the thin moonlight overhead and the multicolored glow of the neon bar signs in the windows behind him, Kade knew that he wasn't playing any kind of game here. He was attracted to her – fiercely attracted – and he wanted her to understand that he wasn't the enemy.

Not precisely, at any rate.

Her outrage cooled to something resembling confusion as she started to take a backward step away from him. 'I really have to go now.'

Kade lifted his hand but stopped short of physically holding her back. 'Alex, whatever secret you're keeping, you can tell me. Let me share some of the burden with you. Let me protect you from whatever it is that's got you so scared.'

She shook her head, her light brown brows knitting together. 'I don't need you. I don't even know you. And if I felt the need to share, I have friends I can talk to instead.'

'But you haven't told any of them, have you.' It wasn't a question, and she knew it as well as he did. 'There isn't another single person in your life who knows what you're keeping bottled inside you. Tell me if I'm wrong.'

'Shut up,' she murmured, her breath steaming on the chill air, her voice cracking softly. 'Just . . . shut up. Leave me alone. You don't know anything about me.'

'Does anyone really know you, Alex?'

She went so still and quiet, Kade thought for sure he'd crossed yet another line that would drive her farther away from him. But she didn't spin around and leave him eating her wake. She didn't curse him out, or strike him, or scream for anyone to come out of Pete's and do it for her. She stood there, looking up into his eyes in a silence that felt so lost, so broken.

His warrior's duty to collect vital intel and erase a potential security risk for the Order collided with the sudden urge he had to offer comfort, to protect this female who professed so strongly to have no need for either.

Kade stepped closer to her, and then he did touch her again. Just the lightest brush of his fingertips over one golden strand of her hair as it caught on the wintry breeze. She didn't move. Her breath had stopped puffing through her parted lips, and this close, Kade could hear the rush of blood pulsing through her veins as her heart rate kicked into a faster beat.

'You asked me in the bar if I was a good guy or a bad guy,' he reminded her, his voice low and rough for the awareness of her body's heat mingling with his as he inched tighter into her space. He shook his head slowly. 'That's not my call to make, Alex. Maybe you'll find I'm some of both. The way I look at the world, everything is just a different shade of gray.'

'No . . . I can't live like that,' she said, the tone of her voice naked with sincerity. 'It would make it all too complicated, too hard to know what's true or not. Too hard to know what's real.'

'I'm real,' Kade said, holding her gaze as he stroked his fingers along the curve of her jaw. 'And you feel very real to me, too.'

She drew in a soft breath at his touch, and as her lips parted, Kade swept his mouth against hers in an impulsive – instantly electric – kiss.

He held her face tenderly in his palm as he brushed his lips over hers and savored the soft, wet heat of her mouth. Alex's kiss was sweet and open and giving . . . so damned good. The feel of her body pressing against his sent a jolt of fire swimming through him, searing every nerve ending with the stamp of her lean curves and the warm, wind-and-woods scent of her.

He wasn't thinking about gathering intel or finding a quiet place to scrub her mind once he had the information he needed. The feeling he had right now had nothing to do with offering her comfort or protection, either.

All he felt was need for this woman, his desire for her startlingly intense.

And a hunger that was growing more consuming the longer Alex remained in his arms.

With a simple, unplanned kiss, she drowned him in a swamping tide of lust and bloodthirst. He hadn't fed since he arrived in Alaska, a careless oversight that now sank sharp talons into him, demanding to be slaked every bit as urgently as the throb that beat hard and hot between his legs.

From somewhere in the hunger-drenched fog of his consciousness, Kade heard the rumbling approach of a vehicle nearing the parking lot. He wanted to ignore the low growl of the truck's engine, but then a male voice called out from the shadows.

'Alex? Everything all right out here?'

'Shit,' she hissed, pulling back now. 'This was a mistake.'

Kade said nothing as she retreated several more steps, but then speech would have proved a bit difficult, given the fact that his fangs now filled his mouth. She wouldn't look at him, which suited Kade just fine, since one glimpse of his eyes right now – transformed from the pale gray they normally were, to the bright amber glow that betrayed him as one of the Breed – would have turned the ill-conceived impulse of kissing her into a catastrophe of huge proportions.

'I never should have let you do that,' she whispered, then ducked around him.

Kade slanted a cautious look over his shoulder at the idling Blazer bearing Alaska State Trooper colors, watching as Alex walked up to it. 'Hey, Zach. What's going on? I thought Jenna was at your house.'

'She just left. Said you were at Pete's, so I thought I'd swing by and have a beer with you.' Tucker's voice carried on the chill wind. 'What the hell are you doing out here? Were you with someone?'

'No, not with anyone,' she said. Kade felt, rather than saw, the quick backward glance that Alex shot into the shadows where he stood. 'I was just leaving. Give me a ride home?'

'Sure, get in,' Zach Tucker said, and Alex opened the door and climbed inside.

Kade clamped his molars together, curbing the lust that was still coursing through him as he watched her close the door and drive off with the human male. He'd detected the trace odor of bullshit in the trooper's casual tone, and had to guess that Zach Tucker wasn't the only man in Harmony who was happy to use any excuse to put himself in close company with – and in the good graces of – sexy Alexandra Maguire. Kade had a very strong impulse to go after her, whether she'd been glad to escape him or not.

But if he needed something to distract him from that idea, he got it in spades as the tavern door banged open and out walked Skeeter Arnold and three of his stoner pals.

Kade observed the knot of twenty-something guys, smiling with satisfaction as the group disbanded and Skeeter was left standing alone while his friends took off in a rumbling old F150. When Skeeter started to walk toward the back lot, Kade peeled away from the shadows to follow him and have a word or two about the hazards of pissing off a bunch of vampires.

But before Kade took two steps toward the asshole,

headlights came on in the parking lot and a black Hummer rolled out behind Skeeter Arnold. The vehicle gleamed under the weak lights of the lot, and compared to the other clunkers parked at Pete's, Kade would bet his left nut that whoever was driving it wasn't local. When the truck slowed down to deliberately keep pace with Skeeter, who paused to stick his head inside the open passenger-side window, Kade's hackles raised along with his suspicion.

What the hell would someone with Hummer-style tastes want with a low-budget loser like Skeeter Arnold? Something was said to the stoner in barely audible tones before he chuckled and eagerly nodded.

'Yeah, sure. For the right price, I might be interested in hearing more about that,' he said, then opened the door and hopped inside.

'What the fuck are you up to?' Kade muttered as the vehicle sped away, kicking up clots of snow in its wake.

He had a feeling that whatever transaction might be taking place between Skeeter Arnold and his newfound business associate, it was going to prove to be much bigger than the small-time dealer's usual fare.

A low, hissing heat and a sentimental old country song drifted from the dashboard of Zach's state-issued Blazer as Alex glanced at the side mirror, watching the parking lot at Pete's fade into the darkness behind her.

'Thanks for the ride, Zach.'

'No problem. I've got to run out for eggs and hot sauce, anyway. Breakfast of champions, you know. And single thirty-five-year-old cops with no nutrition sense.'

Alex gave him a polite smile as they traveled the last of the short two blocks to her house. She felt every bit as relieved as she did foolish for having run off on Kade as she had, but the fact was, she had welcomed the rescue. God knew she'd needed one, before she'd been tempted to do anything more with him right out there in the open, among the pickup trucks and snow-machines.

What had she been thinking, letting a complete stranger put a move on her like that? She wasn't the type to let a guy take advantage of her with empty flattery or free-range hands – and being a young, unmarried woman in the Alaskan interior, she'd known plenty of men who'd tried.

Except with Kade tonight, it hadn't felt like any sort of play or move, as smooth as the art of seduction seemed to come to him. And although she'd never so much as seen his face before he showed up yesterday, she had to admit – to herself at least – that he seemed like anything but a stranger to her.

Kade seemed to know her – to understand her – on a level that astonished her.

He seemed to be able to look deep inside her, into the dark places not even she was brave enough to face, and that's what terrified her about him the most.

It was that unnerving sense of awareness that had made her so desperate to escape him tonight.

'Home sweet home,' Zach said, breaking into her thoughts as he rolled to a stop outside her weathered wood-sided house. 'Jenna probably told you already, but I got word the AST unit out of Fairbanks should be here later this week.' At Alex's nod, he lifted his right arm up onto her seatback and leaned in a bit closer. 'I know this can't be easy for you. Hell, it's not easy for me, either. I knew Wilbur Toms and his family for a lot of years. I don't know how this kind of awful thing could have happened to them. But the truth will come out, Alex. It will.'

Zach's face, half illuminated by the pale lights of the dash, seemed troubled, cautious. And after her blurt at the town meeting, she could hardly be surprised if his cop instincts told him she was holding something back.

'If there's anything more that you recall about the crime

scene, Alex, I need you to tell me, all right? Anything at all. I'd like to know we're on the same page by the time the Fairbanks unit arrives and starts throwing its weight around town.'

'Sure,' she murmured. 'Yeah, Zach. If I think of anything else, I'll make sure to tell you.'

Even as she said it, she knew she would speak no more of the track in the snow or the bone-deep fear she harbored that something terrible was on the loose in the frigid wilderness not far from where they sat now. The thing she feared was worse than any kind of danger posed by man or animal. It was monstrous. It would not be stopped by Zach Tucker or a bunch of Staties, and Alex was going to try her damnedest to forget all about it.

She was going to try to forget everything that had happened in the Florida swamps so long ago, too. Best to just let it all go, bury it deep, and move on.

Or move away.

Run.

'Sleep well,' Zach said as she climbed out of the Blazer and closed the passenger door. 'You call me anytime, you hear?'

She nodded. 'Thanks, Zach. And thanks again for the lift.'

He flashed a quick smile that was there and gone before he put the truck in gear and drove away. As Alex walked toward the front door of the old house she'd shared with her father since she'd been that frightened little girl, uprooted from her entire world – her entire reality – the notion of running away from it all only deepened. It would be so much easier, leaving her memories behind. Starting over somewhere new would be the best way for her to purge the fears that dogged her, that had come back darker now, more dreadful than ever before.

She could not face horror like that again.

Nor could she allow herself to be wooed into a state of false confidence that anyone – even a man like Kade – could stand firm against an evil like the one she knew existed. Getting involved with him on any level was the last thing she needed. Yet that didn't keep her from wondering what he thought of her now, or from wishing she would have apologized before ditching him in the cold.

She tried not to think about the way his mouth fit so perfectly, so electrifyingly hot, on hers. Tried not to think about the way her heart was still racing, her stomach still coiled in an excited knot at the thought of being in his arms. She tried not to imagine what might have happened if Zach hadn't come along when he did, but picturing herself with Kade – maybe naked together in her bed, maybe hastily unzipped and out of control in the middle of Pete's parking lot if they couldn't make it that far – was disturbingly easy to do.

'Oh, this is so not good,' she muttered under her breath as she opened the door and walked in to be greeted by eager wolf dog kisses and much happy tail wagging. 'I know, Luna, I know . . . I'm late. Sorry, baby. It's been a long day for me, too. Come on, let's go take care of you now.'

Alex busied herself with turning the dog loose in the back to pee while she prepared a bowl of food and fresh water. After Luna was back inside and gobbling her kibble, Alex stripped off her parka and clothes while she headed down the hallway to the bathroom for an overdue, but indulgently long and hot, shower.

The heated spray against her bare skin did nothing to quench the lingering heat of Kade's kiss. She soaped up, trying to recall how long it had been since she'd let a man run his hands in slow appreciation over her naked body. How long had it been since she'd been intimate – truly intimate – with someone? The weak moment she'd spent with Zach a few weeks after her father died didn't really count. That had been one night, a couple of hours, really. She'd been an emotional wreck and supposed she'd just needed someone to help her make it all go away, even for a short while.

Is that what she was doing with Kade? Was she latching on to him, manufacturing something between them that wasn't really there – couldn't possibly be there – because of the new trauma she was going through now?

Maybe that's all this was, a temporary feeling of being left adrift and in search of safe harbor. Tonight Kade had told her she'd be safe with him. While part of her believed that – an instinctual, primal part of her – she also knew that the fire he stoked inside her with just a kiss felt anything but safe. She couldn't help feeling that getting close to him might be the biggest risk she'd ever taken. He saw too much about her, knew too much. And tonight he made her feel too much.

Alex groaned as she leaned forward in the tight tub-and-shower combo, bracing her forearm against the slick tiles and resting her head against her arm as the hot water sluiced off her body. She closed her eyes and there was Kade. His chiseled, striking face. His bright, penetratingly intense eyes. The heat inside her was still there, heat that made her whisper his name as she reached down with her free hand to touch herself as she ached to be touched by him.

She relaxed into a blissful state of resignation, letting the hot water and steam and thoughts of him melt away everything else.

❧ CHAPTER TEN ❧

Kade hung back in the darkness, watching from within a tight copse of spruce and pine some five hundred yards from where Skeeter Arnold's fancy ride had taken him. Twenty-plus miles out of Harmony, situated near the base of a small mountain and a narrow tributary that spoked off the Koyukuk, the ten-acre patch of land and squat white buildings sat fenced in and gated by fifteen-foot-high steel links and coiled barbed wire. Security lights and cameras were mounted all around the place, and the pair of uniformed guards trying to keep warm in the shack out front were carrying military-grade assault rifles.

Kade might have guessed the friendly little spot to be a supermax prison, if not for the weathered metal sign bolted onto the gate that read in chipped black lettering: COLDSTREAM MINING COMPANY.

Outside in the yard, a group of workers were busy unloading various-size sealed crates from two large cargo containers parked near what appeared to be some kind of warehouse. Some crates were wheeled into the storage facility, while others were brought into the secured entrance of the mine itself.

Curiouser and curiouser, Kade thought, figuring the more than two hours Skeeter had been inside the main office building hadn't been spent interviewing for a job.

Kade was more than eager to question the human about his business here – along with the rest of his entrepreneurial ventures – but if Skeeter's new friends didn't turn him loose in the next few minutes, his interrogation would have to wait for another time. More important was the need to check in with the Order and let them know what he'd uncovered thus far. He also needed to get his head on straight about Alexandra Maguire.

To his complete irritation, his libido perked up with the eager suggestion that he turn back for Harmony and go find her again. Not that it should surprise him that thoughts of her simmered just beneath the surface of his consciousness. Their kiss still had him on fire inside – banked flames, but embers needing only the slightest trace of fuel to ignite.

And that was bad news.

Bad news to want the female so badly, especially when his mission depended on keeping her silent. Deflecting her suspicions, whatever the cost. Erasing the risk she posed to his mission, the Order's goals, and the security of the Breed nation as a whole.

Whatever Alexandra Maguire knew about the killings in the bush – whatever she knew about Kade's kind in general – had to be shut down, and shut down fast.

Had it only been earlier that day that he'd considered seducing the truth out of her, if necessary? Now that plan had a serious kink in it, because if their kiss had shown him anything, it was that letting himself get close to Alex – even in the name of duty – wasn't going to be easy. She had an unanticipated effect on him already, from the mile-wide independent streak she wore like a carefully placed mask, to the threadbare hint of vulnerability he'd glimpsed in her tonight.

No, going back to find Alex at home right now was not an option. Besides, he doubted she'd look favorably on him stalking her after the way she bolted from him at Pete's. Hell, for all he knew, Zach Tucker might still be with her. Obviously they were friends, and no doubt the clean-cut trooper appealed to her stated need to categorize everything into neat compartments. From his domed hat and meticulously pressed uniform to the tops of his precisely laced boots, Officer Tucker projected cut-and-dried, black-and-white, good-guy appeal.

Except something about the man bothered Kade. Partly the apparent ease of his relationship with Alex, although jealousy wasn't something Kade caved to very often. That didn't keep him from gritting his teeth thinking about the guy, or from wondering if maybe a quick trip back to Harmony just to look in on Alex wasn't in order after all. Picking up where they'd left off in Pete's parking lot was optional. Not to mention sorely tempting.

Before the idea could take root any more than it had already, Kade dismissed it with a curse muttered low under his breath.

Bad fucking news – that's what this entire mission was shaping up to be.

With that thought dogging his heels, Kade slipped away from his surveillance of Skeeter Arnold and his new high-security pals, and started off in the direction of his father's Darkhaven a few hours away on foot. He could wait out the daylight there, check in with headquarters in Boston about his findings so far, and see if Gideon could turn up anything of interest on the Coldstream Mining Company.

Skeeter Arnold had lost all track of time. He rode in the back-seat of the black Hummer, surprised to see the clock on the expensive ride's dashboard up front read 6:00 a.m.

He'd been gone all night?

It felt as though he'd just left Pete's tavern a few minutes ago and now here he was, back again. Only now everything was different.

He was different.

He felt it in the way his body sat so straight on the leather seat, his spine erect, shoulders lifted out of their usual heavy slump. He felt empowered somehow, and knew the source of that power was sitting beside him: motionless, silent, radiating dark menace and cool, lethal control.

Skeeter didn't know his name. He couldn't even recall if he'd been told.

It no longer mattered.

'You will tell no one of what transpired tonight,' said the airless voice from within the deep hood of a black-fur parka. 'You will go home immediately and destroy all copies of the video footage of the slayings.'

Skeeter nodded obediently, eager to please. 'Yes, Master.'

He recalled thinking that when the Hummer driver first approached him about sharing some information with an interested private party, the transaction was sure to involve someone stuffing a sweet amount of cash into his pocket.

He'd been wrong about that.

And when he'd been brought out to the old mining company location to meet the so-called interested private party, he'd been wrong to guess that the tall man in the pricey suit and crisp white shirt was a man at all. He was something more than that.

Something . . . other.

Skeeter had been a little afraid as he was escorted via armed guards from the vehicle and through the main building, into a secured area that looked like some kind of research facility, pimped out in shiny stainless steel exam tables and easily a few million bucks in computer equipment. It was all pretty weird, though the biggest head-scratcher had been the large vertical cylinder that seemed to be some kind of cage with thick metal chains and shackles bolted to the floor of it.

As he had tried to make sense of its purpose, the individual he was to meet with – the same individual seated beside him now – came into the room to question Skeeter about many things. He'd been asked about the cell phone video he'd taken at the Toms settlement. He'd been asked what he knew of the slayings, if he'd witnessed the creature who'd attacked the humans.

Skeeter recalled his confusion over the odd way the questions were phrased, and he worried that he had somehow walked into a situation more dangerous than it seemed. But there had been no opportunity to turn back. He'd walked into something deadly serious. He'd known that, even then.

He'd been questioned about Alexandra Maguire, and what the rumors were around town about the killings. When he'd volunteered about the stranger in Harmony, the big, muscular dude with the jet-black hair and wolfy eyes who showed up out of the blue just a couple of nights ago asking similar questions of the townsfolk, the air in the room had seemed to grow as thick as fog.

Skeeter recalled the dread he'd felt as the tall man in the expensive-looking suit pulled a satellite phone from a nearby table and left the room for a few minutes.

He remembered being antsy, needing to distract himself from whatever disaster might be waiting for him on the other end of that phone call. He'd asked the laboratory workers what the cage was used for, watching as three of them in white jumpsuits tested some of the fittings and clicked computer controls that operated different functions on the thing.

Skeeter had guessed out loud that it wasn't meant to hold a human. The size of the cell, as well as the size of the table inside and the heavy-duty restraints affixed to it, had seemed designed for something much larger than any man. A grizzly, maybe, Skeeter had said, to no reply from any of the workers or the armed guards.

But someone had an answer for him, impossible as it was to believe.

'It was built for one of my kind,' the tall man in the

expensive-looking suit had said as he'd walked back into the room.

And he had looked different to Skeeter then. Still rich and important, still the same current of lethal power about him, but his face had seemed tighter, his features drawn sharper, more pronounced.

Skeeter recalled seeing a sudden spark of amber light flashing in the narrowed gaze that refused to let him squirm, even though every cell in his body was screaming for him to get the hell out of there. He recalled catching a fleeting glimpse of sharp white teeth, recalled thinking that he was only seconds away from dying . . . then he felt the full body blow that knocked him completely off his feet.

Skeeter could not remember much after that moment of pure terror.

Everything slowed down, went black.

But he hadn't died.

He'd woken up a short while ago and all of his confusion – all of his fear – was gone.

Now he belonged to the powerful individual seated beside him, the vampire who had made him into something more than human tonight, as well. Skeeter's loyalty was ensured by blood, his very life tied to that of his Master.

'You will report to me with any and all information you can gather,' said the voice that commanded him in all things now.

'Yes, Master,' Skeeter replied, and when he was given a nod to go, he climbed out of the Hummer and waited as it eased away from the side of the road and departed.

When it was gone, Skeeter walked across Pete's parking lot to the lone snowmachine that still sat parked outside. He hopped on and turned the key in the ignition. Nothing happened. He tried again with the same result, then swore roundly when he realized he'd forgotten to buy gas for the damned thing last night.

'Morning,' a familiar voice greeted him as chain-encased snow tires crunched in the frozen road. 'Need a hand?'

Skeeter shook his head without looking at Zach Tucker. Of all the shitty luck, he had to run into Harmony's sole cop today.

Tucker didn't accept his refusal. The Blazer rolled up next to Skeeter's sled and idled while the trooper got out and went around back to grab a red can of gasoline out of the back of the truck.

'Late night, huh?' he asked as he walked over and unscrewed the cap on the Yamaha's fuel tank. 'Looking a bit ragged this morning, Skeeter. Must have been out partying with new friends from out of town or something. Nice Hummer, by the way.'

Skeeter offered no explanation, watching the red can empty into his snowmachine.

'No charge this time,' Tucker said as he finished. But when Skeeter thought the cop might simply move on, instead he got in his face with a tight whisper. 'I thought I told you to lay low for a while – quit the goddamn dealing and partying until we get this thing cleaned up around here. And for the record, posting that fucking cell phone video on that death fetish website was just about the stupidest thing you could do. Now I've got those assholes in Fairbanks busting my balls about losing control of a crime scene!'

Tucker was furious, and ordinarily that might make Skeeter worry.

But not today.

'Do I need to remind you that our little operation stands a damn good chance of getting blown up in our faces? I've got Staties coming up here later this week to crawl all over this investigation. I won't have you giving them added reasons to stick around and see what else is going on out here. You got that?'

Skeeter ignored him, moving around him to take a seat on the sled.

'Are you that fucking stupid,' Tucker scoffed, 'or are you just stoned?'

'I have never been clearer in my life,' Skeeter replied.

'I want to know who you were partying with last night. Where did you go? Jesus Christ, were you idiot enough to tell them anything about me or our arrangement?'

'None of that is any of your concern. What you want no longer matters. I have other priorities.'

When Skeeter turned the engine over, Tucker's hand came down hard on his shoulder. 'If you fuck with me on this, don't think I won't throw you under the bus. You'll go down faster than you can say felony possession with intent to distribute. Cross me now and I swear to God I will bury you.'

Skeeter held the flinty gaze of his recent silent business partner. 'That would not be wise, Officer Tucker.' He saw the momentary flinch of shock in the cop's eyes and felt a small sense of triumph that he had put it there. 'Thanks for the gas, though.'

Skeeter gave the sled some juice and tore out of the parking lot. By the time he reached his mother's house at the end of the block, he was full of his newfound power and twitchy with the need to carry out his Master's orders. He parked the snow-machine and ran into the back door of the house, aware, but not caring, that his heavy boots clomped loudly on the old wooden floor of the hallway.

Before he was inside his apartment for even as much as a minute, his mother started moving around upstairs, her muf-fled complaints echoing down to him beneath her bedroom. He knew she'd be storming down to bitch at him, and could hardly say that he was disappointed when she did.

'Stanley Elmer Arnold!' she screamed, banging on his door. 'Do you have any idea what time it is? You worthless piece of shit! How dare you stay out all goddamn night, making me worry about you, only to drag your sorry ass back home at the crack of dawn and wake me out of a dead sleep! You're nothing but a loser and a—'

Skeeter was at the door and in the hallway with her, his hand clamped punishingly around her throat and cutting her off before the words had a chance to shriek out of her mouth.

'Be quiet, bitch,' he told her harshly. 'I'm working in here.'

If she'd uttered even one syllable as his hand peeled away from her, Skeeter would have killed her, right then and there. And she knew it, by God. She understood that things would be different now.

Soundless, she stepped back from him, wobbling just a little in her ratty slippers and matted terry housecoat. Slowly she turned around and walked carefully back up the hallway where she'd come from.

Skeeter Arnold cocked his head at her retreating bulk, then smiled as he returned to the more important tasks that awaited him in the shithole apartment he called home.

Kade grinned, seeing Max's angle from a mile away. Like him, Max craved adventure. Unlike him, Max had committed himself to serving as second banana to Kade's father, the leader of the Fairbanks Darkhaven. Max's loyalty had shackled him to this ten-thousand-acre prison, and although he would never shirk his duty or his promise to his rigid, uncompromising brother, Max appreciated the concept of risk and reward, courage and honor, every bit as much as Kade did.

Because of that, and because Kade knew Max's loyalty extended to him, as well, he knew that trusting him with a few details of his experiences with the Order and their current mission would not be misplaced.

'I heard there was some upheaval in the Enforcement Agency out East some months back,' Max said, watching Kade eagerly, waiting for him to elaborate.

'There was,' he admitted, recalling one of the first missions he'd been involved with, and the beginning of the trouble the Order now had with the madman called Dragos. 'Our intel uncovered a high-ranking director of the Agency who wasn't what he seemed. This guy had been operating under an assumed name and seeding a secret rebellion for decades – longer, in fact. We're still trying to figure out just how far the corruption goes, but it hasn't been easy. Every time we get close to the bastard, he goes deeper to ground.'

'So, you pursue him harder,' Max said, talking like any one of the warriors back in Boston. 'You keep hitting him, keep pounding him from all angles, until he's too exhausted from running that he has no choice but to stand and fight. And then you destroy him, once and for all.'

Kade nodded grimly, hearing the wisdom in Max's advice and wishing their pursuit of Dragos was as simple, as clean, as that.

What Max didn't know – what neither he nor anyone else could be permitted to know – was that Dragos was only the tip of a very treacherous iceberg. Dragos had a secret weapon, one he'd been holding for centuries. Around the same time that Kade had joined the Order, they had discovered the existence of a creature long thought to be dead. An Ancient. One of the bloodthirsty otherworlders who'd fathered the entire Breed race on Earth millennia ago.

Dragos was that creature's grandson, and he'd been breeding his army of ruthless, unstoppable vampire assassins off him for longer than anyone wanted to contemplate.

If that news were to get out to the Breed communities in the United States and abroad, it would incite widespread panic.

If it were to leak to the human populations that not only did vampires walk among them, but one megalomaniac intended to put himself in power and enslave them all?

Armageddon.

Kade had to mentally shake himself out of that nightmare scenario. 'While the rest of the Order is doing just what you said, I drew the short straw to come up to Alaska. I've been looking into an attack on some humans in the bush – a whole family settlement, wiped out in one night.'

Max frowned. 'Rogues?'

'That's our guess.' And Kade's hope, although each minute of this assignment led him farther and farther away from that as a viable outcome. 'You haven't heard of any trouble in the Darkhavens, have you? Anyone rumored to be edging toward Bloodlust?'

Max gave a slow shake of his head. 'Nothing like that. There was an incident at the Darkhaven in Anchorage about nine months ago. Some idiot kid nearly bled out a human at a party, but that was the only problem in the region lately.'

The news didn't make Kade feel any better, certainly. Because if there were no Rogues on the loose, then that left only one reasonable place to lay the blame.

'I wonder if Seth has heard anything,' he murmured, trying

to keep the dread and fury out of his voice. 'Sure would hate to miss seeing him while I'm here.'

'He would hate to miss you, as well,' Max said, and Kade could see that he meant it sincerely.

He didn't know about Seth. Like everyone else, he had no clue.

Only Kade knew.

And the burden of that knowledge was sitting heavier in his gut all the time.

Max sat back in his chair and softly cleared his throat. 'There's something I want to tell you, Kade. Something you need to understand . . . about your family, and about your father.'

'Go on,' Kade said, not entirely sure he wanted to hear how much his father adored Seth and wished Kade had been more like him.

'My brother, your father, does not find it easy to show his affection. Especially with you.'

'Funny, I hadn't noticed.' Kade grinned with humor he didn't feel.

'Our family has a dark secret,' Max said, and Kade felt his body go a little numb. 'Kir and I had a younger brother. You never knew that, I'm sure. Not many do. His name was Grigori. Kir loved him very much. We all did. Grigori was a clever, charming boy. But he was also a bit wild. Even at his young age, he rebelled against authority and walked the razor's edge of every situation without any fear.'

Kade found himself smiling, thinking that he might have liked Grigori, too.

'Despite his faults, Kir doted on the boy. But some years later, when it was learned that Grigori had gone Rogue, that in his Bloodlust he had killed, Kir wrote him off completely. Just like that,' Max said, giving a sharp snap of his fingers. 'We never saw Grigori again. Kir never so much as spoke of him after we heard the news about Grigori turning Rogue, nor has he since. From that time forward, Kir was a changed man.'

Kade listened, reluctant to admit the pang of sympathy he had for his father and the loss he suffered.

'Perhaps your father worries that he could not shoulder that kind of pain again,' Max suggested. 'Perhaps it's just that he sees a bit too much of Grigori in you sometimes.'

And he'd apparently decided to write Kade off early, while pinning all of his fatherly hopes on Seth.

'It doesn't matter,' Kade murmured, and he half meant it, too. He was too busy dealing with real life-and-death shit to worry about how low his father's expectations might be for him. 'I appreciate the information, Max. And the insight. I also appreciate that you came by.'

Max, perceptive as ever, took the gentle hint and stood up. 'You have things to do. I should not delay you.'

When he stuck out his hand, Kade grabbed him into a brief embrace instead. 'You're a good man, Max. A good friend. Thank you.'

'Anything you need, Kade, you need only ask.'

They walked to the door together, and Kade opened it just as a pair of women, bundled in winter coats and each carrying a folded down-filled blanket, were walking past the cabin. One of them looked over and did a quick double-take.

'Oh . . . Kade?' she asked, then her pretty face lit up with a bright smile. 'Kade! I heard you'd returned to Alaska, but I didn't realize you were here.'

'Hello, Patrice,' he said, giving a polite smile to the Breedmate his twin brother had kept waiting in the wings for the past couple of years.

Beside him, Max had gone very still. Kade could feel heat radiating from the other male as Patrice continued to chat animatedly, sweet and gorgeous with her bright red hair and dark green eyes illuminated by the firelight pouring out from the door.

'Ruby and I were just on our way to watch the aurora borealis from one of the ledges. Would either of you like to join us?'

Kade and Max both said no together, but it was Max's refusal that dimmed Patrice's smile the most, although she tried to hide it with the edge of the blanket she held. As the Breedmates walked away, Kade noticed that the elder male couldn't keep his eyes off them.

Or, rather, one of them.

'Patrice?' Kade asked, stunned by the carefully restrained longing he'd just seen in both of them.

Maksim snapped out of his stare and looked at him. 'She has promised herself to another. I would never interfere with that, regardless of how long it takes Seth to finally accept the precious gift he's been given. The ignorant, arrogant little bastard.'

Kade watched his uncle walk off the porch and continue on across the snowy grounds to his own quarters.

He didn't know whether to chuckle over the virulence of Max's declaration, or curse Seth for potentially ruining two more lives.

⇥ CHAPTER TWELVE ⇥

Alex poured a kettle of boiling water into the battered old drip coffeemaker on the stove. As the kitchen filled with the aroma of fresh-brewed beans for a second time that morning, she turned back to the little table where she and Jenna were having breakfast. Or rather, Alex was having breakfast. Jenna had only nibbled at her home fries and had left her scrambled egg mostly untouched.

'God, I hate winter,' she murmured, leaning back in the creaky wooden chair and slanting a thoughtful look at the darkness that still pressed thick and deep against the windows at 8:00 a.m. 'Some days it feels like it's never going to end.'

'It will,' Alex said, as she sat across from her friend and watched the haunted look grow deeper in Jenna's eyes.

Of course, it wasn't really the darkness or the cold that was weighing her down. Alex didn't have to look at the calendar on the wall near the telephone to understand Jenna's mounting gloom.

'Hey,' Alex said, forcing a brightness into her voice. 'If the weather stays clear to the weekend, I was thinking about flying down to Anchorage. Maybe do some shopping, go to the movies. You game for a girls' weekend in the city?'

Jenna glanced back at her and gave a weak shake of her head. 'I don't think so.'

'Oh, come on. It'll be fun. Besides, you owe me now. I just

made the last of my Red Goat coffee for you. I need to hit Kiladi Brothers and stock up again.'

Jenna smiled, a bit sadly. 'The last of your beloved Red Goat? Wow, you must be worried about me. You think I'm in pretty bad shape, huh?'

'Are you?' Alex asked carefully, a direct question that required a direct answer. She reached across the table and placed her hand over Jenna's. She watched her friend closely, listening to the instinct inside her that always seemed to know whether she was being given the truth or a lie. 'Are you going to be all right this time?'

Jenna held her gaze as if locked there. She sighed quietly. 'I really don't know, Alex. I miss them. They gave me a reason to get up in the morning, you know? I felt needed, that my life had some higher purpose when Mitch and Libby were in it. I'm not sure I'm ever going to have that again.'

The truth, then, pained as it was. Alex acknowledged her friend's admission with a tender squeeze of her hand. She blinked, releasing Jenna from the invisible hold of her truth-seeking stare. 'Your life has purpose, Jenna. It has meaning. And you're not alone. You have Zach and me for starters.'

Jenna shrugged. 'My brother and I have been drifting apart for a while now, and my best friend has been talking a lot of nonsense lately about picking up and moving away.'

'Just talking,' Alex said, feeling a pang of guilt for both the cowardice that was making her think very hard about running again and for the half-truth she gave Jenna now, in the hope of making her feel better.

She got up and took their coffee mugs with her to the stove.

'So, what time did you end up leaving Pete's last night?' Jenna asked as Alex poured fresh coffee and brought it back to the table.

'I left a little while after you did. Zach came by and gave me a ride home.'

Jenna took a sip from her mug and set it down. 'Did he now?'

'Just a ride,' Alex said. 'He offered to have a beer with me at Pete's, but I was already on my way home.'

'Well, knowing my brother, he probably just wanted an excuse to get you in his truck. He's had a thing for you since we were teenagers, you know. Maybe for all his tough-guy, married-to-his-job talk, he's still secretly got his eye on you.'

Alex didn't think so. Their one night together had been proof enough to both of them that whatever they had together would never go beyond friendship again. She'd known Zach for close to a decade, but he felt more like a stranger to her than Kade did after just a day.

Incredibly, despite the way Kade unsettled her emotionally, deep down, she felt more protected with him on a physical level than she did with Zach, a decorated officer of the law.

Good lord. Just what that said about her judgment, Alex was sure she didn't want to know.

As she pondered that thought over a long drink of her coffee, the kitchen phone started to ring. Alex got up and answered the business line on automatic pilot. 'Maguire Charters and Deliveries.'

'*Hey.*'

That one word – that deep, now intimately familiar growl of a voice – went into her ears and down to the core of her like a current of raw electricity.

'Um, hello . . . Kade,' she said, wishing she didn't sound so dumbstruck. And did she have to sound so breathless besides? 'How did you get my number?'

Across the small kitchen from her, Jenna's brows raised in surprise. Alex pivoted around and leaned over the counter, hoping to hide some of the heat that was creeping into her cheeks.

'There aren't a lot of Maguires in Harmony,' he said on

the other end. 'Not a lot of pilots, either. So I took an edu-
cated guess and called the only listing I could find that
happened to cover both criteria – one Hank Maguire of
Maguire Charters and Deliveries.'

'Oh.' Alex's mouth tugged into a smile. 'And how do you
know that's not my husband?'

His low chuckle rasped like velvet. 'You sure as hell don't
kiss like a married woman.'

Alex's insides went all soft and warm at the reminder, and
it was getting damn hard not to squirm when she thought
about his lips on hers and the steamy mental revisit she had
enjoyed by herself last night in the shower. 'So, um, why did
you call? Do you . . . ah, are you calling on business?'

God help her, she almost tacked on 'or pleasure' but had
the good sense to bite back the words before she'd embar-
rassed herself by blurting them out. The last thing she needed
was to be thinking about Kade and pleasure in the same sentence. She'd gotten a pretty good taste of that already. Enough
to know that it spelled danger and complications, things she
had plenty enough of as it was.

'I'm supposed to meet Big Dave and a few other guys in
Harmony today,' Kade said, casually tossing out the best
reason she needed to not want anything to do with him.

'Oh, that's right,' Alex replied. 'The big wolf hunt.'

And here she was, letting her raging hormones blind her to
the fact that she still wasn't sure what his game truly was. Anger
spiked bitterly in her throat.

'Well, have fun. I gotta go—'

'Wait,' he said, just as she was about to drop the receiver
back in its cradle. 'I'm supposed to go out with Big Dave today,
but actually I was hoping to hire a guide to take me out to
Henry Tulak's place instead.'

'Henry Tulak,' Alex said slowly. 'What could you possibly
want out at his cabin?'

'I just . . . I really need to know how that man died, Alex. Will you take me out there?'

He sounded sincere, and oddly resigned. Because it seemed so important to him, Alex found herself hedging when she likely should be shutting him down flat. 'What about Big Dave?'

'I'll give him my regrets next time I see him,' he replied, sounding anything but concerned about standing up the town blowhard and his pals. 'What do you say, Alex?'

'Yeah, okay.' And dammit, she didn't have to feel so excited about the prospect of spending time with him. 'It will be daybreak around noon, so why don't you meet me here in Harmony at eleven? We'll have light enough for travel, and a couple of hours to check out the site once we get there.'

Kade grunted, as though considering on the other end of the line. 'I'd rather not wait for daylight to head out there, if that's all right with you.'

'You'd rather travel in the dark?'

She could actually feel the slow smile spreading over his features as he answered, 'I'm not afraid of a little darkness if you're not. I'm on the road already, heading your way. I can be at your place within the hour.'

Well, he was bold, she had to give him that. The man set his mind on something and wasn't afraid to go after it.

'Will an hour from now work for you, Alex?'

She glanced at the clock and wondered how fast she could get out of her faded long johns, shower, and make some kind of sense out of her face and hair. 'Um, sure. Okay, an hour it is. I'll see you then.'

As they hung up, Alex could feel Jenna's curious stare at her back. 'That was Kade, huh?'

She turned around, grinning sheepishly. 'Ah, yup.'

Jenna leaned back in the chair and crossed her arms over

her chest, looking like a total cop, even in her sweatshirt and faded jeans, her dark hair loose around her shoulders. 'This is the same Kade from Pete's last night, the same Kade you saw out at the Toms place yesterday and said you wanted nothing to do with? That Kade?'

'That's the one,' Alex replied. 'And before you say anything else, I'm just taking him out to the Tulak place to have a look around.'

'Uh-huh.'

'It's just business,' Alex said, hastily clearing her breakfast dishes and dumping them in the sink. She pulled aside a piece of egg-soaked toast and tossed it into Luna's waiting mouth. 'The way I see it, if it will keep one more gun from being aimed at the area wolf packs, then I'm more than happy to divert Kade with an in-country day trip.'

When she came back to the table to wipe it down, Jenna stared hard at her.

It didn't take Alex's uncanny inner lie detector, or even Jenna's years of training as a cop, to read the plain and obvious fact that Alex was smitten. Turned inside-out by a man she'd known only a couple of days. Tempted to let this man who was a hundred confusing shades of gray into her tidy little black-and-white world.

'Be careful, Alex,' Jenna said. 'I'm your friend and I love you. I don't want to see you get hurt.'

'I know,' she said. 'And I won't.'

Jenna laughed under her breath and waved her hand dismissively in front of her. 'Well, why are you standing around when you need to get ready for this nondate? Go on. Luna and I will handle breakfast cleanup detail.'

Alex grinned. 'Thanks, Jen.'

'But when you get back from this nondate,' Jenna called after her as she raced down the hall, 'I'm gonna want this guy's last name and social security number. And a full medical history, too. You know I'm not kidding!'

Alex did know that, but she was laughing anyway, floating on a welcome, if unaccustomed, feeling of excitement and hope.

CHAPTER THIRTEEN

Kade hadn't realized how much he was looking forward to seeing Alex again until he was watching her through the frosted glass window of her front door as she came to let him in. Tall and lean, dressed in dark jeans and a citrus-green fleece with a white turtleneck underneath it, her warm blonde hair collected into a pair of braids that just cleared her shoulders on either side, she looked fresh as spring in the dead of the frigid winter. She smiled at him through the ice crystals clinging to the window, her naturally pretty face enhanced with only a bit of mascara and the sudden blush that rose into her cheeks.

'Hi,' she said as she swung the unlocked door open for him. 'You found me.'

He inclined his head in a nod. 'I found you.'

'Let me guess,' she said, her smile lingering. 'You walked all the way here like you did the other day in the bush?'

He smirked and gestured toward the snowmachine he'd parked in her yard. 'I decided to ride today instead.'

'Ah, of course you did.' She held the door open for him. 'Come in. I just have to grab my boots and gear and we can be off.'

As she disappeared around a corner of the living room, Kade walked inside the cozy little house, letting his gaze roam over the simple furnishings and the inviting, casual feel. He could smell Alex in this place, could feel her in the clean, unfussy lines of the sofa and chairs, in the rustic, dark woods of the tables and the earthy greens and browns and creams of the woven rug under his feet.

She came back into the room with laced-up Sorels on her feet and a thick khaki-colored parka draped around her. 'Ready if you are. Leave your sled where it is. We'll go out the back and take mine to the airstrip.'

Kade paused a couple of steps behind her. 'The airstrip?'

'Yeah,' she said matter-of-factly. 'No snow in the forecast for the next couple of days, so why waste time sledding out when we can fly there?'

'I didn't realize we were going to fly.' He felt a momentary twinge of uncertainty, something wholly foreign to him. 'It's dark outside.'

'My plane can't tell the difference between day and night,' she said, a playful light dancing in her soft brown eyes. 'Let's go. That is, unless you're uncomfortable with a little darkness, Kade.'

She was goading him, and damned if he didn't enjoy it. He smiled, more than up to any challenge she wanted to toss his way. 'Lead on.'

With Alex in charge and Kade happy to be riding behind her on the sled, if only for the excuse of wrapping his arms around her, they sped through the frozen back lots of town to where her single-engine plane was tethered at Harmony's joke of an airstrip. Aside from the hangar where the bodies of the Toms family still rested in temporary storage, the airport consisted of a short strip of hard-packed snow and landing lights that barely cleared the tops of the highest drifts.

Alex's de Havilland Beaver had one neighbor for company, a small Super Cub that was rigged with fat tires instead of straight skis like Alex's. A wind gust rolled through the cleared land of the runway, pushing a cloud of powdery snow across the ground like a tumbleweed.

'Bustling place, eh?'

'Better than nothing.' She parked the snowmachine and they climbed off. 'Go ahead and get inside. I've got to run the system checks before we're ready to take off.'

Kade might have balked at being ordered around by a female, if he hadn't been so intrigued by Alex's confidence in what she was doing. He climbed into the unlocked cockpit of the plane and closed the door. Even though the Beaver was the workhorse plane of the interior, Kade was struck immediately by the claustrophobic fit of the cockpit. At six foot four and 250 pounds without weapons and clothing, he was a large male by any standards, but sitting in the passenger seat of the single-engine plane, the curved metal panels and narrow windows felt like a tight cage.

Alex came around to the pilot's side and hopped into the seat behind the wheel. 'All set,' she announced cheerfully. 'Buckle up and we'll be airborne in no time.'

This far remote in the Alaskan interior, it wasn't surprising that there was no traffic control, no tower to radio in to for clearance before takeoff. It was all on Alex to get them off the ground and headed in the right direction. Kade watched her work, impressed as hell by the way she took charge of the aircraft and set it moving on the pitifully brief runway. A minute later, they lifted off into the darkness, climbing higher and higher into a morning sky devoid of light except for the distant blanket of stars that glittered overhead.

'Nice job,' he said, glancing at her as she leveled off their ascent and steered them through a few short patches of bumpy, gusting wind. 'I take it you've done this once or twice before.'

She slid him a little smile. 'I've been flying since I was twelve years old. Had to wait to get my official training and license until I was eighteen, though.'

'You like being up here with the stars and clouds?'

'I love it,' she said, nodding thoughtfully as she checked a couple of the gauges on the plane's dashboard, then looked back out at the vast nothingness in front of them. 'My dad taught me to fly. When I was a kid, he used to tell me that the sky was a magic place. Sometimes when I'd get scared or wake up out of a nightmare, he'd take me up with him – no matter what time it was. We'd climb high into the sky, where nothing bad could reach us.'

Kade could hear the affection in her voice when she spoke about her father, and he also heard the sorrow of her loss. 'How long since your father passed?'

'It's been six months – Alzheimer's. Four years ago, he started forgetting things. It got worse pretty quickly, and after about a year, when it started to affect his reflexes in the plane, he finally let me take him to the hospital in Galena. The disease progresses differently for everyone, but for Dad, it seemed to take hold of him so fast.' Alex let out a deep, reflective sigh. 'I think he gave up as soon as he heard the diagnosis. I don't know, I think maybe he was giving up on life even before then.'

'How so?'

It wasn't meant to be a prying question, but she bit her lip as he asked it, a reflexive reaction that said she probably felt she'd already told him more than she'd intended. From the sudden, uneasy look she gave him, he could see that she was trying to size him up somehow, trying to decide if it was safe to trust him.

When she finally spoke, her voice was quiet, her gaze turned back out the windscreen as if she couldn't tell him and look at him at the same time. 'My, um . . . my dad and I moved to Alaska when I was nine years old. Before that, we lived in Florida, down on the 'Glades, where my dad ran seaplane charter tours of the swamps and the Keys.'

Kade studied her in the dim light of the cockpit. 'That's a whole different world from here.'

'Yeah. Yeah, it sure was.'

A sudden metallic clatter sounded from somewhere on the

plane, and the cockpit gave a vibrating shudder. Kade held on to his seat, grateful to see that Alex wasn't panicking. Her attention went laser sharp to her instrument panel, and she gave the plane some added speed. The shake and rattle calmed, and the ride smoothed out once again.

'Don't worry,' she told him, her tone as wry as her expression. 'Like my dad used to say, it's a scientific fact that some of the most alarming aircraft noises can only be heard at night. I think we're okay now.'

Kade chuckled uneasily. 'I'm gonna have to take your word on that.'

They flew over a sloping peak, then made a gradual direction change that brought them back over the Koyukuk below.

'So, what happened in Florida, Alex?' he said, returning to the subject he had no intention of dropping now. Instinct told him he was mining close to pay dirt about the secrets she seemed to be holding, but he wasn't looking to further his mission right now. He was genuinely interested in her – hell, if he was being honest with himself, he had to admit that he was starting to truly care about her – and he wanted to understand whatever she'd been through. Hearing the pain beneath her words, he wanted to help heal some of it if he could. 'Did something happen to your father or you in Florida?'

She shook her head and gave him another of those measuring, sidelong looks. 'No, not us . . . but my mom and my little brother . . .'

Her voice broke, quiet and choked off. Kade could feel a scowl pulling his brows together as he stared at her. 'How did they die, Alex?'

For one stunning moment, as her eyes held his, unblinking and stark with revisited fear, a cold dread began to form in his gut. The small compartment they shared some eight thousand feet off the ground got even tighter, compressed by Alex's terrible silence beside him.

'They were killed,' she said at last, words that only made Kade's pulse beat faster when he considered one possible cause – a terrible cause that would make this whole involvement with Alex even more impossible than it already was. But then she gave a shrug of her shoulders and looked straight ahead once more. She sucked in a deep breath and released it. 'It was an accident. A drunk driver blew a traffic light at an intersection. He plowed into my mom's car. She and my little brother were both killed on impact.'

Kade's scowl deepened as she recited the facts in a rush, as though she couldn't spit them out fast enough. And recite seemed an apt description, because something about the explanation struck him as being too pat, too well rehearsed.

'I'm sorry, Alex,' he said, unable to tear his scrutinizing, now-suspicious gaze away from her. 'I guess it's a small blessing that they didn't suffer.'

'Yeah,' she replied woodenly. 'At least they didn't suffer.'

They flew for a while without speaking, watching the dark landscape beneath them alternate from the lightless patches of tightly knit forest and jagged, soaring mountains, to the electric-blue glow of the snow-covered tundra and foothills below. In the distant sky, Kade saw the eerie green flash of the northern lights. He pointed it out to Alex, and though he'd seen the aurora countless times from the ground in the near century since his birth, he'd never been in the sky to watch the streaking colors dance across the horizon.

'Incredible, isn't it?' Alex remarked, clearly in her element as she navigated in a wide arc to give them a longer look at the lights.

Kade watched the display of colors, but his thoughts were still on Alex, still trying to piece together the facts from the loose bit of fiction she seemed to want him to believe. 'Alaska is about as different as you can get from Florida, isn't it?'

'Yes, it is,' she said. 'My dad and I wanted to start over –

we needed to, after Mom and Richie—' She took a breath as though catching herself from saying something more than she intended. 'After they died, my dad and I flew to Miami to book a flight to someplace where we could start our lives over again. There was a globe in one of the bookstores at the terminal. Dad showed me where we were, then asked me to pick out the place where we should go next. I chose Alaska. When we got here, we figured Harmony sounded like it would be a friendly town for us to make a new home.'

'And was it?'

'Yeah,' she said, her voice a bit wistful. 'It feels different to me now that he's gone, though. I've been thinking it might be time for me to take another look at the globe, see another part of the country for a while.'

Before Kade could probe any further down that path, the single engine's rattle and shake was back with a vengeance. Alex sped them up again, but the noise and shudder persisted.

'What's going on?'

'I'm going to have to take us down now,' she said. 'There's the Tulak cabin below. I'll try to land as close as I can.'

'All right.' Kade glanced out the window to the ground coming up beneath them more quickly than he liked. 'Just try to put it down easy. I don't see anything close to a runway down there.'

He needn't have been concerned. Alex brought the shuddering plane down onto its skis in a soft glide, managing to miss a couple of ancient spruces that seemed to materialize out of the darkness as they coasted over the top of the powdery snow. The cabin was right in front of them now, but Alex slowed the Beaver and steered into a gentle curve, navigating pretty damned tightly on precious little preparation for their abrupt landing.

'Jesus, that was close,' he said as they came to a stop in the snow.

'Think so?' Alex's amused expression spoke volumes as she powered down the engine.

She climbed out and Kade followed her up to the engine. She peered inside. 'Dammit. Well, that explains the problem. A couple of screws must have jiggled loose of the engine cowling and fell out.'

Kade knew as much about engine cowlings as he did knitting. And he had no business hoping the plane's trouble would keep him stranded in the wild with Alex for a few hours. Better yet, a few nights.

'So, what are you telling me, we're grounded until we get some help?'

'You're looking at the help,' she told him, shooting him a grin as she walked back to grab her toolbox from the plane's cargo hold.

Part of Kade's reason for bringing her out with him to the remote location had been to once and for all get to the bottom of what she knew about the Toms killings. Now, after the half-truth she'd told him about the deaths of her mother and brother, he had another reason to question her. And he told himself that if it did turn out that Alex knew something about the existence of the Breed – and all the more so if that knowledge had anything to do with the loss of her family members in Florida – then relieving her of the burden of that memory would be doing her a kindness.

But this wasn't just about his mission. He'd tried to convince himself it was, but duty had taken a swift backseat from the moment he arrived at Alex's place today. The way his pulse hammered around this female sure as hell wasn't part of the plan. His heart was still banging from the sudden landing, but as Alex came back to where he stood, looking smart and capable and too damned adorable as she went to work on the engine, the banging in his chest settled into a heavy throb.

'You mind holding the flashlight for me?' She clicked it on

and handed it to him, then stripped off her glove and fished around in her toolbox for a handful of odd-size screws and bolts. 'A couple of these should do the trick until we get back home.'

Kade watched her carefully hand-thread each screw into the mounting, wondering if the other warriors in Boston felt the same pride and amusement when they watched their mates doing what they did best.

The thought jarred him as soon as it entered his mind . . . since when had he been the type to think about having a mate, let alone place Alexandra Maguire anywhere near that scenario? At best, she was a temporary obstacle in fulfilling his mission for the Order. At worst, she was a security risk for the entire Breed nation – one that he was duty-bound to silence, the sooner the better.

But none of that mattered to his drumming heart, nor to the crackle of awareness that coursed through every vein and cell of his body as she finished her work not a few inches from him. Behind her, far in the distance, the green light of the aurora borealis was joined by a rising ribbon of red. The color framed Alex as she pivoted her head to look at him now, and he wondered if he'd ever seen anything quite so beautiful as her face haloed by the frozen magic of the Alaskan wilderness. She didn't speak, just held his gaze with the same wordless intensity that he felt coursing through himself.

Kade switched off the flashlight and set it down on top of the now-closed engine casing. He took off his gloves and reached for Alex's bare hand, warming her cold fingers between the press of his warm palms. He held her hand in a light grasp, giving her the power to pull away if she didn't want his touch. But she didn't resist.

She entwined her fingers through his, looking up into his eyes with raw, searching intensity. 'What do you want from me, Kade? Please, I need to know. I need you to tell me.'

'I thought I knew,' he said, then gave a slow shake of his head. 'I thought I had it all figured out. God, Alex . . . meeting you has changed everything.'

He freed one hand to cup it along the curve of her cheek, slipping his fingers between the hood of her parka and the velvety warmth of her face.

'I can't read you,' she said, frowning as she gazed up at him. 'It makes me uncomfortable that I can't figure you out.'

He touched the tip of her nose, gave her a wry smile. 'Too much gray in your black-and-white world?'

Her expression stayed serious. 'It scares me.'

'Don't be.'

'*You* scare me, Kade. All my life, I've run from the things that frighten me, yet with you . . .' She released a slow, uncertain sigh. 'With you, I can't seem to stay away.'

He stroked her cheek, smoothed the pads of his fingers over the light creases in her brow as she looked up at him. 'There's no reason to be afraid when you're with me,' he told her, meaning it completely.

But then he bent his head and pressed his lips to hers, and the kiss meant to be tender reassurance ignited into something wilder as Alex kissed him back so openly, teasing his mouth with the tip of her tongue. All of the heat that had leapt between them the night before in Pete's parking lot sprang to life again now, only swifter, more intense for the hours of longing Kade had known in between. He was on fire for this female, dangerously so. Kissing her was risky enough; desire already had his fangs stretching from his gums, his vision going sharp with the flood of amber light that would soon fill his irises.

Seducing her had not been his goal here, no matter what his mission for the Order was, or how badly he wanted to unravel Alex's secrets to satisfy his own personal curiosity.

He drew back, his head held low, face turned away from

her to hide the changes he could not let her see. Changes that would startle her.

Changes that he would not be able to explain.

'What is it?' she asked, her soft voice husky from the kiss. 'Is anything wrong?'

'No.' He shook his head, still cautious to keep his face shielded as he willed his lust to cool. 'Nothing wrong at all. But it's too damned cold to be standing out here. You must be freezing.'

'I can't say I'm feeling any chill at the moment,' she replied, making him smile despite the war raging inside him.

'We should go inside.' He didn't wait for an answer before he walked around to the passenger side of the plane. 'I just need to grab my gear. Go on ahead. I'll be right behind you.'

'All right.' She hesitated for a moment, then started walking toward the cabin, her boots crunching in the snow. 'Bring some firewood while you're at it. Folks use this place as a trail shelter now, so you should find some in the shed out back.'

He waited until she had gone inside the log shelter before he pulled his weapons duffel out of the plane and headed around to look for the woodshed. The Arctic air slapped at him as he strode through the unspoiled snow. He welcomed the chafe of the bitter, cold weather. He needed the clarity of the icy wind.

And still he burned inside for Alex.

He wanted her badly, and it would take nothing short of a glacier swallowing him whole to douse any of the heat that she ignited in him.

⊰ CHAPTER FOURTEEN ⊱

Alex walked into the one-room cabin and closed the door behind her to seal out the cold and, she hoped, steal a minute of privacy so she could deal with the tumult going on inside her. She leaned back against the weathered panel and exhaled a long, tremulous sigh. 'Get a grip on yourself, Maguire.'

She wanted to pretend the kiss didn't mean anything, that the simple fact Kade had pulled away first should tell her that even he thought letting things get heated between them was a bad idea. Except things were already heated. More than heated, and denying it wasn't going to make the fact go away. There wasn't anywhere far enough that Alex could run to outpace the desire she had for Kade. And the kicker was, she didn't want to run from that feeling. For the first time in her life, there was something that scared the hell out of her but didn't make her itchy to bolt.

No, even worse, her feelings for Kade made her want to draw closer to him.

Scarier still, she felt that Kade might be someone strong enough to lean on, strong enough for her to open up to – really open up to – about everything she'd been holding inside her for so long. Some part of her wanted to believe he might be the one man strong enough to stand beside her through any storm, even one thick with monsters, where the night had teeth and the wind roared, bloodthirsty with hunger.

Kade *would* stand with her.

Alex knew that in much the same way she had always known when someone lied to her. Although she couldn't seem to read him as she could other people, the same innate sense of hers told her that it was because Kade was unlike other people in some way. He was unlike any man she'd ever met or might ever meet again.

That same odd but unshakable instinct had been at work on the flight out from Harmony, when she had come so close to telling him the truth – all of it – about why she and her dad had fled Florida. The truth about what exactly had killed her mom and little brother.

It had been a struggle to work against the impulse that wanted her to let Kade in, and as she'd tossed him the polished lie that she'd used on so many others without the slightest compunction, not being honest with Kade had made her feel awful. Imagine that – she'd withheld one of the most fundamental truths about herself from everyone in Harmony who'd known her since she was a child, yet after just a few days of flirting with a stranger, she was ready to lay it all out on the line for him.

But Kade wasn't a stranger to her now. He hadn't felt like a stranger, not even that first night in the back of the church, when his bright silver eyes had met her gaze across the room.

And if all they'd been doing in the time since was merely flirting, then why did her heart feel like it was battering against her sternum every time she was near him? Why did she feel, against all logic and reason, that she belonged with this man?

With the cold of past memories and the uncertainty of the future crowding in on her, she needed something strong and warm to hold on to.

Not just anything, or anyone . . . but him.

She needed Kade's warmth now – his strength – even if only for a little while.

The woodshed in back of the cabin had a decent supply of seasoned, split logs, kept dry and stacked inside the snug out-building that bore Henry Tulak's initials above the door. It was customary in the bush that wanderers looked out for one another, leaving fuel and food for the next person and respecting the land in order to preserve it for others as well as oneself.

As Kade pulled from the supply and set his logs aside, he considered what he might leave in exchange for the fuel he would be burning for Alex in the cabin. He knelt down and unzipped his duffel bag. The only thing he carried that would prove useful to someone in the wild would be his weapons, but the Rogue-killing guns he carried were far too valuable to leave behind. A knife, then. He had more than one in his pack.

As he reached into the duffel in search of a blade he could stand to part with, his boot heel caught on something hard and white, jammed between the floorboards of the woodshed.

'What the hell?'

He moved aside to get a better look at what he might have crushed under his foot. A bear tooth. The long, sharp ivory point was wedged deep into the seam of two boards, as though it had been ground in by countless boots before his. But it wasn't the tooth itself that made Kade's blood go cold in his veins. It was the thin length of braided leather attached to the tooth.

Precisely the same kind of leather band that had been fastened to another bear tooth he'd seen just recently.

The one he'd found stained with dried, aged human blood and hidden in Seth's private cache of little treasures. The twisted collection of souvenirs, kept by a killer.

His brother had been here.

Ah, Christ . . . had Seth killed the human who'd been found dead and scavenged in this spot last year?

Kade wanted to deny the proof in his hand as mere coincidence, but the coldness that settled in his chest told him that his twin had been in this very spot a winter ago, when Henry Tulak took his last breath.

'Son of a bitch,' Kade whispered, sick with the understanding, even though he'd been searching for evidence of it since his arrival in Alaska.

Now that it was staring him full in the face – the certainty that only an identical twin could have about his other half – there could hardly be any more denying what he'd known in his heart for a long time. His brother was a killer. No better than the Rogues Kade had always hated and now hunted as a member of the Order. Fury raked him, outrage not only at Seth but at himself, for still wanting to believe he was wrong about his brother. In his heart, Kade knew there was no mistake. No more doubt to excuse Seth, or the repugnance of his actions.

Kade worked the bear tooth free with the tip of the knife and held it in front of him, staring in revulsion at the evidence that had just damned his brother. That same evidence now compelled Kade to do what was just and right – to do what was his duty, not only for the Order but as a male whose personal code of honor demanded justice.

He needed to find Seth and put an end to his killing.

He needed to leave, right now. He was too on edge with fury and resolve to fly back to Harmony with Alex; he would head out on foot to begin his personal hunt while the noon daybreak was still a couple of hours away. He would cover the whole damned interior on foot if need be – call the wolves to help him find Seth if he couldn't track him down fast enough on his own.

Kade shoved the bear tooth charm into the front pocket of

his jeans and set the knife on top of the logs, an offering in trade despite the fact that he had no use for the wood now. The only thing he needed now was to get the hell out of there and do the job that had brought him home to Alaska in the first place.

By the time he made the trek around from the shed and up to the cabin, he was a powder keg of anger and deadly purpose. But when he opened the cabin door, ready to offer some lame excuse to Alex about why he had to abandon her there, he was greeted by warm air and the golden glow of a fire crackling in the small pipe stove in the center of the cabin.

And Alex, seated within a fluffy nest of sleeping bags and soft wool blankets. Her blonde hair was loosened from its braids, falling down in tousled waves around her bare shoulders. Bare, naked shoulders, just like her long, slender legs, which peeked out from beneath the tattered blanket that only partially covered her.

Holy hell . . . beautiful, sexy Alex, naked and waiting for him.

Kade cleared his throat, suddenly at a loss for words, let alone the excuses he meant to hand her about why he had to leave right away.

'I, ah . . . I found some wood and matches in the bucket over there,' Alex said. 'I thought I'd warm things up in here.'

Warm it up? If she was any hotter, Kade's body would have gone up in flames where he stood. His heart was still pounding from the unpleasant discovery in the woodshed, but now its rhythm took on a deeper, more urgent beat. He felt a muscle jerk violently in his jaw as he watched the soft firelight dance over her smooth, creamy skin.

'Alex . . .'

He gave a weak shake of his head, unable to summon the words to deny her. The dozen or more reasons why this was a bad idea – particularly now, when duty compelled him to put aside his own selfish cravings and focus wholly on the mission he'd been sent there to do – fled from his lust-drenched brain. Hunger swamped him, desire flooding over the rage that had consumed him not even a minute ago outside.

This was bad, this need he had for her. Given its timing, he wasn't sure that taking things between Alex and him to an intimate level could possibly be any worse of an idea right now.

That is, until she stood up and began to walk toward him. The threadbare blanket that draped her form so loosely, trailing behind her, now split open in the front and gave him an unhindered glimpse of her lean, endless legs with every slow step she took. And as she drew nearer, the thin fabric shifting to bare the soft white flesh of her left hip, Kade saw the tiny crimson teardrop-and-crescent-moon birthmark that pushed this entire situation out of the realm of your basic bad ideas and squarely into the disaster zone.

She was a Breedmate.

And that changed everything.

Because Alexandra Maguire wasn't merely a mortal, human woman he could play around with, pump for information, maybe fuck for a while, then eventually mindscrub and forget. She was as good as kin to one of his kind, a female to be honored and revered, as precious as gold.

She was something rare and miraculous, something he damned well didn't deserve, and she had no bloody idea.

'Ah, Christ.' He set the duffel bag down on the floor. His business with Seth and the Order would both have to wait. 'Alex, there's something . . . we need to talk.'

She smiled, a sensual, playful curve of her lips. 'Unless you need to tell me that you have some kind of disease or that you're actually into guys . . .'

He stared at her, wondering if there had been clues he'd missed along the way. But he hadn't been looking at Alex as anything more than a source of information at first, an unwilling witness that he would need to pry open by any means necessary. Once he'd talked to her, he had begun to like her. And once he'd begun to like her, it was hard not to crave her.

And now?

Now he was honor-bound to protect this female at any cost, and that damned well included protecting her from falling into the hands of a male like him. He was putting her in danger just by being with her, dragging her deeper into his mission for the Order and closer, especially after today, to the horror of his brother's sick little games. If he was half the warrior he had pledged himself to be, he would sweep Alex out of this place and get her the hell back home, never to see or hear from him again.

'Kade?' She cocked her head slightly as she came closer, still waiting for his answer, her tone still playful. 'That's, um, that's not what you need to tell me, is it?'

'No. That's not it.'

'Well, that's good,' she said, practically purring the words. 'Because I really don't want to talk right now.'

Kade drew in a breath as she drifted up close to him, no more than an inch and a paltry scrap of wool between them. And the scent of her . . . warm skin, feminine heat, and the spicy-sweet trace of something even more elusive that he now knew had to be the Breedmate's unique bloodscent.

Even without the damned birthmark, hell, in spite of it, Alexandra Maguire was an intoxicating combination that wrapped around him – through him – like the most potent drug.

She looked up at him, her caramel-brown eyes darker than ever, deep pools to drown in. 'I want to be with you, here and now, Kade.' Slowly she opened the blanket, baring herself to him completely as she wrapped her arms around him, ensconcing them both within its folds. The heat of her naked body seared him, imprinted itself on his memory like a brand. 'I'm tired of feeling cold all the time. I'm tired of feeling so alone. Just for now, I want you to touch me, Kade. I just want to feel your hands on me.'

She didn't have to ask twice. He knew the courage it took for her to admit her vulnerability to him, to put herself out to him like this. He couldn't pretend that he wanted this any less than she did. He'd craved her since the moment he first saw her. Now all of his good intentions – all of his thoughts toward duty and honor – incinerated in an instant.

He brought one palm up along the delicate line of her spine; the other rose to caress the graceful curve of her cheek and the silky skin of her nape. Her pulse fluttered against the pad of his thumb as he stroked the tender skin over her carotid. As he played that soft, erotic patch of flesh with his fingers, she closed her eyes and tipped her head back, granting him more access than was wise.

Kade's own pulse hammered, each tick of her heartbeat, each small quiver of her body against him as he stroked her, spurring his most primal hungers. He dipped his head and nuzzled his face in the cradle of her neck and shoulder, daring only the briefest kiss when his fangs were quickly filling his mouth, his tongue eager for a taste of her. He exhaled the urge on a low growl, trailing his mouth around to the front of her throat, then lower, bending as he palmed one perfect breast and lifted the rosy nipple to his lips.

He suckled her, careful not to graze her with the sharp points of his fangs as he tugged the tight little bud deeper into his mouth, rolling it with his tongue and reveling in her breathless gasps of pleasure. He reached down with his free hand, gripping the sweet swell of her rump, then teasing the seam of her body from behind. She felt so good in his arms, so right. He crushed her to him, letting his fingers cleave deeper, into the slick folds of her sex. She was wet and hot, her flesh a welcoming haven as his touch delved within her.

'Oh, God,' she gasped, arching into his embrace. 'Kade . . .'

On a moan, he released her breast from his toying bite and came back to her lips, capturing her sigh in a deep, hungered kiss. Although she matched his fevered pace, he was the one who set it, more urgent than intended, but he was too far gone to take things slowly. He was also too well aware of the changes coming over him – changes that would require some explaining, which would also require talking, something she had not been interested in before and something he was incapable of at the moment.

Still kissing her, unable to take his mouth off hers, he guided her back toward the nest of blankets near the fire. Together they undressed him, a hasty stripping off of his coat and shirt, boots and jeans. Kade shucked the rest of his clothing as Alex broke their kiss and trailed the tip of her tongue down along the side of his neck. He shook with the sudden jolt of desire that flooded his veins, felt the rush of blood racing through his limbs and down to the throbbing length of his cock. His skin prickled with the transformation of his *dermaglyphs*, the pattern of Breed markings that tracked over his chest and arms and down onto his thighs. The *glyphs*, normally a shade or two darker than his own skin color, would surely be saturated with color now, deepening to reflect the desire he felt for Alex.

'Ah, fuck,' he growled, drawing in a sharp hiss as she nipped playfully at the tender skin below his jaw. He didn't know how much more he could take. When she reached down and stroked the length of his shaft, he couldn't bite back his animal snarl. She palmed the blunt head of his sex, her touch both curious and demanding as she slicked his moisture over the sensitive skin.

'Lie down with me,' he said, his voice ragged, his breath sawing in and out of him.

He took her by the arms and sank with her to the blanket-covered floor of the cabin, kissing her as he gently pressed her beneath him. She was so soft and warm against his body, her arms wrapped around his shoulders, her thighs parted where his hips wedged between them. His cock nestled into the wet cleft of her sex, rampant with the need to drive deep, but Kade only played at entering her, sliding between the plush petals of her body as he teased his mouth along the flickering heartbeat at the side of her neck. He reached down to grasp himself, rubbing his hard flesh against her softness, using the broad tip of his penis to stroke the tight little bud of her clit. She moaned, arching to meet his tempo, spreading her legs to invite him deeper. He resisted the temptation, but only barely.

She'd asked him to make her warm, and so she was, but he wanted to make her hotter than she'd ever been. The sudden, unfathomable need to brand himself upon her body – to bring her pleasure unlike anyone had before him – beat in his blood like a drum. Stunned by the feeling, he drew back slightly. But Alex looked too good, felt too good, and before he could remind himself that she deserved better, he was kissing his way down the front of her body. He savored every sweet inch of her from the small mounds of her breasts to the firm muscle of her belly and the damning little birthmark at her hip that made all of this pleasure and selfish need of his so wrong.

But wrong or not, as selfish as it was for him to give in to his desire for Alex, he was well beyond resisting now. The feel of her beneath him kicked the flame in his blood to full boil. The scent of her pulled him like a magnet toward the downy patch of curls between her legs. He kissed her there, using his lips and tongue and teeth until she was writhing against his mouth. And still he didn't stop. He suckled her and stroked her, pleasuring her until she arched up beneath him and cried out with a shattering, shuddering climax.

And still he didn't stop.

He kept kissing and suckling and stroking her, bringing her to the crest of another wild release, and then, only then, did he rise up to cover her with his body, thrusting deep and roaring as the hot, wet walls of her sheath contracted around his pumping shaft. He drove into her, realizing that he too had needed this warmth, this sense – even if temporary – that he wasn't alone. He'd needed Alex like this, in this moment, as much as she only thought she needed him.

Kade's release coiled hard in the base of his cock, intensifying with every fevered thrust. Hotter and hotter, tighter and tighter, until he couldn't hold back a second more. He went taut with the force of it and plunged as far as she could take him, burying his face in her shoulder and giving a hoarse shout of release as his seed exploded from him in a heated, liquid rush.

He couldn't have held back if he'd tried, although there was no threat of pregnancy so long as there was no exchange of blood. But even that proved more tempting than it should be. Kade's fangs punched long from his gums as he lost himself inside Alex's molten heat. He heard her pulse racing, felt it in the frenzied echo of his own heartbeat. And where his mouth rested in a tight grimace against her skin, he felt the rush of her blood pounding just beneath the surface of her delicate skin.

'Ah, Christ . . . Alex,' he hissed, tormented by the flood of sensations she aroused in him.

Everything Breed in him demanded that he make this female his own, that he lay claim to her blood as he'd just laid claim to her body.

Kade clamped down hard on that further need, but damn, it wasn't easy. He rolled her against him, spooning her from behind to help conceal the changes that had come over him in their passion.

'Are you all right?' she asked him as he struggled to get ahold of his impulses and some scrap of rational thought.

'Yeah,' he managed after a moment. 'Better than I have a right to be.'

'Me, too,' she said, her smile evident in the drowsy contentment of her voice as it fanned warm and light over the top of his forearm. 'In case you're wondering, my pilot services usually don't include getting naked with my clients.'

'Good,' Kade said, little better than a growl as he gathered her closer to the front of his still-heated body. He didn't want her getting naked with anyone, he realized with a jolt. He wouldn't have liked the idea before what just happened between them today, and he sure as hell wouldn't take it well now.

'What about you?' she asked as he covered them both with the blankets to shield his *glyphs* from her view.

'What about me?'

'Do you . . . do this often?'

'Get naked with sexy Alaskan bush pilots in the middle of the frozen wilderness?' He paused for a minute, letting her think he was giving the question serious consideration. 'Nope. This was a first for me.'

And so was the fierce sense of possession that still drummed in his blood when he thought of Alex being with any other male. He wondered idly if it was the fact that she was a Breedmate that had drawn him to her from the first. But even as he thought it, he knew that the birthmark that connected her to the shadowy world he inhabited as one of the Breed was the least of the qualities that attracted him to Alexandra Maguire. The last thing he needed right now was an emotional entanglement, least of all with a female bearing the teardrop-and-crescent-moon mark.

But he was entangled. In fact, he had just tied a few more knots in an already impossible situation.

Cursing himself for the first-class fool he clearly was, Kade kissed the top of her head and gathered her close as he waited for his eyes to resume a normal appearance and his fangs to have a chance to retreat.

It took some time, and even after his body settled into a comfortable peace, his hunger for the woman in his arms remained.

✺ CHAPTER FIFTEEN ✺

Daylight broke thin and overcast outside the wide mouth of the woodland cave. The predator had sought shelter there a short while ago, when the sun's first weak rays had begun to claw their way through the winter darkness. Few things existed that were stronger than he, particularly in this primitive world that was so different from the distant one he'd been born into many millennia ago, but as advanced a life-form as his kind was, his hairless, *dermaglyph*-covered skin could not process ultraviolet light, and just a few minutes' exposure would kill him.

From deep within the safety of the dark cave, he rested from the previous night of hunting and wandering, impatient for the thready light of daybreak to exhaust itself and retreat once more. He needed to feed again soon. He still hungered, his cells and organs and muscles requiring extensive rejuvenation after the long period of deprivation and abuse he had suffered while in captivity. The instinct to survive warred with the knowledge he had that he was, wholly and utterly, alone on this inhospitable chunk of orbiting debris.

There were none like him left here now, not for a long time. He was the last of the eight explorers who had crashed on this planet, a lone castaway with no chance of escape.

They had been born to conquer, born to be kings. Instead, one by one, his stranded brethren had all perished, whether by the harshness of their new surroundings or in war with their own half-human progeny centuries later. Through treachery and a secret bargain with his offspring, he alone had survived. But it had been that same treachery and covert dealing that had enslaved him to the son of his son, Dragos.

Now that he was free, the only thing more attractive than ending his time on this forsaken planet was the idea that he might be able to take his duplicitous heir with him in death.

He howled with remembered fury for the long decades of pain and experimentation that had been inflicted on him. His voice shook the walls of the cave, an unearthly roar that ripped from his lungs like a battle cry.

A gunshot answered from somewhere not too distant, somewhere in the woods beyond.

There was a sudden crash in the frozen bracken outside. Then a steady, fleeting beat of animal footsteps – several sets – racing near the mouth of the cave.

Wolves.

The pack split up, half running to the right of the cave's entrance, half darting to the left of it. And behind them by only a few seconds, the sounds of human voices, armed men in dogged pursuit.

'This way,' one of them shouted. 'Whole goddamn pack ran up this ridge, Dave!'

'You men take the westerly path,' a thunderous voice commanded in reply. 'Lanny and I'll take the ridge on foot. There's a cave up this way – good chance one or more of the mangy bastards are hiding inside.'

The buzz of revving engines and the stench of burning gasoline filled the air as some of the men sped off. A few moments later, outside the cave's mouth, in the daylight that barred the only route of escape, the silhouettes of two people holding long rifles took shape. The man in front was large, with a barrel chest and broad shoulders and a belly that might have been muscular in younger years but had since turned to flab. The man with him was a full foot shorter and about a hundred pounds lighter, a timid creature with a thready voice.

'I don't think there's anything in here, Dave. And I'm really not sure it's a good idea for us to split off from the others . . .'

Confined to the shadows, the cave's sole occupant shrank back behind a wall of jagged rock – but not soon enough.

'There! I just saw a pair of eyes glowing inside here. What'd I tell ya, Lanny? We got one of those goddamn bastards right fucking here!' The big man's voice was eager with aggression as he raised his weapon. 'Shine that flashlight and let me see what I'm shooting at, will ya?'

'Uh, okay, Dave.' His nervous companion fumbled the task, clicking on the beam and sending it in a shaky bounce around the floor and walls of the cave. 'Do you see it anywhere? I don't see nothing in here at all.'

Of course he didn't, because the glowing gaze the larger man had seen just a moment ago was no longer low to the ground but looking down on the pair of humans from where the hunter now clung to the rock ceiling above their heads, poised over them in the dark like a spider.

The big man lowered his weapon. 'What the hell? Where the fuck could it have gone?'

'We shouldn't be here, Dave. I think we should go find the others . . .'

The big man took a few more steps into the cave. 'Don't be such a pussy. Give me that light.'

As the smaller man reached out to hand it over, his boot caught on a loose rock. He stumbled, went down on his knees with a yelp of pain and surprise. 'Oh, shit! I think I cut myself!'

The coppery proof of it rose up in a sudden olfactory blast. The scent of fresh blood drilled into the predator's nostrils. He breathed it in and hissed it back out of his lungs through his bared teeth and fangs.

Below him on the floor of the cave, the nervous little man's head jerked upward. His stricken face went slack with horror under the alien, amber glow of now-thirsting eyes.

He screamed, his voice as high and curdled as a human girl's.

At the same time, the big man wheeled around with his rifle.

The cave exploded with a sharp *crack* of gunfire and a blinding flash of light as the predator leapt from his hold on the rocks overhead and launched himself at the pair of humans.

Alex couldn't remember the last time she'd slept so deeply or so uninterruptedly. Nor could she recall ever feeling quite so spent and sated as she did after making love with Kade. She stretched beneath the fluffy pile of blankets and sleeping bags on the floor, then rose up on her elbow to watch him as he added more wood to the fire in the cabin's little pipe stove.

He crouched on his haunches, the thick muscles of his back and arms bunching and flexing as he pivoted to place another log in the stove, his smooth skin bathed in the warm amber glow of the firelight. His short black hair was a bed-rumpled mess of glossy spikes that gave him a wilder air than normal, all the more so when he turned his head to glance her way and she was hit with the chiseled angles of his killer cheekbones and jaw, and the piercing silver of his dark-fringed eyes.

He was gorgeous, a hundred times more breathtaking when he was sitting there naked in front of her, his gaze intense and intimate, locked onto hers. Alex's body still hummed with the memory of their passion, the pleasant ache between her legs pulsing a bit warmer for the way he looked at her now, as if he wanted to devour her all over again.

'Did we sleep through daylight?' she asked, suddenly needing to fill the heated silence.

He gave a brief nod. 'The sun's been gone for a couple of hours.'

'You've been outside, I see,' she said, noting the fresh supply of split logs stacked up beside him.

'Yeah,' he said. 'Just came in a minute ago.'

She smiled, arching her brows. 'I hope you didn't go out there like that. It can't be more than zero degrees in the dark.'

He grunted, his sensual mouth curving with wry humor. 'I don't have any shrinkage issues.'

No, this was definitely not a man who'd have the slightest insecurities about his masculinity. Every inch of him was lean, hard, sculpted muscle. At nearly six and a half feet, he had the brutal form of a mythical warrior, from the thick, ropey bulk of his shoulders and biceps, to the carved planes of his chest and the washboard abs that tapered to narrow, perfectly cut hips. The rest of him was impressively perfect, as well, and she could testify that he certainly knew what to do with it.

Good lord, he was a living work of art, which was only enhanced by the intricate yet subtly rendered pattern of ink – what kind of ink was that, anyway? – that tracked over the golden skin of his torso and limbs like the path of an appreciative lover's tongue. Alex followed the swirling, intriguingly strange designs with her eyes, wondering if it was only a trick of the firelight that made the henna color of his tattoos seem to flush a deeper shade as she stared at him in open appreciation.

Grinning as though he were used to women admiring him, he stood up and slowly walked back over to where she lay in their nest on the floor, totally uninhibited in his nudity.

Alex laughed softly and shook her head. 'Does it ever get boring for you?'

He cocked a dark brow as he dropped into a negligent recline beside her. 'Boring?'

'Women falling all over you,' she said, realizing with a bit of stunned surprise that she didn't exactly like that idea. Hated it, in fact, and she wondered where the pang of jealousy was coming from, considering she had no personal claim on him simply because they'd shared a few sweaty – and, yes, okay, flat-out spectacular – hours enjoying each other's bodies.

He stroked a stray lock of hair out of her face and drew her gaze to his. 'I only see one woman here with me right now. And I can assure you, I am anything but bored.'

He cupped her face in his palms and kissed her, easing her back onto the blankets. His gaze smoldered as he looked down on her, and she could feel the rigid pressure of his erection nudging at the side of her hip where he'd stretched out beside her. 'You're a special woman, Alexandra. More special than you know.'

'You don't even know me,' she protested quietly, needing to remind herself of that fact more than him. They'd known each other for what – a couple of days? It wasn't like her to allow someone into her life so quickly, or so deeply, especially after such a short time. So, why him? Why now, when everything in her world felt as though it were perched on the edge of a very steep cliff? One strong push from the wrong direction, and she was gone. 'You don't know anything about me . . . not really.'

'Then tell me.'

She looked up into his eyes, startled by the sincerity, the raw plea, in his voice. 'Tell you . . .'

'Tell me what happened to you in Florida, Alex.'

All the breath seemed to squeeze out of her lungs in that instant. 'I did tell you—'

'Yes, but you and I both know that it wasn't a drunk driver that took your mom and brother from you. Something else happened to them, didn't it? Something that you've kept secret all these years.' He spoke with gentle patience, coaxing her trust. And God help her, she felt ready to give it to him. She needed to share it with someone, and in her heart, she knew that someone was Kade. 'It's okay, Alex. You can tell me the truth.'

She closed her eyes, feeling the awful words – the horrible memories – rise up like acid in her throat. 'I can't,' she murmured. 'If I speak it, then everything I've tried to put behind me . . . everything I've worked so hard to forget . . . it will all become real again.'

'You can't spend your life running from the truth,' he said, and something haunted crept into his voice. A sadness, a resignation that told her he understood some of the burden she'd carried for so long. 'Denying the truth never makes it go away, Alex.'

'No, it doesn't,' she replied quietly. In her heart, she knew that. She was tired of running and sick of fighting to keep the horror of her past buried and forgotten. She wanted to be free of it all, and that meant facing the truth, no matter how awful – no matter how unfathomable – it may be. But fear was a powerful enemy. Maybe too powerful. 'I'm scared, Kade. I don't know if I'm strong enough to face it alone.'

'You are.' He dropped a tender kiss on her shoulder, then brought her gaze back to his. 'But you're not alone. I'm with you, Alex. Tell me what happened. I'll see you through it, if you'll let me.'

She held his imploring stare and found the courage she needed in the steely strength of his eyes. 'We'd had such a good day together, all of us. We picnicked down by the water, and I had just taught Richie how to do a backflip off the dock. He was only six years old, but he was fearless, and willing to try anything I did. It had been a perfect day, filled with so much love and laughter.'

Until darkness had settled over the swamp, bringing unholy terror with it.

'I don't know why they chose our family. I've searched for

a reason, but I've never been able to find one for why they came out of the night to attack us.'

Kade caressed her carefully as she struggled for the words that came next. 'Sometimes there are no reasons. Sometimes things happen and there's nothing we can do to make sense of them. Life, and death, isn't always neat or logical.'

Sometimes death sprang out of the shadows like a wraith, like a monster too horrific to be real.

'There were two of them,' Alex murmured. 'We didn't even know they were there until it was too late. It was dark, and we were all sitting on the veranda, relaxing after supper. My mom was on the porch swing with Richie, reading us *Winnie the Pooh* before bed, when the first one came out of nowhere without warning and pounced on her.'

Kade's hand stilled. 'You're not talking about a man.'

She swallowed. 'No. It wasn't a man. It wasn't even . . . human. It was something else. Something evil. It bit her, Kade. And then the other one grabbed Richie with its teeth, too.'

'Teeth,' he said evenly, no shock or disbelief in his voice, only a steady, grim understanding. 'You mean fangs, don't you, Alex? The attackers had fangs.'

She closed her eyes as the impossibility of the word sank in. 'Yes. They had fangs. And their eyes . . . they glowed in the dark like bright coals, and in the center of them, their pupils were thin and long, like a cat's. They couldn't have been human. They were monsters.'

Kade's touch was soothing on her face and hair as the terror of that awful night played out again in her mind. 'It's all right. You're safe now. I only wish I could have been there to help you and your family.'

The sentiment was sweet, however improbable, given that he couldn't be more than a few years older than she. But from the sincerity of his voice, she knew he truly meant it. No matter their odds, or the enormity of the evil they faced, Kade would have stood with her against the attack. He would have kept them all safe when no one else could have.

'My father tried to fight them off,' Alex murmured, 'but everything was happening so fast. And they were so much stronger than he was. They knocked him away like he was nothing. By then, Richie was already dead. He was so little, he didn't stand a chance of surviving that kind of violence. My mother screamed for my dad to run, to save me if he could. 'Don't let my daughter die!' Those were her last words. The one who held her sank his huge jaws around her throat. He wouldn't let go, just kept his mouth clamped down hard on her. He was . . . oh, God, Kade. This is going to sound crazy, but he was . . . drinking her blood.'

A tear rolled down her cheek, and Kade pressed his lips to her brow, gathering her closer to him and offering much-needed comfort. 'It doesn't sound crazy, Alex. And I'm sorry for what you and your family endured. No one should have to bear that kind of pain and loss.'

Although she didn't want to relive it, the memories had been resurrected now and after keeping them buried for so long, she found she couldn't hold them back. Not when Kade was there to hold her, making her feel warmer and safer than she ever had before.

'They were like animals the way they tore at my mom and Richie. Not even animals would do what they did. And, oh, God . . . there was so much blood. My father scooped me up and we started running. But I couldn't look away from what was happening behind us in the dark. I didn't want to see any more, but it was so unreal. My mind couldn't process it. It's been years, and I'm still not sure I can explain what it was that attacked us that night. I just . . . I want it to make sense, and it doesn't. It never will.' She drew in a hitching breath, revisiting a fresher pain, a more recent confusion. Looking up into Kade's sober gaze, she said, 'I saw the same kind of wounds on the Toms family. They were attacked, just like we were, by the same kind of evil. It's here in Alaska, Kade . . . and I'm scared.'

For a long moment, Kade said nothing. She could see his keen mind turning over all that she'd told him, every incredible detail that would have made anyone else scoff in disbelief or tell her she needed to seek professional help. But not him. He accepted her truth for what it was, no trace of doubt in his eyes or his level tone. 'You don't have to run anymore. You can trust me. Nothing bad is going to touch you so long as I'm around. Do you believe me, Alex?'

She nodded, realizing just now how resolute her faith in him was. She trusted him on a level that was something more than instinctual, it was blood deep. What she felt for him defied the fact that he had entered her life only earlier that week, nor did it have anything to do with the way that she burned for him physically – hungered for him in a way she wasn't quite prepared to examine.

She simply looked into Kade's unfaltering eyes and she knew, down to her soul, that he was strong enough to carry whatever burden she shared with him.

'I need you to trust me,' he told her gently. 'There are things you need to understand, Alex, now more than ever. Things about yourself, and what you saw, back in Florida and here, as well. And there are things you need to know about me, too.'

She sat up, her heart thudding oddly in her breast, heavy with a wary sense of expectation. 'What do you mean?'

He glanced away then, his gaze following the soft path of his touch as his caress drifted down the length of her naked body, then lingered at the flare of her hip bone. With the pad of his thumb, he traced a skimming circle over the tiny birthmark there. 'You're different, Alexandra. Extraordinary. I should have recognized that right away. There were signs, but

somehow I missed them. I was focused on other things and I
. . . *damn it.*'

Alex frowned, more confused than ever. 'What are you
trying to say?'

'You're not like other women, Alex.'

When he looked back up at her now, the confidence that
normally sparked so brightly in his eyes was missing. He swallowed, the dry *click* of his throat making her blood run a bit
colder in her veins. Whatever he had to say, he was the one
who was afraid now, and seeing that trace of uncertainty in
him made her anxiety spike a bit, too.

'You're very different from other women, Alex,' he said
again hesitantly. 'And I . . . you need to know that I'm not like
other men, either.'

She blinked, feeling an unseen weight press down on her in
the silence that spread out between them. The same instinct
that told her to demand more answers pleaded with her to back
away and pretend she didn't want to know – didn't need to
know whatever it was that had Kade so tongue-tied and antsy.
All she could do was watch him and wait, worrying that he was
about to send her entire world into an even greater tailspin.

The sharp trill of her cell phone jolted her like a kiss from
a live wire. It rang again and she dived for it, welcoming the
excuse to escape the strange, dark shift in Kade's demeanor.

'This is Alex,' she said, recognizing Zach's number as she
flipped the phone open and took the call.

'Where are you?' he demanded, not even sparing a second
on hello. 'I just drove by your house and you're not there. Are
you out at Jenna's?'

'No,' she said. 'Jenna was at my house this morning, before
I left. She must have gone home.'

'Well, where the hell are you, then?'

'I'm out on a call,' she said, bristling a little at his curt tone.
'I had a, um, a charter client book a flight this morning—'

'Well, we've got a bad situation here in Harmony,' Zach cut in harshly. 'I'm in the middle of a medical emergency and I need you to fly a critical injury in from the bush.'

Alex snapped out of the emotional fog that had held her before she took the call. 'Who's been injured, Zach? What's going on?'

'It's Dave Grant. I don't have the whole story yet, but he and Lanny Ham and a bunch of other men from town were out hunting west of town today. They ran into trouble, serious trouble. Lanny Ham is dead, and apparently it's not looking very good for Big Dave right now, either. The guys are afraid to put him on a snowmachine, for fear that they won't get him back here in time enough to save him.'

'Oh, my God.' Alex sat back on her folded legs, a cold numbness crawling over her skin. 'The injuries, Zach . . . what happened?'

'Something attacked them out there, according to the other men. Dave is delirious and he's lost a lot of blood. He's in and out of consciousness, talking a lot of nonsense about a creature lurking in one of the caves west of Harmony. Whatever it was that got ahold of him and Lanny, well, it's bad, Alex. Real bad. Tore both of them up something awful. The news is all over town already and everyone's in a panic.'

She closed her eyes. 'Oh, my God . . . oh, my God . . .'

Kade's hand came to rest lightly on her bare shoulder. 'What is it, Alex?'

She shook her head, incapable of forming the words.

'Who's that with you?' Zach demanded. 'For fuck's sake, Alex. Are you with that guy from Pete's the other night?'

Alex didn't think she needed to answer to Zach Tucker about whom she was spending time with, not when one man was dead and another man's life was hanging in the balance. Not when the horror of her past – the horror she had feared had visited the Toms family just a few days ago – was now raking her heart open all over again.

'I'm out at the Tulak cabin, Zach. I'll leave right away, but I'm probably forty-five minutes out.'

'Forget it. We can't afford to wait on you. I'll track down Roger Bemis instead.'

He disconnected, leaving Alex sitting there, frozen in shock.

'What happened?' Kade asked. 'Who's been hurt?'

For a moment, it was all she could do to concentrate on breathing in and out. Her heart banged miserably, guilt gnawing at her. 'I should have warned them. I should have told them what I knew instead of thinking I could deny it.'

'Alex?' Kade's voice was cautious, his fingers firm but tender as he lifted her face up toward his. 'Tell me what's going on.'

'Big Dave and Lanny Ham,' she murmured. 'They were attacked today in the bush. Lanny's dead. Big Dave might not make it.'

And if Kade had gone with them, instead of coming out with her? The idea that he might have been close to that danger – or worse, a victim of it – made her heart lurch. She felt ill with fear and dread, but it was her anger that she clung to.

'You're right, Kade. I can't run away from what I know. Not anymore. I have to face this evil. I have to take a stand now, before anyone else gets hurt.' Fury buoyed her where fear threatened to hold her down. 'I need to tell the truth – to everyone in Harmony. To the whole damned world, if that's what it takes. People need to know what's out there. They can't destroy an evil they don't even know exists.'

'Alex.' He pressed his lips together, started to shake his head as though he meant to dissuade her. 'Alex, I don't think that would be wise . . .'

She held his stare, incredulous. 'It's because of you that I feel strong enough to do this, Kade. We need to stand together – everyone – and defeat this.'

'Ah, Christ . . . Alex . . .'

His hesitation felt like a cold blade slowly pressing into her sternum. Confused by his change in attitude, but too determined to do what was right – to do what she had to do now – she backed away from him and started getting dressed. 'I have to get back to Harmony. I'm leaving in the next five minutes. You can decide if you're coming with me or not.'

⊰ CHAPTER SIXTEEN ⊱

They didn't speak the whole flight back.

Kade sat beside Alex in miserable silence, torn between wanting to explain to her about the Breed and her place within that world and fearing that if she knew what he truly was, she would lump him into the same category of monster that she abhorred and was now so determined to expose to all of Harmony and the rest of humankind.

The fear that she would hate him kept his tongue glued to the roof of his mouth for the entire forty-five minutes it took for her to fly them back to the snow-packed airstrip on the edge of town. He was a bastard for withholding the whole truth from her; he knew that. He'd proven himself something even worse than that in the Tulak cabin, when he'd let his desire for her trump his duty – his own personal code of honor, flimsy as it might be – that would have compelled a better male to put all of the cards on the table before he'd taken her.

But it hadn't been all about the sex with Alex. It wasn't just about desire, although he had that for her in spades. Things would be a hell of a lot easier right now if it was merely physical.

The fact was, he cared about her. Cared *for* her. He didn't want to see her hurt anymore, least of all by his own words or actions. He wanted to protect her from the things that had harmed her in the past, and he would do whatever possible to see to it that nothing bad could touch her ever again.

Oh, yeah, he was doing a damn fine job there.

Doing a first-class job on everything he'd touched since his arrival back in Alaska.

In light of the evidence he'd found at the cabin, what might have been a simple, sideline mission to rout out a probable Rogue problem in the frozen north country was now a quest to locate a killer in his own family. And now he had at least one more dead human to add to that mix, potentially two, if the report of Big Dave's injuries was accurate.

Another savage attack that Kade prayed against all suspicion otherwise would not have Seth's name written all over it.

He was still chewing on that dread as Alex brought the plane down in a flawless landing. Damn, even as shaken as she had to be, Alex was total cool control behind the wheel. A real professional. Just one more thing that made him appreciate her all the more.

'Shit,' he exhaled low under his breath as he stared out the window of the cockpit. He really did have it bad for this female.

'Looks like half the town is gathered outside the health clinic,' Alex said. 'Since Roger Bemis's plane is in, I'm guessing they must have brought Big Dave and Lanny in from the bush already.'

Kade grunted, looking a block up the center of town at the converted ranch house where a couple dozen people had assembled under the floodlight that lit the yard, some on foot, others seated astride idling snowmachines.

Alex cut the plane's engine and opened the pilot's door. Kade got out with her, walking around the front of the plane as she secured it and locked everything down. Her movements were efficient, her gloved hands working as if by habit more than conscious thought. When she finally glanced over at him, Kade saw that her face was pale as ash, her features stricken and wary. But her gaze was sharp with grim determination.

'Alex . . . let's talk about this before you go in there and say what you think you need to say to those folks.'

She frowned. 'They need to know. I need to tell them.'

'Alex.' He reached out and grabbed her by the arm, more firmly than he'd intended. She stared at his fingers clamped around her, then looked back up at him. 'I can't let you do this.'

She pulled out of his hold, and for a second he considered trancing her to keep her away from the gathered crowd up the road. With a small mental effort and one brief sweep of his palm over her forehead, he could place her into a pliable state of semi-consciousness.

He could buy precious time. Prevent her from jeopardizing his entire mission for the Order by alerting her fellow towns-folk to the existence of vampires living among them, preying on them from the shadows.

And she would hate him even more – rightfully so – for the further manipulation.

She took a step back from him, her brows still knitted together in confusion. 'What's wrong with you all of a sudden? I have to go.'

He didn't stop her when she pivoted around and headed off at a jog for Harmony's small health clinic. On a gritted curse, Kade went after her. He caught up in an instant, then wove with her through the anxious, chattering crowd.

'. . . just terrible that something like this should happen again,' murmured a white-haired woman to the person next to her.

'. . . he lost so much blood,' someone else remarked. 'Tore them up, was what I heard. Not much left intact on either man.'

'A horrible thing,' said another detached voice in the crowd, shrill with panic. 'First the Tomses, now Big Dave and Lanny. I wanna know what Officer Tucker plans to do about this!'

Kade strode beside Alex as she marched toward Zach, who stood near the entrance of the clinic, his cell phone pressed to his ear. He acknowledged her with barely a glance, continuing to bark grave orders to someone on the other end of the line.

'Zach,' she said, 'I need to speak with you—'

'Kinda busy,' he snapped.

'But, Zach—'

'Not now, goddamn it! I've got one man dead and another bleeding out in there and the whole fucking town is going apeshit around me!'

Kade could hardly contain the protective snarl that curled at the back of his throat at the human's outburst. His own anger spiked dangerously, muscles tensed and ready for a fight he realized he was more than eager to initiate. Instead, he subtly took Alex by the arm and placed himself between her and the other male. 'Come on,' he said to her, guiding her away from the trooper and his meltdown in progress. 'Let's go somewhere else until things settle down.'

'No,' she said. 'I can't go. I need to see Big Dave. I need to be sure—'

She broke away from him and dashed up the concrete steps and into the clinic, with Kade fast on her heels. The place was quiet inside, only the hum of the overhead fluorescent lights that tracked from the vacant reception area down the hallway toward the examination rooms. From the sparse look of the clinic and its lack of equipment, it didn't appear that it was set up for dealing with much more than the occasional abrasion or vaccination.

Alex headed down the hall at a determined, brisk pace.

'Where's Fran Littlejohn? She never keeps it this cold in here,' she murmured, at just about the same time that Kade was noticing the temperature, as well.

An arctic chill, blowing up the hallway from one of the rooms in back. The only one with the door closed.

Alex put her hand on the knob. It didn't budge. 'That's odd. It's locked.'

Kade's warrior instincts lit up like firecrackers. 'Get back.'

He was already standing in front of her, moving faster than her eyes could possibly track him. He gripped the doorknob and gave it a hard twist. The lock snapped, mechanisms were crushed to powder in an instant.

Kade pushed the door open . . . and found himself staring into the cold dead eyes of a Minion.

'Skeeter?' Alex's voice was sharp with surprise, and well-placed suspicion. 'What the hell are you doing in here?'

The Minion's business was potently clear to Kade. On the floor next to Big Dave's bed lay a large, middle-age woman – the clinic technician, no doubt. Unconscious, but she was still breathing, which was better than he could say for her patient on the bed.

'Fran!' Alex cried, racing to the unresponsive woman's side.

Kade's focus was centered elsewhere. The room reeked with the overpowering stench of human blood. Had it been fresh, Kade's physiological response would have been impossible to hide, but the odor was stale, the cells no longer living. Nor was Big Dave, who lay on the bed, virtually unrecognizable for the severity of his injuries. All Kade needed was one whiff of the spilled, coagulating hemoglobin to know that the man was several minutes dead already.

'My Master was displeased to hear about the attack today,' the Minion said, his thin face pale and emotionless. Behind him was an open window, his obvious means of entry into the room. And in his hand was a bloodied pair of suture scissors that had been used to speed the consequences of Big Dave's life-threatening wounds.

'Kade . . . what's he talking about?'

Skeeter smiled at Alex, a deviant, rictus grin. 'My Master

hasn't been too pleased to hear about you, either. Witnesses are a problem in general, you understand.'

'Oh, my God,' Alex murmured. 'Skeeter, what are you saying? What have you done!'

'You son of a bitch,' Kade hissed, launching himself at the Minion. He took Skeeter down to the floor in a bone-crushing assault. 'Who made you? Answer me!'

But the human mind slave only stared up at him and sneered, despite the punishing blows Kade delivered on him.

'Who the fuck is your Master?' He hit Skeeter again. And again. 'Talk, you goddamn piece of shit.'

Answers eluded him. Some irrational part of him cast about and latched on to Seth's name, but that was an impossibility. Although Kade and his twin were Breed, their bloodline wasn't old enough or pure enough for either of them to create a Minion. Only the earliest generations of the vampire race had the power to drain a human to the brink of death, then take command of its mind.

'What are your orders?' He pounded the Minion's grinning, bleeding, soulless face. 'What have you told your Master about Alex?'

Behind him now, her voice broke through the violence raging in him. 'Kade, please . . . stop. You're scaring me. Stop this now and let him go.'

But he couldn't stop. He couldn't let the human who had been Skeeter Arnold go, not now. Not knowing what he was. Not knowing what he might be commanded to do to Alex if he was turned loose to carry out his Master's wishes again.

'Kade, please . . .'

With a guttural roar, he grasped the Minion's head in his hands and gave it a savage twist. There was a crunch of bone and sinew, then a hard thump as he let the lifeless bulk fall onto the floor.

He heard Alex's sharp intake of breath at his back. He

thought she might scream, but she went utterly silent. When Kade pivoted his head to look up at her, it wasn't difficult to read the confusion – the complete shock – in her wide brown eyes.

'I'm sorry you had to see that,' he said quietly, feebly. 'It couldn't be helped, Alex.'

'You . . . killed him. You just *killed him* . . . with your bare hands.'

'He wasn't really alive anymore, Alex. Just a shell. He wasn't really human anymore.' Kade frowned, knowing how that must sound to her by the stricken, confused look on her face. He slowly rose to stand and she took a step backward, out of his reach.

'Don't touch me.'

'Ah, fuck,' he muttered, raking his fingers over his scalp. She'd been through more than her share of violence in her life; the last thing she needed was to be a party to more because of her involvement with him. 'I hate that you're here right now, seeing this. But I can explain—'

'No.' She gave an abrupt shake of her head. 'No, I have to get Zach. I have to get help for Big Dave and I have to—'

'Alex.' Kade took hold of her arms in a light but unyielding grasp. 'There's nothing that can be done for either of these men now. And bringing Zach Tucker or anyone else into this is only going to make things more dangerous – not only for them, but for you. I won't risk that.'

She stared at him, her eyes searching his.

In the quiet that seemed to expand to fill the room, the clinic worker Skeeter had knocked to the floor began to rouse back to consciousness. The woman groaned, mumbled something indiscernible.

'Fran,' Alex said, turning back to help the older female.

Kade blocked her path. 'She'll be fine.'

With Alex watching him warily, he went to the woman's

side and gently placed his hand over her forehead. 'Sleep now, Fran. When you wake, you'll remember none of this.'

'What are you doing to her?' Alex demanded, her voice rising as the clinic worker relaxed into his touch.

'It will be easier for her if she forgets that Skeeter was here,' he said, ensuring Fran's mind was scrubbed of the assault on her and any recollections she might have of Kade and Alex being present, as well. 'It will be safer for her this way.'

'What are you talking about?'

Kade swiveled his head to face her. 'There is more to your monsters than you know, Alex. Much more.'

She stared at him. 'What are you saying, Kade?'

'Earlier today, out at the cabin, you said you trusted me, right?'

She swallowed, nodded mutely.

'Then trust me, Alex. Ah, fuck. Trust no one but me now.' He glanced back at Skeeter Arnold's body – the Minion corpse he was now going to have to lose somewhere, and fast. 'I need you to go back outside. You can't say anything to anyone about Big Dave or Skeeter or what happened in here just now. Tell no one what you saw in here, Alex. I need you to walk out there, go back home, and wait for me to come to you. Promise me.'

'But he—' Her voice choked off as she gestured toward the broken body on the floor.

'I'll take care of everything. All I need is for you to tell me that you trust me. That you believe me when I tell you there's no reason for you to be afraid. Not of me.' He reached out to stroke her chilled cheek, relieved that she didn't flinch from him or pull away. He was asking for a hell of a lot from her – far more than he had a right to. 'Go home and wait for me, Alex. I'll be there as soon as I can.'

She blinked a couple of times, then took a few steps backward. Her eyes were bleak on his as she inched toward the open door, and for a moment he wondered if her fear would prove too much for her now.

'It's okay,' he said. 'I trust you, too, Alex.'

He turned around and listened as she walked out and left him there to clean up his mess alone.

❧ CHAPTER SEVENTEEN ❧

In one instant, her world had suddenly shifted on its axis. Alex walked away from Kade, surprised that her legs were functioning when her mind was spinning with the illogic of what she'd just witnessed him do – not only to Skeeter Arnold, but also to Fran Littlejohn. Was it some type of hypnotism he'd used on her, or something more powerful than that to make the woman bend so easily to his will?

And Skeeter . . .

What did he mean, saying all those strange things to Kade, talking about how he was carrying out orders from his 'Master'? It was crazy talk, and yet Skeeter hadn't seemed crazy. He'd seemed very dangerous, no longer the small-time drug dealer and all-around loser she knew him to be, but something deadly. Something almost inhuman.

He wasn't really alive anymore . . . just a shell.

He had killed Big Dave in cold blood, and Kade had snapped Skeeter's neck with his bare hands.

Oh, God. Nothing was making sense to her.

There's more to your monsters than you know, Alex.

Kade's warning echoed in her head as she stepped out into the lightless cold of the afternoon. How could any of this be happening? It *couldn't* be happening. How could any of this be reality?

But she knew it was, just as surely as she had always known

that what had happened all those years ago in Florida was reality, too.

Trust no one but me now.

Alex wasn't sure she had any choice. Who else did she have? What Kade had just done – everything he'd just said in the clinic – had left her with more questions than she was prepared to ask. She was terrified and uncertain, more than ever now. Kade was dangerous; she'd seen that for herself only a minute ago. Yet he was also protective, not only of Alex herself, but of Fran Littlejohn, too – a woman he didn't even know.

In spite of all he'd said and done just now, Kade was a solid anchor in a reality that had suddenly cast Alex adrift. It was his strength and trust that buoyed her as she stared at the small crowd still clustered in front of the clinic. The dozen-plus faces she had known for so long now appeared to her as strangers as she unobtrusively slipped past them. Even Zach, who glanced over when she had just about made it to the outer edge of the throng, seemed less a friend than a source of doubt and unwanted complication.

His eyes narrowed on her, but she kept walking, desperate to get out of there. 'Alex.'

An arrow of sudden, cold panic stabbed her. Zach was the last person she needed to see right now. She pretended not to hear him, walked a bit faster.

'Alex, hold up.' He pushed his way through, catching her by the sleeve of her parka. 'Will you wait a damned minute?'

Given no choice, she paused. It was a struggle to keep her expression neutral as she faced him. There was no containing the tremble that swept her body while Zach scowled at her in the dark.

'Are you all right? Your face is white as a sheet.'

She shook her head, jerked her shoulder in an awkward shrug. 'I'm just a little wrung out, I guess.'

'Yeah, no shit,' he said. 'Listen, I'm sorry I was short with you before. Things seem to be going from bad to worse around here lately.'

Alex swallowed, nodding. He didn't even know the half of it.

Trust no one but me now . . . Tell no one what you saw in here, Alex. Promise me.

Kade's words drifted through her thoughts as Zach watched her expectantly. 'So? You've got my undivided attention, for the moment at least. What did you want to talk to me about?'

'Um . . .' Alex fumbled for a reply, feeling oddly unsettled by the way Zach seemed to peer at her in speculation, maybe even suspicion. 'I just . . . I was concerned about Big Dave, of course. How is he? How do you, um, think he's doing?'

The questions felt clumsy on her tongue, especially when her heart was still banging from everything she'd witnessed in the clinic.

Zach's expression turned a bit more scrutinizing. 'You saw him yourself, didn't you?'

She shook her head, not sure she could deliver a convincing lie.

'Didn't I see you go inside – you and your, ah, new *friend*?' He leaned on the word, unnecessarily hard. 'Where is he, anyway? Still inside?'

'No,' she said, all but blurting it. 'I don't know what you're talking about. Kade and I were out here the whole time. He just left.'

Zach didn't quite seem to buy it, but before he had a chance to press her further, the clinic door opened and Fran Littlejohn came out onto the stoop. 'Officer Tucker! Where's Zach? Somebody call Officer Tucker right away!'

Alex stared, weathering a rising feeling of dread as Fran's head bobbed, searching the crowd.

'Over here,' Zach called. 'What is it?'

'Oh, Zach!' The clinic technician heaved a sigh, her thick shoulders slumping. 'I'm afraid we lost him. I'd just given him another dose of sedative, and I turned away for what couldn't have been more than a minute at most. When I looked back just now, I saw that he had passed. Big Dave is dead.'

'Goddamn it,' Zach muttered. Although he spoke to Fran, he shot a tight glance at Alex. 'No one else with you in there, Fran?'

'Just me,' she said. 'Poor Dave. And poor Lanny, too. God bless them both.'

As a wave of soft murmurs and whispered prayers traveled the crowd, Alex cleared her throat. 'I have to go, Zach. It's been a long day, and I'm really tired. So, unless you have any more questions—'

'No,' he said, but the look he gave her was guarded, filled with a reluctant acceptance of everything he'd just heard. 'Go on home, then, Alex. If I need you, I know where to find you.'

She nodded, unable to dismiss feeling oddly threatened by his comment as she turned and walked away.

Some five miles out of Harmony, deep in the frozen wilderness, Kade shrugged the burden of Skeeter Arnold's lifeless body off his shoulders and dropped it down a steep ravine.

He stood there for a moment, after the Minion's corpse had tumbled out of sight, letting the bitter cold air fill his lungs and steam his breath as he stared out at the vast nothingness all around him. The sky was dark overhead, the snow-covered ground glowed midnight blue under the afternoon starlight. In the distant woods, a wolf cried, long and lamenting, summoning its pack to run. The wildness of his surroundings called to Kade, and for one sharp instant, he was tempted to give in to it.

Tempted to ignore the chaos and confusion that he'd left

behind him in Harmony. Tempted to run from the fear he'd put in Alex, and the unpleasant business of the truth that he would have to deliver to her when he got back.

Would she despise him for what he had to tell her?

Would she recoil in horror when she came to understand his true nature?

He couldn't blame her if she did. Knowing what she'd endured as a child, and now, having seen him kill a man before her eyes, how could he possibly hope that she would look at him with anything more than fear or revulsion?

'Ah, fuck,' he muttered, dropping down into a squat on his haunches at the edge of the ravine. *'Fuck!'*

'Problems, brother?'

The unexpected voice, the unexpected familiarity of it – here, of all places, now, of all times – shot through Kade like a current of raw electricity. He vaulted to his feet and spun around, his hand reaching automatically for one of the blades he wore on his belt.

'Easy,' Seth drawled slowly, inclining his head to indicate the precarious edge of the ravine directly behind Kade. 'Better watch your step.'

Kade's fury spiked as he took in his twin's unkempt, shaggy appearance. 'I could say the same thing to you . . . *brother.*'

He kept the knife gripped in his fist, pivoting around, cautiously following Seth as he strolled toward him to peer into the ravine. Seth grunted. 'Not the most savvy way to dispose of a kill, but I suppose it won't take long for the scavengers to find it.'

'Yeah, you know all about that, don't you?'

Seth looked at him, Kade's own silver eyes – his own face – staring back at him as if in a mirror. Except Seth's short black hair hung limply in dull, matted hanks, his cheeks and jaw sallow, the skin shadowed with grit and grime. His face was leaner than Kade recalled, on the verge of gaunt. He looked strung out, and there was a feral glint in his heavy-lidded gaze.

'Where the fuck have you been?' he demanded. 'How long have you been carrying out your sick killing games?'

Seth chuckled, dark with amusement. 'I'm not the one dumping a human into a snowy grave.'

'Minion,' Kade corrected him, though why he felt the need to explain was beyond him.

'Really?' Seth arched a brow. 'A Minion, all the way out here in the bush . . . interesting.'

'Yeah, I'm all atwitter,' Kade said. 'And you didn't answer my fucking question.'

Seth's mouth curved at the corners. 'What would be the point, when you already know what I'm going to say?'

'Maybe I need to hear it from your own lips. Tell me how you've been stalking and killing humans ever since I left Alaska last year – hell, it's been going on for a lot longer than that, hasn't it?' He ground out a sharp hiss of disgust. 'I found something you might recognize. Here—'

He dug the bear tooth charm out of his pocket and tossed it at his twin.

'Now you have a matched set,' Kade said. 'This one, and the one you took off the Native man when you killed him last winter.'

Seth glanced into his palm at the braided strip of leather and the long, pale tooth attached to it. He shrugged, unapologetic, curling his fingers around the prize. 'You've been home to the Darkhaven,' he murmured. 'Going through my things. How rude of you. Very devious and underhanded, Kade. That's always been more my style than yours.'

'What happened, Seth? Single kills weren't getting you off anymore, so you've had to graduate up to wholesale slaughter?'

Kade watched the dispassionate mask of his brother's face

quirk with confusion. 'I don't know what you're talking about.'

'Now you're going to stand there and try to deny it? You're unbelievable,' Kade scoffed. 'I've seen the bodies, or what was left of them. You slaughtered an entire family – six lives in one night, you sick son of a bitch. And today you added two more to your fucked-up tally when you attacked those men from Harmony.'

'No.' Seth was shaking his head. He had the balls, even, to look insulted. 'You're wrong. If there have been kills like that, as you claim, they're not mine.'

'Don't lie to me, damn you.'

'I'm not lying. I am a killer, Kade. I have a . . . a problem, you might say. But even my perverted morals have their boundaries.'

Kade stared, sizing him up. Even after a year away, he knew his twin well enough to see that Seth was telling him the truth.

'I've never taken a whole family, nor am I responsible for the two men you say were attacked today.'

Kade felt a cold pit opening up in his gut. Twisted though he may be, his brother was being honest about this. He hadn't killed the Toms family. He hadn't killed Lanny Ham and left Big Dave Grant for dead.

If not Seth, then who?

Kade had long abandoned the idea that Rogues might be responsible – not without reports of missing Breed males from the region's Darkhaven populations or some other indicators that there were vampires in the throes of Bloodlust running loose in the area.

So, what possibility was left?

Could it be the vampire who'd made Skeeter Arnold his mind slave? And if so, why would a powerful Breed elder prefer to hunt in the remote, sparsely populated wilds of Alaska when he could choose from countless cities teeming with humans instead? It simply didn't add up.

But none of that excused Seth's crimes, or his unrepentance for his actions.

'What happened to you?' Kade asked him, staring into the face that was so like his own, the brother he still loved, despite everything he'd done. 'Why, Seth? How did you allow yourself to lose so much control?'

'Lose control?' He laughed, shaking his head at Kade. 'When else can we feel more in control than during the hunt? We are Breed, my brother. It's who we are, it's in our very blood. Killing is what we are born to do.'

'No.' Kade spat the denial as Seth began a slow prowl around him.

'No?' he asked, cocking his head in question. 'Isn't that why you leapt at the chance to join the Order? Tell me you don't enjoy your license to kill on behalf of Lucan and your brothers-in-arms in Boston. Say it, and I will be the one standing here calling you a liar.'

Kade clamped his molars tight, admitting, at least to himself, that there was some truth in Seth's words. He joined the Order to escape what he was becoming in Alaska, as much as he had joined to feed the wildness inside him with something that had some degree of honor in it. But there was a higher purpose in his work for the Order now. With the enemy they had in Dragos, his work for the Order had never been more vital. And he wouldn't let Seth cheapen that with the comparison to his own sick games.

'You know that this cannot continue, Seth. You have to stop.'

'Don't you think I've tried?' His lips peeled back from his teeth, baring the tips of his fangs. 'In the beginning, when we were young, I did try to curb my . . . urges. But the wildness kept calling to me. Doesn't it call to you anymore?'

'Every minute that I'm awake,' Kade conceded quietly. 'Sometimes even in my sleep.'

Seth sneered. 'But of course, you, the noble one, can resist it.'

Kade stared at him. 'How long have you hated me, brother? What could I have done differently to make you see that it was never a competition between us? I didn't have anything to prove with you.'

Seth said nothing, merely stared at him in bleak consideration.

'You've made mistakes, Seth. We all do. But there is still some good in you. I know there is.'

'No.' Seth shook his head vigorously, the agitated twitch of a festering mind. 'You were always the strong one. All the good went into you, not me.'

Kade scoffed. 'How can you say that? How can you think it? You, the favored son, the hope of the family. Father never made a secret of that.'

'Father,' Seth replied, exhaling sharply. 'If he feels anything for me, it's pity. I have needed him, where you never did. You're just like him, Kade. Can neither one of you see that the way that I can?'

'Bullshit,' Kade said, certain in his rejection of the idea.

'And then you went off and joined the Order,' Seth continued. 'You were gone and I sank deeper into your shadow. I wanted to hate you for leaving. Hell, maybe I do.'

'If you need an excuse for what you've done, then so be it,' Kade ground out savagely. 'Blame me, but you and I both know you're only looking for a way to justify what you're doing.'

Seth's answering laughter was little more than a growl, deep in his throat. 'Do you really think I'm looking for justification? Or for any kind of absolution? I kill because I can. I won't stop, because it is part of me now. I enjoy it.'

Kade's gut twisted. 'If that's true, then I feel sorry for you. You are sick, Seth. I should put you out of your misery . . . right here and now.'

'You should,' Seth replied without inflection. 'But you won't. You can't, because I am still your brother. Your own rigid morals would never let you harm me and we both know it. That's a line you would never cross.'

'Don't be so sure.'

As he said it, the wolf howl he'd heard a few minutes ago sounded once more, from somewhere nearby. Kade glanced over his shoulder, toward the thick knot of pine and spruce in the crouching darkness, feeling the wild summons coursing through his veins. As it must have been for Seth, as well.

Even though he should hate his brother, he couldn't.

And although his threat was well deserved, he knew in his heart that Seth was right. Kade could never bring himself to harm him.

'We need to sort this shit out, Seth. You have to let me help you—'

When he swiveled his head back around to face his twin again, all that greeted him was the empty winter landscape . . . and the bone-deep, bitter understanding that any hope of saving Seth was gone along with him.

⪥ CHAPTER EIGHTEEN ⪥

Each step was agony.
 Every inch of his naked body was blistered and raw from ultraviolet exposure, his normally rapid healing processes impeded by the added damage he'd sustained from the shotgun blast that had ripped into his thigh and abdomen. Fresh blood would speed the required regeneration. Once he fed, his soft tissue and organs would mend in a few hours, as would his skin, but he could not risk another minute without seeking adequate shelter.

He had barely survived the daylight, having been forced to flee the cave after the humans had stumbled upon him there. He'd run, bleeding and wounded, into the surrounding woods, into the lethal rays of the sun outside the cave. He'd had only enough time to dig a hole in a deep bank of hard-packed snow and bury himself within before the severity of his combined injuries had shut his body down and rendered him unconscious.

Now, a short while after he'd roused to find welcome darkness, he knew only that he needed to seek new shelter before the next sunrise. Needed to find somewhere secure to recuperate further, so he would be strong enough to hunt again and feed his damaged cells.

His feet dragged in the moonlit snow, his pace slow and halting. He despised his physical weakness. Hated that it reminded him of the torture he had endured while in captivity. But animosity drove him now, forced the shredded muscles of his legs to move.

He didn't know how long or how far he had walked. Easily miles from the cave and his makeshift shelter in the snow.

Ahead of him, he saw a dim orange glow through the veil of silhouetted evergreen trunks. A human residence, apparently occupied, and far removed from any other signs of civilization.

Yes, it would do.

He stalked forward, ignoring his pain as he locked all focus on the remote little cabin and the unsuspecting prey within it.

As he neared, his ears pricked with the low, mournful sounds of human suffering. It was faint, muffled by logs and plank-shuttered glass. But the anguish was clear. A female was weeping inside the cabin.

The predator crept up to the side of the domicile and pressed his eye to a crack in the wooden shutter that covered the window to bar the cold.

She was seated on the floor in front of a dying fire, drinking from a half-consumed bottle of dark amber liquid. Before her was an emptied box of printed images, scattered in disarray all around her. A large black pistol lay on the floor next to her bent knee. She was sobbing, incredible sorrow pouring out of her.

He could feel the overwhelming weight of her grief, and he knew that the weapon was not beside her as a means of protection. Not tonight.

The scene gave him pause, but only for a moment.

She must have sensed his eyes on her. Her head snapped to the side, her reddened eyes fixed on the very spot where he stood, concealed by the closed shutter and the darkness of the night outside.

But she knew.

She rose, picking up the gun as she wobbled to her feet.

He backed away, only to move on silent feet toward the front door of the cabin. It wasn't locked, not that it would have barred him if it had been. He squeezed the latch with his mind, pushed the door open.

He was inside the cabin and had his hands wrapped around the woman's throat before she realized he was there.

Before she could open her mouth to scream, before she could command her drink-impeded reflexes to pull the pistol's trigger in defense of the sudden attack, he bent his head and sank his fangs into the soft flesh of her slender neck.

Alex sat at the table in her kitchen with Luna resting at her feet. Every light in the house was turned on, every door and window locked up tight.

It had been nearly two hours.

She didn't know how much more waiting she could take. While Luna slept calmly, blissfully oblivious, across her toes under the table, Alex's mind had been spinning. Churning over questions she hardly dared to ask, and worrying for a man who had left her wondering just who – or what – he truly was.

But the small voice inside her that so often urged her to run from the things that scared her was silent when she thought of Kade. Yes, she was uncertain after what she witnessed today. Frightened that the path ahead of her might be even more unsteady than the past she'd left behind her. But running was the last thing she intended to do – not now. Not ever again.

Idly, she wondered how Jenna was holding up. It couldn't be easy on her, hearing about the deaths in town when she was nearing the anniversary of her own personal grief. Alex reached for her cell phone, wanting to hear her friend's voice. She was just about to punch in Jenna's number when there was a soft rap on the back door.

Kade.

Alex put down the phone and stood up, dislodging her

canine foot warmer, who groaned in protest before dropping her head back down to sleep some more. Alex drifted toward the door where Kade waited. Now that he was there, looking so dark and immense and dangerous through the glass window, some of her courage faltered.

He didn't demand or force his way inside, even though she knew without the slightest doubt that there was little she could do to bar him from entering if that's what he intended to do. But he merely stood there, leaving the decision entirely up to her. And because he didn't force her, because she could see a shadowed torment in the piercing depths of his silver eyes that hadn't been there before, Alex opened the door and let him in.

He took one step inside her little kitchen and pulled her into a hard, long embrace. His strong arms circled her, held her close, as though he never wanted to let her go.

'Are you okay?' he asked, pressing his mouth into her hair. 'I hated to leave you alone.'

'I'm all right,' she said, drawing back to look at him when he finally released her from his hold. 'I was more worried about you.'

'Don't,' he said. Scowling, he stroked her cheek, swallowed hard. 'Ah, Jesus. Don't worry for me.'

'Kade, what the hell is going on? I need you to be honest with me.'

'I know.' He took her by the hand and led her back to the table. She dropped into her chair as he took the one next to her. 'I should have explained everything to you earlier, as soon as I realized . . .'

Her heart sank a bit as his words trailed off. 'As soon as you realized, what?'

'That you were part of this, Alex. A part of the world that belongs to me and those of my kind. I should have told you everything before you saw me kill that Minion. And before we made love.'

She heard the regret in his voice for the intimacy they'd shared, and weathered more than a little sting because of it. But the other part – the peculiar way he'd referred to himself and his kind, and the fact that he was somehow including her in that equation – was what made her mind stutter to attention. And then there was the odd word he'd used to describe Skeeter Arnold.

'A 'Minion'? I don't know what that's supposed to mean, Kade. I don't know what any of this is supposed to mean.'

'I know you don't.' He raked his palm over his jaw, then exhaled around a vivid curse. 'Someone got to Skeeter Arnold before I did. Someone bled him, almost to the point of killing him, before bringing him back so that he could serve. He wasn't human anymore, Alex. He was something less than that. Someone had made him into a Minion, a mind slave.'

'That's crazy,' she murmured, and as badly as she wanted to reject what she was hearing, she couldn't dismiss Kade's grim, sober demeanor. 'You also said that I am a part of this. A part of this, how? And what did you mean back at the clinic, when you said there was something more I didn't know about the attack on my family? What could you possibly know about the monsters that took my mom and Richie?'

'What they did was monstrous,' Kade said, his tone unreadable, too level for comfort. 'But there is another name for them, too.'

'Vampire.' Alex had never voiced the word out loud, not in relation to the murders of her mom and little brother. It stuck to her tongue like bitter paste, foul even after she had spit it out. 'Are you actually trying to tell me – my God, do you really expect me to believe they were vampires, Kade?'

'Rogues,' he said. 'Blood addicted and deadly. But they were also part of a race separate from humans called the Breed. A very old race, not the undead or the damned, but a living, breathing society. One which has existed alongside mankind for thousands of years.'

'Vampires,' she whispered, sick with the thought that any of this could be real.

But it was real. Some part of her had known this truth all along, from the instant her family was shattered by the attack all those years ago.

Kade's eyes remained steady on her. 'In the simplest terms, to say that they were vampires is fair enough.'

Nothing seemed simple to her anymore. Not after everything she had seen. Not after everything she was hearing now. And definitely not when it came to Kade.

She felt some measure of retreat in him as he looked at her, some amount of hurt in his bleak gaze, and it gnawed at her. 'You told me once that nothing is simple. Nothing in your world is simply good or bad, black or white. Shades of gray, you said.'

He didn't blink, just held her in an unflinching look. 'Yes.'

'Is this what you meant?' She swallowed, her voice cracking just a bit. 'Is this the world that you live in, Kade?'

'We both do,' he replied, his voice so gentle it terrified her. 'You and I, Alex. We're both a part of it. I am, because my father is Breed. And you are, because you bear the same birthmark as my mother and a small number of other, very rare women. You are a Breedmate, Alex. Your blood properties and unusual cellular makeup connect you to the Breed on the most primal level.'

'That's ridiculous.' She shook her head, recalling how tenderly he had touched the odd little scarlet mark on her hip when they were together in the cabin earlier today. Without trying, she could still feel the heat of his fingertips on that very spot. 'A birthmark doesn't make me anything. It doesn't prove anything—'

'No,' he said carefully. 'But there are other things that do.

Have you ever been sick in your life? Have you always felt a little bit lost, a little bit detached, different from all the other people around you? Some part of you has always been searching, reaching for something you could never quite grasp. You've never truly found your place of belonging in the world. I'm right, aren't I, Alex?'

She couldn't speak. God help her, she could hardly breathe.

Kade went on. 'You're also gifted in some way that you can't really explain – some innate ability that separates you from the rest of the mortal world.'

She wanted to tell him he was wrong about all of that. Wanted to, but couldn't. Everything he said summed up her experience and her innermost feelings. It was as though he had known her all her life . . . as though he understood her on a level that even she herself had not.

Until this very moment, impossible as it seemed.

'Since I was a child, I have always had an instinct for knowing when someone was telling me the truth or a lie.' Kade nodded as she spoke, unsurprised. 'I can read others,' she said, 'but not you.'

'It's possible that your talent only works on humans.'

Humans. Not him, because he was something . . . *other*.

A coldness swept her as the realization sank in fully.

'Are you—' Her voice cracked, almost wouldn't come. 'Are you telling me that you're like them – the ones that killed my mother and Richie? The ones that killed the Tomses and Lanny and Big Dave?'

'I'm not sure who's to blame for the killings here recently, but I'm nothing like that. And only the sickest, most heinous members of my kind would do what was done to your family, Alex.' He reached out and took her hand in his, brought her fingers to his mouth and kissed them with aching tenderness. His quicksilver eyes held her gaze with an intensity that seared her, deep inside. 'I am Breed, Alex. But I will never harm you, or anyone you love. Never. My God, I sure didn't see you coming – didn't see any of this coming. I never expected I'd end up caring like this.'

'Kade,' she whispered, not knowing what she wanted to say to him after all the things he'd just told her. She was filled with questions and uncertainty, overwhelmed with a confusion of emotions, all of it centered on the man – the Breed male – who held her hand right now, and her heart.

As though he understood the torment she was feeling, he leaned around the small table and gathered her into his arms. Alex went to him, letting him pull her onto his lap.

'I don't know what to think of all this,' she murmured. 'I have so many questions.'

'I know.' He drew her away from him and smoothed the backs of his fingers along the side of her face, the curve of her neck. 'I'll answer anything you ask me. When I come back, you can ask me everything you need to know.'

'When you come back?' The thought of him leaving, now, when her head – hell, her whole life – was turned upside-down, was unthinkable. He stood up, easing her up with him. 'Where are you going?'

'Something has been bothering me about Skeeter Arnold. I saw him with someone the other night, outside Pete's tavern. They took him to a mining company several miles from here.'

'What was the name of it?'

'Coldstream.'

Alex frowned. 'That place shut down about twenty years ago, but I heard new management moved in recently. They're keeping things pretty private out there. Put up a bunch of sur-veillance equipment and security fences around the perimeter.'

'New management, eh?' Kade's dark expression spoke vol-umes.

'You don't think . . .'

'Yeah, I do. But I need to be sure.'

'Then I'm going with you.'

His dark brows crashed together. 'Absolutely not. It could be dangerous—'

'Exactly why I'm not about to wait around and worry. I am going with you.' She walked over and grabbed her parka, pretending she didn't hear his muttered curse behind her. 'Well, are you coming, or what?'

CHAPTER NINETEEN

Since his snowmachine was still parked at Alex's house from earlier that morning, they had each taken a sled and rode out together, heading for the Coldstream Mining Company several miles out of town. Rather than draw undue attention, they'd ditched the noisy machines about a half mile from the secured site and walked the rest of the way on snowshoes.

The reconnaissance would have gone a lot faster if he'd been able to do it alone, but Kade was inwardly relieved to have Alex with him. At least this way she was in sight and within arm's reach. Back in town by herself left her vulnerable, a concept that made his heart squeeze a bit tighter in his chest as he navigated the dark, frozen tundra at her side.

Up ahead of them several hundred yards, floodlights washing over the snow, the mining company's compound was alive with activity. As had been the case when Kade first surveilled the location, tonight a handful of uniformed workers continued to empty one of the two parked cargo containers outside the mouth of the mine itself. Guards with automatic rifles patrolled the barricade out front; mounted security cameras were trained on the land surrounding the tall chain-link perimeter fence.

Kade paused, putting his gloved hand on Alex's arm. 'This is as far as we go.'

'But we need to get much closer to see what's going on in

there,' she whispered, her breath clouding as it penetrated the fleece mask that protected her face.

'Too dangerous for you to get any closer, and I'm not about to leave you here without me.'

'Then let's go back to Harmony and get my plane. We can fly over for a better look.'

'And risk letting them identify you from the ground?' Kade gave a curt shake of his head. 'Not even if Harmony had a hundred pilots who owned little red single-engines. No, there is another way.'

He inhaled deeply, letting a low howl build slowly in his throat. Then he sent it skyward in a long, searching summons. It took only a moment for a wilder reply to answer from somewhere not far off toward the west. Kade sought the lupine voice with his mind, then, with a wordless command, he called the wolf out from the night.

Alex startled when the silver-furred animal stepped into view from the woods and walked directly into their path.

'It's okay,' Kade told her. He glanced at her, his mouth curving at her open astonishment. 'You have your talent; I have mine.'

'Yours is way better,' she murmured on a breathless whisper.

He smiled, then fixed his gaze on the wolf's bright, intelligent eyes. It listened to the silent instructions he gave, then it dashed off in stealth motion to carry them out.

Alex gaped at him. 'What did you just do? And, um . . . how?'

'I asked the wolf to help us. She'll get closer to the site than we can, and through the link she and I now share, she will show me everything she sees.'

Alex got quiet as Kade focused on the temporary connection that put him inside the wolf's senses. Kade closed his eyes, feeling the rhythmic fall of its paws in the snow, hearing the soft huffs of its lungs, the steady, rapid beat of its heart. And through the keen night-sharp vision, he saw the webbed fence and heavy-security outbuildings, the workers – Minions, all of them, he realized now – shuffling in and out of the mine's cavernous entrance, wheeling crated equipment and large, unmarked cartons of God knew what kinds of supplies.

The new management had moved in, all right, and from the looks of it, they wanted to make damned sure that no one got too close to see what they were about.

And speaking of the mining company's new management . . .

The wolf's ears pricked to attention, self-preservation instincts pushing her down into a low crouch as a large male with fair hair and expensive taste in suits strode from within the mine. Although Kade had never seen him before, he didn't miss for an instant that the male was Breed. If his size and demeanor hadn't given him away, the extensive network of *dermaglyphs* would have. The markings tracked out from the rolled-up cuffs and open throat of his white dress shirt, in patterns that clearly declared him an elder of the Breed.

Easily powerful enough to turn a human like Skeeter Arnold into his Minion.

And flanking him like an obedient hound was another Breed male. If the one dressed like a Wall Street banker was formidable simply for the purity of his bloodline, then the individual standing with him trumped him by roughly a mile. Armed to the fangs and dressed from head to toe in black combat gear, his head shaved bald, covered with dense *glyphs*, this was a new enemy that Kade and the rest of the Order had only recently become familiar with.

Through the wolf's eyes, he saw the gleaming black collar that ringed the assassin's neck – an electronic collar rigged with an explosive device that ensured the vampire's loyalty to his creator's deviant initiatives.

'Ah, fuck,' Kade muttered aloud as he remotely observed

the scene from his lupine helper's eyes. 'Dragos has sent one of his assassins here.'

'Who?' Alex whispered from beside him. 'Assassins? Oh, my God. Kade, tell me what you see.'

He shook his head, unable to explain things adequately while his gut was churning with sudden dread and suspicion.

Why would Dragos send a lieutenant of his operations and one of his personal stock of born-and-bred Gen One killers to the middle of the frigid Alaskan interior?

What the hell were they doing here?

Once the vampires were gone inside another building, Kade directed the wolf to change position, to find a safe, concealed spot to dig beneath the perimeter fence and creep inside. He needed a better look at the cargo containers, particularly the one that the Minion workers seemed to take little interest in – the one, he noticed now, that bore huge dents in its sides and smashed, twisted hinges on the double doors at its rear.

He waited, heart pounding in time with the wolf's as she dug her claws into the snow and burrowed deep, then wedged her body beneath the fence. She pulled herself through and began a stealthy crawl, knowing instinctively to keep to the shadows. As she neared the freight containers, Kade's muscles tensed.

He had guessed he would find bad news inside the wrecked cargo hold. He'd been more than right about that. As the courageous wolf poked her head into the gaping ruin of the doors, peering into what had been a refrigerated space, Kade made instant, grim sense of the objects that held little meaning to her.

He saw the smashed, large steel-and-concrete box that sat inside, its lid torn off and reduced to broken rubble. He saw the bloodstains that had dried nearly black on the floor and walls of the hold – bloodstains that reeked of his own kind as the wolf drew the trace scent into her sensitive nostrils. He saw the titanium restraints that had once encircled the thick wrists and ankles of a creature that most of the Breed population believed had been driven to extinction centuries ago . . . a creature that the Order knew firsthand did, in fact, still live.

The Ancient.

One of the alien forefathers who'd sired the entire Breed race on Earth.

The powerful, savage otherworlder that Dragos had been using to further his insane goals.

Had Dragos and his associates moved it north after the Order's recent strike on Dragos's hidden lair? Had they thought to relocate the Ancient as far from the Order's reach as possible, transferring it to the old mine?

Or had that been the plan, until the Ancient somehow found a way to escape his captivity?

Kade thought back on the recent killings in the bush and on today's brutal attack on the two men from Harmony.

Neither Seth nor Rogues had been to blame.

Now he knew that with the gravest certainty. It had been something much worse.

'Jesus Christ,' Kade hissed. 'It's out here somewhere. On the loose.'

He commanded the wolf to abandon her prowl at once, and stayed with her as she made a quick escape from the mining company grounds. As her dark silver shadow vanished into the nearby forest, Kade broke their mental connection and reached for Alex's hand.

'We have to get out of here. Now.'

She nodded at his urgent tone and ran with him, wasting no precious time on questions. He would explain everything to her, but first, he needed to contact the Order in Boston. Lucan and the others needed to know what he'd discovered here, and just how far his mission had veered off course.

Zach Tucker knocked the carbide handle of his state-issued Maglite against the rickety doorjamb a few more times and waited, not with any kind of patience, on the back steps of Skeeter Arnold's run-down apartment.

Since the asshole had been ignoring his cell calls and text messages for the past twenty-four hours, Zach saw little choice but to make an in-person inquiry at the house Skeeter shared with his mother. Five minutes standing in the cold, freezing his balls off while he banged on the door with no reply, but he wasn't going anywhere until he got some answers out of the cocky piece of shit.

Answers, and the five hundred dollars cash that Skeeter owed him from their most recent deal.

If Skeeter thought he could walk away without giving Zach his cut, he was sorely mistaken. And if he'd somehow gotten it into his fool head that he no longer needed Zach – that maybe he'd found himself another source of procurement in the area and suddenly had ideas about severing their association – then Skeeter Arnold might just discover that he was deadly mistaken.

Zach rapped on the door again, hard enough it was a wonder the frozen wood didn't shatter under the repeated blows of his flashlight handle.

Finally, a muffled voice sounded from somewhere inside – not Skeeter, but Ida Arnold, his offensive bitch of a mother. Zach despised the old woman, though not as much as Skeeter must have, being subjected to her piss and venom every day.

'Goddamn it, I'm coming! I'm coming!' she hollered, the heavy shuffle of her footsteps punctuating every syllable. The porch light went on over his head, then the door was yanked open on another coarse grumble.

'Evening, Ida,' Zach said pleasantly as she scowled at him.

'What do you want?' She crossed her arms over her breasts,

tugging at the edges of her old housecoat. 'You come to tell me he's in trouble again?'

'No, ma'am.'

She grunted. 'He dead?'

'No, ma'am. Nothing like that.' He cocked his head. 'Why would you think that?'

'Wouldn't surprise me, is all. I heard what happened to Big Dave and Lanny Ham today.' At Zach's grim nod, she huffed out a breath and shrugged. 'Never did care much for either one of them, tell you the truth.'

'Yes, well,' Zach replied idly. He cleared his throat, adopting his cop voice, the one that Jenna said made him sound like a self-righteous prick. All he knew was, it generally got results. 'I actually came by to talk to Stanley.'

The fact that he'd used her son's given name and not the nickname that all the rest of Harmony had called him from the time he was a skinny, snot-nosed kid made Ida Arnold's scowl burrow a bit deeper on her forehead.

'Is he here, ma'am?'

'No, he ain't. Haven't seen hide nor hair since early this morning.'

'He hasn't called or anything to let you know where he might be, ma'am?'

She barked out a cutting laugh. 'He don't tell me nothin', just like his no-good father before him. Thinks I'm blind and dumb, that boy,' she muttered. 'I know what he's up to, though.'

'Oh? And what's that, Ida?' Zach asked carefully, narrowing his eyes under the glare of the overhead light as he watched the old woman's expression harden.

'He's dealing again, drugs, for sure. My guess is he's also bootlegging to some of the dry Native settlements upriver.'

Zach felt his brows rise, even as his gut clenched into a tight ball. 'What makes you suspect Skeet – Stanley – is involved in something like that?'

She tapped the center of her chest with her finger. 'I raised him, for better or worse. I don't need proof to know when he's up to no good. I'm not sure what he's gotten himself into lately, but he's starting to scare me. I think he has it in him to hurt me one day. In fact, after the way he treated me when he was here last, I don't doubt it for a second. Never seen him act so nasty and arrogant. Acted like he suddenly grew a pair of balls.'

Zach cleared his throat at the woman's crudeness. 'This was yesterday, you said?'

She nodded. 'He came home looking like something the cat dragged in. When I said something about it, he grabbed me by the throat. I tell you, I thought he was going to kill me right then and there. But he just mumbled that he had work to do, then went inside his room and closed the door. That's the last he was home, far as I know. Part of me hopes he never comes back, the way he treats me. Part of me wishes he would just . . . go away. To prison, if that's where he belongs.'

Zach stared at her, realizing that her fear and dislike of her own son could work to his advantage here. 'When he was here at the house last, did he say what kind of work he was doing?'

'He didn't say, but that boy's never done an honest day's work in his life. You wanna have a look inside his apartment? It's a damn pigsty, but if it's proof you need—'

'Can't do that,' Zach said, even though right now he wanted nothing more. 'From a law enforcement standpoint, I can't search his residence. That would require a lot of paperwork and procedures.'

The rounded bulk of her shoulders slumped a bit. 'I see—'

'However,' Zach added helpfully, 'seeing how I've known you folks for the past decade or so since I've lived in Harmony, I suppose if you asked me as a personal favor to come in and have a look around – unofficially, as it were – then I would not be opposed.'

She peered at him for a long moment, then stepped back from the door and motioned him inside. 'It's this way, down the hall. He'll have locked the door, but I keep a spare key tucked behind the baseboard.'

Ida Arnold ambled down to her son's door, retrieved the tarnished brass key from its hiding place, then unlocked and opened the door for Zach.

'I'll be just a few minutes,' he said, dismissing her with both his tone and his unblinking academy-trained stare. 'Thank you, Ida.'

Once she had shuffled back up the hallway, Zach walked into Skeeter's dump of an apartment and began a swift, thorough search of the place. Empty food wrappers, bottles, and other trash littered the floor and nearly every flat surface. And there – surprise – on the counter next to an old police radio, a roll of twenty-dollar bills, secured with a rubber band.

It didn't seem like Skeeter to leave his money lying around. Didn't seem like him to leave his cell phone behind, either, but there it was, jammed into the seat of a tattered light blue recliner. Guess that explained the ignored calls and texts, although it hardly excused Skeeter for being an asshole out at Pete's the this morning.

Zach grabbed the cash and counted it out: fifteen bills. Not the five hundred bucks Skeeter owed him, but he'd gladly take what he could get.

Hell, he'd take the cell phone, too.

If it didn't give him any insight into Skeeter's recent activities or his apparent newfound business associates, then Zach would pawn the damned thing next time he went to Fairbanks to pick up new product from his connections in the city. Skeeter Arnold owed him, and one way or another, Zach intended to collect what he was due.

✠ CHAPTER TWENTY ✠

Alex sat on the sofa in her living room, sharing a piece of buttered toast with Luna, both of them watching Kade walk a repeated track from the kitchen and down the hallway as he spoke on satellite phone to Boston.

In the time since they'd been back to her house, he'd brought her up to speed on a few more things about himself and the work he'd been sent to do in Alaska. Her mind was still reeling over the fact that he wasn't precisely human. Now she understood that he was also part of a group of Breed males pledged to maintain peace between their race and humankind. From the way he described it, the Order sounded almost military, which made some kind of sense to her when she looked at Kade and observed his dark combination of lethal strength and laser-sharp confidence.

And despite the danger that rolled off him in waves, especially what she'd witnessed today, Kade was gentle with her, protective. As shaken as she was by all she had seen and heard in the past few hours – the past few days – she felt secure with him.

Even when he'd gone on to explain the worst of the threats that faced him and the warriors of the Order.

He had told her about the enemy the Order was doggedly pursuing and committed to destroying, a second-generation Breed male called Dragos. Alex had listened in quiet but horrified comprehension as Kade had described the many evils

Dragos had perpetrated, not the least of which being the mass abduction and abuse of an unknown number of women like her – Breedmates, tracked down and collected over a period of decades to be used as vessels for the personal army of assassins Dragos had bred.

What truly gave her pause, and what made her blood run cold in her veins, was one final truth that Kade revealed to her tonight. The fact that a creature not of this world – a creature far worse than the blood-addicted Rogues who'd killed her mom and Richie – was somehow loose in the Alaskan interior.

Even Kade was grim when he spoke of the Ancient to his friends at the Order's Boston compound, describing to them the damaged freight container and the presence of vampires and Minion workers at the old mining company location. Although he kept his voice low, it was impossible for Alex to miss the fact that he and his brethren were preparing for battle against the new threat.

The thought of Kade walking into harm's way made her breath come a little shorter, her heart beat a bit heavier. She couldn't bear it if something happened to him. Not after the time they'd shared, an incredibly short time, in which he was somehow becoming an inextricable part of her life. In just a couple of days, he had become her friend and her lover, her confidant. Somehow he was coming to mean something even more than all of that.

Could she possibly be falling in love with him?

Falling in love . . . with a vampire.

No, he wasn't that.

Kade was Breed, and that was different. *He* was different.

It was hard for her to reconcile that he was cut from the same fabric as the monsters that had attacked her family. Hard for her to believe that somewhere in his DNA, he carried the genes of something completely inhuman, unfathomably lethal.

Something not of this Earth. It was hard for her to reconcile that the strong, proud, devastatingly sexy man prowling her modest little house was actually not a man at all, but something different. Something so much more.

Alex watched him in fascination, all the more so for what she'd seen him do outside the mining company grounds with the wolf. In an instant, he'd become part of the beautiful animal, connecting on some unspoken level that had left Alex gaping at him in awe. Even now, she marveled, feeling the current of wildness, of dark, commanding power, lingering in him still. He was intense and mysterious, strong and seductive. And yes, hot as hell.

Everything about Kade captivated her.

She merely had to look at him and she burned.

And he knew it, too. She saw the spark of awareness light the silver of his eyes as he wrapped up his call and set the phone down on the end table next to the sofa.

'How are you holding up?' he asked, seating himself beside her. 'You must be exhausted. I know this is a lot to handle.'

She gave a vague shrug. 'My head's still spinning, but at least I have answers now. The things that never made sense to me before are clearer. Not exactly reason to jump up and cheer, but it's good to finally have the truth, however terrifying it might be. So, thank you for that, Kade.'

He took her hand in his, their palms pressed together lightly as he ran his thumb over the thin skin of her wrist. His touch was warm, soothing. Achingly tender. 'God, I hate that you've been dragged into this. There are places that you can go where you'll be safe, Alex. The Breed has numerous Darkhavens that would take you in – secure communities where you would be welcomed and protected. Better than what I can do for you now. After seeing what we did out at the mine, this has all gotten too real. Too dangerous—'

'I'm not going anywhere,' she said, curling her fingers

around his and holding his grave gaze. 'I'm not going to run. Don't ask me to, Kade.'

His jaw went tight as he stared at her. His dark brows lowered over his eyes, mouth going flat as he grimly shook his head. 'This is my battle. The Order's battle. Tomorrow some of the warriors will arrive from Boston. I'll be meeting up with them when they get in, and from there we'll launch an offensive strike on Dragos's operations at the mine. We don't know what we're going to find. I just know that I want you as far away from this mission – and any possible fallout – as you can get.' He reached up and smoothed his fingers lightly over her cheek. 'That also means getting you as far away from me as possible, before I put you any further at risk.'

'No.' Alex turned her face, pressing her mouth to the warm heat of his palm where it rested against her. She kissed the heart of his large hand. 'I can't hide anymore, Kade. I don't want to live like that, always looking over my shoulder, afraid of the things I don't understand. You can't ask me to, not when meeting you has given me the strength to believe that I can face my fears. Meeting you has given me the strength to understand that I *must* face them.'

He cursed harshly, but his caress was soft, his gaze penetrating, the pale silver color that ringed his pupils dark with desire. 'You give me too much credit. You were stronger than you realized, to have gone through what you did as a child and not let it destroy you. Not many could. That's courage, Alex. You didn't need me for that. You still don't.'

She smiled, reaching out to hold his face in her hands as she kissed him. 'I do need you,' she whispered against his mouth. 'What's more, I want you, Kade.'

His breath rasped out of him on a sigh as she slanted her lips over his again and moved closer to him on the sofa. His arms went around her, holding her in a loose cage as she climbed up onto his lap and pushed her tongue into his mouth.

He groaned, caught her tongue with his teeth . . . then abruptly broke contact and turned his head away from her.

'What's wrong? Why did you stop?' She panted the words, her lips and tongue stinging with a delicious heat. She tasted blood, only the smallest trace, but instinct brought her hand up to her mouth and the tip of her finger came away wet with a scarlet stain.

She glanced at Kade's downcast face and felt his torment in the way his big body vibrated with barely leashed control, as though he were waging a private war inside himself.

'Look at me,' she whispered. When he didn't immediately comply, she lifted his stubborn chin and physically brought his gaze back to hers. 'Look at me . . . let me see you.'

'Trust me, you will not want to,' he muttered, glancing away quickly.

But not before she noticed the change that had come over his eyes. He hadn't been able to turn quite fast enough to hide the fact that their normally pale gray color was now shot with fiery amber. And his pupils . . . something was different about them, too.

'Kade, please,' she said gently, 'Let me see you as you really are.'

Slowly, he lifted his face. His dark lashes flicked up, and Alex was stunned by a blast of ember-bright color that glowed like lit coals. And in the center of all that fire, his pupils had narrowed to catlike slits. It startled her, the strangeness of his gaze, the way it transformed his face, sharpening the angles of his high cheekbones and squared jaw. She stared, robbed of words. All but robbed of breath.

'I don't want you to be afraid of me, Alex.' His deep voice rasped, sounding oddly thick to her, and then she realized why. She saw the gleam of sharp white teeth behind his lip as he spoke. His fangs. Not quite hidden, despite his obvious effort to conceal them from her view. When he looked at her now, there was a desperation in his amber eyes. Desperation and longing like she'd never seen before. 'I don't want you to hate me, but this is who I am, Alex. This is who I truly am.'

Despite the tiny shiver of wariness that kicked her heart into a more frantic beat, Alex leaned forward and cupped his face in her hands. She held his tormented gaze, then let her eyes travel downward, to his parted lips and the bright points of his fangs, which seemed to have grown even larger now, sharper.

'I'm not feeling anything close to hate,' she whispered, tilting her head up and wetting her suddenly dry lips. 'If you'd just kiss me again, you'd know that.'

Sparks flashed like lightning in his eyes in the moment before he descended on her. Alex felt the leashed power in him, and she sensed the control he exerted to keep that power in check as he took her mouth in a hot, hungered, claiming kiss.

Alex gave herself over to him, reveling in the warm, wet brush of his lips on her mouth, her chin, her throat. She slipped her hands under the black cotton of his long-sleeved T-shirt, running her palms up the firm, satin-smooth muscle of his back. She could feel the vague outlines of his tattoos under her fingertips, a complicated pattern of swirls and arcs that she traced with her nails but really wanted to follow with her tongue.

'Let me see your body. I want to see all of you,' she murmured, tugging at his shirt. She pulled it over his head and could only stare in wonder once she'd unveiled him. 'My God,' she gasped. 'Those are not tattoos, are they?'

'*Dermaglyphs,*' he said, settling back to let her look at the intricate design that pulsed across his torso, shoulders, and arms as though it were alive. The markings that had been only a shade darker than the rest of his skin were now flooded with variegated hues of deepest wine, indigo, and gold. 'We're born with them, the same way Breedmates are born with their mark.'

'They're beautiful, Kade.' His *dermaglyphs* were artful, lacy intertwinings, a glorious web of shifting colors. Alex leaned in to run her finger along a particularly graceful line that tracked around the flat disk of his right nipple. The deep purplish hue blushed darker under her touch. She looked up at him, amazed. 'How'd you do that?'

'You did it.' His mouth quirked. 'The colors of the *glyphs* change according to a male's mood.'

'Oh,' she said, going warm at his dark, meaningful look. 'And your mood is?'

He didn't answer, just moved forward and took her in another long, slow kiss that turned her core molten. He pressed her down onto the sofa beneath him and began to undress her, prompting Luna to jump off the far end and slink into the kitchen on a disgruntled huff.

'Uh-oh. I think you may have just lost points with her,' Alex murmured in between kisses.

He chuckled, a low and deep rumble that vibrated against her mouth. 'I'll apologize later. Right now, there's only one female whose opinion matters to me.'

He took his time stripping her of her double layer of fleece and cotton shirts and loose-fitting jeans. He covered every inch of her with his mouth, kissing a long, hot trail down her neck and breasts and abdomen, stroking her bare limbs as his glowing, fevered gaze drank her in.

By the time he had her naked, Alex was panting and aching with desire. He knelt on the sofa above her, his thick thighs wedged between the spread of hers. He was still in his jeans, which sat low on his lean hips, straining tight across the large swell of his groin.

She raised up and reached out to him, needing to feel his warm flesh under her hands. All over her body.

Deep inside her.

He said nothing as she unfastened the button of his pants

and edged the zipper down. He was naked beneath the dark denim, his rigid cock spilling over as soon as it was freed of its confinement. He rose up as she tugged his jeans off his hips and pushed them down around his knees, a move that brought his gorgeous length within an inch of her mouth.

Alex couldn't resist the temptation. She cupped his shaft and balls and brought him to her, wrapping her lips around the broad head and delighting in Kade's strangled moan as she slid her mouth all the way down to the base of him.

He felt so good against her tongue, hot and earthy, as soft as velvet wrapped around a column of solid steel. Alex drew him deep again, then eased back to suckle at his crest, all the while watching as the *glyphs* on his abdomen and upper thighs churned in ever-deepening hues.

'Ah, Christ,' he hissed as she played her mouth around the rim of his head, then took him all the way to the back of her throat. His fingers speared into her hair, clutching her skull as his body went tight as a cable. 'Alex . . . ah, fuck . . .'

His hands were trembling as he set her away from him. His eyes threw off an intense heat, and his face was stark with passion as he hastily shucked his jeans to the floor. Gloriously naked, he moved toward her once more and gently wrapped his palm around her nape. His touch was firm with possession, yet he didn't simply take. His transformed gaze was hungry yet patient. His kiss passionate yet tender.

There was nothing simple about him.

Nothing simple about the way he made her feel.

Kade was simply a mass of contradictions, each one more fascinating than the last.

He made her feel safe and protected, perhaps the biggest contradiction of all. He made her feel cared for . . . even loved.

And dear God, did he make her burn.

Her body arched into him as he stroked her, every inch of her hypersensitive and greedy for his touch. She couldn't get close enough, couldn't hold him tight enough, as he prowled on top of her and spread her thighs wide with his.

'I want to take this slow tonight,' he said, his voice rough and dark, almost unrecognizable. 'I just want to savor you . . . savor us.'

He watched her as he entered her, thrusting slowly, filling her with deliberate care even though his hips bucked and the tendons in his neck popped tight under his skin. He rocked her gently, stoking her building climax with maddening restraint.

She wanted to scream for him to go faster, to take her as hard as he could if it would ease the coil of need that he'd put inside her.

But making love to him felt too good to rush. She didn't want the feeling – or this night – to end. Neither did he; she could see that in his face. She could feel it in every measured thrust of his hips. In every hot, savoring caress of his mouth as he kissed her breath away.

The hours would pass quickly enough. Tomorrow his mission with the Order would begin again. Tomorrow all the death and danger that lurked outside the haven of this moment would return.

Much too soon, Alex thought.

And so she wrapped her arms around his neck, her legs around the slow, torturously wonderful pump of his hips, and she let herself spin out into a blissful abandon. She welcomed every deep thrust. Sighed with every long retreat. Relished in the weight and warmth of Kade's magnificent body rubbing against her.

When she came, it was a delicious unraveling of her senses. Alex cried out, shuddering as the orgasm rocked her from a place so deep within her, it seemed to detonate from her very soul. She clung to him, catching the muscled bulk of his shoulder between her teeth as an aftershock rumbled through her.

'Kade,' she gasped brokenly. 'Oh, God . . .'

He groaned with sharp force and lifted her pelvis up off the cushions. His thrusts gained strength, driving deeper now, yet still bridled by his rigid control.

'Let go,' Alex whispered. 'Just let it go. I want all of you, Kade.'

He snarled, a raw, animalistic sound of refusal. When he scooped her into his arms and tried to hide his face from her view, Alex pushed back. His face was wild with torment, constricted with pleasure and pain. And his fangs . . . Good lord, the bright white points filled his mouth as he stared down at her, thrust so powerfully, she couldn't hold back her sharp cry.

Her own pleasure was cresting once more, bringing with it a keening hunger that twisted tight in her belly, beginning a slow boil in her blood.

'Oh, God . . . Kade.' She panted with sensation and need, all of it centered on him. She dug her fingernails into the bulk of his arms, buried her face in the curve of his strong neck and shoulder as he crashed into her with long, punishingly intense strokes.

The coil of hunger within her contracted even more, burning into a need so primal it shook her. The scent of his skin, its silky, smooth heat against her lips, against her tongue, made her dizzy with desire. His tempo roughened as he rode her, harder and deeper, grunting with each urgent grind of his pelvis.

Alex sighed his name. She moaned, lost to the swelling rush of another orgasm. She cried out as it washed over her, a quenching flood of pleasure and release that should have doused the smoldering thirst that lived in her now, but only made it explode into a gnawing demand.

She wanted to taste him.

Not in any way that she had already, but in a way that shocked her. In a way that should have terrified her, but only made her blood race hotter, faster, alive with a dark power she could hardly tame.

Beneath her open mouth, she felt the quickened thud of his heartbeat knocking in the vein at his throat. She pressed her tongue against it, then her teeth. Closed them experimentally over the corded tendons and the heated pulse that seemed to beat in the same desperate rhythm within her, as well.

Kade snarled a dark curse but only pumped his hips with more fury.

Alex reveled in the feel of him losing control. She ran her tongue and teeth over the tender skin, then clamped down harder . . .

Kade arced sharply above her, threw his head back, and roared.

❧ CHAPTER TWENTY-ONE ❧

He couldn't hold back another second longer.

His release shot out of him in a scalding rush as Alex's blunt little teeth grazed his throat in a teasing, testing bite that almost – not quite – broke the surface of his skin. She couldn't know how badly he wanted it. How staggering the need he had for her to draw his blood into her mouth, to drink from him. How intensely he wanted to claim Alex for his own and bind her to him forever.

'Fuck,' he gasped as her satiny walls milked his pumping cock and her mouth wreaked holy havoc on his senses. 'Alex . . . ah, Christ!'

He came harder than ever before, lost to his desire for her. Lost to the deafening drum of his pulse that demanded she was already his, blood-bonded or not.

His woman.

The only female he would ever want again.

His forever mate.

Kade raised up onto his knees to look at her, his sex still buried inside her heat, still hard for her and hungry for more. His neck burned from the playful nip of her mouth. He could still taste the sweetness of her blood on his tongue from when he'd so stupidly let his fangs graze her lip as he'd kissed her. That small taste had damned him, and maybe her, as well.

Desire and bloodthirst swamped him, sharpening his vision and making his fangs throb with the urge to penetrate her tender flesh. He clutched her hips and rocked against her, watching as she arched beneath him, following him toward the peak of another shattering release.

She cried his name, her spine bowing upward, blood flushing her pale skin with a pink glow. Kade watched her in tortured admiration, never having seen anything as beautiful as Alex in the throes of erotic bliss.

He wanted to give her more, the kind of pleasure and release – the passion, and, yes, the love – that only a blood-bonded male could give his mate.

God, how he wanted.

'Alexandra,' he rasped, the only thing he could manage when hunger and desire for her swamped him, stripping him of all thought except the want of this female. He wanted to warn her that he was dangerous like this, but all that left his mouth was a sound somewhere between a curse and a moan.

She should have pushed him away, but instead she did the exact opposite. Her hands came up to reach for him, bringing him back down atop her. Breath rushing through her lips in short gasps, she pulled his face to hers and kissed him, a deep, wet, welcoming joining of their mouths.

Kade tried to fight the need – the hunger – but Alex was quickly undoing every bit of his control. Dimly he realized that he hadn't fed since leaving Boston a few days ago, and as much as he wanted to blame his thirst on basic survival, he knew to his marrow that it was the taste of Alex he wanted.

Only her.

He was unhinged now, treading the edge of a very deep crevasse and about to drag her down into it along with him. He knew this. He knew damned well that he should make sure Alex knew it, too.

But then she deepened their kiss, sucking his lower lip between her teeth with a hunger he would not mistake, even at his most sober moment. And he was anything but sober now, when his body was smoldering, his blood racing through his veins like liquid fire.

Kade broke away from her mouth on a growl. He traced his lips and tongue along the delicate line of her jaw, then down to the tender spot beneath her ear, knowing it would doom him but too far gone to stop now. The feel of her pulse ticking against his mouth dug spurs into the soft belly of his need, turning raw ache into fierce agony.

'Ah, God . . . Alex,' he whispered harshly, then took the tender flesh of her throat between his teeth and fangs and slowly pressed down into her vein.

She drew in a sharp gasp as he penetrated her skin, a sudden flinch stiffening her body and halting her breathing. Kade paused as though slapped, horrified at what he'd just done and fearing he would not have the strength to pull away now, even if she hated him.

But then Alex's hands relaxed on his shoulders, began to stroke him. She exhaled a tremulous, pleasured sigh and he responded with a rough, grateful moan as he drew the first sweet taste of her into his mouth.

And, oh, she was sweet.

Alex's blood swept over his tongue like silk, the unique honey-and-almond scent of her mingling with the musky heat of her arousal. Kade drank her in, stunned by the roar of heat and pleasure that flowed into him with each draw he took from her vein. Her blood quenched him, empowered him. Inflamed him all over again, more intensely than before.

She was his. And although it would take a mutual exchange of blood to bond them together as mates, his link to her now was unbreakable. It was a visceral bond, one that could be broken only by death.

And he had just forced it on her.

The thought shamed him, but it was difficult to feel remorse when Alex was clutching at him with greedy hands, panting and writhing against him as another orgasm rocked her. She moaned hotly under the hypnotic spell of his bite, her hips rising up to take him deeper inside her as he drew the honeyed sweetness of her blood into his mouth.

If she'd been merely *Homo sapiens,* she would have felt comfort, even pleasure, as he fed from her. But because she was a Breedmate, and because of the passion that was still coursing through both of them now, Alex's response was exponentially more intense. Her ecstasy was his now, a part of him through her blood he'd taken inside him. Now every intense feeling she experienced would be his, as well, from joy to pain.

As he drank more of her, he felt her desire rising, ratcheting to a fevered yearning she struggled to bear. His thirst had not ebbed, but it was her need that moved him now. With a careful sweep of his tongue over the twin punctures, he sealed the bite closed.

'Come on,' he murmured, gathering her up into his arms. 'I'm taking you to bed now.'

Drowsy and boneless, she rested lightly against his bare chest as he carried her down the hallway and into her bedroom. He placed her on the quilted comforter, kissing her as he settled in next to her on the bed. He caressed every silken inch of her, every curve and muscle imprinting itself on his touch.

'Look at me, Alexandra,' he said when she closed her eyes in pleasure. His voice was rough and dark, almost unrecognizable to his own ears. 'I need to know that you see me now, as I am. This is what I am.'

She lifted her lids and gazed up at him. He waited to see her revulsion, for he would never have looked more feral – more inhuman – than he did at that moment. His *glyphs* pulsed with shifting colors, hues of desire and passion melding with those of his lingering hunger and the torment he felt for everything that had happened here with Alex tonight. Not the least of which being the blood bond he'd initiated and could not sever, even if she despised him for it.

He watched her study him, afraid to speak. Fearful that she would hate him now, or look away, repulsed by what he had become. 'This is me, Alex,' he said quietly. 'This is all of me.'

Her light brown eyes drank him in, unfaltering. She stroked the mutating *glyphs* on his chest, following the pattern with a light, learning touch. She reached down farther, smoothing her palm over his thigh, then back to the erect length of his cock. He exhaled a wordless growl of pleasure as her fingers lovingly caressed him.

Through her blood, the precious part of her that swam inside him, feeding his cells, he read the depth of her desire for him. There was no fear or uncertainty in her as she gazed at him. There was only a soft but fevered demand as she reached up to grip the nape of his neck and guide him back down to her mouth.

'Make love to me again,' she whispered against his lips.

It was a command that Kade was more than willing to oblige. He gently rolled over her as she parted her legs to welcome him once more. He entered her slowly and tenderly as he brought her into his arms. Their kiss was long, passionate, fevered as she traced her tongue over his fangs and his sex erupted deep inside her. Kade shouted with his release and crushed her to him.

God help him, he knew now what the other mated warriors had said about the pleasure – the humbling rapture – of the blood bond. With Alex, with this woman who had awakened feelings in him he'd never wanted to risk before, now Kade knew what forever could be. He craved it, with a ferocity that stunned him.

In that moment, with Alex wrapped around him so warm and content and open to him, he wanted to hold the feeling close . . . even if the wildness within him whispered insidiously that it couldn't last.

The fire that had been slowly dying on the grate a few hours ago had long since gone cold. Jenna Tucker-Darrow lay tightly curled on her side on the floor of the cabin's main room, shivering as she roused from the depths of a dreamless, unnaturally heavy sleep. Her limbs were listless, uncooperative, her neck too weak and tender to let her lift her head.

With some effort, she managed to crack her eyelids open and peer into the darkness of her cabin. Dread crawled up her spine on talons made of ice.

The intruder was still there.

He sat on the floor across the room from her, his head tipped down. He was a massive, menacing presence, even at rest.

He wasn't human.

She still struggled with that awareness, wondered if what she was seeing could be blamed on the single-malt Scotch she'd been drowning herself in – Mitch's favorite, and the crutch she leaned on every year around this time to get her through the awful anniversary of his and Libby's deaths.

But the immense intruder who broke into her home and was now holding her prisoner there wasn't some type of alcoholic hallucination. He was flesh and bone, though she'd never seen flesh like his before. He'd shown up unclothed despite the subzero temperatures outside, and his skin from head to toe was hairless, covered in a dense tangle of red and black markings that were too extensive to be the work of a tattoo artist. And whatever he was, he was stronger than any man she'd ever come across in her time in law enforcement, even though he was unarmed, and nursing some grievous injuries.

Jenna had seen her share of gunshot wounds, enough to know that the shredded chunk of flesh and muscle blown out of his thigh and the smaller one in the side of his abdomen must have been the result of shotgun blasts. His other injuries, the blisters and seeping lesions that covered most of his skin, were less discernible, particularly in the dark. They looked like radiation burns, or a seriously intense sunburn – the kind you could get only if you did your UV baking under a full-body magnifying glass.

Jenna couldn't even begin to guess where he'd come from, or what he wanted with her. She'd thought he meant to kill her when he forced his way inside her house. Truthfully, she wouldn't have cared if he had. She'd been halfway there on her own, anyway. She was tired of living without the people she cared about most. Fed up with feeling so damned useless and alone.

But the intruder – the creature, for that's what he was – did not break in with the intention of killing her. At least, not right away, from what she could tell.

He had done something equally heinous, however.

He'd bitten her in the throat, and to her shock and disbelief, he'd fed on her blood like a monster.

Like a vampire.

Impossible, she knew. Her logic wanted to reject the idea, just as it wanted to reject what her eyes were still witnessing now when she looked across the room at the impossible idea in the flesh.

Jenna shuddered at the recollection of his huge fangs descending on her, tearing into the side of her neck. Thankfully, she couldn't remember much beyond that. She might have fainted, but she suspected he had done something to render her unconscious. Whether she was weakened from blood loss or whatever he'd done to knock her out, she couldn't be sure.

She tried again to move from her tight ball on the floor but succeeded only in getting his attention. His head came up, the fiery twin laser beams of his eyes pinning her from across the room. Jenna stared right back, refusing to cower to him, no matter what the hell he was. She had nothing to lose, after all.

He watched her for a long time. Maybe he was waiting for her to back down, or try to hoist herself up and launch at him in a fit of futile rage.

Belatedly, she noticed that he held something rectangular and shiny in his huge hands. A picture frame. She knew the one it was, didn't have to look to the fireplace mantel above the place where she lay to realize he was holding a photograph of her with Mitch and Libby. The last one she had of them together, taken just days before they were killed.

Her breath came a little faster as a feeling of weary outrage spiked in her. He had no right to touch anything of hers, least of all something as precious as that final image of her family.

Across the room, the hairless head cocked at an inquisitive angle.

He rose, began a slow, painful-looking walk toward her. Idly, she noticed that his gunshot wounds had stopped bleeding. The flesh didn't seem quite as ragged as it had before, almost as if it were healing at an accelerated – almost visibly accelerated – rate.

He paused in front of her and slowly eased himself down onto his haunches. Although she was anxious, fearful for what he meant to do to her now, Jenna worked hard not to show it.

He held the picture frame out to her.

Jenna stared, unsure what to do.

He remained there for the longest time, watching her, his blistered hand holding the photograph of her smiling with her husband and child out to her like some kind of offering. When she didn't move or speak, finally, he set it down on the floor next to her. The glass was cracked, the edges of the silver frame marred with smudges of his blood.

Jenna looked at the happy faces behind the ruined glass and

could not hold back her choked cry. Pain engulfed her, and she dropped her forehead onto the floor and sobbed quietly.

Her captor limped back to the other side of the room and watched her weep, before turning to look out the unshuttered window, up at the starlit sky overhead.

⊰ CHAPTER TWENTY-TWO ⊱

R esisting the pull of wakefulness that would draw her out
of a deep, sensual, very enjoyable dream, Alex sighed lan-
guorously and shifted on her bed. Aside from the black velvet
sleep that caressed her now, she needed only one more thing
to make her state of warm, lazy bliss complete. She sent her
arm out in a slow sweep of the mattress, searching for Kade's
warmth.

He wasn't there.

Had he left without telling her?

Wide awake now, she came up onto her elbows and stared
at the empty darkness of her bedroom. She flicked on the
nightstand lamp, huffing out a disappointed groan that he was
gone. But then, up the hallway, she heard the squeak of the
faucet as the shower turned off.

A moment later, Kade came strolling in, naked except for
her pink bath towel, which was knotted loosely around his trim
hips.

'You're awake,' he said, raking his fingers through the damp
ebony spikes of his hair.

'You're leaving already?'

He sat down on the edge of the bed. Beads of water glistened on his shoulders and chest, a few of them sliding down
his smooth skin and *glyphs* in thin rivulets. He looked and smelled
delicious, and Alex had the strongest urge to lick him dry.

He smiled as if he sensed the lusty direction of her thoughts.

'I have to go. My brothers-in-arms from Boston will be flying into Fairbanks in a couple of hours. We'll be rendezvousing at an old truck stop midway between there and the mining company. We can't risk giving Dragos or his men the chance to know we're on to them, so we're going to hit the mine without delay.'

He spoke so casually about the danger that awaited him and his friends. All Alex could think of was the very real possibility that he might be hurt. Or worse, something she didn't even want to imagine. Just the thought of Kade walking into that mine – potentially into the hands of Dragos, or an even larger evil, should they cross paths with the creature they suspected had been transported to the area – made Alex quake inside with a raw, marrow-deep dread. 'I don't want you to go. I'm afraid if you do, I might never see you again.'

'Don't worry,' he said, and something dark, something ironic, traveled over his handsome face. 'You aren't going to get rid of me that easily, Alex. Not now.'

He placed his palm along her cheek, then leaned down and kissed her, his mouth so tender on hers it opened up an ache in the center of her chest.

She ached in a number of places, all the right places.

By the time his lips left hers, each of her pulse points were lit up as though they'd been touched by lightning. Lower still, a heavy throb in her core sent heat pooling between her legs. After the hours of passion they'd enjoyed, she still burned for him as though she'd had only the smallest taste.

She sighed with the remembered pleasure of all they'd done together. 'Last night was . . .'

'Yeah. It was.' He smiled, but there was a hesitation in his voice. Something haunted about his eyes.

He caressed her bare shoulder, then let his fingers travel up along the side of her neck, the only part of her that felt more alive and heated than the slick cleft of her thighs. Alex nestled into his feather-light strokes, shivering with a growing hunger for him as he ran his thumb across the vein that fluttered more frantically in response to his touch.

'You bit me,' she whispered, feeling an odd thrill just to say the words.

He inclined his head in a grim nod. 'I did. I shouldn't have. I didn't have the right to take that from you.'

Did he mean her blood? 'It's all right, Kade.'

'No,' he said gravely. 'It's not all right. You deserve more than that.'

'I . . . liked it,' she told him, meaning it with a sincerity that shocked even her. 'What you did, it felt good. It still does. Everywhere you touched me last night feels very good.'

He exhaled slowly, his breath hot as it fanned her brow. He hadn't stopped petting her throat. She could have enjoyed his soothing touch for hours more.

'What I did last night has changed everything, Alex. I drank from you. I bonded myself to you, and I can't take it back. Not even if you hate me for it.'

She tilted her head up and kissed the stern line of his mouth. 'Why would I hate you?'

He stared at her for the longest time, as though weighing the impact of what he wanted to tell her. 'I drank from you, Alex, knowing full well that you are a Breedmate. Knowing that once your blood was in my body, there would be no going back. I'm connected to you now, and it's unbreakable. It's forever. I knew what it meant, but I just . . . wanted you so badly, I couldn't stop. I should have, but I didn't.'

Alex listened, seeing the torment in his eyes. She could see the regret, too, and it twisted her heart like a vise.

'Last night, you couldn't stop,' she said, needing to understand, even if it would kill to hear it. 'But now, you wish you could take it back. Because you feel differently . . . about me?'

His head came up sharply, his dark brows lowered over his

eyes. 'No. Jesus . . . no, Alex. What I feel for you—' The words broke off, seemed to catch in his throat. 'What I feel for you is stronger than anything I've ever felt before. It's love, Alex, and it was there before last night. It would be with me even if I hadn't taken your blood.'

She didn't realize she'd been holding her breath until it whooshed out of her on a sigh. 'Oh, Kade.'

He blew out a dry curse as he caressed her. 'I don't know how I let this happen. I sure as hell never expected to find what I have with you. Not now, when everything else around me couldn't be more messed up.'

'Then we'll sort it out,' she said, wrapping her arms around his neck. 'We can sort everything out, together. Because I've fallen in love with you, too.'

He cursed again, but this time it was with reverence, a whispered oath as he gathered her close and pulled her into a deliriously passionate kiss. Alex felt his muscles flex and twitch under her fingertips. She felt the tremor of need that racked him as he eased her onto her back and he crawled over her. The pink towel fell away and Alex drank in the magnificent sight of his body, the thick jut of his arousal, all of that power poised to enter her.

His gaze was fierce, pale silver flashing with amber fire. 'Ah, God . . . Alexandra. I need to hear it now. Tell me you are mine.'

'Yes,' she said, then cried the word again as he thrust deep and ushered her toward the crest of a swift, hot wave of release.

He had stayed in bed with Alex for nearly another hour, much longer than he had intended, but even at that, it had been damn near impossible to find the ambition to leave. Which meant he'd had to haul some serious ass in order to reach the rendezvous point in time to meet the arriving warriors. He'd made it – barely – and had just gotten off his snowmachine to wait for them when the roar of their engines came ripping out of the darkness.

The four vampires were outfitted like him in black winter gear and visored black helmets. As Breed, none of them needed the aid of their sled's headlight to guide them. Their huge forms, each of them bristling with weapons, spilled from the shadows of the night as they flew into the vacant, run-down truck stop. The whine of their snowmachines filled the air, heavy tractor chains throwing off plumes of gray exhaust and chewed-up snow behind them.

The Order's answer to the Horsemen of the Apocalypse, Kade thought with a wry grin as he watched the group of warriors skid to a halt in front of him.

Brock was the first off his sled. He cut the power and swung his leg over the seat, sweeping up his helmet's visor as he strode over and greeted Kade with a broad smile and a hard right cuff to the shoulder. 'You just wouldn't be happy until I had to drag my ass up here to this godforsaken icebox, that it? Gotta tell you, I'm feelin' some hate here, my man. Or I would be, if I could actually feel anything other than Arctic cold gnawing at my vitals.'

Kade grinned at the warrior who had become his closest friend. 'Good to see you, too.'

Directly behind Brock was another of the Order's newer recruits, the ex-Enforcement Agent Sterling Chase – or Harvard, as he was also known, on account of his highbrow civilian education and the stuffy demeanor he'd sported in the beginning of his involvement with the warriors. That cool air of superiority was still there, but sharpened to an icy edge in the year since he'd joined the Order.

Chase was deadly, and took something of an unhealthy sat-isfaction in his work. In fact, Kade was shocked as hell to see the male, considering it had only been a couple of weeks since a street battle in Boston had left him grounded with a nasty gunshot wound to the chest. Looking at him now, Kade couldn't help seeing a bit of Seth's unapologetic arrogance in the male's chilling blue eyes as he pulled off his helmet and bared his brush-cut blond head to the elements. His lean face was almost gaunt and there was a glint of emptiness in the warrior's eyes. An apathy that Kade felt as though he were only truly noticing for the first time.

'Got satellite imagery of the mining company location,' Chase said without greeting, pulling a small laptop out of his gear and firing it up as the others gathered around them. 'It's fresh intel. Gideon procured the images right before we left the compound.'

'Good,' Kade replied. 'You feeling all right, Harvard?'

He glanced up, his expression was unreadable, bleak. 'Never better.'

As Kade considered the warrior, the two others in the unit came over, both of them immense, both ruthlessly efficient weapons in the Order's deadly arsenal. They were both also first-generation Breed, although Tegan was centuries older than the male called simply Hunter. Where Tegan had been one of the Order's founding members along with its Gen One leader, Lucan, Hunter had come on board only a few months ago, an unlikely ally, given that he was a product of Dragos's genetic experimentation labs.

Bred off the last surviving Ancient – the very creature potentially at large in Alaska right now – and one of the many unknown, captive Breedmates whom Dragos had been collecting for decades as part of his grasp for power, Hunter was likely no older than forty or fifty years. But during that short span of life, he'd known only discipline and solitary purpose.

He'd been raised an assassin, an emotionless Hunter, given no name other than that of his function – his sole worth – to Dragos, the one who made him.

Behind the glossy visor of his helmet, Hunter remained his usual close-lipped, automaton self as he and Tegan approached the rest of the group. As for Tegan, he'd never been Mr Congeniality. It wasn't that long ago, little more than a year, that Tegan's involvement in the Order looked dubious at best. But he had proven himself in the end, and earned the love of a good woman besides. Now, as Lucan's second in command, the formidable warrior put all of his merciless, lethal intensity into every mission for the Order.

His bright green gaze was piercing as he stripped off his helmet and gave Kade a curt nod of greeting. 'Nice work, turning up the lead on Coldstream Mining. Gideon tracked it back to an outfit calling themselves TerraGlobal Partners. It's a dummy corporation, a front with about ten layers of bull-shit entities behind it.'

'Let me guess,' Kade said dryly. 'All roads will eventually lead to Dragos.'

Tegan nodded. 'Dante, Rio, and Niko are running with the data, pursuing every bread crumb we can find, no matter how small or spread out. Meanwhile, Lucan and Gideon are holding down the fort in Boston. Had to practically tie Lucan down to keep him from coming with us on this one, but we can't leave the compound unprotected when we still don't have a direct bead on Dragos himself. Too much precious cargo at home.'

Kade nodded, hearing the grim concern in the other male's voice when he spoke about his Breedmate, Elise, and the other warriors' mates who called the Order's headquarters their home.

Kade understood that feeling now.

When he thought of Alex, and the fact that he had to leave her at her house in Harmony while he was on this mission . . .

When he thought there was a chance, if things should go

terribly wrong and he couldn't return to her, that she might fall prey to the Ancient or to any other danger, and he wouldn't be there to keep her safe . . .

Holy hell.

Each thought was worse than the other, an awful spiral that he had to mentally shake himself out of to catch up to what Tegan was saying.

'Based on what we've seen from Dragos already, we have to assume the mine has some kind of self-destruct mechanism in place. If we can't find the nerve center of the lair, we're going to have to detonate the place ourselves.'

Brock grunted. 'Which is why I'm packing enough C-4 to blow a meteor-size crater into the side of that mountain. Gotta tell you, I'll be glad to unload this shit.'

Tegan gave him a wry nod, then set about giving instructions for the raid on the mine. The warriors had already discussed the plan of attack in Boston; now it was just a matter of carrying out the mission.

'Too bad Andreas Reichen isn't here to add some fire to this party,' Chase added, referring to the most recent addition to the Order's ranks, the former Darkhaven leader from Germany. 'Little bit of pyrokinesis would go a long way tonight.'

'Yeah, it would,' Tegan replied. 'But his talent is still too raw. Until he gets it under control, we're better to keep him working diplomatic relations for the Order.'

'Diplomatic relations.' Brock chuckled, a deep, amused rumble in his chest. 'God knows not a one of us standing here now is suited for that kind of work.'

'Damn straight,' Tegan agreed, smiling with cold menace. 'So, let's stop the yammering and go kick some ass.'

As the group broke and prepared to move out, Brock lagged behind the others and gave Kade a questioning look. 'What's going on with you? I've gone on too many patrols with you not to notice that you've got something heavy weighing on your mind, my man.'

'Nah.' Kade shook his head. 'It's nothing. I'm good. Let's roll.'

Brock's dark eyes narrowed. He took a sideways step and blocked Kade's path, keeping his voice too low for the others to hear. 'Now, see, that's the kind of lame-ass thing you say to someone who hasn't watched your back as often as you've watched theirs. So, let me ask it again. What the fuck happened since you got here?'

Kade stared at his comrade and friend – the warrior who was as close as a brother to him. Closer, even, than his own identical twin. The twin Kade no longer knew, and had lost as his kin a long time ago.

It shamed him to think of Seth now, let alone try to explain what he'd discovered about him in the time that he'd been back in Alaska.

He would have to tell the Order all of it at some point – he knew that. He would have to tell Alex about Seth eventually, as well. But there were other things weighing just as heavily on him, not the least of which being the fact that in the midst of all the madness and strife since he'd left Boston, he had somehow dropped his guard and let himself fall in love.

'The woman,' he said lamely. 'Alexandra Maguire . . .'

'You mean the Breedmate,' Brock corrected, having no doubt heard something about her from one of Kade's calls into the compound. 'Did something happen to the female?'

'Yeah, you could say that.' Kade exhaled a short breath, wry and hedging. 'Alex has become important to me. Really important.'

As Brock stared at him, the other warriors were getting on their sleds and juicing up their engines. The roar of machinery rumbled all around them, everyone waiting to get moving.

Brock gaped a minute longer, then let out a whoop of laughter. 'Naah! Oh, hell no. Not you, too?'

Kade grinned, gave him a helpless shrug. 'I love her, man. And she says she loves me, believe it or not.'

'Un-fucking-believable,' Brock said, still chuckling and shaking his head. 'This is becoming a goddamn epidemic lately.'

'Then you'd better watch your step, too.'

'Shit,' he replied, letting the word hiss out of him on a slow exhalation. 'Now who am I going to hang with after patrols – Harvard? Thanks a lot, man. I'll bet Hunter over there would be a barrel of laughs, too.'

From across the way, Tegan tipped up the visor on his helmet and shot them a summoning look. 'Let's do this.'

Brock waved his acknowledgment, then turned back to Kade. 'Ball-busting aside, man, I look forward to meeting your woman. But first, let's go kick some Dragos ass.'

Kade chuckled as he walked over to his snowmachine and prepared to ride out with his brethren, but his light mood was mostly a mask for the unpleasant reality that was settling heavier and heavier on his shoulders. Because assuming he survived the raid on the mine tonight, he would have the unpleasant task of dealing with Seth soon afterward.

He meant to start a life together with Alex, if she would have him, but he couldn't do that without taking care of the business he should have addressed before he ever left Alaska in the first place.

Seth was sliding toward Bloodlust, if he wasn't there already. His madness had to be stopped.

And Kade was the only one who could do it.

❄ CHAPTER TWENTY-THREE ❄

Kade had only been gone a couple of hours, but the waiting was driving Alex crazy.

Sleep was out of the question, even though she hadn't been getting much of it lately. She had already fed Luna breakfast and taken a shower, and if she walked around her tiny house looking for one more thing to dust or scrub or straighten, she was going to scream.

Maybe she could invite Jenna over.

Better yet, maybe she could go to her house instead. God knew, she could use the distraction of some company while her heart was caught in a vise, waiting for word from Kade, letting her know that he was all right.

Ordinarily, she might have just hopped on her snowmachine and rode over unannounced, but this was the one time of the year that Jenna appreciated her privacy – demanded it, even. The November anniversary of Mitch and Libby's deaths had always been a struggle for her friend, and it hurt Alex to think that Jenna preferred to suffer it out alone rather than lean on her for support during the difficult time.

It also bothered Alex that she hadn't heard a word from Jenna since she had seen her last.

Going more than a day or two without at least a phone call or quick drop-in was unusual for Jenna, no matter what time of the year it was.

Alex picked up her phone to call her and noticed that the

message symbol was lit up. Probably Jenna, Alex thought with a relieved laugh under her breath. She'd probably left a voicemail asking Alex why she hadn't called or come around herself. Alex punched in her access code and waited for the message to play.

It wasn't Jenna. One of the clients on her supply route, a new mother with a sick baby and a husband gone some six months doing work on the pipeline, wanted to know if Alex could possibly bring out some formula and more fuel for the cabin's generator. She was just about out of both, and worried that the coming snowstorm would only make things worse. The call had come in yesterday morning. More than twenty-four hours ago.

'Dammit,' Alex whispered.

The woman's cabin was only about ten miles out of town, but the thought of venturing outside Harmony before daylight, especially with the knowledge of the savage creature that likely lurked in the darkness, gave Alex more than a moment's pause.

Then again, could she really sit back in her house and leave everyone else to their own devices simply because she was afraid? Hadn't she just told Kade that she was through with hiding and running, cowering in the corner from the evil she had always known existed but had been too cowardly to face?

She had meant it.

Kade had given her the strength to face her fears.

And the fact that he was out there somewhere, right now, fighting for her – for all of mankind and Breed alike – gave Alex an even greater, renewed sense of power. Noble, courageous Kade was her man, her mate. He loved her. With that knowledge buoying her, there was nothing she needed to fear anymore.

'Come on, Luna.' Alex gestured for the wolf dog to follow her as she headed for the kitchen and grabbed her parka off

the hook. She stomped into her boots, then grabbed the key
to her snowmachine. 'Let's go for a ride, girl.'

And on the way back from her delivery, she would swing
by Jenna's place just to make sure everything was all right with
her, too.

'We counted seven Minions patrolling the areas south and west
of the site,' Kade said as he and Brock came back from a
quick reconnaissance of the mining company. 'From what we
could see, every one of them is armed with semi-auto assault
rifles and wired with comm devices. No outward sign of the
Gen One assassin or Dragos's man, so odds are they're holed
up inside somewhere.'

As Tegan gave a nod in acknowledgment, Chase walked up
with his report from the other side of their operation's target.
'Four Minion guards at the gate out front, and a couple more
staking out the eastern stretch of the perimeter fence. I'm
guessing that's not the extent of them. We're going to find
more of the bastards once we get inside. Only question is, how
many more.'

'No matter.' Hunter's deep voice held no inflection, only
cold assessment. 'Minions have inferior, human reflexes.
Regardless of their numbers or their weaponry, it is doubtful
they can disable us all. They will pose only a temporary
obstacle to our mission.'

'Right,' Tegan agreed, somewhat dryly. 'Once we infiltrate
the site and get past the Minions on guard, our objective is
twofold. Determine if the Ancient is being held inside, and if
so, where. Second, we capture the vampire in charge of the
site. If he's taking orders from Dragos, then he knows where
Dragos is and what he's up to. So, we need to bring the son
of a bitch in and make him talk. Which means we need to
bring him in alive.'

'Doesn't mean we have to bring him in happy,' Chase

drawled, the tips of his fangs already visible in anticipation of the battle to come. 'Just need to make sure his mouth works.'

'We go in stealth,' Tegan continued, turning a brief, narrowed glance on the warrior before addressing the group as a whole. 'We'll split up into teams and clear as wide a path as we can through the mine's security detail – but do it quietly. No bullets unless absolutely necessary. The closer we can get to the mine's entrance without alerting the whole damned place to our presence inside, the better.'

The group of warriors responded with accepting nods.

'We need a frontline team to move in on the guards at the gate,' Tegan said, looking to Kade and Brock. At their agreement, he slanted a look at Chase. 'The two of us will search and secure the outbuildings and cargo containers, and make sure Hunter has a clear path to the mine entrance itself. Once the Minion guards are disabled and the outbuildings are secured, we're gonna need all hands at the ready to move in and breach the mine.'

'Sounds like a plan,' Brock said.

Kade nodded and met his friend's glance through the fine snow that had been kicking up for the past several minutes. 'Let's do this.'

'All right,' Tegan said. 'Everyone knows what needs to be done. Lock and load, and we are rolling.'

The warriors divided into the assigned teams and moved out. Their preternatural speed and agility would benefit their mission, especially since, as Hunter had said, despite the Minions' numbers, they were at the disadvantage in this battle simply because they were human. Their human eyes would not be able to track the swiftness of the warriors' movements as the band of Breed males rushed the perimeter fences and leapt over the nine-foot barrier in fluid, spring-heeled grace.

Kade was the first one to clear the fence. He came down on a Minion who'd been on watch at the shack out front, dropping the guard to the frozen ground and silencing his shout of alarm with a blade drawn instantly across his throat. As he dragged the body into the shack, he glanced over and saw that Brock was also inside, the black warrior's Minion target eliminated with a hard, breaking twist of its neck.

Together the two warriors moved on to their next point of attack, Kade leaping onto the roof of the nearest out-building while Brock disappeared around the corner of another. Kade spotted his quarry on the ground below. The Minion strolled the area between the perimeter fence and one of the corrugated equipment storage trailers, his watchful eyes trained on the empty darkness beyond the fence. He went down with little more than a grunt of surprise as Kade launched himself from the rooftop and put him to a swift death on the ground.

Brock, too, had added another Minion to his tally. He dumped the limp body of his second Minion target beside Kade's.

Up ahead, partially concealed by the flurry of snow that was starting to pick up intensity, Tegan was just releasing the broken, lifeless body of a large Minion guard and stripping him of his weapons. Farther still, toward the pathway that led to the mine's entrance, Kade could just make out the immense form of Hunter as the Gen One male stepped past two freshly dead Minions who lay in slumped heaps at his feet.

Kade shot a look around the site for the remaining member of the team and found him up near the cargo containers. Chase had a Minion clutched by the throat, holding the strug-gling mind slave in a slow and painful death grip, his booted feet several inches off the ground. The Minion flailed and con-vulsed as he began to strangle.

'End it,' Kade muttered in a tight whisper as he watched Chase's expression contort with some kind of wild fury. From beside him, Kade heard Brock growl, a low rumble deep in his throat as he, too, caught sight of the other warrior toying with his prey.

Just then, Chase drew his knife and brought it up, poised to deliver a killing strike.

That's when Kade saw a flash of dark movement across the way – another Minion, stepping out onto an exterior staircase of one of the surrounding buildings. The Minion guard had his rifle aimed at Chase, about to squeeze the trigger.

'Goddamn it,' Kade snarled, bringing up his own weapon and training it on the sudden threat to Sterling Chase's life. Tegan's warning to hold all fire unless absolutely necessary rang through his head.

Fuck it.

He had to do it. If he didn't, in another fraction of a second, the Order was going to lose one of its own.

Kade fired.

The shot cracked like a sudden clap of thunder. Up on the stairwell, an explosion of blood and gore blasted out of the side of the Minion's head as Kade's bullet met its target dead-on. The Minion's corpse toppled over the edge, landing with a hard *thump* on the ground below.

At the same time, an alarm went off inside the buildings. The ringing peal of the sirens echoed all around the exterior of the site, plunging the area into instant chaos.

Before Kade had a chance to regret the move that had spared his brethren's life but possibly put their mission in jeopardy, an army of Minions came pouring out of the place from all directions. Gunfire erupted everywhere. Kade and Brock dived for cover behind the nearest outbuilding, returning fire on the group of Minion guards who moved in on them from across the way.

Through the curtain of thickening snowfall, Kade noticed an additional company of Minions over near the squat brick building that protected the mine's entrance. A dozen of them swept out to fortify the front of the building, while behind them, still more appeared in the narrow windows, which were thrown open and bristling with the long black barrels of high-gauge semi-autos.

Bullets volleyed from all directions as Kade and the others tried to mow down the line and clear a path toward the mine's entrance, the obvious nerve center of Dragos's operation there. The warriors took out several targets, but not without a few hits on their side. Although their Breed genetics gave them the speed to anticipate and dodge an incoming shot, in the heat of battle it was easy to lose track – and potentially lose one's head.

Kade took a nasty graze to his shoulder as he fired on the Minions. Beside him, Brock flinched away from one bullet and barely evaded another. The rest of the warriors were under similar attack and, like Kade and Brock, giving back as good as they were getting. Minions dropped from various positions, until all that was left were a few tenacious guards holding the line at the front of the mine's entrance.

Then, as if to give the challenge an even finer point, the building's steel door opened and an immense, black-clad shape emerged.

'Assassin,' Kade hissed to Brock as the huge Gen One male he'd seen a few days ago with Dragos's lieutenant strode outside to join the fray.

No sooner had he said it than one of the warriors broke out of formation and stalked forward, gun blazing.

Holy hell.

Hunter.

'Cover him!' Tegan shouted, but Kade and the others were already on it, vaulting up from their positions and falling in behind the former assassin to blast at their enemies and storm the mine's entrance in force.

Several yards in front now, Hunter's long, determined strides chewed up the snow-covered ground as he dodged to evade a hail of bullets coming at him from ahead on the right. Another volley answered, and the Gen One took a solid hit to his left thigh. Then another to his right shoulder.

Hunter barely flinched as his flesh tore away with the impacts. Head lowered, he threw down his weapon and bulldozed forward in a streak of speed that only Breed eyes could follow. All of his fury – all of his lethal intent – was focused on the other Gen One assassin, the Breed male who had been born and bred the same as he, and trained to be expert in just one thing: dealing death.

At the same moment Hunter shot forward, the assassin released his gun and launched himself into the air in a great leap. The pair of Gen Ones collided in a crash of pummeling bone and muscle. As they went down onto the ground, locked in vicious hand-to-hand combat that would not cease until one or the other was killed, the rest of the warriors moved in quickly to mow down the remaining Minions guarding the mine.

The dual battles were furious, bloody, and seemed to take place in a vacuum of time that was both agonizingly slow motion and spinning out at the speed of light.

Kade and the others converged on the mine's entrance. Blood and bone and bullets sprayed the snow-filled darkness. Minions fell in greater numbers now, their sharp, agonized screams splitting the night as the mine's alarms continued to blare and howl.

And on the ground nearby, Hunter and the Gen One assassin rolled and twisted in an indiscernible blur of movement, hammering each other with their fists. As Kade took out another Minion near the entrance, he saw the flash of the assassin's fangs in the darkness as the Gen One opened his maw and brought his bite down hard on Hunter's shoulder.

Kade had an opening to fire on the bastard, but in the midst of all the chaos around them, it was a miserably thin chance. If he missed, he could put a bullet in Hunter's head instead.

He blew out a curse and lined up his shot – just as Hunter grabbed the black polymer collar around the assassin's neck and threw him off. Hunter pounced onto the male's chest. Silent, merciless, he grabbed the vampire's huge, hairless head in both hands and cracked it hard onto the snow-packed ground. Kade felt the skull-crushing *thump* reverberate in the ground beneath his boots.

The assassin's fight slowed then, but Hunter wasn't finished. Hands moving with grim efficiency and ruthless strength, he hoisted the heavy bulk of the other male and sent the disabled assassin flying. The body crashed into the side of one of the cargo containers, the assassin's electronic collar shooting off a shower of sparks as it impacted with the corrugated steel.

'Oh, shit!' Kade shouted, having seen firsthand what those collars could do. 'UV blast coming – everybody down!'

His command sent Hunter and all the rest of the warriors straight to the deck. No sooner had they hit the ground than there was a sudden, blinding flash of pure white light. The ultraviolet ray shot out from beneath the assassin's head, cutting a clean line through skin, flesh, tendons, and bone. When it extinguished a moment later, the immense Gen One assassin lay in the melting snow in a broken heap, his hairless, *glyph*-covered head severed cleanly from the rest of him.

Without missing a beat, Hunter drew a pistol from his weapons belt and squeezed off more rounds at the handful of Minions who were staggering around, temporarily blinded by the explosion of light a second ago. Kade and the rest of the group joined in, and, within moments, nothing stood in their way of the mine's entrance except a field of fallen bodies.

Tegan kicked in the steel door and led the push inside the building. The front room was vacant, except for more Minion carnage and a couple of security cameras. At the back of the space was another door, this one steel, as well, but fortified with a heavy latch and turnstile lock, like the door of a bank vault.

'Brock,' Tegan said. 'Give it a bump of that C-4.'

Brock moved forward and swung the black ammunitions satchel off his back. He took out one of the pale cakes of explosive material and cut off a small piece. When he'd pressed it into place on the steel door and set the charges, everyone drew back outside and covered their heads as he hit the detonator and blew the door.

'We're in,' he said, as the rolling smoke and dust started to clear.

They hauled open the blasted interior door and crept into the corridor on the other side. Bunk rooms lined one side of the passageway, presumably for the Minion guards who manned the place. Farther down was a storage room, a modest kitchen, and farther still, a communications room that looked recently vacated of personnel.

The warriors continued their search, past a spartan quarters that was nothing more than a prisonlike room with no light or bunk for sleeping, just a blanket folded neatly on the floor. On a small stool in the corner sat an open box of rounds and a sheath for a large blade.

Hunter looked inside the room with a dispassionate eye. 'The assassin slept here.'

The cold cell was in stark contrast to the plush living quarters the group encountered a few yards down the corridor. Through the partially open door, Kade glimpsed a lot of dark, polished wood and luxurious furnishings. Behind a gleaming cherry desk a leather wing chair was still spinning, in motion from its recent occupant's apparently hasty departure.

No doubt, this fancy suite belonged to Dragos's lieutenant.

Kade gestured down the passageway, toward the last

remaining room before the corridor opened into the mine shaft itself. 'Only one way he could have run.'

'Yeah.' Tegan's green gaze slid to him in agreement. 'Right into a trap.'

He motioned for the others to fall in behind him, then led the way into the shadowy maw of the corridor.

⫷ CHAPTER TWENTY-FOUR ⫸

The snowstorm that had started as a teasing flurry was worsening into heavy, persistent flakes as Alex and Luna were riding back from making the delivery out to the bush. Alex was glad to have been able to help the young mother who'd been counting on her today, but she fretted that she hadn't yet been able to touch base with Jenna. She took out her cell phone and tried calling Jenna's cabin once again.

No answer.

The niggle of worry she'd been carrying for her friend had only increased in the time Alex had been out, turning into a full-fledged jab of concern. What if Jenna was taking things harder this year than before? Alex knew that she struggled, that she despaired still, over the loss of her husband and child. What if that despair had deepened to something worse this time?

What if it had become something dangerous and she'd harmed herself?

'Oh, God . . . Jenna. Please let me be wrong.'

With Luna running alongside her, Alex gave the sled more speed as she diverted from the game trail that would eventually lead into Harmony. She headed away from town instead, toward Jenna's cabin a mile outside.

She was still an easy fifteen minutes away when she saw something moving in the trees up ahead of her. She couldn't quite make out the shape in the dark, but it looked to be . . . a person?

Yes, it was. Someone crashing through the snow-laden underbrush of the forest. Incredibly, in spite of the bitter cold, he was utterly naked.

And he wasn't alone.

Several other shapes materialized from the shadows to run alongside him, four-legged, dark forms . . . a pack of half a dozen wolves. The sight of the man and wild animals together didn't so much shock her as it confused her.

Kade?

Alex cut the gas and slowed her sled to a crawl, Luna drawing to a pause at her side.

'Kade,' she called, his name rushing out of her mouth on a breath of pure instinct. She felt a brief moment of elation to see him, but then logic crashed down on her like a cold hammer. Kade had left hours ago to meet the other warriors from Boston. What would he be doing out here, like this?

Something about him didn't seem quite right . . .

It couldn't be Kade.

But . . . *it was.*

The headlight of her snowmachine pinned him in its beam. The wolves scattered into the forest, but he stood there now, alone, one arm raised to shield his brightly glowing amber eyes from the glare. His *dermaglyphs* were so dark they seemed black against his skin, and something almost as dark – something her mind refused to acknowledge at first – slickened his naked body from head to toe.

Blood.

Oh, Jesus.

He was injured . . . badly injured, by the horrific look of him.

Alex's heart gave a sick lurch in her chest. He was wounded. His mission with the Order must have gone terribly wrong.

'Kade!' she cried, and leapt off her sled to run toward him. Luna circled in front of her, blocking her way as she barked in a high-pitched whine, a warning to her, or maybe even the dog could see that something was very wrong with him.

'Kade, what happened to you?'

He cocked his head at her and stared as though transfixed, his black hair wild about his head and slick with wetness. Even from the hundred feet that separated them, Alex could see that blood splattered his face, streaked off his chin in gory lines.

Why wouldn't he answer her?

What the hell was wrong with him?

Alex paused, her feet suddenly refusing to move. 'Kade? Oh, my God . . . please, talk to me. You're hurt. Tell me what happened.'

But he didn't utter a single word.

Like a creature of the forest himself, he bolted away from her, vanishing into the dark woods.

Alex called after him, but he was nowhere to be seen now. Her sled's headlight cut deep into the trees where Kade and the wolves had been. She took a couple of hesitant steps forward, trying to ignore the knot of dread in her gut and the low, tentative warning of Luna's growl beside her.

She had to find Kade.

She had to know what had happened.

Alex's uncertain steps became a jog, her boots dragging in the snow. Her heartbeat was racing, lungs squeezing for each breath as she ran through the frigid darkness, following the piercing beam of her snowmachine's headlight.

She sucked in a gasp when she saw the bloodstains in the snow. So much blood. Kade's footprints tracked it everywhere. So had the pack's many paws.

'Oh, God,' Alex whispered, feeling sick, about to retch, as she ventured deeper into the forest, following the trail of gore.

The snow was stained almost black the farther she went. Blood as she'd never seen. Far too much for Kade to have lost

and still be able to stand upright, let alone run off as he had
when he'd realized she was there.

Alex walked numbly, all of her instincts clamoring for her
to turn around before she saw something she would never be
able to purge from her mind.

But she couldn't turn away.

She couldn't run.

She had to know what Kade had been doing.

Alex's feet slowed as she reached the place where the carnage had begun. Her vision swam as she stared down at the
bloodied aftermath of a vicious attack. A vampire attack –
worse than any savagery she'd witnessed before. Another
human being, another innocent person, brutalized by the monstrous killers of her nightmares.

By Kade, though she never would have believed it had she
not seen him with her own eyes.

Alex couldn't move. God, she could barely feel a thing as
she stood there, numb with shock and a horror so profound
she couldn't even summon the breath to scream.

Kade felt the oddest sensation in his chest as he and the other
warriors pushed farther into the corridor of the mine's shaft.
He crept forward in the dark, weapon held at the ready, trying
to dismiss the chill feeling that was knotting up tight behind
his sternum.

Jesus, had he taken a chest hit in the earlier fracas?

Surreptitiously, he felt around for a wound or the stickiness
of spilling blood but found nothing. Nothing but the phantom
ache that seemed to want to suck a lot of the air out of his
lungs. He shook it off, struggling to keep his attention on the
pitch-black cavern that stretched out ahead of him and the
other warriors.

The alarm sirens continued to wail from behind them;
nothing but quiet awaited in the depths of the mine shaft.

Then – the most minute scuff of a footstep came from some-where deep within the shadows. Kade heard it, and he was certain all the rest of the warriors had, too.

Tegan held up his hand to halt their progress in the pas-sageway. 'Looks like the damn place is empty,' he said, fishing for Dragos's lieutenant as he cast the line into the murky abyss ahead. 'Hand me some of that C-4. Let's blow this mother—'

'Wait.' The detached voice was begrudging and arrogant, an airless grunt of sound in the dark. 'Just . . . wait, please.'

'Show yourself,' Tegan ordered. 'Walk out nice and slow, asshole. If you're armed, you'll be eating lead before you take the first step.'

'I do not have a weapon,' the voice growled back in reply. 'I am a civilian.'

Tegan scoffed. 'Not today. Show yourself.'

Dragos's associate came out of the darkness as instructed, but only barely. Dressed in tailored gray pants and a black cashmere sweater, he looked to be more of a boardroom strate-gist than a military tactician. Then again, from what the Order had seen in the past of Dragos's handpicked associates, he seemed to recruit his lieutenants based on pedigree and apti-tude for corruption more than anything else.

Hands held up in surrender, Dragos's man hung back near the shadows of the mine shaft. He moved with slow deliber-ation, his carefully cultured expression not quite able to mask his fear as his eyes took stock of the five Breed warriors holding him in their killing sights.

'Who are you?' Tegan demanded. 'What's your name?'

He said nothing, but his gaze seemed to slide almost indis-cernibly to his side.

'Is there anyone else left inside?' Tegan asked. 'Where is the Ancient? Where is Dragos?'

The male took a hesitant step forward. 'I would need some

kind of assurances from the Order,' he hedged. And there went
that quick, telling dart of his eyes again. 'I would require sanc-
tuar—'

A gunshot exploded out of the darkness, cutting short his
words as it blew away a sizable chunk of the vampire's head.

'Assassin,' Hunter snarled at the same sharp instant, but his
warning was eclipsed by more gunfire blasting out of the
shadows.

Dragos's lieutenant – the vampire who might have given
the Order their best lead on their enemy – was collapsed on
the floor in a pulpy, boneless heap. Kade and the four other
warriors opened fire on the black maw of the mine shaft, pep-
pering the area with rounds as they dodged the gunfire coming
back at them.

'Take cover!' Tegan shouted as the incoming bullets showed
no sign of stopping.

Kade and Brock dived into the nearest chamber in the corridor of the shaft, Tegan right behind them. Chase and Hunter
took posts farther up on the other side of the passageway,
returning fire on the relentless hail of bullets that ripped out
of the darkness.

'Brock,' Tegan said, his fangs gleaming in the darkness.
'Throw some boom down the corridor. We'll shoot it from
here and set it off.'

Brock put down his gun and grabbed a pack of C-4 from
his satchel. Working quickly, he stuffed a blasting cap and a
small detonator into the pale cake. When it was done, he gave
Tegan a nod. 'Gotta hit this shit pretty square. If we miss the
embedded detonator, we get no spark.'

Kade caught the warrior's dark gaze. 'No spark, no boom.'

'Right.'

'Toss it,' Tegan said.

Brock moved to the opening of the door. He threw the
C-4 in a high arc, and as it disappeared into the shadows of

the mine shaft, the three of them opened fire. It was hard to tell if they'd hit the cake, until a spark cracked brightly in the darkness. Then the material exploded with a shuddering blast.

A billowing cloud of smoke and pulverized rubble pushed forward like a tsunami, blowing bits of concrete and choking dust into the room where Kade, Brock, and Tegan had taken cover.

And then, charging through the blinding wave of debris, came the Gen One assassin.

He was nothing more than a blur of motion and momentum, all of it crashing forward like a cannonball. Tegan leapt out to intercept him, and soon both Gen One males were engulfed in a deadly fight. The darkness and the churning cloud of debris swallowed them up as the struggle intensified, weapons clanging against the stone floor, fists crunching against flesh and bone.

The sudden, pungent scent of blood rose up from the confusion of movement.

A roar of fury – Tegan's low bellow of rage . . . then silence.

Someone found a light switch and flicked it on. Fluorescent tubes lit the corridor in a hazy fog of bluish-white light.

And there was Tegan, his thigh bloodied from a deep wound, his serrated titanium knife slipped between the assassin's thick neck and the black polymer collar that ringed it. 'Slowly, now,' he cautioned Dragos's homegrown killer. 'Stand up very carefully.'

The bald Gen One growled, his eyes flashing pure hatred. 'Fuck you.'

'Get up,' Tegan commanded. 'Careful. It's real easy to lose your head in a situation like this.'

Grudgingly, radiating menace, the assassin rose to his feet. With Kade and the others holding their weapons on the vampire, Tegan slowly walked him into the nearby chamber. The room's function was familiar enough to Kade since he and the

Order had encountered a similar one when they'd raided Dragos's headquarters in Connecticut just a few weeks ago. It was a holding cell, the cylindrical cage at its center, with its electronic restraints and computerized control panel designed for the containment of one particular captive.

'Where is the Ancient?' Tegan demanded as he guided the assassin over to the heavy-duty restraints that had been built to hold the otherworlder. Tegan glanced at Kade and Brock. 'Lock this son of a bitch down.'

They each took a hand and slapped the shackles around the Gen One's wrists. While they secured his arms, Chase walked over and fitted two more cuffs around his ankles.

'Where is the Ancient?' Tegan asked once more, his words tightly clipped. 'Okay, how about this. Where's Dragos? He's obviously diversifying his operation now, moving his pieces around instead of keeping them all together in one place. So, he moves the Ancient into cold storage up here, but what about the rest of it? Where is he hiding now? Where are the Breedmates he's holding prisoner?'

'He won't know.' Hunter's deep voice cut through the din of the alarms outside and the tension mounting inside the Ancient's containment chamber. 'Dragos tells us nothing. As his Hunters, we serve. That is all.'

Tegan snarled, looking like he wanted to snap the assassin's collar then and there. Keeping one hand on the blade that pressed against the UV collar, he put his other hand on the assassin's brow and pushed the big head backward. 'Motherfucker. He knows something.'

The assassin's mouth curved with private amusement.

'Start talking, you lab-spawned piece of shit, or you go up in smoke right here and now.'

The assassin's gaze was glacial. 'We are all about to go up in smoke,' he hissed through his teeth and fangs.

Kade glanced at the control panel on the opposite wall, only just that second realizing that there was a digital timer counting down on a five-minute clock. On top of the gnawing cold that was still chewing away at his chest, now a sick sense of déjà-vu gripped him as he watched what had to be the mine's self-destruct mechanism ticking off seconds. 'Shit. He's already dropped the switch. This whole place is gonna blow.'

Tegan growled, low and deadly, as he withdrew the knife from under the assassin's chin and left him standing in the Ancient's holding cell. Kade and the others stepped back as he strode over to the control panel and punched the button that operated the ultraviolet light bars. The vertical beams of light went live, circling the Gen One assassin inside and imprisoning him more securely than any amount of metal could.

'Let's get out of here,' Tegan said, stalking out the door. The rest of the warriors fell in behind him, Kade and Brock at the rear.

Brock paused to give the captive assassin a broad smile. 'Don't go anywhere now, you hear?'

Ordinarily, Kade would have gotten a good chuckle out of his partner's grim humor, but it was damned hard to appreciate anything when his heart was hammering like he'd just run a hundred miles and his veins were lighting up with the same odd chill that had made a home in his chest.

He ran with the rest of the group, out of the mine's building and into the main yard of the site, which looked like a war zone. The alarm sirens howled the loudest outside, screaming into the night. The snow was coming down at a furious pace now, blanketing the field of dead Minions and dropping visibility to next to nil.

'We need to *adios* these bodies, make sure there's nothing left to identify once this place blows,' Tegan said. 'Come on, let's drag them inside one of the outbuildings and send them off with the rest of that C-4.'

'On it,' Brock said.

Kade joined the rest of the warriors as they worked to clear the yard before the self-destruct clock wound down to zero. It was getting hard for him to breathe now, his blood throbbing with alarm sirens of its own, awareness seeping through the wash of adrenaline and battle focus that had swamped his senses for much of the combat at the mine.

As he and his brethren dragged the last of the Minion dead into place, and the first rumblings of the coming explosion began to shake the ground, the cause of his internal distress hit him broadside.

Alex.

Holy hell.

Something had happened. She was upset, shaken. Something had terrified her . . . horrified her. And he felt her trauma like his own now, because he had taken her blood into his body, and it was that blood bond that had been clamoring in his own veins.

Her name was a plea – a prayer – as the ground beneath him gave a mighty shudder, and the mining company blew sky high behind him.

CHAPTER TWENTY-FIVE

'Okay, Alex. Now, hold on here. Slow down, all right?' Zach Tucker carefully closed the door of the shed in back of his house and looked at Alex in stunned disbelief. She couldn't really blame him. No one in their right mind would believe what she'd just told him – not unless they'd seen it with their own eyes. 'You're telling me you just found another dead body in the bush, and you think it was . . . a vampire attack?'

'I know it was, Zach.' Her heart ached to say the words, but the image of Kade, and the image of the hunter's savaged body he'd left behind, tore at her with icy talons. 'Oh, God, Zach. I know you don't believe me, but it's true.'

He frowned, staring at her for a long moment. 'Why don't you come inside? It's freezing out here, and you're shaking like a leaf.'

Not from the cold of the outdoors, but from the confusion and horror of discovering that Kade had betrayed her. He'd sworn he was different from the monsters of her nightmares, and she had believed him. She would have believed everything he'd told her, if she hadn't seen the blood-soaked proof of his deception for herself just a short while ago.

'Come on,' Zach said, wrapping his arm around her shoulders and guiding her away from the shed, toward his house. Luna got up to follow, keeping pace at Alex's heels, but before the wolf dog could make it into the house, Zach closed the door in her face. 'Sit down, Alex. Let's take this slowly now, all right? Help me make sense of what you think you saw.'

Numbly complying, she sank down onto the sofa in his living room. He took a seat beside her. 'I don't *think* I saw anything, Zach. I *did* see it. It's real, everything I told you. Vampires do exist.'

'Listen to yourself. This isn't like you, Alex. You've been acting strangely ever since the attack on the Tomses. Ever since that guy – Kade – showed up in Harmony.' Zach's eyes narrowed on her. 'Has he been giving you drugs? Is that what his business is in Harmony? Because if some asshole thinks he can come into my town and start dealing—'

'No!' Alex shook her head. 'God, is that what you think? That I'm telling you all of this because I'm high or something?'

'I had to ask,' he said, still watching her with an intensity that unsettled her. 'I'm sorry, Alex, but all of this sounds a little . . . well, crazy.'

She exhaled a sharp breath. 'I know what it sounds like. I don't want to believe it any more than you do. But it's the truth. I've known it was the truth since I was nine years old.'

'What do you mean?'

'Vampires, Zach. They're real. Years ago, they killed my mom and my little brother.'

'You always said it was a drunk driver.'

She slowly shook her head. 'It wasn't. I saw the attack with my own eyes. It was the worst thing I've ever witnessed. And I didn't need to see the attack on Pop Toms and his family to know that the same evil killed them, too. I should have said something then. Maybe I could have stopped what happened to them, or to Lanny Ham and Big Dave.'

Zach's frown deepened to a questioning scowl. 'You're saying it was vampires that attacked them in that cave?'

'One vampire,' she corrected. 'The same one that probably

killed the Toms family. It's stronger than other vampires, Zach.
It's one of the fathers of the entire vampire race. And it's not
. . . from this world.'

Zach leaned back and barked out a loud guffaw of laughter.
'Oh, Christ, Alex! What the fuck are you on right now? You
look sober enough, but you must be completely stoned to sit
there with a straight face and expect me to believe this shit.
Alien vampires, that's what you're talking about?'

'I know it's hard to imagine something like that could exist,
but I'm telling you, it does. Vampires exist, and they call themselves the Breed.' She stopped short of naming Kade in their
number, not quite ready to betray him, even though he seemed
to have had no difficulty when it came to her.

Zach stood up and threw out his hands at her. 'Go home.
Sleep it off.'

'Listen to me,' she cried, desperate that he not dismiss her
as wasted or crazy. She could see that she was losing this battle,
she was afraid that her failure to convince him now might cost
other lives before long. 'Zach, please! We have to warn people.
You have to believe me.'

'No, I don't, Alex.' He whirled around to face her, something brutal in his expression. 'I'm not even sure I can believe
anything you've said today, including your claim of another
dead body in the woods. I don't have time for this kind of
bullshit right now, okay? I have my own problems I'm dealing
with! Folks are already worked up over everything that's going
on around here lately. I've got troopers arriving tomorrow, and
the last thing I need is you adding to my headaches with a lot
of crazy talk about bloodthirsty, killer aliens running loose in
the bush!'

Alex looked away from him, unable to hold the sharp fury
in his gaze.

She'd never seen him so angry. So . . . unglued. He was
in a state of near panic himself, and it didn't seem due to

anything she'd told him. As she turned her head, she noticed a folded wad of cash on the coffee table and a cell phone that looked vaguely familiar. She stared at both items, a peculiar inkling of suspicion worming its way up her spine.

'Isn't that Skeeter Arnold's cell phone?'

Zach seemed caught off guard by the question. 'Huh? Oh. Yeah, I confiscated it off the little bastard this morning.'

He picked up the roll of twenty-dollar bills without offering an explanation and stuffed it into his pocket, his eyes on her the whole time. Alex's blood slowed in her veins, oddly chilled. 'I haven't seen Skeeter around all day. When did you see him?'

Zach shrugged. 'I guess it wasn't long before you got here. I figure the Staties are going to want that phone for their investigation, seeing how he used it to record that video of the Toms settlement.'

The explanation made sense to her.

And yet . . .

'How long ago was it that you saw him?'

'About an hour ago,' he replied, his answer clipped. 'What does it matter to you, Alex?'

She knew why he sounded defensive, even without having to reach out and confirm it with her gift for divining the truth with her touch. Zach was lying to her. Skeeter was dead hours before now – dead at Kade's hands, after Skeeter had finished off Big Dave.

Why would Zach lie about seeing him?

As the question sifted through her mind, she thought about the cash Zach had tucked away, and the cell phone he couldn't have gotten when he said he had . . . and the fact that although most of Harmony and the communities roughly a hundred miles out knew that Skeeter had connections in bootlegging and drug-dealing, Zach had never found sufficient evidence to arrest him. Maybe Zach hadn't been looking hard enough.

Or maybe Zach had no desire to remove Skeeter Arnold from his line of work.

'Oh, my God,' Alex murmured. 'Did you and Skeeter have some kind of arrangement, Zach?'

That defensive gaze narrowed even further now. 'What the hell are you talking about?'

Alex stood up, feeling some of her horror from everything that had happened today begin to melt under the heat of her outrage. 'You did, didn't you? All your trips to Anchorage and Fairbanks. Is that where you picked up supplies for him? What kind of commission did you skim off the top of his drug deals, or off the backs of the Native kids who threw their lives away on the alcohol he peddled to them on the side? Good kids, like Teddy Toms.'

Zach's eyes blazed with anger, but he offered her a sympathetic look. 'Is that really what you think of me? You've known me for years, Alex.'

'Have I?' She shook her head. 'I'm not so sure. I'm not sure of anything anymore.'

'Then let me take care of you,' he said, his voice gentle, but she was hardly convinced. 'I'm going to get my coat, and I'm going to take you home so you can get some rest. I think you need it, Alex.' He pressed his lips together and gave her a vague nod. 'I'll be right back, okay?'

As he walked out of the room, Alex stood there, overwhelmed with uncertainty.

Everything in her life had tilted beneath her. She didn't know whom she could trust now.

Not Kade.

And apparently not Zach, either.

She didn't think it would be wise to trust him at all now.

Flames and debris shot high into the darkness as the mining company exploded behind him.

Kade threw a glance backward, feeling the push of the expanding heat against his face, heat that turned the snowstorm that swirled around him and the other warriors into a brief, warm spittle of rain. The warmth didn't last. Frigid cold roared back in, all of it settling in Kade's chest.

'Alex,' he whispered.

He had to reach her.

Brock shot him a concerned look. 'What's going on?'

Kade rubbed at the icy hurt under his breastbone. 'I'm not sure. It's Alex, and whatever I'm feeling, it's not good.'

Even though he could tell from his blood bond to her that she wasn't in mortal danger, every instinct within him screamed for him to go to her. But he had a duty to the Order, and a duty to the warriors he still might have failed by losing sight of the ball on this mission. Dragos's Alaskan outpost was destroyed, a few more of his assets eliminated, but the Ancient was still at large. The warriors' mission here would not be complete until that deadly otherworlder was located and contained.

'Shit,' Kade hissed.

This was not good. He couldn't go another second without talking to Alex at the very least. He had to reassure himself that she was all right. And part of him just needed to hear her voice.

'Call her,' Brock said. When Kade hesitated, wondering why the ice in his chest was crawling up to his throat to taste like dread, Brock gave him a stern look. 'Call your female.'

Kade took out his cell phone and walked until he was several yards from the other warriors. He dialed Alex's number. It rang three times before she answered.

'Alex?' he said into the silence on the other end. At his back, the crackle of flames and the soft hail of falling shrapnel seemed deafening when she was so quiet. 'Alex . . . are you there? Can you hear me?'

'What do you want?' she sounded a bit out of breath, as if she were walking somewhere at a good clip.

'What do I want,' he echoed. 'I . . . are you okay? I know you're upset. I felt it. I've been worried that something happened—'

Her scoff cut him off at the knees. 'That's funny. When I saw you earlier, you didn't seem to care that I was upset.'

'What?' He gave himself a mental shake, trying to make sense of what she was saying. 'What's going on with you?'

'Did you want me to see you like that? Is that what you meant when you said you were afraid I might hate you one day? Because right now I don't know what to think.' Her voice was tight with anger, and with hurt. 'After what I saw, I don't know how I feel. Not about you or us or anything.'

'Alex, I don't have any idea—'

More huffing breaths, her boots crunching in the snow. 'What was all that talk about a mission with the Order? Was it all bullshit, Kade? Just a game you played to make me think you were something better than what you are?'

'Alex—'

She sucked in a sob. 'My God, was everything between us just a bunch of bullshit, too?'

Kade stalked farther away from the settling destruction behind him and the other warriors who had taken notice of his departure from the group. 'Alex, please. Tell me what the hell is going on.'

'I saw you!' she burst out sharply. 'I saw you, Kade. In the woods, covered in blood, running with that pack of wolves. I saw what you did to that man.'

'Ah, Christ,' he muttered, comprehension dawning in a smothering wave. 'Alex . . .'

'I saw you,' she whispered now, her voice breaking. 'And I know you saw me, because you looked right at me.'

'Alex, it wasn't me,' he said, his heart sinking. 'It was my brother. My twin, Seth.'

'Oh, please.' She scoffed. 'How convenient for you to just remember him now. Let me guess, you're Dr Jekyll and he's Mr Hyde.'

Kade understood her doubt. He understood her anger, and her disdain of him. Her emotion swelled in his own chest, squeezing his heart as though it were caught in a vise. 'Alex, you don't understand. I didn't want to tell you about Seth because I am ashamed. Of him, of what he's done. Of myself, too, and the fact that I have not put a stop to his madness before now. I didn't tell you about him because I thought you would think I was just like him.' He blew out a harsh sigh. 'Shit . . . maybe it was only a matter of time before you realized that I *was* like him.'

She was silent for a long moment, her footsteps halted. In the background, he could hear Luna's soft whine. 'I'm hanging up now, Kade.'

'Wait. I need to see you. Where are you, Alex?'

'I don't . . .' She inhaled a deep breath, blew it out in a rush. 'I don't want to see you. Not right now. Maybe not ever again.'

'Alex, I can't let you do this. I want to talk to you, in person, not like this.' He closed his eyes, felt some of his hope drifting away. 'Tell me where you are. I can be at your house in a few minutes—'

'I'm not at home. After what I saw today, I didn't know what to do, or where to go. So I went to Zach's.'

The human police officer. Ah, fuck.

Panic drilled into the center of Kade's being. 'Alex, I know you're upset and confused, but do not tell him any of this—'

'Too late,' she murmured. 'I have to go now, Kade. Stay away from me.'

'Alex, wait. Alex!' The cell phone beeped as the connection ended. She hung up on him. 'Goddamn it.'

He tried her back again, but there was no answer. Three rings, four . . . her voicemail picked up and he hung up.

Tried again. Same result.

'Shit!' Kade roared with anger, frustrated and raw with self-directed fury for what Alex had been through. Trauma he'd had a hand in, and which had likely lost him the one woman he hoped would be at his side for the rest of his life.

When he pivoted around, Tegan was standing there. 'That doesn't sound good.'

Kade gave a vague shake of his head.

'A female, obviously,' Tegan said. 'The Breedmate from Harmony?'

Kade held the grim gaze of the Gen One warrior. 'I am bonded to her. I love her.'

Tegan, also a mated Breed male, grunted. 'There are worse things.'

'Yeah,' Kade agreed. 'There are worse things. She thinks I betrayed her. I didn't, but I wasn't honest with her, and I let her down. She said she never wants to see me again.'

'Go on,' Tegan said.

'Alex knows about the Breed,' Kade said. 'She knows about the Ancient, too. Shit, she knows everything. And I think she may have told it all to the state trooper stationed in Harmony.'

Tegan didn't blink. His stare was bleak, calculating. Ruthless. 'That would be unfortunate.'

Kade nodded, blew out a curse. 'I think it's too late to stop her. She told me she went to his house today. She's upset, and scared. I think she might have gone to the human for help.'

'I see.' Tegan's growl was so deep it was hardly audible. 'Then it looks like we're going to Harmony now. We need to contain the situation. And if need be, we'll have to contain your female, as well.'

CHAPTER TWENTY-SIX

‘Come on, Luna. Let's go.'

Alex sat on her snowmachine outside Zach's house and waited for Luna to get situated in front of her on the sled. With her cell phone turned off after the repeated calls from Kade, Alex pocketed it and could only sit there for a moment in the snow-flurried darkness, willing herself to simply breathe in and out.

She couldn't talk to him anymore. Not now. Her heart felt weak, and even as she'd been telling him to stay away from her, there was a part of her that wanted to let him back in, even though everything around her was in turmoil. Perhaps because of that fact, she still wanted the comfort of Kade's strength around her.

She still wanted his love.

But she didn't know if she could trust her feelings right now. Nothing seemed clear. Since meeting Kade, gone was her comfortable black-or-white, good-or-bad world. He had changed everything. He'd opened her eyes, and she could never go back to living as she had been.

She was changed forever, most significantly because no matter how much she wanted to fear him, to hate him for what he was, her heart refused to let him go.

Alex started up her snowmachine. She just needed to get away from everyone so that she had some room to think, and clear her head. She needed safe haven, and could think of only one place to find it now – Jenna's cabin. In all the upheaval of the past few hours, her plans to check in on her friend had been derailed. If there was one person she could trust right now, Alex knew it was Jenna.

Behind her, the door to Zach's house banged shut.

'Hey, where are you going?' he called to her, coming down across the yard at a brisk clip. 'I said I wanted to take you home, make sure you got there safely. I don't think you're in any condition—'

'I don't want your help, Zach.' Alex turned a hard look on him, disgusted to think she had ever considered him a friend. Worse, that she'd once allowed herself to be intimate with him. If Kade was dangerous because of the Breed blood that flowed in his veins, then Zach was a far more insidious threat for the way he was willing to use innocent people – to corrupt them and ruin lives – for the benefit of his own personal gain. 'How much money did you and Skeeter make together over the years? How little value do you place on the people you've been sworn to protect and serve, when you're willing to sell them out like you have?'

Zach glared. 'You don't know what you're saying, Alex. You're delusional.'

'Am I?'

'Yes, you are.' He stepped nearer. 'I'm concerned you are a danger to yourself.'

'You mean a danger to your livelihood, don't you?'

He chuckled, but there was no humor in it. 'As an officer of the law, I cannot in good conscience let you leave my custody like this, Alex. Now, step off the sled.'

She shook her head and gave the engine some gas. 'Fuck you.'

Before she could take off, Zach's hand went around her wrist. He jerked her arm tight, nearly unbalancing her. Alex glanced down in alarm to see that he had drawn his pistol from the holster belted around his waist.

She gasped in stunned terror, at the very same instant that Luna swiveled her big head around and clamped her jaws onto the arm that held Alex.

Zach hollered a pained cry. His bruising grasp fell away, and Alex, wrapping one arm around her beloved Luna to hold her steady in front of her on the sled, gave the snowmachine a thrust of power that sent it leaping into a fast escape.

She sped through the swirling curtain of snowfall, not daring to look back.

Not even when she heard Zach shout her name, followed by the buzzing whine of another snowmachine as he came after her.

The woman lay prone on the floor of the cabin, unmoving, except for the relaxed rise and fall of her breathing. She was tranced, unaware of the small incision he'd made in her nape a short while ago.

That careful incision now trickled a thin stream of blood as he crouched beside her and brought the edges of her delicate human skin together. He bent over her and licked away the coppery rivulet, then pressed his tongue against the wound and sealed the flesh closed.

His own body was mended, as well. The ultraviolet burns were cooled, his skin no longer festering with blisters and ripe with pain. The gunshot wounds in his thigh and abdomen were knitted tight with new, regenerated flesh. And the thirst that had been his fevered companion since his escape from captivity had, at last, subsided.

Now that his mind was clear, he had the opportunity to reflect, to consider what lay ahead of him.

More running. More hiding, struggling to stay one step ahead of the progeny that sought to either capture or destroy him. More of the same existence he had known since he and his brethren had taken their first step in this inhospitable human world.

He would survive.

But to what end?

While his instinct assured him he was far from defeated, his logic calculated that there was no way for him to ever win. There was no end in sight, only more of the same.

He and the other seven conquerors who crash-landed here so long ago should have been kings among the lesser, human life-forms that inhabited this planet. They might have been kings, if not for the uprising of their half-human sons. If not for the war that had left only him, his survival dependent on the treachery of the son who had secreted him away in a mountain cave.

He shouldn't have been surprised that treachery awaited him once he'd been awakened.

After his period of hibernation, he had expected the world to be different, laid out like a bounty for him to feast upon. Instead he'd been shackled and starved, weakened by chemicals and technology he'd imagined would have been far out of the grasp of the crude humanity that existed when he last knew it.

Earth had advanced. It was nothing remotely close to the world he had left behind, but enough so that life here for him would forever be a trial. An endless monotony of days and nights, pursuit and retreat.

He wasn't sure he had the will or the desire.

The woman lying before him was caught in a similar snare. He had witnessed her despair, and he had tasted her defeat in each pulse of her heartbeat as he had taken his nourishment from her. He tasted her loneliness, her hopelessness, and it plucked at something deep inside him.

She, too, was a warrior. He saw it in the few, scattered images in frames within her domicile. This woman in a human warrior's uniform, carrying weapons and a look of determination in her eyes. That look was not gone, even when she'd been weakened from blood loss and terrified. She was still strong, still a warrior in her heart, but she no longer saw it in herself.

She, too, was lost . . . alone.

But where she had been prepared to give up in those moments before he intruded on her plans, his advanced genetic makeup would permit no such surrender. He was born a conqueror, born for war. He was the ultimate predator. Whether he desired it or not, his body would resist death to its final gasp . . . no matter how long it took to get there.

And he was also driven to see his enemies defeated, by whatever means required.

It was that drive that compelled him to take the measure he had a few moments ago with this woman lying unconscious, and wholly unaware, on the floor of the cabin.

Now he moved back from her in grim consideration. Idly, he brought his left forearm up to his mouth and sealed the small cut he'd made there. His tongue swept over the faint indentation in the muscle beneath his skin as the wound closed up and vanished, as if the incision were never there.

As he got up and stalked to the other side of the room, he heard the approaching roar of gas-powered engines not far from the cabin.

Had they found him so soon?

Whether his pursuers were human or Breed, he couldn't be sure.

But as he tested the newly regenerated sinew and skin of his arms, he smiled grimly, satisfied that he was prepared to meet any incoming threat.

⊰ CHAPTER TWENTY-SEVEN ⊱

Alex flew as fast as she dared through the snow and wilderness on the way to Jenna's cabin. She could still hear Zach behind her, gaining on her. Cutting a hazardous path back and forth, praying she might lose him in the nearly blinding storm, she hoped that the gun he'd pulled on her in town had just been a momentary lapse of good sense on his part.

But she'd seen the dangerous gleam in his gaze. He was furious, and he was desperate to protect his secret. Probably most of all from Jenna. But would he be desperate enough to kill Alex in the process?

The knot of dread that was lodged in her throat said he would.

Alex's heart was beating like it wanted to leap out of her rib cage by the time she reached Jenna's property. She skidded into an abrupt halt and killed the engine. Luna jumped off with her and the pair of them started running for the cabin's front porch.

'Jenna!' she called. 'Jenna, it's me!'

Almost to the steps, Alex heard Zach's snowmachine grind to a halt behind her. 'Don't take another step, Alex.'

Oh, God.

'Jenna!' she cried. 'Are you there?'

There was no answer. No movement of any kind came from inside the cabin.

Behind her, the soft *click* of the pistol's hammer.

'Goddamn you, Alex.' Zach's voice sounded wooden, utterly devoid of emotion. 'Why are you making me do this?'

'Jenna,' she called again, quieter now, realizing the futility of it.

The cabin was silent. Jenna either would not, or could not, hear her. What if her earlier dread for Jenna's well-being was accurate? Alex hardly dared imagine it.

Nor would she even have the chance, because Zach was apparently out of his mind and Alex was likely about to die here and now.

Then, from within the stillness ahead of her, Alex heard the faintest sound – a small moan, barely audible even as close as she was to the door. Alex's heart gave a hopeful stutter.

'Jenna?' She braved the smallest step forward, one foot on the bottom step of the porch. 'If you can hear me, please open—'

The gunshot rang out like a cannon blast behind her. Alex felt the heated whisper of the bullet as it sang past her head and lodged into the wooden doorjamb not even three feet in front of her.

Oh, Jesus. Oh, holy Christ.
Zach had shot at her.

Alex's body froze with shock and a fear so deep and cold it left her shaking all over. She exhaled a shuddering breath and slowly pivoted her head, not about to let Zach shoot her in the back. If he was going to do it, then, by God, he was going to do it looking her in the eyes.

But no sooner had she turned than there was an explosion of movement behind her. Something huge blasted out of Jenna's cabin in a blur of speed, splintering the door right off its hinges. Zach screamed. His gun went off again, the bullet ripping audibly through the thick, snow-laden canopy of pine boughs overhead.

Alex grabbed Luna and hit the ground, her face buried in

the warm fur of the wolf dog's neck. She didn't know what just happened. For an instant, her mind struggled to process the guttural snarl and the sickening, wet sounds that followed.

Then she knew what it had to be.

Slowly she raised her head. The scream that crawled up to her lips died as her gaze locked onto a deadly creature that eclipsed anything she'd ever seen before.

The Ancient.

Through the steady fall of snowflakes in the darkness, his amber gaze burned laser bright, searingly savage. He was naked, hairless, covered from head to toe in *dermaglyphs* so dense and intertwining they all but concealed his nudity. His enormous fangs dripped with blood – Zach's blood, taken from the gaping hole that had once been his throat.

A terrible thought slammed into her: Had this monster also gotten to Jenna?

Alex closed her eyes, whispering a prayer for her friend and hoping desperately for some kind of miracle that might have spared her from the brutal savagery that had just befallen Zach.

Luna growled in Alex's arms and the creature cocked its head at an exaggerated angle, staring at the animal. He started to prowl away from Zach's lifeless body, a low growl ticking in the back of his alien throat.

Alex's lungs compressed, squeezing out what little air was in them. She thought for certain the Ancient was about to kill her, too, but its questioning stare lingered for an agonizing few seconds. Time during which the distant buzz of more snowmachines carried on the wind.

Alex sent a nervous glance toward the sound.

When she looked back again, the Ancient was gone, nothing but the sway of a few low-hanging branches at the edge of the forest to tell which direction he'd fled.

The knowledge of Alex's fear hit Kade like an anvil driven into his gut.

He and the other warriors were hauling ass on their snow-machines, nearly to Harmony when the feeling gripped him that they were moving farther away from Alex, not closer. He quickly redirected the group, leading the way along a game trail that rambled to the west of town.

Fresh sled tracks told him he was on the right path, but no more so than the homing strength of his blood bond to Alex, which pulsed more powerfully as his snowmachine chewed up the trail, heading toward a small log cabin up ahead in the dark a few hundred yards.

Kade's heart soared that he had reached her, only to crash an instant later when the copper stench of human blood tickled his nostrils. It wasn't hers – he'd know her honey-sweet blood-scent anywhere – but the idea that Alex was near any kind of death sent fear arrowing through his veins.

Kade goosed the throttle of his sled, but the damn thing was still too slow for his liking. He steered off the trail and ditched it, vaulting in a fluid leap before hitting the ground running, using every ounce of his Breed agility to reach her.

'Alex!' he shouted, speeding past the carnage in front of the cabin and glancing around only long enough to note the bru-talized corpse of Zach Tucker and the splintered ruins of what had been the cabin's front door. 'Ah, God . . . Alex!'

He ran inside and found her on folded knees beside her friend Jenna, who lay on the floor of the darkened cabin. Kade flicked on a lamp, not so much for himself as for the two women. Jenna seemed confused, her eyes drowsy, her voice groggy as though she were just coming to after having been unconscious.

'Alex,' Kade murmured gently, his voice breaking with emotion.

She turned to face him then, and slowly rose to her feet.

She took one hesitant step forward, and that was all he needed. Kade went to her and pulled her against him, wrapping her in his arms. He kissed the top of her head, so damned relieved to see that she was unharmed.

'Alex, I am so sorry. For everything.'

She drew back and glanced away from him. He could read the emotion in her eyes. The quiet uncertainty that said she wasn't sure she could trust him fully yet. It crushed him to see that doubt in her eyes. Even worse was knowing that he was the one who put it there.

She led him away from Jenna, who was still murmuring incoherently, in and out of wakefulness.

Alex's gaze held his with bleak calm. 'It was the Ancient, Kade. He was here.'

He swore, though he was unsurprised, given the condition of the body outside. 'You saw him? Did he touch you? Did he . . . ah, Jesus . . . did he do anything to you at all?'

She shook her head. 'He must have been hiding in Jenna's cabin when Zach and I arrived a few minutes ago. He exploded out the front door after Zach tried to shoot me—'

'What?' Kade's blood went from the icy chill of his fear to the boiling heat of rage. If Tucker wasn't already dead, Kade would have torn his lungs out. 'What the hell happened? Why did that son of a bitch want to hurt you?'

'Because I realized what he was up to. Zach and Skeeter were in business together, dealing drugs and selling alcohol to the dry Native settlements in the bush. I knew something was wrong when I saw Skeeter's cell phone and a lot of cash at Zach's house today. He tried to lie about it, but I knew.'

'He picked the wrong person for that, eh?'

Her smile was faint and fleeting. 'I don't want Jenna to see . . .' She gestured toward the front yard as her words trailed off. 'She'll have to know the truth, of course, but not like this.'

Kade nodded. 'Yeah, of course.'

As they spoke the rest of the warriors roared up to the cabin on their sleds. Kade went out to intercept them, informing them that the Ancient had been there just a short while ago and that the victim outside was the brother of Alex's friend.

Chase and Hunter fell in to perform a discreet cleanup, while Tegan and Brock walked with Kade back inside.

'This is Alex,' he said, making quick introductions to the two warriors. It was difficult not to touch her as he explained what had occurred before they arrived, just to reassure himself that she was whole and unharmed.

'Are you and your friend all right?' Tegan asked, the Gen One's voice deep with respect despite the fact that he'd come there to assess a situation that had gone from mildly screwed up to fucked up beyond all recognition.

'I'm okay,' Alex replied. 'But I'm worried about Jenna. I didn't see anything wrong with her, but she doesn't seem quite right to me, either.'

Tegan glanced at Brock, but the big warrior was already heading over to have a look at the woman across the room.

'What's he going to do to her?' Alex asked, worry creasing her brow.

'It's all right,' Kade said. 'If something is wrong, he can help her.'

Brock smoothed his hands over Jenna's back, then gently swept aside her hair and placed his dark fingers against the wan paleness of her cheek. 'She's been tranced,' he said. 'She's coming out of it, though. Gonna be fine.'

Chase and Hunter strode into the cabin and looked to Tegan. 'The yard is cleared. The two of us can start searching the area for the Ancient's trail.'

Tegan pursed his lips, blew out a sharp sigh. 'He's miles away from here by now. A needle in a haystack. We'll never catch him in this wilderness. It's not like we can track the son of a bitch across the whole damn interior in this blizzard.'

Kade felt Alex's gaze light on him. 'What about Luna? If you used your talent with her, would she be able to help us track the Ancient?'

Tegan eyed the wolf dog that had come over to nuzzle Kade's hand. 'It might be our best shot, man.'

'Yeah, I can do it,' he said, 'but what about the rest of you? Are we all going to run with her, fully loaded with weapons in case we catch up to the bastard?'

'I can fly you,' Alex suggested.

'No way.' Kade shook his head. 'No fucking way. I'm not going to put you any farther into this whole thing than I already have. That's a risk I'm not willing to take.'

'I want to do it. I'm not going to leave Luna, and I can carry all of you in my plane while she tracks the Ancient on the ground.'

'It's dark, Alex,' he bit off harshly. 'And it's snowing like a bitch.'

'I'm not seeing your point,' she countered. 'And the longer we stand here arguing about this, the farther that creature can run. That's a risk that *I'm* not willing to take.'

Tegan leveled a questioning look on Kade. 'She's right. You know she is.'

Kade slanted his gaze to Alex, seeing in her eyes all of the courage and determination that had made him fall in love with her in the first place. The fact was, the Order needed her right now. He was proud of Alex and petrified at the same time. But he exhaled a low curse and said, 'Yeah. Okay, let's do this.'

'What about the human?' Chase asked, gesturing toward Jenna. 'We'd better scrub her before she sees anything more than she already has.'

When the ex-Enforcement Agent started to walk toward her, Brock wheeled his head around, fangs gleaming behind his lips. 'Back off, Harvard. You don't touch her. Got it?'

Chase paused at once. He gave a negligent shrug and withdrew as Brock turned his attention back to the human female.

As the tension in the cabin subsided, Alex kneeled down beside Luna and wrapped the wolf dog in a loving hug, whispering something to her before she looked up at Kade. 'All right, she's in your hands. Promise me you'll be careful with her.'

'I promise,' he said, meaning it completely.

As Alex moved away, Kade took Luna's chin in his palm and met her intelligent gaze. He established his connection with the canine's mind, then gave her the silent command to show him where the Ancient fled.

Alex had her arms crossed over her chest, one hand pressed to her mouth, as Luna took off running from the cabin and into the swirling snowstorm outside.

CHAPTER TWENTY-EIGHT

Not long afterward, Alex was flying them over the dark wilderness landscape, with Kade in the copilot's seat and three of his Breed brethren huddled in the cargo area behind them. Kade called out directions to her, navigating their course through his mental link to Luna on the ground.

Alex couldn't see her. They were too far up, the snow too thick in the darkness, for her to make out anything much farther than the nose of the plane. These were dangerous conditions to fly in – potentially deadly – but Alex knew this terrain intimately. She followed Kade's directions, practically able to anticipate the path Luna was tracking along the Koyukuk, the most logical route the Ancient would have taken into the bush.

'Keep following the river,' Kade told her. 'The trail is getting fresher now. We're gaining on him.'

Alex nodded, focusing on her flying and the heavy gusts that blew down off the Brooks Range as they pushed farther north along the frozen river below. Although she could barely see the icy ribbon of water, she knew that they were coming up on a spot where the fleeing Ancient would have been forced to make a choice: stay low to the ground and trust the thickening woodlands to conceal him from pursuit, or veer to the west and take his flight to higher terrain, up into the craggy ridges of the mountains. Neither option would provide the best landing conditions, but in this weather, there was little more treacherous than attempting a short landing on high, potentially unstable rock.

'The trail is turning,' Kade announced. 'We need to bank left.'

'Okay,' Alex replied, sending up a silent prayer as she changed course away from the river and headed toward the mountain range instead. 'Hang on, everyone. There are going to be some bumps as we turn into the headwinds.'

'How you doing up there?' Tegan asked from behind her. 'You sure you can handle this?'

'Piece of cake,' she said – not quite the truth – and felt Kade's hand slide over to brush hers.

It felt good, the contact of his touch. Even though she still carried the chilling vision of what she'd seen in the woods, her stomach still coiled with ice from that experience and the even greater terror of having seen the Ancient at Jenna's cabin, Alex could not deny her feelings for Kade. He was the one person who knew her, better than any other now. Despite everything that had occurred between them and around them, her heart could not completely seal itself off from the comfort that only he could give her.

Some of the betrayal and anger she'd had for Kade and the rest of his kind had melted when she'd seen how he and his friends from the Order had handled the awful situation at the cabin. Kade had been tender and loving with Alex, respectful and considerate with Jenna. The other warriors had been, too. Especially the one called Brock, who had stayed behind to tend to Jenna.

It was difficult to reconcile a race of beings that could show so much humanity yet belong to the same ruthless, otherworldly line as the creature that had killed Zach and so many others in recent days. Or the blood-addicted Rogues who'd killed her mom and little brother. Or the twin Kade had been too ashamed to admit he had until Alex had seen Seth's savagery for herself.

But Kade and the other Breed males he'd introduced her to were different. They were good men, regardless of the genes that made them something other – something more – than men.

They had honor.

Kade did, too. And now, as she flew him and his brethren of the Order through a patch of gusty air, toward the jagged crag of the mountain and an imminent battle with a creature not of this world, she only hoped that she and Kade would have the chance to sort out the tangled mess of what they meant to each other. She could only pray there would be some kind of future waiting for them on the other side of the danger that lay ahead right now.

'Luna's tracking the Ancient's scent up the base of the mountain,' Kade said from beside her. 'Ah, shit . . . it's rough rock and it's damned steep. Son of a bitch is escaping up the ridge. We're gonna lose him on the mountain.'

'Just tell me where Luna's heading,' Alex said. 'I'll worry about getting us there.'

She flew the plane along the dark ridge, following Kade's directions, straining to see through the windscreen as the fine flakes of snow danced and rolled in her line of vision.

'Damn it,' he snarled a moment later. 'The scent is gone. It just went cold. Luna's circling around on the ledge below us, but she can't pick up the Ancient's scent anymore.'

'Because he leapt from that point,' Hunter remarked evenly. 'The Ancient is now either above the animal, or below her.'

'We're close enough to pursue him on foot,' Tegan said. 'The Ancient can't get far now without us right on his ass. But we need to set this plane down now.'

'Okay, here we go,' Alex said, and peered through her window, seeing limited options for anything more than the shortest of short landings.

She aimed the little plane toward a small patch of pristine snow on the rocky tableau, and began the descent.

Kade had seen Alex in action behind the controls of her plane before, but it didn't diminish his awe for her as she brought the small plane down onto a narrow, snowy ledge on the mountain. It wasn't until they had landed that Kade noticed she'd successfully touched them down into a gentle glide that left barely a few feet of room for error on any side.

None of the warriors uttered a word as the single-engine growled into idle and the plane came to a delicate rest on the ridge.

Not even Hunter, who sat stock-straight in the cargo hold, his face imperturbably calm, even though his knuckles looked a bit white for their grip on the netting above his head.

Finally, Chase muttered a ripe curse.

Tegan chuckled low under his breath. 'Hell of a landing, Alex.'

'Hell of a woman,' Kade said, looking across the cockpit at her and taking a personal pride in her that he probably had no right to feel. But her gaze was soft on him, although brief, and it gave him a surge of hope that maybe he hadn't lost her completely.

Maybe there was a chance for them yet.

As the group climbed out of the plane and suited up with weapons and ammunition, Luna came bounding up the sloping incline and straight into Alex's open arms. For a moment, Kade selfishly held onto his telepathic connection to the wolf dog, letting himself savor the warmth of Alex's love for the animal.

When he broke the link, Tegan was standing next to him, armed for war. 'We're going to split up: Hunter will take the incline, Chase and I will cover the ground below.'

Kade gave him a grim nod. 'Where do you want me?'

Tegan glanced over at Alex, who was talking in low, praising tones to Luna. 'Stay here and make sure your female is safe. That's more important than anything else you can do, yeah?'

Kade considered the comment, feeling duty spurring him to say that the mission was the most important thing right now. That nothing mattered more than his pledge to the Order, his brethren, and their goals. Part of him believed that. Part of him knew without the shadow of a doubt that he would give his life for any one of the warriors, just as they would lay down their lives for him. They were family, as tight as any bond he'd ever known.

But Alex was something even more.

She owned his heart now. He wouldn't even attempt to deny that. And he knew that when Tegan spoke about her, the mated Gen One warrior drew from a point of personal experience, as well.

'Yeah,' Kade admitted to him. 'Without Alex . . . ah, Christ. Without her, nothing else would matter.'

Tegan nodded, mouth pressed in a thin line. 'Maybe you ought to make sure she knows that.'

He cuffed Kade on the shoulder, then gestured to the other warriors to fall in and begin the next leg of their pursuit. When Hunter had vaulted up to the next ledge and Tegan and Chase had dropped to the one below, Kade strode over to Alex.

'I guess the three of us make a pretty good team,' he said, reaching out to scratch behind Luna's ears only because it distracted his hands from reaching for Alex instead.

She wrapped her arms around herself. 'You're not going with the others?'

'Tegan wanted me to stay behind and look after you. He knows how much you mean to me, and he knows it would kill me if anything happened to you.'

A small line formed between her brows as she looked at him. For the longest time, there was only silence between them.

The quiet of falling snow and the faint cry of a wolf baying low in the distance.

When Alex finally spoke, her voice was barely above a whisper. 'I wanted to hate you. When I saw you in the woods, covered in blood—'

'Not me,' he reminded her. 'It wasn't me, Alex. It was Seth, not me.'

She nodded. 'I know that. I believe you. But it was you I saw in that moment. It was you, Kade, seeming just as monstrous as the Rogues who killed my mom and Richie. I wanted to hate you in that moment . . . but I couldn't. Part of me refused to let go of you, even then, when you couldn't have seemed more hideous and evil to me. I still loved you.'

He exhaled a relieved sigh and pulled her into his arms. 'Alex . . . I'm so sorry for what you thought. For what you saw. I'm sorry for everything.'

'That's what scared me the most, Kade. That I could love you even if you were a killer. Even if you were a monster, like . . .'

'Like my brother,' he answered softly. 'I'm not him. I promise you that. You never have to be afraid of me. I love you, Alexandra. I always will.'

Gingerly he took her beautiful face in his hands and kissed her. She felt so good in his arms, against his lips, he could have kissed her forever.

But behind them, Luna's throaty growl put Kade's combat instincts on high alert.

He felt the slightest shift in the air as he drew away from Alex and moved her behind him on reflex –

Just as a large, dark shape dropped out of the sky.

Several yards away from them, the Ancient landed with fluid grace on his feet in the snow. Baring his teeth and enormous fangs, the deadly creature fixed his amber gaze on Kade and hissed with murderous intent.

❧ CHAPTER TWENTY-NINE ❧

Alex screamed.

Terror clenched her as the Ancient's *glyph*-covered legs contracted into a low crouch, amber eyes bathing Kade in awful light.

'Alex, get out of here.'

She swallowed on a throat gone bone dry. 'W-what?'

'Go!' Kade ordered her, his eyes rooted on the threat in front of him. 'Get back in the plane, take off. Get as far away from this rock as you can. Go now!'

Fear poured through her veins, but her legs refused to move. She couldn't abandon Kade like this, no matter what he said. No matter what he faced. They would face it together. 'I'm not leaving. I won't—'

'Damn it, Alex, go!' he snarled, reaching for one of the big semi-automatic pistols holstered under his parka.

He moved with a speed she could hardly follow. One second his hand was slipping into his unzipped coat, the next he was holding the gun in front of him, squeezing off a hail of several rounds.

But the Ancient was faster, even than Kade.

He dodged the gunfire, and then his powerful legs pushed off the ground in a lunge that would have sent him crashing into Kade – should have, if not for the sudden blur of movement that was Hunter. The immense Gen One warrior careened into the Ancient from the ledge above, tumbling them both to the snowy ground in a confusion of tossing, rolling chaos.

They struggled together, nearly an even match in terms of strength and power, both of them fighting as though prepared to battle to the death.

Kade moved into the fray just as Hunter took a severe swipe to the base of his neck and shoulder. Blood spurted from his wound, which only seemed to make the Ancient grow more frenzied, its eyes wilder now, fangs elongating further. It reared its great head back and opened its jaws on a furious howl.

Kade fired a shot, and instead of the Ancient striking again at Hunter, he had to spend precious effort dodging Kade's bullet.

Alex blinked, which was all the time it took for the Ancient to have his fingers wrapped around Kade's pistol. Metal crushed in his fist, then, using a power she could hardly fathom, the otherworlder flung Kade bodily through the air. He landed at the sheer edge of the cliff, his head split open on the rock, bleeding above the temple.

'Kade!' Alex cried, heart freezing to ice.

He tried to get up, but it was a clumsy, disoriented attempt. He slumped back down with a groan.

One misstep and he would be lost.

'Kade! Oh, God – don't move!'

Snow swirled all around, the storm having worsened to near blizzard conditions since they'd landed. She could just make out Hunter's large shape as he came up off the ground to lunge at the Ancient again. On a vicious hiss, the creature wheeled around and thrust the big Gen One away from him.

Then the Ancient began to prowl toward Kade at the edge of the cliff's steep drop.

Alex's heart wanted to explode out of her breast as she inched her way nearer and nearer to her plane. She wasn't about to run, not even now. She was scared as hell, more than she'd ever been in her life, but she had to do something – for Kade, and for his brethren – no matter how insignificant her actions might prove to be against this threat.

She grabbed the loaded rifle she kept in the back of the plane.

Raised it as the Ancient stalked closer to where Kade was now trying to drag himself up once more. She couldn't let the creature reach him.

Alex pulled the trigger.

The gunshot cracked like thunder in the snow-tossed darkness.

The Ancient hadn't seen it coming. His large hand was pressed to his chest, but blood seeped through his fingers.

The otherworlder curled his lip back and snarled. Then he started prowling forward again . . . no longer toward Kade, but toward her and Luna near the plane.

Alex heard the howl of wolves from somewhere close. So many voices. At least half a dozen or more. She heard them, and could almost hear the beat of their paws rising up through the bitter cold of the storm and the chilling terror of the situation playing out on the ledge.

Alex knew the wolves were near, but she hadn't been at all prepared for the sight of them, suddenly rushing up from the craggy slopes below. The pack charged en masse, leaping in tandem at the same target: the alien creature who roared with outrage as the eight predators attacked.

And as the wolves bit and tore and jumped at the Ancient, another adversary came over the ridge from below.

Seth.

Alex's breath caught as the Breed male who looked so much like Kade emerged out of the shadows and the swirling chaos of the storm. He didn't seem so much identical to Kade now as he did a mirror image – reversed somehow, as though he were the wilder, more dangerous half of the Breed male she loved.

Seth's huge fangs gleamed as white as bone. His eyes threw off a feral amber light that seared like lasers. Alex swallowed as he gave her a brief, sidelong glance. She thought she saw an apology written in the stark expression on his face. Perhaps some measure of remorse.

But then, with a battle cry that made her blood run cold, he surged into a powerful leap and threw himself onto the Ancient.

They were too close to the edge of the cliff.

The forward momentum was too great to be stopped.

Alex's eyes flew wide when she realized what was about to happen. She squeezed them shut an instant later, as Seth and the Ancient careened over the ledge together.

'Seth!'

Kade shouted his brother's name, the cotton in his head from the blow he took having cleared instantly when he saw Seth locked in battle with the Ancient. Horror choked him not a second later, as they sailed past him at the cliff's edge and plummeted into the darkness.

There was a great rumbling that seemed to come from all around him, like the roll of thunder, only he felt it in the ground beneath him. Above him, too.

Then, the violent crack of ice and hard-packed snow giving way from the rocky crag overhead.

The avalanche roared off the cliff, tons of crushing snow and ice, sweeping like a tidal wave past Kade's head and down, into the mountain's steep cleft below. A blinding, choking cloud of fine, powdery crystals rose up in its wake, chilling Kade's face and forcing him to look away from the snow-filled crevasse where the Ancient and his brother had fallen. Nothing could survive the suffocating weight of that much snow.

Kade felt soft hands coming around his shoulders, the warmth of Alex's body catching him in her embrace, holding him close. And behind them on the ledge, he heard the low sounds of voices. Hunter, Tegan, and Chase, a hush of murmured disbelief for everything that had just occurred.

'Kade,' Alex whispered, her tone quiet and comforting. 'Oh, God . . . Kade.'

All he wanted was to wrap his arms around her and accept the love she offered him now, but his heart cried out for his twin. The thought of losing his brother raked him; Seth's sacrifice was too difficult to process. Too terrible to be real.

Kade extracted himself from Alex's sheltering arms and scrabbled to the sheer edge of the cliff.

'Seth!' he yelled into the rocky void, straining to find even the slimmest thread of hope that his brother might not be dead.

And then . . . a dark, broken form, lying on a jagged outcrop about a hundred feet down. Moving only slightly, but alive.

Hope soared in Kade's chest.

'Jesus Christ. It's him.' He got to his feet. 'Seth, hang on!'

Alex gasped. 'Kade, what are you doing? Kade, don't—'

He stepped off the edge.

Alex's scream followed him as he dropped at a calculated leap, down into the cleft of rock. His booted feet came to a rest beside his brother. Kade crouched and swept the ice and snow away from Seth's battered face and body.

'Goddamn you, Seth.' His voice cracked with a mix of relief and pain as he took in the extensive injuries that his brother had sustained in both the fight with the Ancient and the fall. Seth bled from multiple contusions on his head and limbs, but it was the vicious gash in his torso that concerned Kade the most.

Regenerating from that kind of damage would be a challenge for the fittest Breed male, but for one in Seth's gaunt, emaciated condition? Shit. It didn't look good for him at all.

Seth's eyes were closed, his body limp and broken. He was barely breathing, except for the thin rasp of air that wheezed out of his lungs when he parted his lips and tried to speak to Kade.

'G-go,' he huffed out after a moment. 'You can't . . . can't save me, brother.'

Kade exhaled a sharp curse. 'Like hell I can't. I'm going to get you out of here.'

'No. Leave me . . . I am dying. Already dead. You and I both know it.'

'Not like this, brother,' Kade ground out. 'You will heal. I'll take you home to Father's Darkhaven, and you will recover from all of this.'

'No,' Seth murmured quietly. His eyes peeled open slowly on his pained hiss. 'No, Kade. I won't.'

The sight of his twin's gaze almost made him glance away. The pupils were needle-thin, vertical slits bathed in bright amber. Seth's gaze was hot with anguish, a feral gaze. His fangs were still extended. The *glyphs* that were visible through large rips in his clothing were dark and pulsing with color, as though he starved for blood.

All the signs were there, but it killed Kade to recognize them. From the time he'd last seen him, his brother had succumbed to Bloodlust.

Seth was Rogue.

'There's no going back for me now,' Seth murmured. 'You tried to warn me . . .'

'Ah, fuck,' Kade whispered. 'Ah, damn it, Seth. No. No, this can't be.'

Seth sucked in a short gasp and a violent cough racked him. His body shuddered. His skin seemed to grow paler before Kade's eyes. 'Let me go, brother. Please.'

Kade shook his head. 'I can't. You know that. I wouldn't have given up on you, not before . . . not now. You saved my life up there, Seth. Now, goddamn it, I'm gonna save yours.'

He turned his head and shouted up the cliff to Tegan and the others above. 'I need some ropes. My brother's wounded. He can't make it up his own. I'm going to need a harness to lift him back to the top.'

The warriors peered down at them, then vanished to carry out Kade's request. Then Alex's face appeared in their place, just the sight of her a haven to him, giving him a feeling of pure, honest love – something he'd needed more than anything in that moment.

Seth's cracked, bloodied lips parted in a weak smile. 'You're in love,' he said, something wistful in his wheezing voice.

'Yeah,' Kade replied. 'Her name is Alexandra. I'm going to make her my mate, if she'll have me.'

Seth closed his eyes, gave a weak nod. 'I would have liked to have met her.'

'You will.' Kade stared down at him, seeing a stillness washing over his broken body. 'You have to hang on, Seth. Come on . . . open your eyes. Keep breathing, damn you!'

But Seth's eyes remained closed.

He breathed, but only one final time. His chest compressed with his last exhalation, and then he was gone.

Seth's pain was over.

Kade gathered his twin's ravaged body into his arms. He sat with him on the frozen ledge and gently rocked him, praying that Seth had finally found peace.

➤ CHAPTER THIRTY ➤

No one said a word as the warriors helped Kade lift Seth up from the ledge. They worked soberly, handling the lifeless body like precious cargo even though it had to be obvious, even in death, that Kade's twin was Rogue.

Seth's *dermaglyphs* were still dark with angry color, his fangs still protruding behind his slack lips. Although his eyes were closed, beneath the lids, his pupils would still be elongated, his irises still swamped with furious amber.

All marks of the Bloodlust that had owned him and that declared him an enemy to every law-abiding member of the Breed. All the more so to the warriors of the Order, who were sworn to rid the population of all killers in their midst.

Yet despite that, Tegan and Chase lay Seth down with reverent care on the snow-covered ground before Kade, while Hunter went to the edge of the crevasse and surveyed the deep chasm far below. He turned a level look on Tegan and gave a mild shake of his head. 'I can find no sign of life whatsoever down there. The Ancient is surely dead.'

Tegan nodded. 'Good. Even if the fall didn't kill him, a few thousand tons of snow and ice will certainly finish the job.'

Just then, Alex walked back from the plane with a folded blanket in her hands. She had tears in her eyes as she glanced at Kade, then began to gently shake out the shroud that would cover Seth's bloodied, broken corpse.

Kade held up his hand. 'Wait. I need to see him like this.

I need all of you to see him, and to know that this could have just as easily been me.' He glanced at the grim faces of his brethren from the Order, from Hunter's impassive golden eyes, to Chase's narrowed scowl, and then to Tegan's steady, unreadable regard. Finally, Kade looked at Alex, the person whose opinion mattered more than any other. 'Seth – my twin – was a killer. I've known it for a long time, but I didn't want to admit it. Not even to myself. What I really didn't want to admit was that he and I were not so different.'

'He was Rogue,' Tegan said. 'There is a difference.'

'Yes.' Kade lifted his shoulder in acknowledgment. 'But it took many years for him to fall. And during those years, he hunted like an animal. He killed in cold blood. Seth was sick with a wildness that he couldn't curb. I knew he was, because the wildness lives in me, too.'

Kade saw Alex swallow hard, saw her hold the blanket to her as if she suddenly needed its warmth. He felt the little spike in her pulse as she stared at him in wary silence. Through his bond to her, he could feel her fear as if it were his own.

He hated like hell knowing that he was causing it, and the urge to soothe her worries with a comforting lie was nearly overwhelming. But he was through with secrets. He couldn't hide anymore, or pretend he was something stronger than what he was, even at the risk of losing Alex here and now.

She had to know the truth, and so did the group of Breed males standing before him.

'From the time Seth and I were boys, we let our talent rule us. It was hard to resist the freedom it offered, and the power. It was heady stuff back then – to command other deadly predators, to run alongside them. To hunt with them. Sometimes, to experience the precision of a kill as seen through their eyes. And once the wildness had called to us, it only got harder to rein it in. At times, it still is.'

Although Alex didn't so much as blink, Kade felt the twist

of her stomach as she listened to him. She was repulsed, not by Seth this time, or by some misunderstanding that Kade could smooth away with charm or well-meaning promises. She was seeing the truth now, at last, and as terrible as it felt to know that he was pushing her away with his honesty, he couldn't stop until she knew it all.

'Too much power is never a good thing,' Chase interjected into the long silence, the ex-Enforcement Agent's voice deep with reflection. 'It corrupts even the strongest.'

'Yeah, it does,' Kade agreed. 'It corrupted Seth early on. I don't know when he first started killing humans. It doesn't really matter now. Eventually, I found out, and I should have stopped him then and there, but I didn't. Instead I left Alaska. I got the call from Niko that the Order was looking for new recruits, and I couldn't get out of here fast enough. To save myself from turning into what Seth had become, I ran to Boston and left him to fend for himself.'

Tegan eyed him gravely. 'That was just last year. Seth was no child then. How long would you have considered him your responsibility?'

'He was my brother,' Kade said, casting a pained look at the corpse of the Rogue that had once been his mirror image. 'Seth was a part of me, almost an extension of who I was. I knew he was sick. I should have stayed here to keep him in line. And if he didn't quit the killing, or if it turned out he couldn't, then I should have made sure he was stopped for good.'

Tegan's green eyes narrowed. 'It's no easy thing, to kill a brother, no matter what he's done. Ask Lucan, he'll tell you.'

'Is it any easier to break a father's heart?' Kade scoffed, a bitter sound that grated in his throat. 'My father would have expected this of me, not Seth. All his hope and attention has always been pinned on Seth. He'll be devastated to see him like this. Just as he would have been if I'd exposed Seth's secret instead of protecting it all this time.'

Tegan grunted. 'The truth only gets uglier the longer you try to hold it down.'

'Yeah. I know that now.' Kade's gaze strayed to Alex, but she had turned away from him. Handing the blanket over to Chase, she strode back to her plane in silence with Luna trotting at her heels. Kade cleared his throat. 'I need to take my brother home to his family. That's where he belongs. But first I want to make sure Alex is all right. Her friend Jenna, too.'

'There's also the added problem of one dead trooper back in town,' Chase put in.

Kade nodded. 'Not to mention several more people on ice after the attacks by the Ancient, and a unit of Staties currently on the way in from Fairbanks to look into those recent killings in the bush.'

'Shit,' Tegan said. He gestured to Chase to cover Seth's body. 'You and Hunter bring him to the plane. And be careful, yeah? Rogue or not, Kade's brother saved his life today. What Seth did more than likely saved all our asses up here.'

The two warriors nodded in agreement as they carried Seth away. When Kade took a step to follow them, Tegan held him back with a meaningful look.

'Hey,' he said, his voice pitched only for Kade's ears. 'I know something about what you're dealing with, so you're not alone. A long time ago, I gave in to a similar wildness, only my drug of choice back then was rage. It nearly killed me. It would have, if Lucan hadn't pulled me out of it. Now it's Elise who keeps me grounded. But it's always there. The beast never fully goes away, but I'm here to tell you that it can be mastered.'

Kade listened, recalling what he'd heard of Tegan's own struggles, both in the Order's earliest days in Europe centuries ago, and the more recent events that had brought Tegan and his Breedmate Elise together in the past year.

'I'm not gonna say I'm happy to hear all of this today,' the

Gen One said, 'but I respect that you trusted us enough to put it out there.'

Kade gave him a short nod. 'I owed it to you.'

'Damn straight you did,' Tegan replied. 'You need to remember one thing, my man. You lost a brother in Alaska today, but you're always gonna have family in Boston.'

Kade held the intense gem-green stare. 'Yeah?'

'Yeah,' Tegan confirmed, his broad mouth breaking into a brief smile. 'Now let's get the fuck off this frozen rock and go take care of business.'

Alex could not pretend that hearing Kade's admission hadn't frightened her. Seeing his brother – the twin who looked so much like him – transformed into the same kind of monster that had killed her mother and Richie only made things worse.

Could Kade one day turn into a monster, too? He certainly believed he could, and the worry put an ache in Alex's chest, not so much out of fear for herself but out of concern for Kade.

She didn't want to see him in pain. She didn't want to lose him to the disease – or to the addictive wildness – that had claimed Seth.

With the exception of Jenna, whom she could only pray would be all right, Alex had already lost everyone she loved. Now Kade could be next. He feared the seductive nature of his talent. Seeing what it had done to Seth, Alex feared it, too. She wasn't sure she could handle letting herself fall any deeper in love with Kade, only to lose him later to something she could never compete with and hope to win.

But the problem was, she did love him.

It was the depth of that love that terrified her the most as she flew him and the other warriors back to Harmony. She couldn't dismiss the knowledge that Kade's Rogue brother lay dead and shrouded in the cargo hold, a grim warning of the future that might await Kade one day.

Losing her loved ones to Rogues had been difficult enough. Losing Kade to the same vicious enemy that had robbed her of her family was a prospect too terrible to consider.

Alex dragged her thoughts away from those dark worries and searched for a place to land near Jenna's cabin outside town. They had decided on the way to avoid using Harmony's airstrip when it would risk drawing more undue attention from the upset residents. Instead, Alex brought the plane down in a small clearing not far from Jenna's property.

'The trail to the cabin is just through those trees,' she told Kade and the others as she brought them to a stop and killed the engine.

Kade turned to look at her from the passenger seat, the first time he had done so since they'd left the mountain to head back into Harmony. His eyes flicked down for a moment as he cleared his throat. 'After we sort things out here in town, I'd like to return Seth to my family's Darkhaven near Fairbanks. I know it's a lot to ask of you. Too much, probably, especially after—'

'It's not too much to ask,' Alex replied. 'Of course, Kade. I'll take you there whenever you're ready.'

His expression was sober, contrite. 'Thank you.'

She nodded, feeling a bit sorry herself for the way he seemed to be pulling back from her with his silence, and his carefulness when he did speak to her. Or maybe it wasn't so much that she felt him pulling back but, rather, pushing her away.

Alex climbed out of the plane with him and the other three Breed males, leaving Luna to stand watch over Seth's body while the rest of them went to check on Jenna and Brock.

As soon as her friend's cabin came into view with the door smashed open and Zach's blood still visible beneath the freshly fallen snow, the reality of what had occurred there rose up on Alex in a swell of emotion.

'Oh, my God,' she gasped, breaking into a run as they drew closer. 'Jenna!'

Brock appeared in the open doorway, his huge Breed body blocking the entrance as Alex dashed up the steps of the porch. 'She's doing fine. Confused and not exactly coherent yet, but she's unharmed. She's going to be okay. I put her in the bedroom so she could rest more comfortably.'

Alex couldn't help herself from throwing her arms around the big male's shoulders in a grateful hug. 'Thank you for taking care of her, Brock.'

He nodded solemnly, his dark brown eyes warm with a kindness that seemed incongruous with the warrior's immense, lethal appearance. 'What happened?' he asked as Alex moved past him into the cabin and Kade and the other warriors came in behind her. 'Did you find the Ancient?'

'Long story,' Tegan said. 'We'll fill you in later, but suffice to say the Ancient is dead. Unfortunately, not without casualties on our side. Kade lost his brother in the battle.'

'What?' Brock's expression fell as he put a comforting hand on Kade's shoulder. 'Ah, Jesus. Whatever happened, I'm sorry.'

Alex was moved by the true emotion – the tight bond – shared between Kade and Brock, between all of the warriors gathered in the small space of the cabin. It humbled her to see such strong men – men who were, at their core, something far more extraordinary than that, in fact – looking out for one another like family.

Feeling something of an outsider in that moment, Alex drifted into the bedroom where Jenna lay curled up on the bed where Brock had placed her.

Jenna stirred as Alex sat down gently on the edge of the mattress. 'Hey,' she murmured, her voice groggy, barely above a whisper. Her eyelids lifted the smallest fraction.

'Hey.' Alex smiled and swept a bit of hair from Jenna's pale cheek. 'How are you feeling, honey?'

Jenna murmured something indecipherable as her eyes fluttered closed once more.

'She's been in and out of consciousness since you guys left.'

Alex turned her head and found Brock standing behind her. Kade and the other warriors came into the bedroom, as well, all of them looking on Jenna with quiet concern.

'She's still weak from blood loss,' Brock said. 'The Ancient must have been with her long enough to feed from her. She's luckier than most. At least she's still alive.'

Alex closed her eyes at that, regret for Jenna's ordeal squeezing some of the air out of her lungs.

'I put her in a light trance to calm her,' Brock added, 'but something's not quite right. The trance isn't keeping her down completely, which is particularly odd, considering she's human.'

'Not a Breedmate?' Tegan asked.

Brock shook his head. 'Just your basic *Homo sapiens* from what I can see.'

Tegan grunted. 'I guess that's good news, at least. What's going on with her?'

'Damned if I know. She's not in any pain, but she keeps drifting awake, mumbling a lot of nonsense. Not even words, just a strange, incoherent rambling.'

Alex glanced back down at her friend and caressed her softly. 'Poor Jenna. She's been through so much. She didn't deserve this on top of everything else she's endured. I wish I could just snap my fingers and erase everything that happened here today.'

'That can be arranged, actually,' Tegan said. When Alex pivoted a startled, questioning look on him, he went on. 'We can scrub her memory of all of this. It's painless, and it's fast. She won't even know we were here. We can make it so that she remembers nothing of the past day, or two, a week . . . longer than that, if necessary.'

'You can do that?'

Tegan shrugged. 'Comes in handy from time to time.'

Alex looked at Kade. 'What about me? Can you erase my memory of all this, too?'

Kade held her gaze for what seemed an endless moment. 'Is that what you want?'

There was a time when Alex would have jumped at the chance to toss away all of the awful memories that had plagued her. To be able to blink her eyes and recall none of the loss or grief, none of the fear.

There was a time, not that long ago, in fact, when she would have given anything to forget all of it.

Not anymore.

Her past was part of who she was now. The things she witnessed, terrible as they had been, had shaped her life. She couldn't willingly discard her memories of her mother and Richie, not even the memories of the night they were killed. To do that would be just another form of running away, of hiding from the things she didn't feel strong enough to face.

She didn't want to be that person anymore.

She couldn't go back to living that way, never again.

Before she could say as much, Jenna began to toss on the bed. She flexed and contracted her limbs, her face pinched in a frown, breath huffing through her parted lips. She murmured something unintelligible, then her movements became more agitated.

Brock moved up beside Alex and placed his big hand on Jenna's back with the utmost tenderness. He closed his eyes, concentrating as he caressed her, and some of Jenna's distress seemed to ease under his touch.

'Brock,' Tegan said, giving a faint shake of his head. 'Don't trance her just yet. I need to hear what she's saying.'

The warrior nodded but kept his hand on Jenna's back, still stroking her with a light motion. She relaxed on the bed, but her lips kept moving, whispering more of the peculiar ramblings as she drifted into a calmer state.

Tegan listened for a moment, his face growing more grave with every strange syllable that spilled out of Jenna's mouth. 'Holy shit. We can't scrub this female's mind of anything. And we can't risk trancing her any more, either.'

'What's going on?' Alex asked, worried by the stunned look on the warrior's normally impassive face. 'Is something wrong with Jenna after all?'

'We won't know that until we get her back to Boston.'

Alex stood up, alarmed now. 'What are you talking about? Take Jenna to Boston? You can't make that decision for her. She has a life here in Harmony—'

'Not anymore,' Tegan said, his voice brooking no argument. 'When we leave here, the woman will be coming with us.'

Kade moved over to stand beside Alex. 'What is it, Tegan?'

The elder Breed male tilted his head in Jenna's direction, where she continued to murmur softly under Brock's gentling hand. 'Alex's human friend is not incoherent. She's speaking in another language. The Ancient's language.'

❧ CHAPTER THIRTY-ONE ❧

It took a while for the aftershock to wear off, following the bomb Tegan had dropped about Jenna. While Kade and his fellow warriors had connected via satellite phone with the Order's headquarters to brief Lucan on the various developments and potential disasters in Alaska, Alex had remained in Jenna's bedroom with her friend the entire time.

She was worried about Jenna; Kade knew that.

Alex had tried to argue with Tegan and him that it wasn't fair to yank Jenna out of her world in Harmony and carry her off to Boston as if Jenna had no say in the matter whatsoever. But Tegan would not be swayed, nor would Lucan, once the Order's leader had been informed of the stunning revelation concerning Jenna Tucker-Darrow and the fact that the human female was suddenly speaking a language that hadn't originated on this planet nor been heard here for several centuries at that.

A language that was recognizable only to the few, very oldest of the Breed, and one the Order hoped might somehow prove useful in their efforts against their enemy, Dragos.

Alex had been reluctant to leave Jenna alone with Kade's brethren when the time came for her and Kade to leave for his family's Darkhaven. Tegan had given his word that Jenna would be safe with them, but Kade noticed it was Brock's personal reassurance that finally eased some of the worry from Alex's eyes.

'He'll take good care of her until we get back,' Kade said
now, seated beside Alex in the cockpit of her plane as they
passed over the lights of Fairbanks a few thousand feet below.
Alex had also entrusted Luna to the warrior, having sent the
wolf dog back to Jenna's cabin before she and Kade departed.
'You don't need to worry, Alex. I've fought beside Brock for
the past year, trusting him to watch my back as I've watched
his. When he gives his word, you can count on him to keep
it. Jenna couldn't be in better hands.'

Which was more than he could say for Alex, Kade thought
grimly. If he hadn't needed the plane to transport Seth's body
to his family's domain, he would have insisted that Alex stay
behind in Brock's care, too. The reception that awaited him
at his father's Darkhaven would not be pleasant – he knew
that. The last thing he wanted was for Alex to witness his
shame, or to see the pain his return was sure to cause in his
kin when he brought Seth's corpse back to them.

That was a path he wished he could walk alone, but there
was a small part of him that was grateful for her company
beside him. Selfishly, he took a measure of comfort just in her
presence at his side.

Alex glanced over at him in his silence. 'What about the
rest of the people in Harmony? I heard Tegan say on the
phone that he and Chase and Hunter were going to contain
the situation while we're taking care of Seth. What exactly
does 'contain the situation' mean? They won't . . . hurt anyone
in town, will they?'

'No. No one will be hurt,' Kade said, having been part of
the discussion with Lucan and the others as they'd strategized
the mission's final steps in Alaska. 'You know how you said
you wished there was a way to erase Jenna's memories of the
Ancient and what she might have been through with him?'

Alex shot him an incredulous look as understanding dawned
on her. 'You mean the whole town? There are nearly a

hundred people in Harmony. What are Tegan and the others going to do, walk down every street, knocking door to door?'

Kade smiled despite the gravity of the situation, including the chasm of unresolved issues that still gaped between Alex and him. 'I'm sure they'll find a way to get the job done. Tegan is nothing if not efficient.'

Kade glanced out the window as the dark landscape below the plane changed from the uniform terrain of city with its plowed streets and snow-covered rooftops, to the rugged, far-reaching wilderness of the bush. 'My father's ten thousand acres begin just at that ridge ahead. There's a clearing where we can land on the other side of those tall spruce to the north. The Darkhaven compound is within an easy walk of the clearing.'

Alex gave a nod of acknowledgment as she guided the plane to the ground where he had indicated.

Once they had landed, Kade went back to the cargo hold and retrieved Seth's bloodied, blanket-wrapped body. He carried the lifeless bulk in a careful grasp, Seth's weight a precious burden he would never know again. As much as he intended to bring his brother home alone, as was his duty, he had to admit Alex's presence as he made the trek to the Darkhaven compound lent a comfort he hadn't expected he would need.

She walked beside him in sober purpose, into the snowy yard of the main residence. It had to be late morning by now, probably only a couple of hours before the noon daybreak. Most of the Breed population of this small community would be inside their private quarters, sleeping perhaps, some of them making love.

Kade paused in front of the large house where his mother and father lived, reflecting that in just a few minutes, he would shatter their lives with grief and pain. The very things he had sought to protect them from in keeping Seth's secret for so long.

'Are you okay?' Alex hesitated beside him. She put her hand

on his shoulder, a tender, warm touch that gave him more strength than she could have possibly known.

He needed that strength in the moment that followed.

From within the Darkhaven came the sound of footsteps traveling swiftly over the wood-plank floors. His mother's voice called from somewhere inside. 'Kir? Kir, what is it? Where are you going?'

Kade's father did not answer.

The doors of the main residence burst open with the force of the elder Breed male's emotions alone. He stalked over the threshold like a tempest, clearly roused from his bed and having paused only long enough to tug on a pair of loose flannel lounging pants before he flew outside to face the news no parent wanted to hear.

Alex gasped at the sight of him, though her shock came as no surprise to Kir's surviving son.

Six and a half feet of muscled fury, *dermaglyphs* seething with the dark hues of anger and alarm, stood frozen on the porch of the large log residence. Gray eyes burned with amber, flicking questioningly over Alex before landing on Kade in searing judgment.

'Tell me what has happened to my son.'

Kade had never heard his father's voice shake, not even at Kir's worst. The tremor in that deep baritone now was like a knife to Kade's gut.

'Father . . . I am sorry.'

Kir thundered down the steps and into the snow. He stopped in front of Kade and Alex, reached out with a shaking hand to lift the blanket that covered Seth's face.

'Ah, Christ. No.' The words choked in the back of his throat, raw with anguish. He looked once more, longer now, as though forcing himself to take full measure of the Rogue's face that had been hidden beneath the shroud. 'I prayed this wouldn't happen again. Goddamn it, not to one of my sons.'

'Kir!' Kade glanced up as his pregnant mother strayed out to the porch, her silk nightgown engulfed by the large parka she'd apparently grabbed and thrown on inside the house. Her steps faltered as she saw Kade standing there in the snow, his arms filled with an unmistakable bulk. 'Oh, my God. Oh, no. Oh, dear lord, no! Please tell me that's not—'

'Stay back,' Kade's father barked. Then he gentled his voice to a heartbreaking softness. 'Victoria, I beg you . . . don't come any closer. Please, my love, go back inside. Do as I say. You don't need to see this.'

With a sob, she inched back toward the door, aided by Maksim, who'd just come outside in that moment, as well. Max took her arm to steady her as he brought his brother's mate back into the Darkhaven.

'Give him to me,' Kade's father said once the doors had closed and both Max and Victoria were back inside. 'Let me have my dead son.'

Kade released Seth to him, and watched as his father carried the body, barefoot through the ankle-deep snow, toward the Darkhaven's chapel that stood near the center of the compound. There, as was custom, Seth's corpse would be prepared for the funeral rites to be carried out at the next sunrise.

Kade felt Alex's arms come around him in a warm embrace, but it did little to ease the cold regret that gnawed at him like a vulture on carrion.

In just a couple more hours, nothing but a pile of sun-scorched ash would remain of his brother – or of Kade's place among his kin.

Back in Harmony, the warriors were hauling ass to clean up the situation with the locals, which had begun some time ago with the task of disappearing several dead bodies from cold storage at the airstrip and at the town's tiny clinic.

'One nice thing about all this snow and wilderness out here

is there's a lot of goddamn snow and wilderness out here,'
Tegan remarked dryly as Chase and Hunter met up with him
at their waiting snowmachines on a game trail several long
miles into the bush.

They'd sledded out of Harmony with the Toms family, Big
Dave, and Lanny Ham in tow, carrying all of the Ancient's
recent victims to a cavern in the area mountains. A few strategically fired gunshots had collapsed the ice and rock at the
cavern's mouth, sealing it off and ensuring that the dead would
not be found until sometime well into the next ice age.

'Any word from Gideon about Phase Two of this operation?'
Tegan asked Chase, who'd been charged with coordinating the
in-town portion of their task list for the day.

'Everything's in place,' Chase said. 'Gideon has spoken with
one Sidney Charles, Harmony's acting mayor, informing Mr
Charles that the unit dispatched from the Alaska State Trooper
division in Fairbanks should be arriving within the hour to
address the townspeople as a group and collect statements.'

'And I take it the good mayor was agreeable to that?'

Chase nodded. 'He told Gideon he would personally see to
it that every citizen was in attendance. They're gathering at
Harmony's church to wait for us as we speak.'

Tegan chuckled low under his breath. 'So, where does that
leave things? Breaking and entering, evidence tampering, compromising a crime scene, impersonating police officers,
scrubbing roughly a hundred human minds in one fell swoop
and getting it done before first light . . .'

Chase grinned. 'All in a day's work.'

Kade wasn't sure he would be welcomed in the Darkhaven
chapel where all of the compound's residents had gathered to
say their good-byes to Seth in the remaining minutes before
daybreak. He had intended to sit the damned ritual out completely, pacing his quarters in front of Alex like a caged animal

as the hour crept closer and closer to noon, when the winter sun would finally make its brief appearance. Finally, he couldn't stand it anymore.

'I have to be there,' he blurted, stopping in front of Alex where she sat on the sofa in his cabin's living room. 'Whether they think I belong with them now or not, I need to be there. For Seth. And for myself, too. Goddamn it, they all need to hear what I have to say.'

He stormed out of the cabin and headed across the frozen grounds. The faintly blue-tinged snow, lighted by the approaching sunrise, crunched under his boots with each long stride that carried him toward the chapel.

The windows of the small log building were already shuttered tight in anticipation of daybreak. As Kade drew nearer, he heard the soft murmur of voices lowered in private prayer, mingled with the intermittent sounds of the grieving inside.

Even before he reached for the latch of the door, he could smell the paraffin odor of the eight candles that would be burning at the altar, and the fragrant scent of the perfumed oil that anointed Seth's body in preparation for the infinity rites about to take place.

Eight ounces of oil to bless and cleanse him. Eight layers of pristine white silk to shroud him until his body would be surrendered to the sun. Eight minutes of scorching ultraviolet exposure for the one who would be chosen from among the living to attend Seth in private for the final moments of the funeral ceremony.

'Fuck,' Kade whispered, paused at the chapel doors as the reality of it all settled on him.

His brother was dead.

His family was in mourning.

And Kade felt more than partly to blame for all of it.

He opened the chapel door and stepped inside. Nearly every

head swung in his direction, some looking on him in pity, others staring at him like the stranger he had become in the year he'd been gone with the Order.

Everyone gathered in the chapel was dressed in ceremonial attire – females draped in black hooded gowns, males in belted long black robes. He found his parents in the front row of pews, standing with Maksim and Patrice, all of them garbed in black, their faces pale with shock, eyes rimmed in red, moist with grief. Had Seth been mated to Patrice, as his widow, she would have been gowned in hooded scarlet to signify their blood bond. His body, cocooned in white silk on the altar, would have borne a single crimson kiss where his Breedmate would have scored her own lips then pressed her mouth to his in one final good-bye.

As Kade considered the solemn traditions of his kind, he couldn't help thinking of Alex. He couldn't keep from flashing forward to a future where he was the one laid out on the funeral altar, his face transformed as Seth's was, frozen by Bloodlust under the shroud of white silk. Would Alex love him then?

Could he really ask her to love him now, after everything she knew about him? After everything she had seen and heard in the past several hours, could he ever expect to have her trust or affection ever again?

For that matter, what about the people gathered in this chapel? Would his kin at this Darkhaven have anything but scorn for him, once he'd said his piece?

Kade didn't know. At the moment, he didn't damn well care. He strode to the center aisle, knowing how out of place he must look in his combat-worn, bloodstained black fatigues, guns and blades bristling from the belt around his hips while his lug-soled boots echoed hollowly over the polished wood path toward the altar.

His father's gaze narrowed darkly as Kade began to walk

toward the front of the chapel. As he passed the rows of filled pews, he heard the quiet murmurs of prayers and softly whispered praises for his brother.

'Always such a charming boy, wasn't he?' someone reflected in a barely audible voice. 'How tragic that something like this could have happened to him.'

'Seth was the studious and responsible one,' another detached whisper recalled. 'He might have made a fine Darkhaven leader himself one day.'

'Poor Kir and Victoria, they must be heartbroken,' remarked yet another grief-choked resident, voice lowered so that Kade could hardly hear as he passed. 'Would anyone have imagined that Seth could turn Rogue? What a waste, and what a disappointment for his family.'

'Kir has refused to speak of it' came a hushed reply. 'I understand he is so ashamed, he would let no one near the body after Kade brought Seth home.'

'That's right,' someone else chimed in confidentially. 'It's only because Victoria insisted that Kir even permitted a gathering for the funeral rites. It's as though he wanted to simply sweep Seth away like he never existed.'

Kade ignored the quiet wave of whispered speculation behind him as he made his way to the altar at the front of the chapel. His father's shame and disapproval didn't surprise him. The fiercely disciplined, rigidly perfect Kir would never tolerate a Rogue in the family, let alone willingly deign to admit that his favored son had fallen to Bloodlust.

Kade was ashamed, too, not so much for his brother's weaknesses and unforgivable misdeeds but for his own failure to help Seth turn his life around before it was too late.

'This moment belongs to my brother,' he said, addressing the assembled group of his relatives and the other residents of the Darkhaven. 'I have no wish to take even a second of this time away from Seth, but there are things you all should

know. Things all of you need to understand before you con-
demn him for what became of him in the end.'

'Sit down, Kade.' His father's voice was low and level, but
his eyes crackled with command. 'This is neither the time nor
the place.'

Kade nodded. 'I know. I should have come forward a hell
of a lot sooner. Maybe if I'd said something earlier, my brother
would've had a chance. Maybe he wouldn't be dead.'

His father rose, coming up off his seat on the bench.
'Nothing you say here will change a goddamn thing. So hold
your tongue, boy. Let it be.'

'I can't,' Kade said. 'I've carried Seth's secret for too long.
I've been carrying my own secrets, too. It's long past time I
let them go.'

Kade's mother blinked back a fresh rush of tears, one
slender hand cradling the swell of her stomach, where another
pair of twin boys was growing inside her. 'What are you talking
about? What secrets, Kade? Please . . . I want to know.'

He looked past the disapproving glare of his father, to the
plea that swam in his gentle mother's moist eyes. Maybe what
he said in this room, before all of these witnesses, would
someday help the new pair of brothers who would soon be
born with the same talent – the same seductive, wild calling
– that he and Seth possessed. For that reason alone, he had
to speak.

And then, there was Alex.

Kade's gaze strayed to the back of the crowded chapel,
where she had entered in silence and now stood near the closed
doors, her steady gaze as tender as it was strong. She nodded
faintly, the only approval that truly mattered in this room.

'My brother was not well,' he told the quiet gathering. 'From
the time we were boys, we both struggled with the ability we
inherited at birth. Maybe in someone else, like you, Mother,'
he said, glancing at her as he spoke about the unique gift she

also possessed, 'the talent might have been a strength. For Seth and me, it became a curse. It was too much power for boys who were stupid with arrogance and too naive to understand the consequences. We abused the talent we inherited from you. At first, we treated it like a game, running with a pack of wolves in the woods, hunting with them . . . killing with them. We let the wildness rule us. At some point, I realized Seth could not stop.'

'Oh, my son,' she gasped. 'I am so sorry. I had no idea—'

'I know that,' he said, interrupting her before she could assume any more blame that wasn't hers. 'No one had any idea. It was wrong for Seth and me to conceal the truth. I made it worse when I left Alaska last year.'

Kir's scowl deepened. 'Worse, how?'

'Seth had killed a human.' Kade ignored the horrified gasp that traveled the congregation, his eyes rooted on his father. 'He'd killed, and I knew he had. He promised me it was a mistake he would never repeat. I didn't believe him. I wanted to, but I knew my brother too well. I should have done something then. I should have found a way to ensure he wouldn't do it again. Instead, I left.'

Silence fell over the room as Kade spoke. It stretched endlessly, a cold, sodden weight that bore down on his shoulders as he weathered his father's unreadable gaze. Kade's mother rushed to fill the terrible quiet.

'You had to leave, Kade. The Order needed your help in Boston. You had important work to do there—'

'No,' Kade said, shaking his head in slow denial. 'I was glad to join the Order, but that's not why I left. Not really. I left Alaska because I feared that if I stayed, I would become like Seth. To save myself, I abandoned my brother – abandoned all of you – and I ran to Boston for my own selfish reasons. There was no honor in what I did.'

He glanced to the back of the chapel as he said it, meeting

Alex's gaze. She was listening without judgment, the only pair
of eyes in the room that wasn't fixed on him in contempt or
stunned disbelief.

'What Seth did was wrong,' Kade continued. 'He was sick,
maybe beyond help, even before his weakness turned him
Rogue. But despite all that, he died with honor. Because of
Seth's sacrifice a few hours ago, I am alive. More important,
there is a beautiful, extraordinary woman standing at the back
of this room who's also alive because of Seth's actions in the
final moments of his life.'

As a whole, the group turned to look on Alex. She didn't
flinch at the sudden attention, nor at the whispers of speculation and curiosity that traveled the chapel on Kade's
announcement.

'Seth wasn't perfect,' Kade said. 'God knows, I'll never be.
But I loved my brother. And I owe him everything for what
he did today.'

'You honor him well,' a male voice murmured from somewhere on Kade's left. He glanced over and found Maksim
standing now. He nodded soberly. 'You honor all of us here
today, Kade.'

The praise from his uncle – his friend – was unexpected,
and tightened Kade's throat. Then similar murmurs rose up
from others in the room.

Kir walked forward and placed his hand on Kade's shoulder.
'It's time. Daybreak is coming, and I must take Seth into the
sun.'

Kade reached up, wrapped his fingers around the thick
strength of his father's wrist. 'Let me. Please . . . it should be
me, Father.'

He expected a curt refusal. A dark glare that would force
Kade to insist on taking the burden – the final honor – of
accompanying Seth's body for the eight minutes of solar exposure required by Breed funeral tradition.

But Kir did not argue. He took a step back, saying nothing as Kade stripped off his soiled combat shirt and weapons belt, then set them down on the wooden bench nearby.

No one uttered so much as a syllable as he went to the altar and lifted his brother's shrouded bulk into his arms, then began the walk through the corridor that emptied onto the chapel's snowy back garden, where the noontime sun was just beginning to break through the winter gloom overhead.

⊰ CHAPTER THIRTY-TWO ⊱

Alex waited in Kade's cabin, anxious with concern for what he was subjecting himself to in the yard behind the Darkhaven's chapel. Eight full minutes of ultraviolet light on his exposed skin. Eight minutes of excruciating pain, before duty would permit Kade to leave his brother's body to the consuming rays of the sun.

Alex wouldn't have had any idea about the funeral tradition of the Breed had it not been for Kade's uncle, Maksim, and the young Breedmate named Patrice, both of whom had walked back to introduce themselves in the moments after Kade had carried Seth's body away. The pair had been warm and welcoming, waiting with Alex while the rest of the congregation departed via underground tunnels that connected all of the buildings in the Darkhaven compound.

Max and Patrice had offered to keep Alex company in Kade's quarters to await him and help tend his burns, but Alex had declined as politely as she could. She didn't think Kade would want to be fussed over. She wasn't even sure he would want her there now, a worry that made the wait for his return drag out all the more.

But thoughts for herself blew away like cinder on the breeze when she heard Kade's footsteps coming up the front porch of the cabin.

Alex ran to the door and opened it, stricken by the sight of him standing there with daylight blazing behind him.

Incredibly, after the eight minutes he'd given his brother, Kade had not taken the tunnels but had instead apparently walked across the grounds from the chapel to his quarters.

'Oh, my God,' Alex whispered as his pale silver eyes stared out at her from the reddened, blistered skin of his face. Her throat squeezed up like it was caught in a fist. 'Come inside now.'

As he walked past her, his bare shoulders, arms, and torso radiated palpable heat that she could feel a foot away from him. He was obviously in agony, but he showed no sign of it beyond the visible UV damage of his skin.

'Come with me,' Alex said. 'I have a cool bath waiting for you.'

He shot her a questioning look.

'I met Maksim and Patrice in the chapel. They told me what you might need when you came back.' His mouth curved slightly at that, but when he tried to speak, his voice was nothing but a raspy croak of sound. 'Come on, Kade. Let me take care of you.'

He walked with her to the bathroom down the hall. He put up no resistance as she helped him undress, removing his boots and socks one at a time as he stood on the tiled floor, his broad palm feeling like an electric iron against her shoulder as he held on to her for balance. Alex carefully stripped him of his black fatigues and briefs. She couldn't contain her soft gasp, struck as always by the masculine perfection of his body and the complex artistry of his *glyphs*, even though at the moment she was too concerned about soothing his burns to take much pleasure in the sight of his nakedness.

She helped him step into the tub, watching as he slowly sank down into the cool water on a hiss that stretched into a long, deep sigh.

'Is that all right?'

He moaned and gave a faint nod, his eyes drifting closed

as steam from his heated skin curled over the surface of the water. 'Thank you,' he murmured thickly, settling deeper into the bath.

Alex picked up a soft cloth and submerged it in the tub. 'Just relax now. I'll do the rest.'

Gingerly she trickled the clear, cool water over the blistered bulk of his shoulders. She did the same to his burned back and chest, then his strong, bare arms. As carefully as she could, she brought the cloth to his face and cleansed the raw, reddened skin of his lean, angled cheeks and the strong, stern lines of his chin and brow.

As he relaxed deeper, Alex gently tipped his head back so she could wet his ebony hair and run cool water over his scalp. 'The things you said in the chapel today about Seth, and about yourself . . . I was very proud of you, Kade. It took a great deal of courage to stand up there like you did.'

He grunted, a wordless sound of denial.

'You may not think so, but you were a good brother to Seth. I think everyone saw that today. You are a good son to your parents, too.'

His eyelids flicked open even as his dark brows lowered in a frown. 'A few minutes of talk,' he rasped on a dry voice. 'That's all it was. Doesn't erase the past. Doesn't mean a damn thing.'

Alex squeezed more water into his hair and tenderly ran her fingers through the silken strands. 'Why are you so hard on yourself?'

'Seeing what my brother was should tell you the answer to that,' he said, all but growling the words. 'I'm sure I don't have to remind you what he was capable of. You saw that firsthand in the woods outside Harmony.'

'Yes,' Alex agreed softly. 'I did. But that was Seth, not you. Or do I have to remind you that those were your very words to me when I told you what I saw? Seth was a killer, not you.'

He exhaled a vivid curse, but Alex ignored his rising anger.

'Seth was the one who went Rogue, Kade. That doesn't mean you will, too.'

He shifted in the tub, lifting his head so that he was looking her squarely in the eyes. 'Most of my life, Alex, I have been hiding from the truth, living in denial. Running from the things I couldn't control. I thought if I put enough distance between myself and my problems, they would just . . . go away. Well, they don't.'

Alex nodded. He could just as well be talking about her life. 'I know now that running away doesn't solve anything,' she whispered. 'You have to stand up and face the things that scare you the most. You've taught me that, Kade.'

His scowl deepened. 'That's what I intend to do. But I need to do it alone, Alex.'

'What do you mean?'

'The things I talked about in the chapel today, and on that mountain when we brought Seth's body up from the ledge. I can't risk putting you in the middle of my problems.'

'It's a bit late for that, don't you think?' She caressed his tight jaw, only the barest skate of her fingers over the tender skin. 'I've heard everything you've said. I've seen what happened to your brother. I understand your fear, Kade. But I'm not going to run away. Not ever again. And I won't let you push me away, either. I love you.'

He expelled a harsh breath, and when he looked at her now, sparks of amber lit the silver irises of his eyes. She saw the glint of his fangs behind his lips, sharp white points gleaming with deadly power.

'I love you, Kade,' she insisted, refusing to back down. 'And unless you tell me here and now that you don't love me, too, then I can think of no reason why either of us should be alone.'

He stared hard at her, his jaw held tight. 'Goddamn it, Alex.

You know I can't say that. I do love you. And that has complicated everything.'

She smiled with a humor she barely felt. 'A little too much gray for you?' she asked softly. 'And here I thought I was the one who liked to keep things simple, black and white.'

He didn't return her smile. He was too far gone for that. As Alex drew back, she saw his eyes move from her lips to the base of her throat.

Her pulse was fluttering there, a fast tick that intensified to a heavier throb as she watched Kade stare hungrily at that spot. He caught her looking at him and abruptly glanced away. Tried to hide his awareness of her blood, pounding below the surface of her skin. Tried to hide his thirst from her.

Alex brought his gaze back to her with a coaxing touch. 'You don't have to deny who you are or what you need, Kade. Not from me. Not anymore.'

Silently she put down her wet cloth and positioned herself against his mouth, sweeping her hair away from her neck.

Her name was a reverent whisper on his lips as he drew in his breath, then blew it out in a heated rush against her skin. Kade descended on her in a swift motion, his sharp bite filled with need and a desperation that he made no effort to conceal.

Inside Zach Tucker's house in Harmony, a pair of Alaska State Troopers recently arrived from the post in Fairbanks slumped in subdued silence, both men tranced on the living room sofa.

In a recliner next to them, Mayor Sidney Charles snored softly, tranced, as well. The elderly Native man had proven immensely cooperative, albeit unwittingly so, to the Order's mission objectives in town. Not only had he delivered on his promise to summon every citizen of Harmony into the church a few hours ago, but he'd also had the good manners to escort the newly arrived Staties to Zach Tucker's place when their plane had touched down from Fairbanks around daybreak.

With Brock still on post at Jenna's cabin, Tegan, Chase, and Hunter had since relocated their operation to Tucker's house. They'd waited out the scant few hours of daylight there, using the idle time to dig into the dead trooper's computer records and look for further evidence of his corruption in the house. They hadn't had to look very far.

Zach Tucker might have been a bush cop but he had an accountant's eye for record keeping. He'd logged every drug deal and bootlegged bottle of booze that had passed through his hands and into Skeeter Arnold's for distribution around the area.

When the two Staties woke up, they were going to find every handwritten ledger and computer-stored spreadsheet in Zach Tucker's ransacked house. They were going to find the safe where Zach kept all of the considerable cash he'd made from his little side business over a period that had to have been several years.

The uniformed troopers were going to follow a hunch neither one of them could shake that would lead them to a remote area of the bush where they would discover Harmony's sole police officer, brutally murdered and scavenged by animals. Near the body, they would find Skeeter Arnold's cell phone, showing a history of plenty of calls to and from Trooper Tucker. With Skeeter nowhere to be found, nor heard from, the Staties would conclude that Tucker, and possibly Skeeter, as well, had apparently found themselves on the losing end of a deal gone horribly, fatally wrong.

What the troopers from the Fairbanks unit would not find was evidence of any other strange happenings in Harmony. With no one in town recalling the spate of recent deaths, let alone the names of the victims, and with a strategically placed computer worm originating from Boston that wiped out half of the AST's dispatch logs for the past week, there would be no reason for the Staties to look for anything more than a disappointing matter of police corruption in the otherwise peaceful town of Harmony.

'That's gonna do it,' Chase said as he came out of Tucker's home office. 'The computer password is disabled and there's a spreadsheet of our boy's current-year transactions conveniently left open on the monitor. These troopers are going to think Tucker was not only an asshole, but a complete moron besides.'

Tegan chuckled. 'I'll finish in here with the humans. Tell Hunter we're rolling out in five minutes.'

Chase nodded. He took a step, then paused. 'Any word from Kade?'

'Nothing yet.'

'Damn shame about his brother,' Chase said, his voice oddly wooden.

'Yeah,' Tegan said. 'It is a shame.'

When the ex-Enforcement Agent pivoted to walk away, Tegan cleared his throat. 'Hey, Harvard. I've been meaning to talk to you about what happened out there at the mine.'

'What about it?'

'Just wondering what the fuck you were thinking when you held that Minion by the throat for a while instead of going for a clean, quick kill.'

Chase's grin seemed somehow too tight for his face. 'Just having a little fun, is all.'

Tegan stared, assessing the once-straitlaced agent who'd proven to be a valuable asset to the Order, if a bit reckless at times. 'Fun can get you killed, my man. You'd do well to remember that.'

Chase's expression was nonchalant, the lift of his shoulders casual, unconcerned. 'Sure, Tegan. Thanks for the advice. I'll keep it in mind.'

Tegan watched him walk outside, then he turned his attention toward instructing the tranced humans to awaken once he and the other vampires had time enough to get several miles out of town.

⫷ CHAPTER THIRTY-THREE ⫸

Kade stood outside his quarters at the Darkhaven compound in a black silk robe, leaning against the timber post of the back porch that looked out over the property's vast acreage. It was now a few hours after the sun had retreated, and darkness blanketed the region once more. He was lost in his thoughts, staring out at the far horizon, where the greenish glow of the aurora borealis streaked across the starlit sky.

Alex drifted outside to join him. He heard her walking up softly behind him, closed his eyes as she gently wrapped her arms around his waist. She made a soft noise in the back of her throat, then sighed when he skimmed his fingers tenderly under the white satin sleeve of her robe to stroke her bare arms.

They had spent most of the day in his bed, lying in each other's arms. His body was still healing from the funeral rite, though much improved, thanks to the blood Alex had given him. Now his skin was merely red and tender, no longer blistered and searing with pain. His libido reminded him that he was well enough to want Alex. God knew, there was nothing that would keep him from desiring her.

'I didn't mean to wake you,' he murmured as they stood together as one under the starlit sky and watched the aurora dance in the distance. 'You've been through a lot the past few days. You should rest some more.'

Alex moved around to the front of him and burrowed into

his warmth. 'I came out here to tell you the same thing. How do you feel?'

He grunted, gave a brief nod. 'Better, thanks to you. And all the more so when I have you in my arms.'

She lifted her head to meet his gentle kiss. The brush of her lips was warm, inviting. Filled with tenderness for all they'd been through, and ripe with a tentative hope for what may still lay ahead for them.

'I needed you today, Alexandra,' he whispered against her mouth. 'I tried to convince myself that I didn't, but you are all that I need. Thank you for everything you did for me today. Thank you just for being here.'

She smiled up at him, her voice soft with emotion. 'You never need to thank me for that.'

'God, I love you,' he murmured, his chest tightening as he gazed down at her. 'You honor me, Alex. You humble me. I don't think you realize how much. You could have any male you choose—'

She reached up to caress his cheek with aching sweetness. 'There is only one male I would choose. Only one male I could ever love.'

His words perished on a low moan as he bent his head to hers and caught her mouth in a deep, passionate kiss. Need surged within him, hot and demanding. He wanted Alex – wanted her in his bed, beneath his fangs. He wanted her in every way he could have her.

So total was his desire, he hardly heard the rapid knock that fell against the front door of his cabin.

He would have ignored it completely if Alex hadn't drawn back, breathless. 'Someone's here.'

'I don't care.' Kade moved to kiss her again.

The knock came again, louder now. Insistent and demanding.

Kade snarled a curse as he caressed her beautiful face, then withdrew to stalk toward the door. He knew who he'd find on the other side, even before he opened it.

'Father,' he said, his clipped tone hardly able to be interpreted as a greeting.

Kir stared at him, then glanced past Kade's shoulder to where Alex had drifted in from the back porch. 'We need to talk.'

Kade stood firm, blocking the threshold with his body. 'I've said all that I needed to.'

'But I have not.' Another look went in Alex's direction. 'Hear me out. Please, son.'

Kade had never heard his father utter either one of those words in conversation with him before. Perhaps that was why he finally loosened his death grip on the door handle and stepped aside to permit his father entry.

But he wasn't about to budge where Alex was concerned. 'Anything you have to say to me can be said in front of Alexandra. She is my mate. I will keep nothing from her.'

Kir's brows rose ever so slightly on his proud forehead. 'Of course.' He inclined his head in Alex's direction, a gesture of respect that won him a few small points with Kade. 'Is it all right with you if we sit for a while, son?'

Kade nodded, then held his hand out to Alex in a motion for her to join them. She glided over and sat beside him on the sofa, Kir taking the leather chair across from them. For a long moment, the elder male merely looked at the both of them, his expression unreadable, his shrewd eyes unblinking as he silently appraised them.

'Today was a day I prayed would never come,' he said at last. His deep voice sounded hollow, still raw from grief. 'For a very long time, since you were mere boys, I have lived in fear of the thought of losing your brother.'

Kade dropped his gaze, fresh shame rising up on him. 'I know you're disappointed, Father. I know . . . ah, Christ.' Alex slipped her hand into his, her fingers wrapped around his own. Kade swallowed past the ash that seemed to have settled in his throat. 'I know you must wish that it was me, not Seth.'

'You know nothing,' Kir snapped. Kade's head came up at that, and his father's voice gentled. 'You don't know what I wish, or what I feel. How could you know, when I never gave any of myself to you? I poured everything into Seth instead. I gave him too much.'

Kade shrugged. 'He was your son. You loved him.'

'You are also my son,' he replied. 'And I love you both, Kade. But it was Seth who needed it more. He never had your independence. He wasn't born with your courage.'

Kade frowned. 'You doted on him. Everyone did.'

'Yes,' he admitted. 'Because you were stronger than he, Kade. In every way, you were his better. Seth knew that as well as I did. I tried to compensate for his failings by giving him more attention than I did you, but it spoiled him even more.'

'You let him handle Darkhaven business for you,' Kade pointed out. 'You seemed to be grooming him for a Darkhaven of his own.'

Kir slowly shook his head. 'A father's futile hopes, nothing more. I tried to give him the chance to make something of himself. Time and again I tried. Seth would never have made a good leader. He was too weak, too insecure.'

'And me?' Kade asked, the question blurting out of him before he had the chance to bite it back.

'You,' Kir said, thoughtful as he looked at him. 'You were untamable. You were unstoppable, from the moment you came howling and kicking out of your mother's womb. You were a force of nature, Kade. Everyone who looked upon you saw that you were something unique, something special. I knew a child once who was not so different from you.'

'Grigori,' Kade murmured, watching his father's expression mutate from mild surprise to remembered regret.

'Grigori,' Kir repeated quietly. 'I presume you heard something about him from my other brother, Maksim.'

Kade nodded. 'Max told me a little. I know that Grigori meant a lot to you, and I know that he went Rogue.'

Kir's brows rose a fraction. 'Yes, he did.'

'And you thought I would end up like him one day.'

'You?' He scowled, then gave a small shake of his head. 'I never thought that of you. It was Seth I worried about. You reminded me of Grigori, that is true. Everything vibrant and robust and strong in him, I saw in you, Kade. Seth, however, had none of those qualities. He was only like my brother in that he possessed the same flaws and insecurities that eventually doomed him. I knew it, and I lived in dread of what might become of Seth. As for you, I could only hope that you would never be put into the position that I had been with Grigori. I prayed you would never be faced with that kind of decision.'

Something cold coiled around Kade's heart at his father's words. Alex's fingers tightened around his as if she, too, felt the dread of what Kir might say. 'Tell me what happened, Father.'

'I never wanted you to have to shoulder the burden of having to destroy something you loved.' Kir's eyes dimmed with regret. 'I thought that if I kept Seth close enough, if I gave him every opportunity to prove himself, my strength might be enough to hold him up. If I could keep Seth from giving into the weakness I saw in him from the time he was a child, then maybe he wouldn't end up like Grigori. Maybe you would not be forced to do what I had to do.'

'Max said Grigori was never seen or heard from after your family received word that he'd gone Rogue and killed someone in his Bloodlust. Max said you refused to speak of Grigori after that.'

Kir nodded grimly. 'There was no need to speak of him

again. He was dead. As his brother, I felt it was my duty to make sure that he could never kill again.'

Alex exhaled the smallest gasp at the sober confession. Kade was stunned to discover how similar his father's path had been to his own, how much he never knew about the male who'd sired him or the life his father had led before Kade and Seth had been born.

He muttered a curse, but there was no venom in it. There never could be again, not after tonight. 'I have resented you nearly all my life,' he admitted. 'I thought you despised me.'

Kir clucked his tongue, gave a remorseful shake of his head. 'Never. I only wanted the best for you. For both my sons. And now, for the two new ones who will be born in a few short weeks, as well.'

'We have wasted a lot of time on secrets and festering fears,' Kade said to him. He turned a look on Alex, swamped by love for the female who owned his heart. 'I can't waste another minute like that.'

Kir stood up. 'Nor should I waste any more of your time when you and Alex could be spending it together. I want you to know that I am proud of you, Kade. And I am glad to see that you have found happiness. You've found love, and next to all your other strengths, that is the one that will see you through any challenge.'

Kade swallowed, gave an awkward nod. 'Thank you, Father.'

'How long will you and Alex be staying here at the Darkhaven?'

'Not long,' Kade replied. 'A few more hours at the most. Some of my brethren from the Order are waiting in a town not far from here. We have a mission to wrap up, and then we'll be heading back home.'

'Both of you?' Kir asked, glancing from Kade to Alex.

'I guess I'd better make it official and ask her,' Kade said, smiling as he stroked Alex's cheek. He drew her gaze to his. 'What do you think, Alex? Any chance I can convince you to come back with me to Boston?'

Her soft brown eyes gleamed. 'I've never been to New England. I think I'd like to see it.'

Kade's grin burst across his face. 'I'll show you the whole damn world if you'll let me.'

They kissed, interrupted a moment later by Kir's slightly awkward clearing of his throat. Alex was blushing furiously. Kade felt no embarrassment for his affection, meeting his father's amused look with an unapologetic quirk of his brows.

Kir smiled, then strode to the door, Kade and Alex walking at his side. When they paused at the threshold, Kade held out his hand, but his father didn't take it. Instead, he pulled Kade into a firm embrace. 'I know that you have made a family in Boston with the Order,' he said as he drew back to meet Kade's eyes. 'I'm glad for you. But you have a family here, as well. You and your beautiful Alexandra both have family here.'

'May I hug you, too?' Alex asked, turning her warmth on Kade's gruff father.

Kir's mouth curved into a rare smile. 'I would be honored if you did.'

As Alex embraced him, the elder male glanced at Kade, his gaze filled with too many emotions for Kade to name. Pride, forgiveness, regret, hope . . . years of emotions that went unspoken between father and son. Maybe now they would have the chance to repair the things that had been buried under so many secrets, so many useless fears.

And then there was Alexandra.

Kade looked at the female he loved – his female, his mate. His heart overflowed with all the things he wanted to say to her, things he wanted to share with her . . . promises he intended to give her now, in the hope that he would have the rest of his life with her to make good on them.

Kade wrapped his arm around Alex's shoulders as they stood together and watched his father stroll across the moonlit snow toward the main house. When he was gone, Kade turned to Alex and swept her up into his arms.

She gasped as her feet left the ground, then laughed as he pivoted around and started walking with her toward his bedroom. 'Put me down! You're hardly recovered from your burns, Kade. You really shouldn't be doing this.'

'Oh, yes, I should,' he replied, gazing into her eyes with a hunger he wouldn't have been able to mask even if he'd tried.

They made love together, at first a tempestuous, fevered joining, both of them lost to the swell of their emotions and to the urgent demands of their desire for each other. Kade ravished her body, made her climax so many times she finally gave up trying to keep count.

Alex's senses were filled with him, her body thrumming as she came down from the crest of another wave of pleasure, nestled in the protective shelter of Kade's arms.

She loved him so deeply she ached with her devotion. And in the afterglow of their passion, she knew that he loved her, too.

His touch was tender as he stroked the sensitive skin of her neck, his fingers skating like velvet beneath her ear. 'I haven't done right by you,' he murmured quietly. 'When I drank from you that first night at your house in Harmony. It should have been your choice, Alex. I took that from you. I should have told you what it meant before I bonded myself to you. I should have had honor enough to earn the right, not steal it the way I did.'

'It doesn't matter to me,' she murmured. 'All that matters is that we are together now. I want you forever, Kade. I want . . .' The words trailed off, not out of fear or uncertainty, but out of the depth of her longing. She turned her head to look at him. 'All I want is you, to be bonded to you as your mate.'

'And all I want is to make you happy, and to know that you are safe and protected.'

'I am. There's nowhere I could be happier – or more secure – than here in your arms.' She caressed his handsome face, seeing the torment that still lingered in his expression. The measure of self-doubt that hadn't quite faded from his eyes, and might never fully disappear. 'Together we are strong, Kade. Stronger than the wildness inside you. You heard what your father said: Love is the greatest strength. Nothing is more powerful than that.'

'You really believe that?'

'More than anything,' she replied. 'But the question is, do you?'

He stared at her for a long moment, his silver eyes searching. 'So long as I have you beside me, I can believe that anything is possible. I love you, Alexandra. You are everything to me.'

He brought her closer and kissed her – the most tender, reverent kiss she had ever known. Alex melted into him, her body responding in a fluid rush of warmth that pooled in her core. She tipped her head back as his mouth traveled down the line of her jaw, to the side of her throat.

Kade reared his head back on a growl. He stared at her, his eyes blazing with amber sparks, his fangs glowing white. Already he was panting with need, fierce with hunger for her.

He scowled, dark emotions tossing in the depths of his silver eyes. 'Forever?'

'Forever, Kade.' She let her fingers drift over his sensual mouth, where the points of his fangs glinted behind his parted lips. 'Bind me to you now. I want to taste you. I want to have forever with you.'

On a deep growl, his gaze locked on hers, he brought his wrist up to his mouth. He parted his lips, then sank his fangs into the flesh and muscle. Blood dripped from the punctures and down his chin. Tentative, he held his arm out to her.

Alex took him in her hands and brought his wrist to her lips.

The first taste of him was a shock. She didn't know what she'd expected, but none of her imaginings had prepared her for the reality of drinking from Kade. His blood was a sweetness that rolled over her tongue, a stunning wildness that stole her breath. She drank in the scent of his skin and the earthy spice of his blood as she drew from his open vein.

Power surged through her like lightning.

Kade groaned with pleasure and she drank more, greedy now, desire pulsing through every nerve ending and making all of her senses come vividly to life. Heat roared deep inside her, and she whimpered as the first wave of orgasm rose up on her and swept her away.

Kade's growl was purely male, purely triumphant.

Alex was still riding the crest of rapture as he licked the wound at his wrist, then spread her body, opening her thighs to the searing heat of his hungry gaze.

'You are mine now, Alex. God help you, you are mine forever now.'

'Then show me,' she whispered, her voice roughened from pleasure. She swept her tongue along her lips, savoring every last taste of him on her mouth. She tipped her head to the side, presenting her throat to him. 'Show me that I will always belong to you, Kade.'

His lip curled away from his fangs, which shone as sharp and pristine as diamonds in the dim light of the aurora dancing in the distance outside the cabin. Alex took in the savage beauty of his face, feeling nothing close to fear when she looked at him now.

He was her heart, her lover, her mate.

Her everything.

'Love me, Kade,' she murmured.

'Forever,' he replied.

Then, with a groan of pleasure and surrender, he bent his head and sank his bite deep into her flesh and showed her just how pleasurable their forever was going to be.

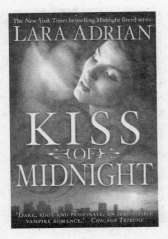

Reality shifts to a dark and deadly realm when Gabrielle Maxwell witnesses a murder outside a nightclub; in a shattering instance she is thrust into a world where vampires stalk the shadows and a blood war is set to ignite. Her future bound to a black-haired stranger who stirs her deepest fantasies, she must confront a destiny of danger, seductions and the darkest pleasures of all...

Robinson

978-1-84901-106-8

£6.99

www.constablerobinson.com

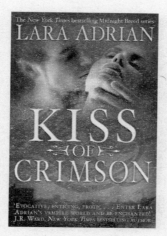

He comes to her more dead than alive, a huge black-clad stranger, mortally wounded and rapidly losing blood. As she struggles to save him, Tess is unaware that the man calling himself Dante is no man at all, but one of the Breed of vampire warriors.

In a single erotically charged moment Tess is plunged into his world. His touch has awakened in her hidden gifts and desires and a hunger she never knew she possessed. Bonded by blood, Dante and Tess must work together to overcome the deadliest of enemies . . .

Robinson
978-1-84901-107-5
£6.99

www.constablerobinson.com

The *New York Times* bestselling Midnight Breed series

LARA ADRIAN

MIDNIGHT AWAKENING

'A THRILLING BLEND OF DARK PASSION AND HEART-POUNDING ACTION. LARA ADRIAN ALWAYS DELIVERS A KEEPER'
GENA SHOWALTER, *NEW YORK TIMES* BESTSELLING AUTHOR

Elise Chase prowls the street of Boston seeking retribution against the Rogue vampires who took her beloved son from her. Using her psychic gift, she stalks her prey, well aware that the power she possesses is destroying her.

In her desperation for vengeance she turns to Tegan, who slays his enemy with ice in his veins. He is perfect in his self-control – until Elise seeks his aid.

An unholy alliance is forged, one which will plunge them into a tempest of danger, desire and the darkest passions of the heart . . .

Robinson
978-1-84901-108-2
£6.99

www.constablerobinson.com

Journalist Dylan Alexander finds herself at the centre of a gathering storm of violence. But nothing is as dangerous as the scarred and lethally seductive man who appears from the shadows to plunge her into his world of dark desire and endless night.

The warrior Rio has pledged his life to a war against the Rogues. Fuelled by pain and rage over a shattering betrayal, nothing will stand in his way, least of all a mortal woman.

When an ancient evil is awakened, Dylan is faced with a choice: either to leave Rio's midnight realm, or risk everything for the man who has shown her infinite pleasures of the heart?

Robinson
978-1-84901-110-5
£6.99

www.constablerobinson.com

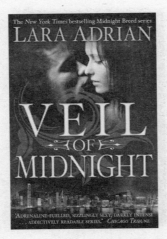

The New York Times bestselling Midnight Breed series

LARA ADRIAN

VEIL
OF
MIDNIGHT

'ADRENALINE-FUELLED, SIZZLINGLY SEXY, DARKLY INTENSE
. . . ADDICTIVELY READABLE SERIES.' *Chicago Tribune*

Bound by blood, addicted to danger, they'll enter the darkest
and most erotic place of all . . .

A warrior trained in bullets and blades, Renata cannot be
bested by any man – vampire or mortal. But her most powerful weapon is her extraordinary psychic ability – a gift both
rare and deadly. Now a stranger threatens her hard-won independence – a golden-haired vampire who lures her into a realm
of darkness . . . and pleasure beyond imaging . . .

Robinson
978-1-84901-109-9
£6.99

www.constablerobinson.com

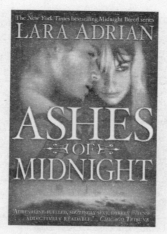

As night falls, Claire Roth flees, driven from her home by a fiery threat that seems to come from hell itself. Then, out of the flames and ash, a vampire warrior emerges. He is Andreas Reichen, once Claire's lover but now a stranger consumed by vengeance. She cannot escape his savage fury – or the hunger that will plunge her into his world of eternal darkness. So a dangerous seduction begins, blurring the line between predator and prey, love and hatred . . .

Robinson

978-1-84901-105-1

£6.99

www.constablerobinson.com

To order any of the **Lara Adrian** titles simply contact The Book Service (TBS) by phone, email or by post.
Alternatively visit our website at www.constablerobinson.com.

No. of copies	Title	RRP	Total
	Kiss of Midnight	£7.99	
	Kiss of Crimson	£7.99	
	Midnight Awakening	£6.99	
	Midnight Rising	£6.99	
	Veil of Midnight	£6.99	
	Ashes of Midnight	£7.99	
	Shades of Midnight	£7.99	
		Grand total	

FREEPOST RLUL-SJGC-SGKJ, Cash Sales Direct Mail Dept.,
The Book Service, Colchester Road, Frating, Colchester, CO7 7DW

Tel: +44 (0) 1206 255 800
Fax: +44 (0) 1206 255 930
Email: sales@tbs-ltd.co.uk

UK customers: please allow £1.00 p&p for the first book, plus 50p for the second, and an additional 30p for each book thereafter, up to a maximum charge of £3.00.

Overseas customers (incl. Ireland): please allow £2.00 p&p for the first book, plus £1.00 for the second, plus 50p for each additional book.

NAME (block letters): _____

ADDRESS: _____

_____

_____ POSTCODE: _____

I enclose a cheque/PO (payable to 'TBS Direct') for the amount of £ _

I wish to pay by Switch/Credit Card

Card number: _____

Expiry date: _____Switch issue number: _____

CHAPTER ELEVEN

It was strange being back in his old quarters at his father's Darkhaven, as though he'd somehow walked into a distant, remembered dream of home that no longer seemed to fit him quite the same way. True to her word, however, Kade's mother had made sure nothing was out of place since he'd left a year ago. After the long night he'd had in Harmony, he could appreciate the thick, engulfing cushion of his leather mission-style recliner, which was perfectly situated in front of the massive, river-rock fireplace that roared with freshly laid logs.

Kade leaned back and chuckled into his satellite phone as Brock caught him up on everything he was missing in Boston the past couple of nights.

'I'm telling you, man, if we aren't careful, these females around here are gonna show our asses up. The way they've been tackling daytime missions topside, they're starting to make the rest of us look bad.'

Since Kade had phoned in to the Order's compound headquarters a few minutes ago, Brock had been regaling him with stories about some of the other warriors' Breedmates and their current efforts to assist in what had been, until very recently, something of an all-boys club. Now Order missions had become all-hands-on-deck kinds of operations – solely devoted to stopping a power-hungry Breed maniac named Dragos from unleashing his personal brand of hell on both humankind and Breed alike.

Dragos's resources were as deep as his pockets and, so it happened, as black as his plans. His most heinous act had been the capture and imprisonment of an unknown number of Breedmates, whom he'd been collecting for decades and using to give birth to an army of savage assassins. With Dragos's headquarters sacked by the Order just a few weeks ago, his operation had been disrupted – disassembled and diverted, the Order suspected.

Finding the captive Breedmates before he could harm any more of them was the Order's primary objective now. Because timing could mean the difference between lives lost or saved, Lucan had agreed to utilize every weapon in the Order's arsenal, which included the very special, uniquely gifted, females who'd taken some of the warriors as their mates.

There was Rio's mate, Dylan, who had the ability to see the spirits of other Breedmates who'd passed and, when she was lucky, obtain critical information from them. There was Elise, who was mated to Tegan and who had a talent for hearing corrupt, dark human intentions. She accompanied Dylan to area shelters, private homes, and flophouses, her ability helping her assess the motives of the folks they met with along the way.

Gideon's mate, Savannah, used her tactile skill for reading the history of an object, hoping to find traceable links to some of the missing. Nikolai's mate, Renata, whose power to mind-blast even the strongest vampire made her a formidable ally on any mission, provided armed bodyguard service to the other Breedmates for their daytime missions.

Even Andreas Reichen's mate, Claire, who'd only recently recovered from her own ordeal at the hands of Dragos and his associates, was apparently getting involved in Order business. Using her gift for dreamwalking, she'd been trying to make contact with some of the known Breedmates who'd been reported missing over the years.

'You know,' Brock added wryly, 'when Niko recruited me for this gig a year ago, I was expecting it to be just a great excuse to kick some Rogue ass.'

Kade grinned, recalling their initial patrols around Boston, which typically involved taking out the city's feral blood addicts and making things go *boom*. 'Kind of makes you miss the simplicity of the first few months on the job, doesn't it?'

Brock grunted in agreement. Then, 'Speaking of Rogues, how's it going up there in the icebox? Been two days and counting. You got that situation swept up yet?'

'I'm following up on a few leads, but nothing solid right now. I'll probably be here another few days, maybe a week.'

Brock's exhaled curse told Kade what he thought of that prediction. 'Better you than me, my man. Better you than me.' There was a pause before he asked, 'You have a chance to see your family yet?'

'Yeah,' Kade said, tipping his head back to stare at the thick beam rafters of the cabin. 'My arrival home went over about as well as I expected.'

'That good, huh?'

'Put it this way, I get a warmer reception stepping outside in the twenty-below darkness.'

'Harsh,' Brock said. 'I'm sorry, man. Seriously.'

Kade shook his head. 'Forget it. I don't need to talk about my welcome homecoming. Just wanted to touch base and pass along another bit of info that Gideon might find interesting.'

'Okay, shoot.'

'I found the asshole who posted the video clip of the attacked humans. His name is Skeeter Arnold, local burnout, probable small-time dealer. I watched him leave a bar and take off in a shiny new chauffeured Hummer. He was brought to some kind of mining company office out in the sticks. The name on the gate was Coldstream Mining Company. Put

Gideon on that when he gets a chance. I'm curious to know what kind of business this loser might have with them.'

'You got it,' Brock said. 'You take care out there. Don't freeze off anything you might need later.'

Kade chuckled despite the unease he felt just thinking about this whole assignment. 'I'll be in touch,' he said, and ended the call.

As he set the phone down on the lamp table beside him, a firm rap sounded on the cabin's front door.

'Yeah, it's open,' he said, expecting to see his father. He steeled himself for the disapproval that would follow. 'Come on in.'

Maksim entered instead, sparking a relief Kade could hardly hide. He rose, smiling, and gestured for his uncle to join him in front of the fire.

'I didn't think you'd come back,' Max said. 'At least, not so soon. I hear it did not go well between you and my brother the other day. I wish he wasn't so hard on you.'

Kade shrugged. 'We've never seen eye to eye. I sure as hell don't expect us to start now.'

'Now that you are one of the Order's warriors,' Max said, his eyes lighting with eager conspiracy, his deep, slightly accented voice edged with unhidden admiration, 'I am proud of you, nephew. Proud of the work you are doing. There is honor in it, just as there has always been honor in you.'

Kade wanted to dismiss the praise as unneeded, but hearing it – particularly from Max, who, although he was a couple centuries older than Kade, had always felt like a brother to him – felt too damn good to pretend it didn't matter.

'Thanks, Max. It means a lot, coming from you.'

'No need to thank me. I speak the truth.' He stared at Kade for a long moment, then leaned forward, his elbows planted on his spread knees. 'You've been gone a year. You must be doing important things for Lucan and his Order.'